THE
SUMMER
WE BURIED

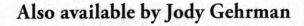

Also available by Jody Gehrman

Triple Shot Bettys
Triple Shot Bettys in Love
Confessions of a Triple Shot Betty

Audrey's Guide
Audrey's Guide to Black Magic
Audrey's Guide to Witchcraft

Other Works
The Girls Weekend
Watch Me
The Truth About Jack
Bombshell
Babe in Boyland
Notes from the Backseat
Tart
Summer in the Land of Skin

THE SUMMER WE BURIED

A NOVEL

JODY GEHRMAN

CROOKED
LANE

NEW YORK

Published in the United States by Crooked Lane Books, an imprint of The Quick Brown Fox & Company LLC.

Crooked Lane Books and its logo are trademarks of The Quick Brown Fox & Company LLC.

Library of Congress Catalog-in-Publication data available upon request.

ISBN (trade paperback): 978-1-63910-243-3
ISBN (hardcover): 978-1-64385-923-1
ISBN (ebook): 978-1-64385-924-8

Cover design by Kara Klontz

Printed in the United States.

www.crookedlanebooks.com

Crooked Lane Books
34 West 27th St., 10th Floor
New York, NY 10001

Trade Paperback: January 2023
First Edition: March 2022

10 9 8 7 6 5 4 3 2 1

For my mom,
Charlotte Garner,
who sparkles.

1

S HE WALKS INTO the room, and I know it's her. In spite of the big Jackie-O sunglasses, the fake name, I'd know that walk, that smell, that *hair* anywhere. She glides into my office with the long, confident strides of a runway model, bringing with her a faint cloud of amber. The hair is the real giveaway, though. She could have a paper bag over her head, and I'd know her so long as I could see her hair. It's the inky dark of raven feathers, a blue-black, and it falls to the middle of her back, slithering like a cat's tail—that same unconscious animation, like it's somehow both under her control and separate from her.

How long has it been? Fifteen years? Twenty?

"Hello, *Jasmine Jones.*" I do nothing to disguise my sarcasm. "What brings you here today? Are you looking to map out an ed plan?"

She takes off her sunglasses with one quick jerk. Her fingers, as always, are covered with rings. "Hello, Tansy."

"Selene." I lean back in my chair and take her in.

She's wearing a floaty blue sundress, scuffed cowboy boots, and a butter-colored leather jacket. She's still beautiful, I note, though the years have left their mark. She's got a scar above her eyebrow

I never noticed before, and parentheses around her mouth. Her body is still lithe and compact as ever—five feet of muscle and sinew. The tendons in her neck are taut, giving her the aggressive look of a cobra about to strike.

"Been a while." Her eyes move over me, over my office, taking it all in.

"Sure has. Did you move back to Sonoma?"

"I'm renting a little yurt outside of town. Don't worry, though, I'm not here to catch up. I came to ask a favor." She sits in the chair opposite my desk. She doesn't perch on the edge as if ready to bolt, like most of my visitors. She leans back into it, settling in like she plans to order a round of martinis or three.

I fondle my paperweight, a mermaid under glass. "Cutting right to the chase, as usual."

"It's not a social call."

An eruption of laughter escapes from me, sounding nervous and shrill. "I'm not expecting social niceties, okay? This is where I work. You came here under an assumed name. I don't appreciate being ambushed and I—"

"Don't be so dramatic." She stares out the window, distant and arctic. "I need something. You owe me. I came to collect my debt."

"Your *debt*?" I say it louder than I mean to. With a quick glance around—these walls are thin—I lower my voice. "Are you serious right now?"

"Let's not play games, Tansy." Her hazel eyes hold mine. There's something there I don't like—something hard and determined that tells me I can't just brush this off as a weird thing that happened at work. "We both know it's true. I saved your life. You're welcome. Now I need something, and it's time to pay up."

"That is—" My voice shakes. I take a deep breath to steady it. "—a gross oversimplification."

"You can tell yourself whatever you like, but it doesn't change the facts." The hardness in her jaw reminds me of warriors, of samurai. She glares at me, willing me to back down.

I say nothing.

She lounges again, taking my silence for agreement. "I have a daughter. She's a student here."

I return my attention to the mermaid paperweight. The concept of Selene with a daughter is incomprehensible. I shudder to imagine what that was like—growing up with her tests, her mind games.

Again, Selene takes my silence as an invitation to go on. "Her name's Jupiter. She's in a thoroughly messed up relationship. I want you to help me get her out."

"Out?" My eyes widen at that. "What do you mean, *out?*"

"He's abusive." She leans forward, the tendons in her neck going even more taut. "I'm going crazy with worry."

For a moment, as our eyes meet, I feel myself softening. I steel myself against it. This is the slippery slope I always fell down in the past. Give Selene an opening and she'll have you dancing like a puppet before you know it.

"I think you have a fundamental misunderstanding about what we do here," I say, trying to sound distant and professional. "I'm a college guidance counselor. Breaking up relationships— even abusive ones—is way outside my job description. Have you thought about going to the police?"

She huffs out a breathy, incredulous laugh. "Cops? Yeah, right."

"If you think she's in danger . . ."

"She's in love with the little bastard. He's rich and entitled, with a powerful family." She shakes her head. "You think I'd come here if you weren't my only hope?"

Would she? I don't know. During our whirlwind two-year friendship, Selene manipulated me all the time. I was eighteen when we met in a creative writing class at the local community

college. She was twenty-eight, exotic and fascinating in ways I
didn't even know human beings could be. Her life contained so
much more than mine. She'd been a stripper in New Orleans, a
speed freak in San Diego, a money launderer in Seattle. She'd been
married to a bank robber who ended up in jail. I was drawn to her
hard edges, her grit. She was a survivor, already tested by life in a
thousand ways. By contrast, I felt sheltered and unformed, as soft
and bland as a lump of dough. The stories she told as we sat in
her candlelit geodesic dome, drinking wine and listening to Bob
Dylan, beguiled me. Only later, once I'd run from our friendship
and gotten some distance, did I understand the many ways she
had controlled and manipulated me from the very beginning.

"How old is your daughter?" I ask, cautious.

"Eighteen."

The number registers with a hollow thud in my belly. Our friendship imploded eighteen years ago. Could Selene have been pregnant
when all of that went down? Did she have a baby growing inside her
the whole time, an unseen witness to the terrible things we did?

I shake my head. I don't want to think about any of that. I've
been blocking out memories of Selene for almost two decades; for
my own mental health, I plan to keep blocking them, thank you
very much.

I circle back to my reason for asking the question in the first
place. "Eighteen makes her an adult. I know it probably doesn't
feel like it—she'll always be your baby, right? But legally—"

"He won't let me see her," she blurts, raising her voice to talk
over me. "He could have her locked in the basement for all I know."

This throws me. "Wait, what?"

Her fingers grip the arms of the chair, knuckles white. "The
little shit blocked my number on her phone, so I couldn't get in
touch with her. Naturally, after weeks of silence, I show up at
their place, just wanting to make sure she's okay. You know what
he did?"

I blink at her, pulled into the story in spite of myself. "He has the nerve to meet me at the door and tell me I'm a 'toxic influence' on my daughter and that she's 'disconnecting' for a little while. *Disconnecting!* Like I'm an appliance she can unplug and not the woman who carried her for nine months."

In the pocket of silence, I ask, "How long has it been since you've talked to her?"

"Months." Selene glares out the window, simmering with resentment.

I get the feeling there's something she's leaving out here. "Have you thought about 'running into' her away from the boyfriend? Say, here on campus, or her favorite café?"

Her lips curve into a moue of distaste. "I shouldn't have to stalk my own daughter."

I shrug, like, *It's worth a shot.* Again, I sense she hasn't told me the whole story. The Selene I knew would use any means necessary to confront someone she cared about. I let the silence stretch out, wondering if she'll get to the real issue or keep dancing around it.

Selene meets my eye, and for the first time since she walked in, I see something vulnerable there—a complicated mixture of need, fury, and embarrassment. "There's a restraining order. I can't get within three hundred feet of her or I could be arrested."

"Jupiter took out a restraining order against you?" I say it softly, knowing this is hard for her to admit.

"Colton did." She spits out his name like something rotten. "He got her in on it, too. Because of the day I went to their apartment."

With creeping dread, I ask, "What happened?"

I catch another flash of sheepishness before she buries it under righteous indignation. "I may have pushed him. Not hard, but he's a lawyer's son and a spoiled little snowflake, so he knows how to make the most of it. According to the police report, I assaulted him in the foyer of his own home."

Neither of us says anything for a long moment.

Selene inches closer, lowering her voice to a whisper. "I need you to help me do this the right way, or so help me God, I will do it the wrong way. You know I will."

I swallow. The aura of danger Selene always carries with her fills the room, making the silence dense. I turn in my chair and open my window, desperate for air. The muted cacophony of campus reminds me I'm here, in my world. I'm safe. A cool breeze pushes through the screen, and the tang of coming rain catches at the back of my throat.

"I don't see how I can—" I begin, but she cuts me off.

"Get her to come see you," she says. "Become her counselor."

"Normally, students initiate contact." I try to make my tone brisk, matter-of-fact, a *case closed* shrug just starting to take shape in my shoulders.

She shakes her head. "I know you can figure it out. You like to play by the rules, but you also know how to bend them when you feel like it." Each syllable gets harder and more staccato, like a hailstorm building on a tin roof.

I look away. She's got me pegged.

"And what then?" I keep my gaze fixed on the green stretch of lawn outside. Students wander across it in shorts and T-shirts, underdressed for the storm that's moving in from the west, closing fast. The clouds hang low on the horizon, and I can see gray streaks of rain bleeding into the hills.

From the corner of my eye, I see her stand and shove her sunglasses back on. "One step at a time, Tanzanita."

Hearing her old nickname for me, I can't help twisting back around to look at her.

But she's already at the door, yanking it open with that same maddening confidence she walked in with, that runway model-meets-commanding-officer strut.

When she's got one foot in the hallway, she looks back over her shoulder and smiles with a radiance that startles me. I'd forgotten she could turn that sort of thing on and off at will. It's one of her more frightening superpowers.

"Good meeting," she said. "I'll be in touch."

I have a terrible feeling this is one promise she's going to keep.

* * *

I turn onto Moonview Road around six that evening, my Subaru full of groceries. Dust rises under my wheels as I curve through the oak grove and drive over the bridge that spans the swollen creek. It's Friday, and my brother Tim is coming to visit tomorrow with his husband Jay. Tim's an amazing cook. I know he'll bring plenty of provisions, but I've stocked up on wine, sugar, and carbs just to be safe.

Marius stands in his driveway as I pull up, wearing mustard-colored Dickies, his Carhartt jacket, and a wool beanie. His pants sit low on his skinny hips. He's staring up at the roof of his house.

I slow my car and zip down my window as I pass. He turns, and his dear, gingery face lights up in a smile. It's a sad smile—the same sort of smile he's offered me ever since Scottie died. We're comrades in the same war, and we greet one another with the weary melancholy of soldiers.

"How's it going?" I say, loud enough to be heard over my engine. The evening sun has painted the sky in syrupy pinks and smears of amber. He's backlit, so it's hard to read his expression. The golden red of his stubbled jaw lights up like neon.

"You mind if I ride with you?" His hazel eyes scan my face as his hand thumps the top of the Subaru.

I flinch at the sound, thrown. Usually we just call out hello and I cruise past. The last time I had a real talk with Marius was before Jessica moved in.

"Ride where?"

He squints toward my place, about a quarter mile down the road, on the western edge of the property. Marius doesn't like to use words if he doesn't have to. It's one of the many things I both love and hate about the man. He's economical with language, as if every word he utters costs him thousands.

"Of course," I say without thinking. "Hop in."

Marius is my ex. We were together for almost eleven years, off and on. Our band, The Insatiables, was a pretty big deal, at least with a certain crowd. We were never on the cover of *Rolling Stone*, but we did get little sidebar mentions once or twice. The summer Marius and I were twenty-eight, we toured the country in a run-down van, performing everywhere from dive bars to concert halls. We had a bluegrass-tinged R&B sound that struck the right note for a certain quirky fan base.

I miss making music with Marius. Sometimes I even miss the feel of his arms, the easy cave he made when he wrapped me up and held me tight. Plus, Marius and I were always good together in bed. I miss that too. Mostly, though, I miss the music.

And, of course, our bass player Scottie. I'll never stop missing him.

As we bump along the dirt road, Marius stares out the window, squinting at the setting sun. His reddish stubble is turning into something more like a beard. He has a rugged profile, Viking-like, his eyes turning greener in the glare of sunset.

"What's up?" I'm trying to stay calm, but there's something about the set of his shoulders I don't like. After my encounter with Selene, my nerves are already a little jangled. I'm not sure I'm up for whatever bombshell he has planned.

"I just wanted to let you know . . ." He hesitates, yanking off his black beanie and rubbing a hand over his short hair, palming it so it spikes in crazy directions. "This is harder than I thought."

I can't stop the impatient huff that escapes me. Then I realize, rushing him will only make him more inhibited. Better to get this confession over with, whatever it is, and to do that I need to make him comfortable. I recognize the agitation in his face, the nervous hands working at the insides of his coat pockets.

We pull up in front of my cottage and he shoots out the door. As if this little car ride was my idea; like he's a prisoner escaping. Masking his discomfort as helpfulness, he waits for me to open the hatchback. As soon as I do, he fills his arms with groceries and lugs them toward my cottage. At least I'll get some help. It seems like a poor bargain, though, given how nervous Marius's silence is making me.

Marius walks right into my cottage without hesitation. The property is twenty-three acres, and the nearest neighbors are a mile away, so we never lock our doors. I cast a wistful glance at the two bottles of red wine in the grocery bag I'm carrying. A big glass is just what I need to sand off the edges of this jagged day. I wonder if it will seem rude to pour myself a drink right away, a little liquid courage to help me endure the bad news Marius is about to deliver.

That makes me sound like an alcoholic. I'm not. It's after six on a Friday and I just saw Selene Rathbone again for the first time in eighteen years. If this isn't a good excuse for a drink, I don't know what is.

Marius has my fridge already half full of milk and eggs and cheese by the time I get to the kitchen. He takes my bags from me as I round the corner, putting the groceries away with an efficiency that startles me. I guess over the years, he's memorized the layout of my kitchen. It's not like he's here all that often, which is why this catches me off guard. We moved onto this property ten years ago, back when Marius inherited it from his parents. I moved out of the main house and into the cottage seven years ago, when Marius and I broke up. By then, we'd been together so long we were like family. Besides, I'd grown so attached to the land I couldn't imagine living anywhere else. Sonoma County rents had skyrocketed, too, so I couldn't afford much more than a shitty, soulless apartment in a dicey neighborhood.

Then Marius started seeing Jessica. She's a perky, clean-living brunette with dewy skin and a smile that glows in the dark. A yoga teacher and holistic living guru on YouTube, she spends her days doing downward dog and making delicious vegan recipes for her ever-present GoPro. She's got like a million followers. Between that and their organic, sun-grown weed farm, Marius and Jessica (*Messica*, as I like to think of them) do pretty well. Plus they have zero overhead, aside from property taxes. Their house is three thousand square feet of walnut floors and built-in bookcases, wall-to-ceiling windows looking out over Valley of the Moon. Their deck has been featured in *Sunset* magazine for its innovative raised beds and eco-friendly solar-lit water fountains. It's a stunning place.

My cottage, by contrast, is five hundred square feet of cuteness. It's compact, abbreviated, with the same walnut floors and expansive windows as the big house, but scaled down to a dollhouse miniature. It's a studio with a decent kitchen, a trundle bed, a clawfoot tub and an outdoor shower. I've always loved small spaces. It feels cozy to me, safe, like living on a boat. Plus it keeps me from acquiring too much shit. Only my shoe collection is out of control; everything else in my life is remarkably minimalist. Okay, I have way too many scarves, too. And teas. And teapots. But those are my only indulgences, really.

While Marius deposits my spaghetti sauce on a top shelf—not where I'd put it; I'll need a chair to retrieve it, and I practically live on that stuff—I watch him with raised eyebrows, waiting for him to speak.

He casts a glance over his shoulder at me and flashes his little-boy face, a bashful grin playing at the corners of his mouth. This really confuses me. What could he have to tell me that he's both terrified of sharing and proud of? A thread of understanding weaves its way into me, and I feel my face going slack with shock.

"Jessica's pregnant," I say before I can stop myself.

He whips around, eyes wide. If I didn't feel sick, it would be funny.

"How the hell did you—?"

"Marius, come on." I shake my head at him. "We've known each other a long time. I hate to say I can read you like a book, but—"

"You could tell just by looking at me?" He ducks his head and runs his palm over it again, his eyes still astonished. "That's amazing."

"How far along?" I fill the electric kettle and turn it on. Outside, the sunset's getting serious. It fills my west-facing windows with an autumnal palette of tangerine and amber.

"Two months. She's due in April."

"A spring baby." I can hear something not quite natural in my voice, overly bright and chirpy.

Marius and I were pregnant once—or, rather, I got pregnant when we were still together. I had a miscarriage five months in. We'd just started painting the nursery. I was twenty-eight, still young enough to know we could try again, if we wanted. Not that we were doing much trying when it happened. As it turned out, that miscarriage was the beginning of the end for us. It wasn't the end of our friendship, but it took all the juicy sweetness between us as lovers and dried it to a bitter, pithy husk.

I feel his large, calloused hand land on my back. The heavy heat of it is half balm, half brand. My instinct to flinch away fights with my instinct to curl toward it like a cat. It's not like I'm still in love with him—nothing like that. It's just, sometimes my hunger to be held by him again, to feel protected, is stronger than my much healthier instinct to keep my distance.

"I know this is hard for you." His voice is low and gravelly, honeyed at the edges with compassion. I listen for the dreaded note of pity, but it's not there. This is Marius my friend, the one who knows the ghosts that haunt me, the one who remembers my pain. Those kinds of friends are rare, and even though his status as my ex is often inconvenient, that hassle doesn't outweigh the value of our deep, shared history.

With shaking hands, I reach for the cupboard of tea. It bulges with glass bottles filled with tiny black squiggles, cardboard boxes of teabags, a row of mugs in every shape and size, a jar of honey, and four different teapots. These are my everyday teapots. The display of special-occasion teapots sits on a shelf a few feet away, sharing a sunny corner with a few succulents. There are seventeen pots all together.

What can I say? I have a thing for tea.

"You must be so excited." I pull out a couple of mugs, then realize this is all wrong. "Actually, you know what? Screw tea. Let's have a drink." I flip off the teakettle and reach for the bottle of wine still nestled in its recycled grocery sack. "Pinot noir okay with you?"

His face melts into a relieved smile that liquefies my heart. He was worried about what I'd think, how I'd react. There's a mild insult buried in there, I guess, but mostly what I see is how much he cares about me, how much he dreads opening old wounds. For this, I want to hug him.

On impulse, I do. I take a step toward him, my hands landing on his chest, and he doesn't even hesitate before encircling me in his arms. I can smell the damp canvas of his jacket, the green, dank scent of weed. It's the smell of home.

"You doing okay?" he murmurs into my hair.

I just nod, not trusting my voice.

Neither of us says anything for a long moment. With my face pressed sideways against the zipper of his jacket, I watch the windows turning a bruised plum. A raven caws and swoops past the glass, its black feathers reminding me of Selene's hair.

"I saw Selene today," I say on a sigh.

He pulls away from me, studying my face. "*The* Selene? Your Crazy Stalker Friend?"

"Yep."

I met Marius soon after my friendship with Selene imploded. The experience was still fresh enough in my history to warrant a fair amount of airtime in our getting-acquainted conversations. It had taken me years to sort through the wreckage Selene left in her wake, and Marius had hovered on the fringe of that cleanup. I recounted to him almost everything about our friendship, except how it ended. That was something I couldn't bear to think about, let alone drag out into the light for my boyfriend—who was occasionally virtuous to the point of judgy—to examine.

There was even one time a few months after I moved when Selene showed up in Santa Cruz unannounced. Though Marius never met Selene, he knew how spooked I was by her sudden reappearance in my life. She charmed my landlord into letting her into my apartment and scared me half to death. I told Marius about it afterward, and ever since then he referred to her as my Crazy Stalker Friend.

"How did that go?" He leans against the counter, watching me.

I uncork the wine, pull glasses from the cupboard, and give us both a generous pour. Taking a long swig before I answer, my voice comes out thick, coated with wine. "It scared the shit out of me, tell you the truth."

"What did she want?"

It's so Marius, the way he homes in on the dynamic without being told. Somehow, he can tell we didn't just run into each other; he knows she sought me out, looking for something. That's my ex for you—laconic but perceptive.

I wave a dismissive hand, not wanting to get into it. "Something to do with her daughter. It might be nothing. I don't know."

He tilts his chin down to catch my eye as I take another sip of wine.

"It doesn't sound like nothing."

I bite my lip. The truth is, ever since Selene came to see me, I've felt an anxious, ugly dread churning up silt in my stomach, putting me off food and making me crave the numbing warmth of wine. It's not a feeling I want to discuss, though, so I just shrug with a helpless little shake of my head.

"How is Jessica feeling?" I ask, changing the subject.

He tilts a hand back and forth. "So-so. Pretty woozy, most of the time. Hopefully that part will be over soon."

A sad smile passes between us, and I suspect we're both remembering my first trimester. I was sick all the time. The smell of anything more pungent than water made me wretch. Maybe we should have known then my body wouldn't hold on to the life taking shape inside it. We were on tour, and I had to keep running off stage to throw up into a bucket we kept there for that purpose. Scottie called me their puke-cussionist. Leave it to Scottie to nickname my misery.

"Anyway," Marius says, fascinated now by the bottom corner of my fridge. "We're going to get married."

"Oh. Right."

He risks a quick look up, meeting my gaze for just a second, like a dog waiting to be scolded. I wish he wouldn't do that. The puppyish innocence of it slays me. It makes me feel like a ticking time bomb he's dismantling. I'm not in love with Marius anymore. I haven't been, not really, for years. But I still feel my heart swelling with pure affection at the care he's taking, even as I register the sting of it.

"Congratulations." To my surprise, it comes out warm and sincere.

Marius shoves his hands into his pockets and grins. A single word of approval, and his shoulders deflate—not in disappointment, but in relief. That's how much he cares about my position in all of this. We're family, even now. We've been through too much together to let each other wander off into the wilderness. We hold each other's secrets. We know where the bodies are buried.

I get that it's weird to live on your ex's property and be a front-row spectator to his grand new life. I know it smacks of dysfunction. My only defense against all of this is *Marius and I are different*. But then, that's what they all say, right?

"Thanks for telling me." Fondness makes my eyes sting.

"I didn't want you hearing it from someone else." The unspoken hangs in the air between us: *from Jessica*. Sweet and earnest, Jessica has no filter. Whatever she's got in her head, it's hitting the airwaves, like it or not.

Marius is right. I would have hated hearing it from her.

"You set a date yet?"

He studies his fingernails before pushing away from the counter, downing the last of his wine, and heading for the door. "We're trying to throw something together before she gets too pregnant, but I don't know. Maybe we'll do it after."

"Keep me posted."

At the doorway, with him out on the porch, the remnants of that fiery sunset glinting in his scrubby half-beard, I grab his hand and squeeze his calloused fingers. "You're going to be the best dad ever."

He half grunts, half laughs. Tears sparkle in his green-gray eyes. "How do you feel about Auntie Tansy? It's got a nice ring to it, right?"

"Auntie Tansy," I say, rolling the syllables around in my mouth. I lean back on my heels with a grin. "I like it. I sound like the crazy stoner granny with a bong on a crocheted doily."

This pulls a laugh from Marius—not a cynical chuckle but his hearty belly laugh. The sound warms me. I let go of his hand

and he strolls back toward his gleaming home on the hill. Marius leads a charmed life. Aside from the thing with Scottie, nothing ever seems to mar his fairy-tale existence.

I watch him go for a good minute or two, enjoying the sweep of tree shadows across the hill as his figure gets smaller. The air smells of fall leaves and coastal rain. I take a deep breath, then shut the door.

2

IT'S FIVE TWENTY on Sunday morning, and my brother is playing "Bohemian Rhapsody" at top volume. Irritated at this rude
interruption of my beauty sleep, I stumble out of bed and glower
down at him from my sleeping loft.

"Good morning, sunshine." Tim grins up at me, all innocent
ebullience, making it impossible to stay mad. That doesn't stop
me from complaining a little.

"It's Sunday morning," I whine.

Jay appears beside Tim with a cup of steaming coffee. "We've
got caffeine, if that helps." He shoots a look at my brother. "I told
you not to play it so loud."

I pull a robe on over my pajamas and make my way down the
stairs, lured by the smell of coffee. Jay hands me the cup he's just
prepared. Honey and a touch of soy milk. He knows just how I
like it.

"You promised we'd go hiking at dawn," Tim reminds me,
turning off the music.

"No fair," I pout. "I was under the influence."

"Under the influence of Tim's baked chicken." Jay pulls some
berries from the fridge.

"God, that was so good!" The buttery tenderness comes back to me, and my stomach growls audibly.

"Waffles in ten." Jay cracks an egg into a bowl. "Can you wait that long?"

I nod, flashing him a grateful smile before drinking more coffee. One of the things I love about having Tim and Jay over for the weekend is the way they transform my underutilized kitchen into a fully functioning clearinghouse of seriously delicious meals. Tim always does dinner and Jay specializes in breakfast. I never feel pressure with them to play hostess; they know my kitchen better than I do.

Being around my brother and Jay is my favorite form of therapy. Our conversations range from bacon to Buddhism, Sophocles to cat videos. A weekend with Tim and Jay is a high-octane retreat full of amazing meals and long walks. The two of them are so perfect together, they make me sick. They're both lawyers; Tim's in criminal defense and Jay does divorce law. They're brilliant conversationalists, and they love it when I pull out my guitar to play a few songs by the fire. When I'm with them, the soundtrack is gentle and acoustic, a nice change from my frantic weekday pace.

"You want berries *in* your waffles, or on them?" Jay asks as he stirs the batter.

"On." I'm not very loquacious in the morning. Before the caffeine kicks in I'm downright monosyllabic, especially with a hangover. Last night we killed two—God, maybe three?—bottles of wine. Jay hardly drinks, so I know Tim and I managed the lion's share. The coffee is doing little to address the sour, cotton mouth stickiness coating my tongue.

My guitar's hanging on the wall, where I usually keep it. I played for Tim and Jay a little last night, but I was appalled at how rusty I was. I gently unhook it from the wall mount and carry it to the couch before cradling it in my arms and plucking the first notes of "Morning Brew," my brother's favorite song.

Tim roars, mimicking a crowd going wild, and watches me from his chair.

It's a song I wrote when we were just kids, a silly, sophomoric tune that pays tribute to our dad's elaborate Sunday morning breakfasts. It's far from my best work, but there's a poignancy there I can't deny—at least, for Tim and me. Folded into its simple G-C-D chord structure are a thousand memories of my father in our sunny kitchen, flipping pancakes and sizzling bacon while lip-syncing to his favorite album, Bruce Springsteen's *Born in the USA*.

When I'm finished, Tim's face creases into such a sad, tender smile, I have to clear my throat to speak. "Good times."

Dad died three years ago, when I was thirty-five and Tim was thirty-seven. Mom left us when we were toddlers, flitting off to Chicago, where she still lives, a stranger to us both. Dad raised us, sometimes with girlfriends in the picture, though never for very long. I suspect he was better at being a dad than a boyfriend. Just before his seventieth birthday, Dad was diagnosed with a brain tumor. He didn't linger—there were just a few months between the bad news and his death. He was surprisingly serene about the whole thing, smoking more weed than ever to combat the pain. When he died, Tim and I were both there in the room, each of us holding onto one of his big paws, flanking him like acolytes.

"I still miss him every day," Tim says, tilting his head back to look at the ceiling.

"Me too." It comes out hoarse, choked.

Just then, Jay saves us from more maudlin displays with a hearty "Come and get it!"

I rise from the couch, coffee cup in hand, careful not to spill. As I pass Tim on my way to the bacon, hot and crispy on a paper towel, he touches my back—just once, gently, near the nape of my neck.

* * *

Late September is a gorgeous time in Sonoma, when the light ripens to a mellow gold and the vineyards turn scarlet. Today is no exception. Jay stayed back at the house to get some work done, allegedly, though I suspect his real agenda was to give Tim and me a little time together. We haven't managed a weekend like this since July. As much as I love Jay, I'm eager to have my brother all to myself.

We hike north from my place through a redwood forest, then through a sunlit meadow and back into the primordial gloom of the woods. The trail is little more than a deer path through the ancient trees. Beams of sunlight spear the branches here and there, illuminating lazy dust motes swirling like miniature solar systems. I breathe in the cool scent of blackberries and redwoods. A thin ribbon of creek meanders beside us, babbling as the water slips over mossy rocks and forms tiny waterfalls.

Tim is a good listener. It's part of what makes him a great lawyer—his innate curiosity about other people's lives. I tell him about Jessica's pregnancy, which he teases out of me with just the right note of righteous indignation. He thinks Marius is making a huge mistake, tying himself forever to Shakti Jess, as she's known online. Tim's only been around Jessica a handful of times over the years, but he has strong opinions about her, none of them very positive. Though I'm not sure he's right about Marius making a mistake, I can't help savoring Tim's snarky quips. It's a balm for my tangle of complicated feelings about the whole thing.

"How are you feeling about the news?" Tim asks as we pant our way up a steep, blackberry-lined slope.

I know Tim's not just inquiring about my reaction to Jessica's pregnancy; he's also asking about my ticking clock, the *now or never* deadline looming as my window for having kids closes year by year. He knows I spend a lot of time worrying at this particular tangle of conflicting desires. The miscarriage left a lot of scar tissue behind, physically and emotionally. I've experienced a good portion of pregnancy—more than half of it, long enough to feel her squirming and fluttering inside me. That sensation was so real, so visceral. It still haunts me.

I'd never asked for a baby. Sure, when I was a girl I saw motherhood as part of my inevitable future. It was one of those things we all assumed about our lives: house, husband, baby. In college, though, studying music at UC Santa Cruz, I started to question the wisdom of motherhood.

The creative life I'd forged there was rich and multifaceted, all-consuming. Jam sessions late into the night, bongs of elaborate blown glass, African dance classes and Co-op shopping and beach barbecues and organic beeswax candles—these were the currency of my world. Baby wipes and Goldfish crackers and sippy cups were not in the cards for me, I decided. I wanted to stay in this land of artists as long as I could. I had a friend who'd dropped out sophomore year to have a kid, and she'd never come back. To me, her life looked like a whirlwind of drudgery. My escape to college had given me a fresh start, one I dove into with deep abandon. I loved my life in Santa Cruz. It was gritty and colorful. And probably unsustainable, but at the time I couldn't see that. Anything that might rip me away from the utopia I clung to I deemed dangerous and ill-advised. Babies fell into this category.

But then Astrid happened. That's what we'd decided to call her. It was my grandmother's name. It means "divine beauty." Sometimes I can still see her, with my dimples and blonde curls, Marius's green eyes and straight, slender nose. My half-pregnancy and its traumatic, abbreviated conclusion left behind a Celtic knot of wishes and fears. Sometimes I want a baby so badly it's a physical ache. Sometimes the notion is so repulsive I feel a wave of relief that I've never gotten pregnant again.

I breathe out a sigh, running my hand over a patch of velvety moss as I pass an oak. It feels plush and cool under my fingers. A dragonfly zips above my head, iridescent blue body glinting with flecks of amber in a lozenge of sunlight. I pause to trace its trajectory with my eyes before it races off into the gloom.

"I'm happy for them, I guess." I hesitate, searching for an answer that's true. "But it's complicated."

"Always is," Tim says.

We hit another steep climb, conversation pausing as we dig our hiking boots into the damp hillside for traction. By the time we're close to the top of the hill, our T-shirts cling to us and our foreheads are damp with sweat. Tim turns to me and stretches a hand down to tug me up the final few steps, which are so steep they're basically vertical. I welcome the help and clamber onto the ridge with an unladylike grunt.

Suddenly, we're looking out over a wonderland of rolling hills, forests, and deep red vineyards. Far below us, the town of Sonoma looks small and dainty. A blanket of fog hovers at our backs, cooling the morning air and carrying a whiff of the sea.

"Gorgeous." I flash Tim a smile. "I hate to admit it, but I'm glad you dragged my lazy ass up here."

He smirks a silent *I told you so.*

"Selene came to see me." It's been on the tip of my tongue all weekend, but the moment hasn't felt right until now.

Tim's brown eyes study me, something tensing in his jaw. "Why? How?"

I open my mouth to answer, but he says, "Hold on. We need sustenance for this."

He tugs me over to an oak with a trunk that bends so close to the ground it forms a mossy bench. Then he takes off his backpack, unzips it, and produces a water bottle, a Ziploc baggie of cheese slices, and a box of Ritz crackers.

Once we're settled onto the tree trunk, each of us with a cheese and cracker sandwich, I tell him about the appointment, the fake name, the Jackie-O sunglasses, the restraining order, the weird command to interfere with her daughter's love life.

"Selene has a kid?" he asks around a mouthful of crackers, incredulous.

"I know. She was challenging enough as a friend. I can't imagine what she'd be like as a mom."

Tim shakes his head and swallows, wiping his mouth with the back of his hand and reaching for the flask of water between us. "I don't like it, Tansy."

"You and me both."

He looks at me, squinting like I'm an equation he's trying to solve. "You said no, right?"

My hesitation tells him everything he needs to know.

He throws his hands up, spilling a little water from the flask as he jiggles it in his lap. "No, no, no, tell me this is not happening."

"I didn't tell her *yes*," I argue, defensive.

"You know that woman! If you don't tell her no, a thousand times no, what she hears is yes."

I shrug. "I can't help what she *hears*. She's going to hear what she wants to hear, no matter—"

"You're doing it." He points a finger at me. "It's happening."

"What am I doing?" My voice comes out as a squeak.

Tim's eyes widen like he can't believe my stupidity. "You're letting her manipulate you."

"No, I'm not."

"You are." He nods, agreeing with himself. "You're playing the innocent little Dorothy to her Wicked Witch of the West."

"Fuck off. I'm not Dorothy."

He stands, handing me the water bottle, and blocks my view of the valley with a wide-legged stance, forcing me to meet his gaze. "This is not okay, Tans."

"I'm older now. Wiser."

He pulls a face, which I ignore.

"I'll admit, I felt a tiny bit . . ."—I search for the right word— "intrigued, but I kept my distance. I agreed to nothing."

Tim studies me for a long moment before puffing out an exasperated breath. "I remember what you were like last time this
woman crossed your path. It was not pretty."

"I was eighteen! Tell me you didn't do stupid shit when you
were—"

"Not the point," he declares, holding up a finger. "This was
different from everyday teenage bullshit. It was like you'd joined a
cult, only it was even creepier because you were the only follower.
She was your Charles Manson. That woman's evil."

"Evil? Come on." But even I can hear the lack of conviction
in my protest.

A red-tailed hawk shrieks, pulling our attention. We watch it
ride the updrafts before gliding off over the valley. We stand side
by side, close to the ridge's edge, the vertigo-inducing drop making
something flutter in my belly.

"Do not give her an opening." Tim keeps his gaze fixed on the
view, his tone somber. "I mean it. That way lies madness."

"I hear you."

He shoots me a side-eyed squint. "In my experience, when
somebody says 'I hear you,' what they really mean is 'I'll do whatever I want.'"

"I'll be careful," I assure him.

All the way back down the hill, though, I wonder if he's right.
Maybe, by not saying no to Selene loudly enough, I've already said
yes.

*   *   *

When Tim and Jay head back to the city Sunday evening, it's
almost dark. After they leave, I take my guitar and a beer out onto
the porch. The sky's a deep periwinkle blue, speckled with stars,
and the air has a clean, foggy smell. I sip my Scrimshaw and set
the bottle on my rickety little outdoor table, a couple of wooden

crates with a door screwed on top. I balance my Martin on my
knee, quickly tune up, and start to play.
     First I run through the old stuff—The Insatiables' greatest
hits. I played rhythm guitar on some numbers, congas or tambou-
rine on others. I wrote about eighty percent of our songs. Well,
I wrote the lyrics. Scottie came up with most of melodies, and
Marius refined the arrangements. We were like three cogs in a
well-oiled machine, each of us slotted into our groove.
     Back then, songwriting was my obsession. All through my
twenties, I channeled my angst into music, pouring it into the
lyrics that unspooled from my brain like an endless ball of
twine.
     Except it wasn't endless. I haven't written a song in years. It
pains me to admit that, because anyone who knows me will tell
you, songwriting is what I *do*. It's the core of my identity. I started
playing guitar when I was eight years old, started writing songs
at nine. Everyone in high school knew me as "that weird hippie
girl who's always dragging around a guitar." In college I double-
majored in music and psychology. People assumed psych was my
safety net, my backup degree, but I thought of it as research for
lyrics. The more I understood about the psyche, the more prepared I'd be to map it in my songs.
     Seven years ago, I gave up touring and went back to school
for a master's degree in career counseling. I may have a day job,
but I still think of myself first and foremost as a musician. Being
an academic counselor at Valley of the Moon University isn't as
exhilarating as writing and touring, but it's also a hell of a lot less
precarious. I don't miss tiptoeing around Scottie's mood swings,
or sharing a bathroom with two hygiene-challenged guys. I don't
miss not being able to pay rent on the shitty little apartment Marius and I shared—with Scottie, more often than not, sleeping on
our couch. I don't miss finding Scottie with a tube around his

arm, looking alarmingly pale as he nods off in a deck chair. I don't miss the sickening nerves just before a big show, my clammy hands shaking so badly it felt physically impossible to form a single chord.

But there's so much I do miss. I miss the nights when Marius, Scottie, and I all curled up on the mattress we kept in the van and told each other funny stories until two in the morning. I miss the deep satisfaction I felt when a song came together, every harmony and rhythm fitting perfectly, like an intricate clock. I miss the pure delight of opening my mouth and hearing my own voice pouring into the microphone and out of the speakers in a cool river of sound. I miss the power I felt when the crowd's drunken roar poured over me like a great, warm wave.

A soft breeze pushes against my face, and I pause to sip my beer. The usual Sunday night sadness creeps up on me. An owl hoots from the forest across the meadow, a melancholy plea. My cat, Diego, pushes against my leg with his hard little forehead. I reach down and run my fingers along his striped back, tugging gently on his tail. He circles back for another round. I repeat the action, murmuring my hello.

Turning my attention back to my guitar, I try a couple of chord progressions, taking a stab at a melody. I can feel the urge welling up like it used to. Everything that's happened in the last few days mixes inside me, and the need to distill it feels like a physical ache. Selene's reappearance, Marius's announcement about the baby, Tim and Jay's visit—it all competes for space and begs to be turned into a song. Somewhere along the way, though, I've lost the alchemy, the ability to take the ingredients of my life and transform them into music.

Defeated, I lay my Martin down gently on the deck and lean back into my Adirondack chair, fixing my gaze on the stars. They've multiplied since I last looked. Now they're crowding each other, the Milky Way a smear of powdered sugar across the inky blue. I think about my brother and his warning today on our hike. Is he overprotective, or am I naïve?

I wonder if Selene will check in on me soon, see if I've done her bidding. How long will she give me? A week? Three days? If she's anything like she used to be, patience is not one of her virtues. The thought of seeing her again sets off a complicated cacophony of feelings—fear, dread, excitement, affection, repulsion. The mental real estate I've allotted to her in the two days since she invaded my office makes me think Tim was right to issue dire warnings. I'm in dangerous territory. I need to watch myself.

The owl hoots again and its silhouette appears above a towering pine about fifteen yards away. Its wings form a ghostly shape against the blue as it glides west. I remember my father's superstition about owls, how he swore he heard one every time big trouble was headed his way. The thought sends an unpleasant chill down my spine.

I swig the rest of my beer, scoop up my guitar, and head inside. The frustration about my failure to write a song lingers, but I try not to get too down on myself. After all, I played music this weekend for the first time in months—that's a step in the right direction. Still, it's hard not to mourn the loss of my singer-songwriter self. Back in the day, writing a song was my way of finding out how I felt. Each melody became a map of my inner life, every chorus a big X marking my emotions. Maybe if I carve out more time to practice, the songs will come again, and with them, clarity. Now that Selene's barged back into my life, I'll need that clarity more than ever.

As I climb the stairs to my loft and crawl into bed, though, I can't shake the uneasiness clinging to me. I keep hearing that owl hooting into the night, calling out a warning of things to come.

CHAPTER

3

BY WEDNESDAY, I'VE almost convinced myself that Selene will leave me alone if I do nothing. She's always been impulsive. Okay, yes, she booked an appointment with a fake name, so there was some planning involved, but surely in the five days that have passed since she ambushed me, she's decided that involving me is a mistake. If she's really concerned about her daughter's well-being, there must be more direct and effective ways to intervene.

Then I hear her voice in my head: *You think I'd come here if you weren't my only hope?*

I brush this aside. Whether I'm her only hope or not, she can't order me to do something antithetical to my work as a counselor. I'm here to guide students, to help them reach their academic goals. Sure, if somebody comes to me and shares something more personal, I listen. I'm not a mental health counselor, specifically, but we all have the basic training to lend a sympathetic ear, and we do.

Still, all of our sessions rely on students coming to us. They book appointments and tell us what they need, not the other way around. Selene's suggestion that I utilize my position here at the university to meddle in a student's personal life makes me profoundly uncomfortable. The whole idea is ass-backwards. No matter what Selene tries to pull, I won't violate my professional ethics just to placate her.

At twelve fifteen, I wrap up a session with Travis, a student struggling to keep his GPA up in the midst of a hectic football season. He's here on an athletic scholarship, and if he doesn't get at least a C in biology, he'll lose that. A lot of what I do is hand holding—showing students how to manage their time and get their priorities straight. We've just finished signing him up for extra tutoring sessions and allotted a specific time slot every day for him to chip away at the readings.

Over the course of our sessions, Travis has told me a lot about his sick mom and his workaholic father, his anorexic girlfriend and his meth-addled brother. Most of the students I work with tell me personal details about their lives. Time management is meaningless if you ignore all the messy shit life has strewn in your path. Planning your schedule pretending those messes won't slow you down is just setting yourself up for failure. I always keep a box of Kleenex on my desk, in case a discussion of career and educational goals veers into messier territory. Travis didn't need any this time, but he wouldn't be the first burly football player to dissolve into sobs in that chair.

I've got a faculty meeting at twelve thirty, so I grab a panini at the campus café and hurry toward the lecture hall across the quad. Less than a third of the faculty are in attendance, leaving the room sparsely populated, about seventy people total. Angela Darby, our academic senate president, facilitates a heated debate about changes to the calendar for the following year. I can't bring myself to care, so I munch on my panini and furtively check my phone.

When the meeting finally ends, I realize I've spent the entire hour wondering about Selene's next move, and I haven't really heard a word anybody said. Walking out into the dazzling autumn sunlight, I feel irritated that Selene's already planted her flag in my psyche so firmly. I'm still preoccupied as I make my way back across campus, so I don't notice the person walking right behind me at first. When a hand touches my arm, I flinch.

"Yes?" I snap, whipping around to face the stranger.

His eyebrows arch in—what? Surprise? Amusement? "Hey. You're Tansy Elliot, right?"

I scan his face, trying to place it. There's something familiar about him, but I can't put my finger on it. He has grayish-blue eyes, short dark hair and stubble, a dusting of freckles across his cheeks. He's taller than I am by a few inches, his chest thick beneath a dark blue sweater. His nose is strong, decisive, but it swerves just a little where it must have been broken years ago. He looks about my age, maybe a little older.

A breeze pushes one of my curls into my eyes, and I brush it away, annoyed. "Do I know you?"

"Not yet." He shoves his hands into his pockets. "That's why I'm introducing myself. Hope you don't mind—I followed you out of the faculty meeting. Are they always that mind-numbingly boring?"

I cock my head to the side, still trying to place him. "Pretty much."

"This was my first one. Don't think I'll be back anytime soon." He grins, rocking back on his heels.

"I take it you're faculty?"

He nods. "Psychology. My first semester."

"First semester teaching?"

"Oh no." He runs a hand over his face. "I was at Berkeley for six years."

"You came *here* from Cal?" I blurt before I can stop myself.

He gives me a quizzical smile. "I did. You find that suspect?"

Everything about this man is throwing me off my game. Not to be dismissive of VMU, but it's no UC Berkeley, that's for sure. Coming here had to be a step in the wrong direction for him, career-wise. Sure, Sonoma is beautiful, and our campus in the hills overlooking the valley is idyllic, but academically it's got nothing on Cal.

"Not suspect, just . . . I mean, why?"

"I take it you don't think too highly of this place." His tone is light, teasing.

I cringe. "It did kind of sound like that, huh?"

"Actually, I do have an ulterior motive for making the move." He squints in the autumn sunlight. Flecks of darker blue are illuminated in his irises. "I have family here."

I find myself glancing at his left hand. No ring. Not even the telltale whiteness of a ring tan line. "Yeah? Are you from here?"

Sonoma's not a big town, and I've lived here most of my life— aside from my years in Santa Cruz. I'd remember if I grew up with a guy who looked like this.

He chuckles. "Why do I have the feeling everything I say to you is regarded with suspicion?"

"Sorry." I flash a sheepish grin. "I'm not being very collegial."

"No worries. After that meeting, I can't blame you."

"So, did you grow up here?" This time I consciously remove any hint of suspicion from my voice.

He shakes his head. "No, I'm from Vermont."

"Oh." This rings distant alarm bells. "So what brought you to—?"

His hands go to the back of his neck, elbows splayed. "I'm, uh, Zack Rathbone. Selene's brother."

I can feel my mouth falling open in an involuntary gape. Selene talked a lot about her baby brother, Zack, but back when I knew her, he was living in Europe. She said he was a photographer, tending bar in Amsterdam. I don't know exactly what I pictured, but this is not it.

"Do you have a minute? Maybe we can grab a cup of coffee?" He puts his hands out, like I'm a wild horse he just spooked and he's trying to keep me from bolting.

I glance across the quad at the student services building, where my office is. "Not really. I have appointments all afternoon."

"Okay, look, this isn't how I wanted to do this, but—can I walk with you, at least?" He ducks his head a little, deferential.

I nod and start walking, my boots clicking on the pavement. One of my counselees calls out my name in a greeting, and I wave, distracted. The quad, swarming with students, suddenly feels like an obstacle course. It's warm for late September, the sunlight tinged with an autumnal gold, the last gasp before winter. Students mill in shorts and little dresses, making me feel overdressed in my sweater and boots. A guy with dreads sitting on the edge of the fountain at the center of the quad is playing guitar, and the girl beside him starts to sing, crisp and clear—a John Prine song, I think. My brain's racing to catch up with this new bombshell: Selene's brother, here. On faculty. And *cute*. So damn cute. Which is totally irrelevant.

"What do you mean, 'do this'?" I blurt as he struggles to match his pace to mine.

Zack looks confused. His forehead wrinkles, a series of lines that are well worn.

"You said, 'This isn't how I wanted to do this,'" I clarify. "Do what?"

He shoves his hands into his pockets. "I wanted to talk to you about Selene, but I was hoping we could sit down and—"

"What about her?" My tone's gone brittle.

He sighs. We've almost reached the doors to my building. I'll either have to finish this conversation out here or let him follow me inside. I stand to the side of the entrance, out of the light traffic of students moving in and out. A girl in a yellow sundress laughs as her friend yelps in surprise at something she's said. Their youthful exuberance is jarring, a sharp contrast to how testy and apprehensive I feel.

Zack stares up at the sky. Dappled sunlight filtered through the branches of an oak dances over his blue sweater. "I don't know a lot about your relationship with my sister. I wasn't even in the country when you two were . . ." He glances at me, searching for the right word, and finishes with "close."

I watch him, saying nothing.

"I moved here because I—well, I'm worried about her. She's not doing too great, and even in the best of times, she's no walk in the park." He squints at me, looking for a reaction.

I nod, acknowledging the understatement.

"Our mom died last year." His voice catches a little, and he clears his throat. "Selene took it pretty hard."

"I'm sorry," I murmur. "I didn't know that."

"Mom was almost eighty. It happens." He looks down at his shoes. "My niece, Jupiter—she's a great kid. I know Selene's worked up about her boyfriend, which may or may not be grounded in reality. Sometimes Selene gets ideas that are way off, and nothing anybody tells her can change her mind. I guess you might know a thing or two about that."

Again, I nod.

"You have any experience with borderline personality disorder?" he asks.

I blink. "Not a lot."

"Selene's a textbook case. Undiagnosed, of course, but then most of them are." His expression is sad as he studies the oak above us, the leaves dancing in the breeze casting shadows across the lightly freckled planes of his face. "I don't know what she has planned. She's secretive, especially with me."

"Why especially with you?" I ask, surprised. Twenty years ago, Selene talked about her brother with deep affection peppered with awe. She'd never been out of the country; I got the feeling his globe-trotting turned him—for her—into a mythical hero, her baby brother Odysseus off dodging giant boulders and resisting the call of sirens.

"She knows I'm not afraid to step in if she's headed for crazy town." He winces at his own phrasing. "I know a trained psychologist shouldn't use the c-word like that, but she's my sister. I reserve to the right be a little irreverent."

A breeze stirs my hair, sending my curls swirling around my face. I push them back with my hands and glance at the door, aware that my next appointment is minutes away; I'll be late if I don't hurry.

"Sorry, I know you have to go." He picks up on my body language and rushes to get to his point. "I think she's trying to drag you into this crusade she's got against Jupiter's boyfriend."

I bite my lip and look down.

"I'm here to tell you, don't get involved. She's persuasive, I get that—very persuasive." His gaze bores into me, imploring. "You've got to resist, though. Selene is dangerous. If you give in to her, you're only feeding her psychosis."

We stare at each other for a long moment. He's not telling me anything I don't know, exactly. Until now, I've never applied the label of borderline personality disorder to Selene's peculiar brand of mind fuckery, though I have to admit it kind of fits. I vaguely recall studying the disorder in one of my abnormal psychology courses, but I never connected the dots until now. All the signs were there in Selene, even when I knew her: troubled childhood, intense fear of abandonment, impulsive behavior, disproportionate fury at any sign of disloyalty, suicidal tendencies, self-harm. I feel a little stupid for never having made the connection myself.

I break his gaze, folding my arms in front of me. "I get it. Steer clear. That's what I was planning to do anyway." It's true, though a little voice inside my head whispers, *Easier said than done.*

"Good." He smiles, but it's a sad smile, and—if I'm not mistaken—a little leery. I don't think my declaration has convinced either one of us.

What he doesn't know—what nobody knows, except Selene and me—is the leverage she has over me. The secrets neither one of us can afford to say out loud.

"I'll let you get back to work," he says.

I shield my eyes from a ray of sunlight as it spears through the swaying branches. "Thanks for introducing yourself. And for the warning."

His smile turns bashful. "I've heard a lot about you over the years. It's kind of like meeting a character from a book."

"Hope I didn't disappoint."

He's already turning to walk away, but he flips around, walking backward a few steps as he looks me right in the eye. "Not even a little."

*   *   *

Driving home that night, I notice a car I don't recognize parked at Marius's house. It's a midnight blue MG convertible. I figure they must have a friend over. I haven't seen Jessica or Marius since he shared their big news. I'm glad to have had the space to digest the information at my own pace. Even though we live on the same property, we lead separate lives; sometimes I don't interact with them for weeks.

I barrel past their house and park in a cloud of dust at the end of the road. My sweet little A-frame cottage looks different, somehow. I can't put a finger on it. The windows on this side are pretty minimal. The entire back wall, the one facing the meadow, is all glass. It gives me a lovely, sweeping view of the glade, the forested hillside, and the valley below. Since it's a totally open floor plan, the wall of windows also sends sunlight streaming through every room. From this side of the house, though, the place looks shuttered and secretive. The windows, opaque in the evening light, reveal nothing but reflections of the evening sky.

A shiver of apprehension washes through me as I get out of the car, still trying to detect what's different about the house since I left it this morning. Diego jumps onto the hood of my Subaru, and I drop my keys in surprise. Feeling ridiculous, I bend to pick them up, stuffing them into my hobo bag and turning my attention to the cat, who stretches on the hood as the engine ticks.

"Hello, handsome," I coo, scratching him under the chin. "Catch any rats today, you bloodthirsty maniac?"

I make my way to the front door, Diego leading the way with an imperious strut. The doorknob turns easily, and I let myself in, hitting the light switch and looking around. Everything seems normal. The homey smell of beeswax candles and this morning's oatmeal linger in the air. I chide myself for being paranoid, hang my bag on a hook near the door, and go to the fridge. Pulling out a bottle of Perrier, I drop a cube of ice into a tall glass and pour.

It's annoying, how much I've thought about that brief encounter with Zack Rathbone today. I keep seeing the way he ducked his head in apology as he walked with me across the quad. *This isn't how I wanted to do this.* He must have anticipated I'd be thrown by his appearance. How did he want to "do this," anyway? If I'd had time to go for coffee, would he have told me more about his sister and why I should stay away?

Is there a chance he knows what Selene and I did, all those years ago? How close are they, anyway? I remember the smile she always wore when she talked about him, a kind of wistful pride. She had photos he'd taken all over her little geodesic dome, some of their mother, some of places he'd explored in Europe. I remember one black-and-white photo of the two of them standing on a porch, her arm wrapped around him protectively.

My thoughts still replaying the afternoon's conversation, I pour food into Diego's bowl and give him fresh water. He digs in, ravenous, purring as he eats. I pull a block of cheese from the fridge, slicing off a few squares and stuffing them into a baguette

I find in the breadbox. Something about the quiet of the house unnerves me, and I'm just about to turn on some music when a voice cuts through the silence.

"You really should lock your doors, Tanzanita."

I scream, spilling the contents of my glass all over the counter. There's Selene, leaning in the doorway to the back porch, her head canted to the side. She looks pleased with herself, amused by my outburst.

"What the fuck, Selene?" I struggle to catch my breath, adrenaline knocking the wind out of me. My hand clutches my chest, trying to keep my heart from bounding free of my sternum. Perrier drips from the counter; I snatch a tea towel and mop it up.

Selene chuckles. "I was going to say, 'Don't scream,' but I knew that was useless."

"What are you doing here?" I swipe at my forehead, feeling cold sweat there. "How do you even know where I live?"

She makes a clucking sound with her tongue, chiding me. "Come on, Tansy. You know there's no such thing as privacy anymore."

I take a deep breath, trying to pull myself together. My heart goes on racing, my hands trembling as I pour myself more water and take a long sip, stalling for time, trying to decide how to play this. Calling the cops seems melodramatic. Selene used to be one of my closest friends, after all. If I'm being honest, she's one of the only women with whom I've ever been truly close. After her, Marius and Scottie became my world; Tim and Dad have always been my only family. I live in a mostly male world, which always leaves me off balance with women, unsure of their rites and rituals.

Then I catch myself. This is not some "chick thing." She broke into my home. It's a blatant invasion of my privacy, an act of aggression. A power play.

Adrenaline continues to gush through my system, my body refusing to get the memo that imminent death is unlikely.

I decide firm and reasonable is the way to go. Let Selene know this is unacceptable, but don't escalate the situation with histrionics. That's what she expects from me, right? A big scene? She always did feed off drama, goading people until she worked them into a frenzy. Once, after a few too many glasses of wine, she admitted that it soothed her to see other people surrender to the howling anguish she experienced internally all the time.

No calling the cops. No more screaming. I need to be the adult here.

"You scared the shit out of me," I say.

She covers her mouth with one hand, hiding a smirk. "You know I can never resist the element of surprise."

"This is out of line. You do realize that, right?" It comes out hollow, not quite stern enough. I try again. "I could call the cops and charge you with breaking and entering." Dammit, what am I doing? I just told myself I wasn't going to bring the cops into this.

Her thin eyebrows arch, all innocence. "Oh, I didn't come in. I waited on your porch."

"Please don't pretend this is—"

"Your lovely neighbor, Jessica, assured me you'd be home any minute. She's the one who suggested I *hang out*." She infuses these last two words with ironic emphasis, as if to highlight how normal and chummy this all is, while simultaneously acknowledging it's anything but.

Of course Jessica welcomed her. I can just see Jess's guileless brown eyes taking one look at Selene and registering nothing but friendly curiosity. Selene's wearing a pretty embroidered top, cropped jeans, and expensive-looking sandals. Why on earth would Jessica doubt whatever story Selene cooked up?

Selene flips her long hair over one shoulder and smiles. "Aren't you going to offer me something to drink? I've been here half an hour, resisting the urge to help myself to some of that wine." She nods at a bottle on my countertop.

I sigh, feeling defeated. So much for stern and resolute. With my heart still hammering and my hands shaking, that bottle of wine does look mighty tempting. Despite my tendency to avoid drinking during the week, I find myself uncorking the bottle and filling a couple of glasses.

"That's more like it." Selene takes her wine and saunters back out to the porch. "It's a gorgeous evening. Come sit with me."

I roll my eyes at her back. For fuck's sake, this is so Selene. She breaks rules of social etiquette and common decency—breaks laws, even—then makes you feel like an idiot for balking at her audacity. I think of Tim and Zack's warnings to stay away from her schemes. I can't help griping inside my head that they have no idea how insidious she can be.

Resigned but cautious, I follow her out to the porch, taking a healthy swig of wine as I do. The warm glow in my chest goes a long way to slowing my runaway heart.

Selene takes a seat on the outdoor couch, slipping off her sandals and propping her bare feet on my table. "Great place you've got here."

I sit in the Adirondack chair, cautiously balanced on its edge. "Thanks."

"Does Jessica own the whole spread?" She gazes out over the valley, her expression relaxed as she sips more wine.

An impatient huff escapes me. "Selene, I'm not going to sit here and make small talk with you, okay? Tell me whatever it is you came to say—or was this all an elaborate way of proving you can pop up anytime, anywhere? Because if that's the point, I got it. You know where I live. Message received."

She reels back, though her relaxed expression remains. "Damn, girl. I thought the chilly reception you gave me the other day was because I invaded your sacred 'workplace.'"

"So, naturally, you figured I'd be much more receptive if you broke into my *home?*"

Her hazel eyes spark for just a second, but she keeps her grin in place. "We were friends, Tansy. Real friends. Does that mean nothing to you?"

I swallow hard, fighting the lump in my throat. "I think I made it pretty clear our friendship is over."

"That you did." She studies me, head tilted. "While we're on the subject, why *did* you cut and run like that?"

"You know why."

"I'd like to hear you say it." She speaks quietly, but I can still make out the cold edge of menace underneath her words.

I sigh. "I couldn't reconcile the things we did."

"So you blame me for what happened?" She raises an incredulous eyebrow. "Doesn't that strike you as a bit unfair?"

I sip my wine, struggling to find the right words, just as I did eighteen years ago, when she was my idol. "I don't blame you. We both had a part in it. I know that."

"Yet I'm the one you punished." Her tone is bitter.

"Honestly? I felt healthier away from you." This isn't an easy thing to say, but the wine is loosening my tongue. Maybe a little brutal honesty will help her accept my decision. "It was the only way for me to move on."

She considers me for a long moment, then waves a dismissive hand. "All of that happened ages ago. We were so young— especially you. Now we're grown-ass women. Don't you think we could start again? I've changed since then. I've done so much work on myself."

I feel the old sick desire to believe her blossoming inside me. This is one of the mysteries of Selene. She's forever *working on herself, dealing with her issues*, yet the fundamental truth about who she is never changes. Her cruel streak, her ruthlessness, is so much a part of her, no amount of *work* could ever alter it. She knows me well enough to understand this is the card to play, though. I was always a great believer in transformation, so much so that it took two years of cycling through her dramatic demands, tests, and mind games to see that cutting her out of my life like a tumor was the only way to feel better.

"I'm sure that's true," I say, cautious. "I'm just not willing to try again. I'm sorry."

She smooths back her hair and stares out at the valley. "Look at little Tansy. All grown up."

"What's that supposed to mean?" I know I shouldn't ask—I'm just playing into her hands—but I can't resist.

"The old Tansy would have given me a second chance—though I can't for the life of me understand why I should be the one begging here." Her eyes glint in the twilight, catlike. "What I did was the ultimate proof of loyalty. I think you know that, deep down."

I say nothing. This is old territory, a path we've walked down so many times, it's well worn beneath our feet. Back when I ended our friendship, she wrote me countless letters stating this same basic tenet in a thousand different ways. When I didn't answer those letters, she showed up at my apartment in Santa Cruz and screamed about her loyalty until I threatened to call the cops. I know from experience there's no way to talk her out of this conviction. That's why I gave up and went silent, choosing to move in with Marius so she wouldn't know where to find me.

She stares at me, her eyes welling with tears. "Everything I did was out of love."

I steel myself against her attempt to draw me in, remembering my goal here: keep the drama minimal, find out what she wants, get her out.

"Why don't you just tell me what you want." My voice sounds flat, hollow.

Her eyes glimmer, but she blinks the tears away. In the evening light, the shadows beneath her cheeks are more pronounced, making her look almost gaunt. She shakes her head, sending her hair shimmying around her shoulders. "You know what I want. I made that very clear."

"I can't interfere with your daughter's life." I make my voice as firm and defiant as I can. "That's not on the table."

"My baby is being held hostage by a control freak with a violent temper." Her eyes plead with me to understand. "I can't even check in on her or I'll be arrested."

I feel a pang of sympathy, in spite of my resolve. "That must be terrible—I get that—"

"You know what these guys are like—they all have the same MO. He's cut her off from everyone so he can do whatever he wants with her." Her frustration makes her words come out in a tumble, like she can't get them out fast enough. "The very least you can do is meet with her and let me know how she's doing."

"Selene, that's not how it works." I try to keep my tone firm and rational. "College counselors don't report back to parents. It violates student privacy laws."

Her neck muscles tense. "This is nonnegotiable. You're doing it."

"Or what?" I can't keep the goading note from my voice. She thinks I'm still eighteen years old, in awe of her. Well, I'm not. She doesn't hold all the cards anymore, and I'm not the insecure little girl I was when she learned to push me around.

She leans back, suddenly calm. Her throat relaxes, the taut wires smoothing to a gentle curve. "I'm this close to bringing us both down, Tansy."

We stare at one another, her eyes shining with a dare.

I put my wine on the table. "What are you saying?"

"I'll go to the cops, if I have to." She tightens her grip on her glass, knuckles going white. "I'll tell them everything."

My pulse skyrockets again. I shake my head, like I can negate what she just said. "You wouldn't do that. You would lose everything, more than—"

"I have nothing to lose." She spits the words out with such venom, I flinch. With an impatient toss, she throws back the rest of her wine. "And a woman with nothing to lose is the most dangerous thing in the world."

Selene always did have a knack for exit lines. She rises, crosses the deck, pulls open the back door, and strides through my house, letting herself out the front. The heels of her sandals strike my hardwood floors in hard, staccato beats.

I sigh and run my hands through my hair, wondering how I'll ever go to sleep tonight. My body hums with fear, my system drenched in adrenaline. Selene just raised the stakes, and she knows it. Does she really have nothing to lose? Is she reckless enough to risk everything?

More importantly, do I call her bluff? Or do I fold to her demands?

I think about the restraining order Selene reluctantly explained that day in my office. I'm willing to guarantee Jupiter and Colton have a very different story about what happened there. Selene made it sound like Colton was the puppet master keeping Jupiter from her mother, but given my experience with Selene, I have to wonder. There were times during our traumatic "breakup" when I would have loved to get a court order keeping her away from me. Selene has serious issues with boundaries, and Jupiter is probably grateful to have some distance from her drama.

Though I have no way of knowing what prompted Jupiter to bar Selene from her life, it's obvious Selene is mortified by her banishment. I'm sure it messes with her ego. Maybe I can use Selene's fear of losing face to my advantage. If she sees herself as the victor in our struggle, it might be enough to defuse the conflict. There's no real harm in meeting with Jupiter, assuming I can arrange it. Whatever we discuss in our counseling session will be confidential, after all. I won't interfere in her relationship; I'll just talk to her. Sound her out. See what's going on. Any kid who grew up with Selene for a mother could probably use a little counseling.

Selene won't get what she's asking for, but it will look like she's won, which could be enough to get her off the destructive path she's on. I recognize that glimmer in her eye. It's the look she gets right before she burns everything to the ground. I don't want to be the one in flames when she douses my world with gasoline and lights the match.

I go inside and start for the stairs, but something about my fridge catches my eye. With my heart in my throat, I creep closer, trying to read the words spelled out with my alphabet magnets. The lurid primary colors and the slightly crooked letters give it the creepy vibe of a ransom note.

HARVEST MOON BALL

SUMMER 03

U-O-ME

CHAPTER

4

JUPITER RATHBONE SITS across from me, her expression placid. The sunlight from my third-story office windows catches in her hair, bringing out the gold. It's parted down the middle, hanging straight and smooth in two curtains that frame her face. She watches me with that blank-faced innocence only the very young can manage, a trusting serenity in her wide-set, crystal blue eyes.

I can't help seeing something of myself in her. Not my current self, but the girl I was when I first met Selene at eighteen. Back then, I'm sure I had this same beguiling air of naïve trust. She sits in my visitor's chair with perfect posture, her narrow shoulders erect in her pale yellow tunic. A gold necklace, gossamer thin, drapes over her pronounced collarbones and disappears into her V-necked bodice. Her hands rest in her lap, one wrist adorned with an equally delicate bracelet.

"I usually meet with Mr. Hernandez," she says. Her voice is surprisingly deep for such a little slip of a thing. "Your office is nicer than his."

I chuckle. "Is it?"

She nods, looking around at the small room, taking in the shelves lined with books, the bright yellow filing cabinets, the plants in ceramic pots, the framed prints of botanical illustrations: a passionflower on one wall, a dandelion on another. I can't help the little flicker of pride I feel at her compliment. It took me the better part of a week to move into my office. I wanted to create an inviting haven for students, a place that would feel like a slice of home. Most of my colleagues treat their offices like sterile receptacles for files and paperwork, sometimes tacking up a cheesy inspirational poster as an afterthought. I detest those things, photos of mountain climbers with vague, condescending commands like *Dare to dream!*

"I like your hair," Jupiter says, studying my curls.

Again, that little flutter of pride in my chest. This is a girl who deals in compliments, I note. She's got an instinct for delivering what a person wants to hear.

"Thanks. I like yours, too. I guess everyone always wants what they can't have, when it comes to hair, huh?"

She gives me an earnest look. "You could totally straighten yours, if you wanted."

"True." I smile. "I'm just lazy, I guess."

"Not that you should." She backpedals, apparently afraid she's offended me. "It looks amazing. I could never get those kinds of curls in a million years."

I decide we've exhausted the topic of hair and move on. "I appreciate you coming in to meet with me on such short notice."

She regards me with solemn interest. "I was a little surprised when you guys called. Is it time to sign up for spring classes already?"

Her face shows no sign of wariness or resentment. If anything, she looks a little nervous, like she's worried she might be in trouble. I'm relieved she doesn't see me as the enemy. If her uncle knows about Selene's plans to involve me, it's possible Jupiter might know too. After a minute in her presence, though, I can tell this worry is unfounded. I had visions of a pissed-off teenager trudging into my office, rebellious and truculent, angry that her mother had interfered with her life yet again. Of course, I have no proof that Selene makes a habit of this sort of thing, but knowing what I know about her, it seems unlikely this is a first.

"No, we won't start registration for another month." I hesitate, trying to find the right tone for what I'm about to say. I've rehearsed it in my head over and over all morning, but hitting just the right note—friendly and interested, but not cloying—is harder than I imagined. "Once in a while, we like to reach out to students and check in, see how things are going. Academically, or—you know, in general."

"Oh." She nods, but I can see confusion clouding her clear, wide-set eyes. "Okay. Is something wrong with Mr. Hernandez?"

"No, no, he's fine." To my annoyance, I can feel my neck going hot with a creeping blush.

She touches my desk with one hand. "Not that I mind switching counselors. Not at all. To be honest, I like you better."

I'm getting flustered, but I fend it off with a deep breath. "Not everyone ends up with the right counselor on the first try. We like to mix things up sometimes, see if we can find the best fit."

This is a patent lie, something I promised myself I wouldn't do in this meeting. It pops out because her calm, steady gaze unnerves me. There's something so familiar about her face, and I don't think it's a resemblance to Selene. She doesn't actually look like Selene at all. Does she take after her uncle? I search for similarities, but I don't see any. No, she must resemble her father, whoever he is. So why do I have this niggling feeling that I've stared into those eyes before?

Trying to get back on familiar ground, I launch into a series of questions about her major, her classes, her career goals. All standard fare. She answers with calm, unwavering poise, a preternatural serenity most girls her age couldn't hope to possess. I learn she's a psychology and criminal justice double major. She wants to be

a criminal profiler for the FBI someday—either that or a homi-
cide detective. She mentions that her uncle, who teaches here, was
a consultant for the FBI on some high-profile cases, which got
her interested in the field. That, and shows like *Mind Hunter* and
Criminal Minds, she admits with a self-deprecating giggle.

I listen to all of this with genuine interest, guarding my expression when she mentions her uncle. His involvement with the FBI
raises intriguing questions about the dynamic between Zack and
Selene. Given her sketchy past and her chronic distrust of law
enforcement, I doubt Zack's connection with the FBI would have
endeared him to his sister. I recall what he said when we talked
two days ago: *She's secretive, especially with me.* Could Selene be
extra wary about sharing details with her brother because of his
affiliation with the feds?

"How are things going at home?" I ask, going for casual and
receptive. "Do you live in the dorms, or off campus?"

"I live with my boyfriend." Her hand reaches up to touch
the delicate gold chain around her neck. It's the first time she's
fidgeted since she got here. Throughout her monologue about her
career goals, she sat perfectly still, her hands folded in her lap like
someone interviewing for a job.

I nod, saying nothing, hoping she'll jump in to fill the silence.
She obliges. "He's a student here too. He's going to be a lawyer."

"Nice." I offer a bland smile. "So, you two rent a place together?"

She hesitates. "Well, his family owns the Stanton Building,
downtown?" It comes out as a question.

The Stanton Building is a handsome old brick complex near
the plaza, filled with high-end shops and a classy boutique hotel. I
nod to let her know I'm familiar with it.

"There's an apartment on the top floor." Her expression is
hard to read—almost apologetic, the way people sometimes look
when they admit to some unearned good fortune, like a trust fund
or a huge inheritance. "We've been living there."

I widen my eyes at her in appreciation. "That sounds lovely."
"It really is." She gives me a conspiratorial look and leans a little closer. "It has four bedrooms, views of the whole downtown—and the kitchen! It's like a full-on professional chef's kitchen. I've never seen anything like it."

It's hard not to warm to her girlish awe. She's so earnest in her appreciation. "That's great. You like to cook?"

"Love it." She looks down at her lap, her fingers going to the gold bracelet around her wrist. "I'm not very good at it yet, but I'm learning. I watch videos online to make all kinds of things— chicken cordon bleu, pot roast, stuffed salmon. I even made my own raviolis from scratch. Colton says they're better than his grandma's."

"Is that your boyfriend?"

For a second, her expression clouds over, but it clears almost immediately. "Yeah. He loves to eat, but he hates to cook."

I wait for her to say more, but she leaves it at that.

I wade in carefully, not wanting to seem invasive. "How long have you two been together?"

"Seven months." She looks out the window. "I know it's not that long, but we just really clicked."

"When did you move in together?"

"A few months ago. June, I think?" She gives me that conspiratorial look again as she returns to the topic of the apartment. "Every day I wake up and I'm like, *I can't believe I actually live here.* I've never even had a living room before."

"Do you come from a big family?" I know she doesn't, of course, but I decide this tiny lie of omission is an acceptable transgression.

She shakes her head. "No, it was just my mom and me. We never had nice places to live, is what I mean. Like, one time we stayed in this tepee for over a year. She's kind of . . . well, she's hard to explain. Not a hippie, exactly, just not . . . conventional."

"Sure," I say. "That makes sense. Did you grow up around here?"

She nibbles at her bottom lip, her gaze going out the window again. "We moved around a lot. My mom gets restless. She's a massage therapist? So, like, anyplace that had a spa was fair game, I guess. We were up in Washington for a couple years, then San Diego, then Oregon. She says she's a free spirit, but really she just messes up a lot, and when that happens, she's got to move on. My uncle says she never crosses a bridge without burning it behind her."

"That sounds hard." I can't say any of this is surprising. It's exactly the kind of instability I imagined when Selene told me she has a daughter. Selene was constantly moving when I knew her, finding peculiar, quirky places to rent. She always made them homey, no matter how squalid or impractical, but that sort of nomadic, unstable lifestyle couldn't have been easy for a kid. No doubt the financial stability Colton offers feels like an antidote to all that chaos for Jupiter.

She pastes on a thin smile. "It was okay. I'm sick of moving, though. I just want to settle down."

I see my opening and nudge the conversation back to her relationship. "Are you and Colton pretty serious, then?"

"Well, we live together." She chooses her words carefully, a hint of wariness edging into her voice. "I guess that's serious, in a way."

"Do you get along pretty well?"

She nods, but her smile looks insincere. "Yeah. He says all my cooking is going to make him fat, but I doubt that. He works out like three hours a day."

"Wow. Is he an athlete?"

"Not, like, team sports right now. I mean, in high school he played football, but these days he's focused on law school." She smirks. "He's just obsessed with going to the gym."

I try to picture him, this wealthy, muscle-bound boyfriend. "So he's in law school already?"

She nods. "Yeah, it's his first year. He's four years older than me. He's pretty focused."

"It can be tough, living with a boyfriend for the first time," I venture. She seems determined to keep the conversation away from any signs of trouble with Colton. It's hard to tell whether this is because there is real trouble, or she's protective because her mom's been judgmental about their relationship. Either way, I'm careful to keep even the slightest note of criticism from my questions.

Her gaze falls to her lap again, her pale, slender fingers worrying at her bracelet. I wonder if the matching set of jewelry was a gift from him; she seems to fidget with it whenever he comes up.

"It's not all sunshine and roses, I guess." The sadness in her voice catches me off guard. There's a deep pool of melancholy there that contradicts her earlier, perky, everything-is-great tone.

I don't respond, waiting for her to go on. The silence stretches for several more seconds, her eyes fixed on her lap with the blank, preoccupied stare of someone replaying memories—difficult ones, if the tightness around her eyes and mouth is any indication.

Her gaze floats up to meet mine, and there is something so vulnerable in her face, so naked my heart melts a little. Her next words catch me off guard.

"I hate sharing a bathroom," she admits, her tone a disarming mixture of confession and disgust.

I recall my own experience of moving in with Marius and Scottie back in college. Though I'd shared a bathroom with my brother growing up, Tim's a neat freak, so nothing prepared me for the level of grossness young guys are capable of.

"Is it dirty?" I ask with a sympathetic smile.

"No!" She waves her hand as if erasing this image. "Nothing like that. We have a cleaner that comes once a week, and Colton's incredibly neat. Like *super* neat. It's just . . ." She trails off, blushing.

"You have trouble doing your business there?" I guess.

She nods, her head bobbing up and down emphatically. "I don't want him to hear, you know? Or *smell* . . . it's so gross. I don't know how married people get used to that."

"I get it," I say, because I do. After living with Marius and Scottie for a few months, I lost most of my inhibitions around bodily functions, but I remember how awkward that adjustment was.

"Sometimes I'm like, *Why would this amazing guy choose me,* you know? Out of all the people in the world, why me?"

"It sounds like you feel a lot of pressure to be perfect with him," I suggest, my tone cautious.

"Exactly." She sighs, and that deep melancholy appears again. Her whole body wilts with a sadness she hasn't put words to. I can feel it emanating from her just the same.

Then, like flipping a switch, she flashes a radiant smile. It's the first time since meeting her that she reminds me of Selene. Her abrupt transformation from listless to full-on luminous is exactly like the one I witnessed in her mother last week—that final, thousand-watt smile she flashed right before she left my office.

"I feel really lucky, though." Her teeth gleam. "I *am* lucky. Everything's going great."

"Glad to hear it," I murmur, too thrown by this transformation to offer much more.

She stands, heaving her bag onto one slender shoulder. "Thanks so much for taking the time to meet with me."

"Of course." I stand too, a little belatedly.

In spite of her deferential, innocent persona, it's clear to me now that Jupiter Rathbone has no problem taking charge of a situation when she's motivated. She has her mother's uncanny ability to transform herself at will, turning sadness into sunshine so quickly you're left wondering if you imagined the dark shadows chasing each other across her face moments before.

Once she's gone, I go to my window and stare out at the cumulus clouds drifting across a bright blue sky. I'm intrigued by this girl, I have to admit. There's something oddly familiar about her, something I can't put a finger on. Though she showed no obvious signs of abuse, her relationship with her boyfriend sounds complicated, at the very least.

Now that I've met Jupiter, I can feel the beginnings of protectiveness taking root, despite my efforts to keep my distance. She's not in any obvious danger, but there's something troubling about the way she kept deflecting when Colton came up—that odd mixture of pride in her new lifestyle and a desire not to talk about their relationship in depth.

It's not definitive, but it's something. Selene or no Selene, the girl I just spoke with may truly be in trouble.

I make a decision and go to the receptionist's desk. I let her know that if Jupiter Rathbone calls to make another appointment, she should rearrange my schedule to fit her in as soon as possible.

I'm not going to force anything, but if Jupiter wants to talk, I'm ready to listen.

*　　*　　*

"Tansy needs to get laid." Gabby raises her margarita glass, like this is something worth toasting. Jo and Viv follow suit.

I shake my head at them. "Why don't you say that a little louder, Gabby? I'm not sure the entire bar heard you."

Gabby raises her voice obligingly. "Tansy needs to—" But I cover her mouth before she can finish.

After work, I agreed to hit happy hour with a few of the girls from the office. Gabby's the receptionist in counseling, Viv is a counselor, and Jo works in financial aid. They're all younger than I am—early thirties, I'd guess. Friday night at Pedro's, a festive Mexican restaurant near campus, is their weekly ritual. This is the first time I've joined them, and though the margaritas are delicious, I'm feeling a little old and out of my element. The music is loud, the place is crawling with students, and they've each downed three margaritas while I'm still halfway through my first.

How we got on the unfortunate topic of my sex life, I have no idea. It's true I've been in a bit of a dry spell. My last relationship was well over a year ago, and since then I haven't had the energy to actively look. The whole dating app world feels overwhelming, an exhausting form of shopping where I find myself digging through the bargain bins. The few times I tried I ended up on weird, stressful dates with men who looked nothing like their profile pictures and showed no real interest in me as a person, but got all truculent when I didn't put out, never mind that we had zero chemistry. As a result, I've been celibate as a nun for way too long.

Not that I told Gabby, Jo, and Viv all of this. Gabby's reading between the lines. Also, she's drunk. Mortified at the direction our little girls' night seems to be heading, I turn the conversation back to Gabby's budding romance with a contractor from Calistoga. That does the trick. She gabbles on about their recent trip to Miami while I excuse myself to run off to the ladies' room.

En route, I feel someone touch my back, and spin around to find Zack Rathbone staring down at me. He's wearing a T-shirt and jeans, his tan arms muscular in a ropy, understated way I can't help but notice. In his hand he carries a bulging brown sack, probably a to-go order.

"Hey there." I beam at him, but my smile fades when I see his frown.

He doesn't look happy. "I got a text from Jupiter today. She mentioned a surprise counseling appointment. Tell me it wasn't with you."

Thrown by his hostility, I take half a step back, jostling a guy behind me with a pint of beer in one hand. I apologize, flustered, before turning my attention back to Zack. "Actually, it was, though I can't see it's any of your business."

"I thought you assured me just two days ago you'd stay out of this." He runs a hand over his face like he can't believe the mess I've made.

"Give me a little credit." Even I can feel how defensive my posture's getting, arms crossed in front of me, shoulders hunched like I expect him to hit me. "Just because I met with your niece doesn't mean I'm doing your sister's bidding."

"That's exactly what you're doing, from what I can see."

I uncross my arms and take a step closer. "Maybe there are complications in this situation you're unaware of. Did that ever occur to you?"

A muscle in his jaw tightens as he studies me. This close, I can see the stubble on his chin, the flecks of navy in his gray-blue eyes, the fan of crow's feet. I can smell him, too—a musky, male scent, unsullied by cologne, that makes me breathe in more deeply. He's out of line, but the urge to bury my nose in his neck, to investigate that smell, is stronger than I care to admit.

Maybe Gabby's right. I really do need to get laid.

"What kind of complications?" he asks.

I raise one eyebrow. "Complications I can't discuss."

He sighs, annoyed, and looks around the bar. The music is way too loud, some kind of rap that makes conversation impossible.

"What are you doing right now?" He searches behind me, maybe looking for a date.

Something flutters in my stomach—something other than the hunger my margarita has done little to assuage. "I'm out with some friends. Why?"

"Can we go out on the patio for a second?" Someone carrying a pitcher of margaritas elbows him and he steps so close to me I get another whiff of him. God, he smells good. It makes me think about his skin, which is very distracting.

I hesitate, but not for long. "Sure. Give me a couple minutes, okay? I'll meet you out there."

After a hasty pee and a quick explanation to my too-inebriated-to-protest drinking buddies, I slap a twenty on the table and take my half-melted margarita out to the patio. There are heat lamps humming in every corner, even though Indian summer is still in full swing. It's almost six o'clock and still seventy degrees out here. A bunch of the outdoor tables are full, but the music's not as loud. I spot Zack at a table for two in the far corner, nursing a beer and sitting in front of a margarita.

I take a seat. "You drinking for two?"

"I took a guess at what you might want." He looks at the mostly empty glass I brought with me. "Looks like I did okay."

"Indeed." I take a sip of the fresh margarita, enjoying the sting of salt on the rim and the chill of the crushed ice. "Are you always this hostile with women you buy drinks for?"

He huffs out a laugh. "Sorry. Temperamental runs in our family."

"I noticed." There's a basket of chips and a dish of salsa on the table. I take one and dip it in the chunky pico de gallo, shove it in my mouth and chew.

"So, what kind of complications?" He leans a little closer, his expression both curious and worried. A couple of lines form between his furrowed brows.

I continue chewing, my slightly buzzed brain searching for a way out of this line of questioning. Jupiter said Zack was a consultant for the FBI. There's no way I can tell him about the leverage Selene has on me. He looks kind and compassionate now, so different from the pissed-off glare he offered inside, but he's still the last person I should admit anything to. I swore to Selene I'd take that secret to my grave. So far I've kept that promise, though she's threatening to renege on our deal.

"I told you, Zack, I can't talk about that." I search for a way to distract him, but my food-deprived, margarita-blurred brain can't seem to get traction. I settle for a clumsy non sequitur. "Sounds like you and your niece are pretty close."

He blinks at me, and I can see the wheels turning behind his eyes. He knows I'm changing the subject. I've done it with all the finesse of a four-year-old trying to distract her mom from the missing cookies. He wants to find out what Selene's got on me, but he suspects grilling me directly is only going to shut me down. I see the exact moment when he surrenders to my ploy—for now. There's still a glint of determination that lingers, an *I'm not giving up* tightness to his jaw that tells me I've got to keep my guard up. If this guy has the skills to work with the FBI, surely he's a force to be reckoned with.

"Jupiter's a good kid." His expression softens into an affectionate smile. "She's been through a lot."

I sip my margarita, licking salt from my lips. "Yeah, I got that impression. Selene doesn't strike me as the easiest mom in the world."

Zack puffs out a breath. "You could say that. Jupiter's been to so many different schools, it's a wonder she managed to get into college. She's smart, though. And determined."

"Who's her father? Is he in the picture at all?"

He scoffs. "Your guess is as good as mine. Selene's very elusive on that particular subject."

"Have you and Jupiter spent much time together?" With Selene and Jupiter zigzagging from state to state, I'm guessing Zack couldn't have seen them very often. I recall him saying he'd taught at UC Berkeley for the last six years. Full-time faculty at universities almost never get hired without a doctorate, so he must have been working on his PhD for ages before that. It's hard to imagine he's had much time for active uncle duty.

He takes a swig of beer and shovels some salsa onto a chip. A complicated look drifts across his face, one I can't read. There's sadness there, but also something else that's more subtle. Tenderness? Wistfulness?

"Selene went through a rough patch when Jupiter was little." He eats the chip before adding, "She lived with me for a few years."

I lean toward him, interested. "You mean the three of you lived together, or . . . ?"

He shakes his head. "Jupiter lived with me in Oakland from the time she was three until about six. I'd just gotten back from living in Europe and I was starting grad school. Selene went off to—God, I don't know where all she went. It was a crazy time."

"So you helped raise her," I say, impressed. Professor, FBI consultant, now part-time single parent? This guy's full of surprises.

He shrugs, modest and self-effacing, though it's easy to see by the way he studies his beer that he's remembering those years and they weren't easy.

"What do you think of Jupiter's boyfriend?" It seems likely Zack knows more about all the players in this drama than anyone else. He's made it clear he doesn't want me to do Selene's bidding, but that doesn't mean he endorses Jupiter's relationship, either.

His gaze flies up to meet mine. "If I thought Jupiter was in danger, I promise you I'd do something about it."

"Of course." I catch the warning note in his voice and put up my hands to show I'm not prying, even though I kind of am. "I was just curious about your impression of the guy."

"Do I love Colton Blake? No. Not at all." He grimaces and drinks more beer. "The kid's an entitled asshole, Selene's right about that."

A child at a nearby table screams in delight, pulling both of our attentions for a second. There's a breeze picking up, tumbling a discarded napkin across the patio and sending my hair swirling.

I smooth it away from my face and turn my attention back to Zack, who's watching me with a look I can't quite read.

"But you don't think he's abusive," I prompt.

He squints at me, choosing his words carefully. "He's manipulative. I think Jupiter's attracted to his stability, his lifestyle—not that she's after his money, nothing like that. She's in love with him, but I think the intensity of her feelings for him has a lot more to do with her messed-up childhood than any particular charms Colton has to offer. With a mom like Selene, it's not surprising she has a slightly skewed vision of what love looks like."

I lean back in my chair. "I can't help noticing you didn't answer my question."

"Is he abusive?" He sighs. "I haven't seen any evidence of that, no."

"But you think it's a possibility?" I press.

"I think Jupiter is an adult. She's smart and kind and yes, vulnerable in some ways, but she has a right to make her own mistakes." He drinks more beer, watching me over the rim of his pint glass. "Speaking of not answering questions, you're completely avoiding mine."

I give him an innocent look. "Did you ask me something?"

His expression says *give me a break*, but he keeps his tone polite. "What does Selene have on you?"

"Funny thing about secrets," I say, sloshing my margarita around in the glass and studying the ice like it's a delicate experiment I'm conducting. "If you tell them, they aren't secret anymore."

He plants his elbows on the table and leans closer, his eyebrows knitting together in a frown. "Let me explain something about my sister. She's dangerous. Not *theoretically* dangerous, but actually dangerous."

"I know that," I say, my voice quiet.

"I don't think you do." He shakes his head, leaning back. "Not really. Otherwise you'd take my advice and stay as far away from both Jupiter and Selene as possible."

I put my glass down and throw him an exasperated look. "She broke into my house."

For a second, he doesn't say anything, just stares at me, his eyes wide. "Seriously?"

"I mean, she didn't smash any windows or break down doors," I amend, "but she was waiting for me on my back porch when I got home. As you can imagine, it freaked me out. And then she started throwing down threats, and I figured—"

"What kind of threats?" he cuts in.

I don't see any advantage to lying outright, so I edge as close to the truth as I can without revealing too much. "Something happened years ago, when we were friends. Something bad, okay? Something irreversible. She threatened to tell—" I'm about to say "the cops" but I stop myself. Margarita-addled brain aside, I have just enough sense not to confess that to a guy who moonlights as a consultant for the FBI.

"Threatened to tell who?" He looks like he knows the answer, but he wants me to say it.

I shake my head. "That's not the point."

"Isn't it?" His eyebrows arch, a mixture of incredulity and annoyance in his face.

"The point is," I say, giving him a stern look, "she broke in, she threatened me, and I decided this was the only way to de-escalate the situation."

"De-escalate?" He looks dubious.

"Hear me out," I tell him. "If Selene thinks she's won this battle, maybe she'll back off."

"That's not how she works. I think you know—"

"I'm really good at my job," I say, interrupting. "Jupiter needs someone to talk to. Of course I'm not going to orchestrate a breakup—Selene's crazy if she thinks I can get an eighteen-year-old in love to do anything she doesn't damn well want to do. But if Jupiter wants to talk, I'm going to listen."

He appears to consider this, squinting up at the sky. "Selene's not going to let you off that easy. She wants what she wants."

I throw up my hands. "Exactly. She's also not going to give up if I say no to her demands. But if she *thinks* she's getting what she wants . . ."

"It will buy you time, nothing more."

I press on, warming to my subject. "If Jupiter's relationship is messed up, maybe talking it through with someone who doesn't have a stake in her life will help her see that, and she *will* break up with him. Selene gets what she wants, Jupiter's better off, everyone's happy."

He closes his eyes like he's searching for patience. It's the first thing he's done that reminds me of his sister. "Don't you see? This is how she does it—reels you in, inch by inch, until you're playing her game."

"I get that," I say. "I really do. But given the circumstances, I don't see that I have much choice."

He looks unconvinced.

I add something I don't even know I feel until I hear myself say it. "The truth is, Jupiter reminds me a little of myself at that age. I was eighteen when I met your sister. I have some experience navigating Selene's particular brand of manipulation. If I can help Jupiter, even a little, it will be worth it."

Before he can respond, Gabby totters across the verandah, unsteady in her high heels, cheeks pink with a margarita flush.

"Oh my God!" she gushes, her voice so loud everyone on the patio looks over. "No wonder you bailed on us. Who's *this*?"

I want to hide under the table; instead, I make my voice as normal as I can. "Gabby, this is Zack Rathbone, psych professor. Zack, this is Gabby Gomez, receptionist extraordinaire."

Gabby's gaze rakes over Zack with a look so lascivious, she's basically dry humping him with her eyes. I pray a bus will lurch up the sidewalk and mow us all down, thus saving us from this excruciating exchange.

Zack looks amused and, I can't help noticing, totally unsur-prised. Apparently, women undress and molest him with their eyes all the time.

"Nice to meet you, Gabby." He holds out a hand.

She shakes, holding on to him a little longer than is socially acceptable. Then she turns and gives me a conspiratorial wink, whispering sotto voce, "When I said you need to get laid, I didn't mean, like, before we'd even finished our round."

"Okay," I say, standing. "On that note, I think it's time I head home."

Zack tosses back the rest of his beer, throws some money on the table, grabs his to-go bag, and stands. "I'll walk you out."

As we make a beeline for the exit, Gabby trills, "I want a full report on Monday, Tansy."

I wave without turning around and practically run for my car.

Zack stops me before I can take refuge in the driver's seat. He continues our conversation as if that mortifying little interlude had never happened. "I see what you're saying about Jupiter. She could use someone to talk to."

I nod. "I'm good at that. It's my job. Plus, I like her. I want to help."

He gives me a look that says he's not sold on this plan, but he's not going to try to stop me, either. He rests one hand on the top of my car as I open my door. "You're okay to drive?"

"I only had a margarita and a half." I can't help feeling a little touched at his protectiveness. "I'm good. Thanks for checking, though."

"Listen, can I . . ." He hesitates, then seems to decide some-thing and pulls out his phone. "Can I get your number?"

I raise an eyebrow.

He hurries to explain. "We both want the same thing."

"Which is?" Trying not to get flustered, I take a seat behind the wheel and close the door, rolling down the window to hear his response.

He leans down. "To help Jupiter."

"Oh. Right." I shake my head and reel off my number, annoyed at the blush I can feel burning my cheeks.

As I drive away, my phone pings with a text. I check it when I'm stopped at a red light.

Sorry I was a dick at first, it reads. Blue dots chase each other as he adds something else. I hold my breath. *Maybe I can buy you a drink again sometime—though I can't promise the same level of hostility.*

All the way home, I can't wipe the stupid grin off my face.

5

Saturday, Tim and I go shopping for his annual Finnelicious Dinner Party. I've driven down to the city early so we can make it to the farmers market at the Ferry Building. Tim and Jay have a dinner party in late September every year to honor Finn, a friend of theirs who died a decade ago. Finn was a true gourmand, so they vowed when he died to celebrate his life and his recipes every autumn. Tim stresses about it every year, spending most of September drafting and revising the menu, experimenting with recipes from Finn's tome of a cookbook, and generally agonizing over whether or not the food will be up to Finn's impeccable standards.

I watch as Tim fondles organic avocados beneath a striped awning. It's foggy, the brine of the bay thick in the mist that drifts over us. A couple of kids chase each other at the edge of the table, dangerously close to a tower of Asian apple pears, while their parents argue in low voices. I try to decide if the language they're speaking is Farsi. Tim's scrutinizing the avocado in his hand like a surgeon feeling for a tumor.

"You're going to eat it," I say, "not marry it."

Tim holds up a finger. "I'm going to serve it. That's very different."

"I need more coffee," I say, looking around. "You want anything?"

He waves me away, turning back to the avocados with a worried frown. I forge my way through the crowds of tourists and foodies to Blue Bottle, where the line is ten people deep. When at last I've procured my latte, I wander to a stand selling hot, cream-filled Italian pastries and buy two. Tim's trying to lose ten pounds, so he'll protest, but he's the fittest person I know, and I refuse to enable his neurotic mission to get even fitter. He makes the rest of us look like undisciplined slobs.

It's good getting out of town, feeling the youthful throb of the city, the gentle chaos of the farmers market. Usually, coming down here helps me forget everything, and I return refreshed, with a new reserve of energy to tackle the week ahead. Today, though, thoughts of home keep creeping in. Every few minutes, I check my phone for texts from Zack, which is ridiculous. He's not going to text me. Besides, I can't afford to be distracted by Zack right now. Selene's the one I need to keep my eye on.

When I finally locate Tim again amid the throngs of shoppers, he's examining a bin of chanterelle mushrooms with the same intensity he brought to the avocados. He spares me a glance when I hold up the white bakery bag and shake it.

"Get 'em while they're hot."

He scowls at a mushroom, plucks it from the bin and sniffs it before depositing it into a bag he's brought for this purpose. "I'm trying Finn's corn-and-chanterelle crostini this year as an app, but I can't decide which bread to use."

I push the bag of pastries under his nose. "You need sustenance before making such a life-altering decision."

For a second, he looks like he's going to wave me off again, but then he gets a whiff of the hot, fresh pastries and I know I've got him. He buys the mushrooms and we make our way to a bench by the water. I hand him one of the pastries and his eyes light up.

"I really shouldn't," he says, just before he shoves half of it into his mouth.

I wipe away the trace of powdered sugar on his upper lip with my thumb. "You've been starving yourself, haven't you?"

He groans as he chews. "My God! What is this?"

"I think they called it a sporcamuss, but they should totally rename it." I chew, the vanilla cream filling my mouth, thick and rich. "Mmm. How can they saddle something this good with a name that sounds like a fungal infection?"

"It's probably more appetizing in Italian," Tim says, licking cream off his fingers. "So, who's the new guy?"

I do a double-take. "What are you talking about? There's no new guy."

He gives me a *bitch, please* look.

"There's not! Why would you even—?"

"You're distracted, checking your phone every four seconds, and you're *glowing*." He ticks the symptoms off on his fingers. "I haven't seen you like this in years. You could double as a flashlight. He must be pretty hot."

I laugh. "Okay, there might be someone I'm a teensy bit . . . intrigued by, yes, but it's not—"

"I knew it!" He finishes off his sporcamuss and brushes the powdered sugar from his T-shirt, turning toward me with an eager grin. "Tell me everything."

A pair of seagulls land on another bench nearby, squabbling over the remains of someone's falafel. The ferry chugs toward the dock, churning the dark bay in its wake. A couple in matching sweatshirts pose for a selfie in front of a stand selling orchids.

I'm scared to articulate the tangle of attraction and dread I feel for Zack Rathbone. Crushing on him is a profoundly stupid idea for so many reasons. He's Selene's brother, for one—that alone should be a deal breaker. I know enough about their childhood to glean it was traumatic and violent. Those scars run deep.

Though he seems to have found ways to deal with his past that are healthier than Selene's dysfunctional coping mechanisms, he's still a man with serious baggage. And anyway, why do I assume he's not as messed up as Selene? I've had exactly two conversations with the guy, after all. What do I really know about him?

More importantly, there's no way I could ever let my guard down with Zack. Selene will always be present in our conversations, if not the focal point. And given his apparent affiliation with law enforcement, I can't afford to be honest with him about my friendship with his sister. It's simply not an option. I've never told anyone about that dark chapter, and opening up to a guy who's got a direct line to the FBI is unthinkable.

"Wow," Tim says, his smile wry and knowing. "You really like this guy."

"Why do you say that?" I hide my grin in a big bite of pastry.

He pivots in his seat to study me, turning the same laser stare on me he used on the avocados and mushrooms. "It's pretty obvious."

"*What's* obvious?"

"You're all broody and at the same time glowy. It's fascinating. Something about this guy has you all tangled up in knots." His eyes light up with scandalous glee. "Is he a student? That's it, huh? Or wait, no, maybe he's married. Your very married, smokin' hot boss made a pass at you and you're trying to decide if it's worth the risk."

I shove him, almost spilling my latte in the process. "No! It's nothing like that."

"Oh, but it is." He rubs his chin, scanning my face. "It definitely is. You know I won't let it go until you tell me."

I turn my attention to the ferry emerging from the fog, carving through the tranquil bay. Passengers queue up on the dock, juggling shopping bags, bikes, and babies. The temptation to tell Tim everything, even the horrors that unfolded eighteen years

ago, is stronger than it's ever been. So many times I've longed
to unburden myself, to set my terrible secret down at my brother's feet like a cat delivering a dead rat. Every time, though, I've
stopped myself, remembering my promise and my fear of what
will happen if I break it.

It's a genie I'm afraid to release from its bottle. Once it's out,
there's no putting it back. A superstitious part of me half believes
Selene will know the second I utter it aloud—that she'll sense I've
betrayed her and will exact some terrible revenge.

I decide to tell Tim the basics and hope that's enough to sat-
isfy his curiosity. "His name is Zack. He's a professor at VMU."

"A professor," he repeats, nodding in appreciation. "That
sounds promising."

"He's also done some consulting for the FBI." I don't mean
to share this, but it's too juicy not to. Oh, the irony. One of the
immutable facts about Zack Rathbone that makes him the worst
person for me to be attracted to is, in and of itself, attractive.

Tim cackles with glee. "A professor who works for the FBI?
That's so made for TV! On a scale of one to ten, how hot?"

"Like a nine point nine three."

He whistles, then reaches out and snags my latte, stealing a
sip. "Coming from you, that's remarkable. You're so picky. What's
the problem?"

I snatch my latte back. "I offered to get you your own."

"Do not change the subject," he scolds. "You were about to
explain why Special Agent Professor Hottie Pants has you all
twisted up like a pretzel. Is he married?"

"Nobody in this story is married," I say, exasperated.

"What then?"

I sigh. "He's Selene's brother."

His teasing smile vanishes. "*The* Selene?"

"Not a lot of Selenes in my life, so that would be a yes." I can't
look at him.

"Shit. Really? That's not good." He cocks his head, an ominous pause as something occurs to him. "You didn't take my advice, did you?"

"What do you—?"

"You're getting caught up in her shit. I can tell."

"I'm not," I protest, but he's having none of it.

"Dammit, Tans, I told you—do not mess with Charles Manson."

I laugh in a way that sounds nervous and guilty, even to me. "She's no Charles Manson."

"What is it with you and that woman?" he asks, irritated. "Why can't you just stay away?"

"She didn't leave me much choice." I stand and toss my now empty coffee cup into the bin. "Come on, let's go scrutinize more mushrooms."

"That was not a rhetorical question," he says in a tone that leaves no room for discussion.

I look at him finally. He's wearing that fierce, protective, older brother frown that I both love and hate, the scowl that tells me no matter how hard I try, I can't escape this interrogation.

I give in and tell him about Selene's surprise appearance on my porch. I recount our conversation there, explaining that her threats convinced me counseling Jupiter would be the only way to keep her from blowing up both of our lives. This leads to the question I both yearn for and fear.

"I don't understand," he says. "*What exactly* did she threaten you with?"

I hesitate. "She said she'd tell the cops . . ." I trail off.

"Tell them what?" He looks bewildered, his coppery, thinning hair growing damp in the fog.

My mouth feels dry. I sit back down on the bench. "If I tell you something I've never told anyone, do you promise to keep it a secret forever?"

Now he looks genuinely alarmed. "Jesus, what is it?"

"Not even Jay," I insist. "Nobody, ever."

"I swear to God."

"Okay." I look around. "I think we should walk, though. I can't tell this story unless I'm in motion."

* * *

During the summer that changed my life, Selene and I worked as massage therapists at The Springs, a beautiful, funky old spa just outside Calistoga. I was twenty and she was thirty, both of us rounding the corner of our respective decades with giddy optimism. I'd just gotten certified in massage, something Selene suggested I do. The Springs was an amazing place to work, full of stylish guests from all over the world who stayed in the little cabins dotted around the property. We had the biggest hot spring pool in the country, a bath house with a steam room and mud baths, and adorable little enclosed gazebos in the back where we did massages and facials. It was a slice of paradise, tucked into the rolling hills a short bike ride from town. The land itself was supposedly an ancient place of healing among the Wappo, the Native Americans who populated that area for thousands of years. Sometimes, when Selene and I floated in the hot springs at night, listening to the owls and the crickets, I thought I could feel the old spirits watching over us, bubbling up through the champagne tickle of the springs.

All summer, Selene and I worked hard, raking in the tips during the day and spending most nights at her geodesic dome, listening to music, drinking, and telling stories. To be fair, Selene was the storyteller; I was the listener. She would light candles and incense and make enormous salads and pasta with sauces she invented: creamy Alfredos and earthy mushroom pestos and even a vodka marinara. I kept one of my guitars there, and sometimes I would pluck away quietly while Selene cooked and talked.

Her stories held a dark fascination for me, exotic tales of the clubs where she danced and the many characters who populated those places. Some of my favorite stories took place in New Orleans, at a bar on Bourbon Street, where Selene rode a swing from a second story window out over the street in lacy negligees to entice customers inside. She often talked about Danny, her ex-husband, and when she did her face became a symphony of wistful memories and thunderous resentment. Danny had been her first true love, a restless, charismatic whirlwind of a man who had blown into Vermont, whisked her away from her suffocating hometown and introduced her to a high-stakes world of speed, forgery, cons, and bank robbery. In my mind he had the reckless charm of Jesse James and the slow-burn sexiness of Kurt Cobain. He was also a feckless and unrepentant breaker of hearts; when Selene talked about catching him with other women, her eyes became luminous with a potent mixture of hatred and adoration.

Sometimes, when I look back on that summer, it's hard for me to reconcile the pure, deep pleasure of June, July, and August with the horror of September. The beginning was so fresh and alive, so sensual. Selene and I would take lunch breaks in our favorite little Japanese tea house, spreading out food on the massage table like a picnic: avocado and watermelon and rice cakes piled high with hummus and dandelion sprouts. We would eat with the single-mindedness of animals, ravenous from our bike ride to work and the deeply physical labor of kneading people's muscles for hours. We would wash our food down with the icy cucumber water the spa kept in big glass pitchers, talking in low voices so we wouldn't disturb the massages taking place in the other tea houses all around us.

Our connection with everyone at work was thin and porous compared to the impenetrable bond we shared with one another. Though we were embedded in a community at The Springs, we were wrapped in our private world. The one person who crossed that line, piercing our bubble, was Rob Marsden.

Rob is the hardest person for me to remember clearly from that summer. When I try to picture his face, it's a blurry snapshot. Sometimes, though, in my dreams, I see his blue eyes with vivid clarity, so lucid and bright they're seared into my subconscious. He was in his mid-thirties, a tall, lanky man with dirty blond hair that flopped down over his forehead like James Dean. He drove an old BMW motorcycle from the seventies and wore a tobacco brown leather jacket he'd peel off as soon as he arrived, revealing a white tank top and faded Levi's—his daily uniform. Rob was a massage therapist like us, with huge hot hands that could melt even the stubbornest knots. He had a black belt in aikido and taught classes at the local dojo. His wife, Karla, worked as a waitress at Luigi's, the pizza joint in town, a place Selene and I sometimes went to after work.

Selene was obsessed with Rob Marsden all spring. She said he looked like a young Willem Dafoe, an actor she had always loved. It was true, there was a likeness there—the craggy face, the laser blue eyes, the enigmatic smile that always seemed to know more than you did. By midsummer, Rob and Selene were engaged in a highly charged flirtation, a roller-coaster ride of tortured attraction that never quite spilled over into a full-blown affair. Rob and Karla lived in a Buddhist community near St. Helena. I got the impression Rob saw Selene as a temptress trying to lure him back to the lawlessness of his checkered past. She was a carnal distraction from the pure, simple life he'd chosen with dour and unhappy Karla as his fellow seeker of enlightenment.

The holistic health community was riddled with these characters—damaged refugees running from their shady former selves. Recovering addicts, reformed outlaws, survivors who had suffered unthinkable loss; they flocked to The Springs in droves. Unless you counted my innocent childhood in Healdsburg, I had no former self, so I found their shadowy histories beguiling. I envied their storied pasts, the depths of depravity they'd pulled themselves up and out of. I craved their depth, something I saw myself as lacking.

In that world, I was a rare, unspoiled flower, clean and dewy and oblivious. I was just self-aware enough to sense the child-like allure I held for this ragtag crew of misfits. What I didn't yet have was fear. Like most people under thirty, I casually assumed I was invincible. I had no idea the darkness I found so compelling could, in a matter of minutes, pull me down into itself and swallow me whole.

*   *   *

The Springs had an event they called the Harvest Moon Ball at the first full moon in September. They hired a local band to play Rolling Stones covers on a makeshift stage, and local wineries donated truckloads of wine. The grounds, always beautiful, became extra festive, with twinkling strands of lights festooning the gazebos and tiki torches around the pool.

As lovely as it was, the mood was bittersweet. Early September marked the beginning of a long dry spell for the spas. Business would peter out after Labor Day. Though I wasn't worried about the lack of work, I had other reasons to consider the occasion both exciting and sad. School started at UC Santa Cruz in a couple of weeks, and I was planning to move there in a few days. The summer hung like a bubble in the air, shimmering with oil-slick colors before it inevitably popped and disappeared forever.

Selene and I got ready for the party back at her place. We'd scored a couple of dresses at a little secondhand boutique in Calistoga. Mine was pale and gauzy, with spaghetti straps and a pattern of yellow roses swirling up from the hem. Selene's was the real show-stopper, though. It was lipstick red and fit her curves in a way nobody could ignore. With an open back and a halter top that tied behind her neck, it had a retro, 1940s nightclub singer vibe. She'd never looked so amazing.

We were putting on makeup in front of her mirror, Bob Dylan warbling in the background, when Selene said, "Rob is going to love you in that dress."

I was so surprised, the eyeliner I was applying slipped, slashing a jagged squiggle along my upper lid.

Selene chortled at my confused expression. There was something a little mean in her laughter, a note of ridicule. "Come on, Tanzanita. You must have noticed how he looks at you."

I had noticed, but I was trying hard not to. More than once, I'd caught Rob eyeing me with a hungry, vacant stare, scanning my body with blank, impersonal yearning. He and Selene were only about five years apart, but he was fifteen years older than I was, and his languorous glances creeped me out.

Before I could answer, she went on. "It's okay. I'm not jealous, if that's what you're worried about."

For some reason, this didn't reassure me. I busied myself repairing my eyeliner with a Q-tip, saying nothing.

Selene sipped some wine and uncapped her lipstick. "If anything, it's kind of hot."

"Hot?" I couldn't keep the note of disbelief from my voice. I had a hard time seeing how her married boyfriend lusting after her best friend could be hot.

"We talk about it sometimes." Selene sipped more wine before applying a coat of scarlet lipstick. She pressed her lips together and studied the color in the mirror, turning her face from side to side. "What it would be like. The three of us."

I picked up the blush, eager to do something with my hands, but when I looked at my reflection, I saw my cheeks were already flushed with wine and embarrassment. Our eyes found each other in the mirror, and I couldn't quite read the glint in hers. The nervous flutter in my chest told me we were in dangerous territory, a landscape full of shadows and hidden ravines.

I put the blush down and poured myself more wine.

"Don't tell me you've never thought about it." There was that edge again, an undertone of malice. I'd heard her use that voice with other people, but never with me.

"Having sex with you and Rob?" My incredulity came out sounding childish and naïve, which only made me more flustered. I took a healthy swig of my drink, trying to gather my thoughts. "Not really, no."

Selene swept her hair into a bun and held it up on top of her head, considered the effect, then let it swing loose again. "I just don't see Rob getting this fixated on a menage à trois without a little encouragement."

My eyes widened in bewilderment. "You think I've been flirting with him?"

She turned from the mirror, her gaze locking on mine. "Have you?"

"Of course not." I took half a step back.

There was something dangerous about the way she studied me, a calculating look that made her face hard and unyielding. It was impossible to miss the accusation in her eyes.

I swallowed hard. "He's so much older than me—plus he's married."

"His marriage is a farce," she scoffed. "They don't even have sex."

"Still, I wouldn't . . ." I trailed off, spotting the trap a second too late. Selene had no qualms about making out with Rob in storage closets and vacant massage rooms. They still hadn't had sex, but there had been a number of steamy encounters. If I expressed disdain for sleeping with a married man, I knew Selene would hear that as judgment about her own peculiar moral code. The conversation was riddled with land mines everywhere I turned.

Something slammed shut behind her eyes. "I'm just teasing you. Ignore me. Ready to go?"

Without waiting for my response, she tossed back the rest of her wine and strode outside to her truck. I followed, relieved our conversation was over, but still left with a gnawing anxiety about the night ahead. There were so many things I loved about Selene, but her hunger for histrionics made me nervous. If she was in a certain mood, she could decimate the happiness of everyone around her. She wasn't big on harmony. Tranquility bored her. She wanted everything alive and bristling with intensity.

We settled into the truck, me pulling the janky old sun-faded seat belt across me and buckling it with effort. Selene started the truck; she didn't believe in seat belts.

"Are you mad?" The ball of nerves in my stomach forced the question out of me.

She turned to me, her smile radiant, the hardness I'd seen in her face earlier gone without a trace. "Of course not. It's Harvest Moon Ball. Best night of the year."

We wound our way down the country roads, dust rising under our wheels. Selene took the curves too fast and blasted Bob Dylan's "Everything Is Broken." The breeze coming through the open window fanned her long dark hair out and blew it around her face. She gripped the wheel and stared at the road ahead with a tiny crease of concentration between her brows. There was something fierce and determined in her gaze. It made me think of Athena in her chariot, charging into battle.

* * *

When we got to the party, the sky had the two-toned depth of twilight, robin's egg along the horizon, Prussian blue overhead. A few stars sparkled, mimicking the tiki torches and the strands of white lights. My dress was so light and airy it whispered around my hips and thighs as we got out of the truck and strolled around back. The meadow behind the spa looked beautiful and festive. At least two hundred people milled about, plucking bacon-wrapped figs and puff pastries from the platters offered to them by catering staff. Somehow its beauty only made me melancholy; I was already homesick for this place, and I hadn't even left yet.

Selene poked me in the ribs. "Why the sour face, Tanzanita? The Harvest Moon Ball is no time for pouting."

"I'm not pouting." I leaned in close so she could hear me over the music. "It's just a little sad, you know?"

"What is?" Her eyes studied me. The hazel sparked with gold in the light of the torches.

"End of summer." An imploring note crept into my voice when I added, "End of *our* summer."

I wanted her to make this night about us.

Selene tucked a curl behind my ear and tilted her head, her smile warm and amused. "This is just our first summer. There will be so many more."

"Still . . ." I trailed off, unsure how to finish.

A waitress passed with a tray of wine. Selene grabbed two glasses and handed me one. I held it up and admired its ruby red density.

Selene raised her glass in a toast. "To summers and summers and summers—each one more beautiful than the last."

I smiled and we touched our glasses together, the soft clink lost in the final strains of the song. *Wild, wild horses, we'll ride them someday.* I took a swallow of wine and felt the way it warmed my chest, loosening the hard knot of sadness into something waxy and malleable.

* * *

Hours later, I stumbled into the oak grove that stretched out behind the springs, looking for a place to pee. The spa bathrooms were open, but they seemed so far away. Besides, I didn't want to go inside, as if losing sight of the stars spread out in a vast, sparkling canopy overhead for even a moment would break the spell of the night. I'd had three glasses of wine, enough to make me desperate to relieve my bladder. I knew this crowd wouldn't blame a girl for peeing behind a bush; we spent so much time kneading the flesh of naked strangers, a little public exposure was nothing to us. Already, half the guests had stripped off their party clothes and left them in rumpled little piles as they plunged into the hot springs pool, whooping with delight.

I navigated the oak forest, the moon casting lacy shadows through the twisted branches. An owl hooted. A moody blue light gave the sloping hills the melancholy cast of a black-and-white photo. Veils of Spanish moss twisted in the breeze. Bullfrogs croaked in mournful harmony with the crickets. In the distance, a driving guitar solo wove through the trees. The lead singer raised his voice to join in: *Pleased to meet you, hope you guess my name.* My sandals slipped a little as dead branches crunched like brittle bones underfoot. The air was perfumed with oak leaves, wheaty summer grass, and the earthy tang of weed.

I found a thick tangle of manzanita and crouched behind it, hiking up my dress and pulling down my underwear. Squatting low, looking down to make sure I didn't ruin my sandals, I peed.

As soon as I'd pulled my panties back up and fluffed out my dress, a voice to my left startled me.

"A woodland sprite on the full moon. Lucky me."

I spun around and saw Rob sitting on a rock about twenty feet away, smoking a joint. My whole body went hot with shame. How had I not seen him there? He was draped in shadow, the branches throwing intricate patterns over his body. He wore his usual faded Levi's, but had replaced his tank with a white linen shirt. It seemed to glow in the moonlight, making me feel stupider than ever for failing to notice him. I wondered, with a twist of unease, what other signs and omens I might have missed throughout the night.

"I didn't see you there." It came out sounding prim.

He unleashed one of his slow, knowing smiles. In the moonlight his teeth gleamed. His voice sounded even more gravelly than usual. "I'm lurking."

"Yeah?" I tried to relax my shoulders and ease my voice into a less alarmed-sounding register. "Is that something you have to study, or does it come naturally?"

"Lurking is pretty basic. Skulking—now that's more challenging." He leaned back, supporting his weight on one hand as he took another drag off the joint, held the smoke in his lungs a moment, and exhaled. It poured from his mouth in a pale, silvery stream. "It's not recommended for amateurs."

I took a step closer. A part of me knew I should get back to the party. Rob's wife, Karla, hadn't shown. Rob and Selene had danced for the better part of an hour, then slipped off somewhere, probably to one of the empty gazebos.

I'd never had an opportunity before now to talk with Rob all alone, and I didn't want to waste it. In a week, I'd be living in Santa Cruz. I was a little drunk, and that emboldened me, making me think this was the perfect chance to find out what he planned to do with my best friend's heart. It seemed to me he was playing her, and I knew that couldn't end well.

I suspected he had no idea just how intensely Selene worshipped him. To be fair, Selene was intense about everything, but with Rob, she was also illogical and savage. She probably downplayed the depth and breadth of her feelings for him, but the truth was, he dangled her from a thread.

I wanted to sound him out, warn him Selene wasn't someone to be trifled with. Even though Selene was ten years older than I was, in some ways I felt protective of her. She was almost childlike when it came to Rob. She talked about him with a fierce possessiveness I'd only ever heard in her voice when she talked about Danny, her ex-husband. She refused to believe he might continue to resist her. In her mind, they were meant to be together, end of story.

The memory of my earlier conversation with Selene flitted through my mind, planting doubt about the wisdom of being alone with Rob, but I brushed it aside. Selene sometimes tested me with tricky, labyrinthine hypotheticals to gauge my loyalty. That was probably all it was. Maybe I could prove that loyalty once and for all by making Rob see he couldn't string her along.

As I moved in Rob's direction, my sandal caught on the edge of a stone and I stumbled a little. Rob launched himself off the rock and appeared at my side. He gripped my elbow. "You okay?"

"Yeah," I said, embarrassed.

A breeze riffled through the oaks, making the dry, golden grass around us shimmy. I felt goose bumps rise on my arms. Back at the party, the lead singer belted out: *Let me please introduce myself, I'm a man of wealth and taste.*

"Can I show you something?" Rob asked suddenly.

I blinked at him, surprised by the abrupt question.

"It's not far." He looked like a little boy begging his mother to come see his sandcastle. "It's worth it. I promise."

I tried to consider this rationally, but three glasses of wine on a mostly empty stomach had impaired my logic. His eager expression looked wholesome enough. Anyway, I wanted to talk to him about Selene, and a little more distance from the rowdy party would only help with that.

The truth is, though, I was twenty years old and too polite to deny a man something he clearly wanted. This tiny fact would haunt me for decades. He was thirty-five, intimidating and mysterious, with his motorcycle and his leather jacket and his Willem Dafoe swagger. Nothing in my experience had prepared me to refuse a man like that. I went with him because I didn't know how to say no.

*   *   *

"Oh my God," I breathed. "It's beautiful."

Rob had led me on a steep climb. True to his word, it wasn't that far—maybe a quarter mile from The Springs—but it was almost vertical in places. He'd turned to offer me a hand when the tall grass turned to rocky shale that slipped beneath my sandals. His calloused fingers felt strong and reassuring.

When at last we reached the top of the rocky outcropping, we had an amazing view. We stood on the edge of a cliff now, suspended above the valley by a good three hundred feet of sheer rock face. A ribbon of river, silver in the moonlight, meandered far below. The faintest traces of music floated toward us every now and then, thin and ghostly. An owl hooted, and I wondered if it was the same one I'd heard earlier. Was it following us? Its call sounded urgent, searching, like it was trying to locate another owl in vain.

"A Wappo elder I know showed me this place." Rob squinted at the hills and vineyards, the distant lights of Calistoga. There was a hint of pride in his voice, like a king showing off his kingdom. "He told me it's a power spot, where people came to pray and worship."

The wine and vertigo made me feel a little dizzy, so I stepped back from the edge. There was a large slab of rock covered in lichen and patches of moss. It was flat as a table and still warm from the day's sun. I sat there and looked up at the stars. From up here, they seemed close enough to touch.

"Thanks for making the trek." Rob sat beside me. A breeze washed over us, balmy and warm. It smelled like the dry summer grass all around us, sunbaked and thirsty for rain.

I tried to organize my thoughts into an acceptable opener. "I've been wanting to talk to you, anyway. I'm glad we got a chance."

"Oh, yeah?" He angled toward me, his expression curious and maybe just a little wary. "What about?"

I hesitated. Now that we were here, in this isolated spot, it felt odd to broach a topic so intimate. I didn't really know this man. He seemed more intimidating than ever, with his perfect posture and his slow, devilish grin.

"About Selene," I said at last.

He looked up at the sky and laughed.

"Why are you laughing?" I asked, bristling a little.

He shook his head. "I'm sorry. I really shouldn't. Life is just so funny sometimes."

I waited for him to explain. When he didn't, I said, "What do you mean?"

"I've been waiting all summer to get you alone, and the second I do, you want to talk about Selene Rathbone."

My brow furrowed in confusion. The pall of uneasiness I'd been hoping to banish all night with wine returned with fresh intensity. "I don't understand."

He took my hand in his. "You can't be that clueless, Tansy. You have to know how much I want you."

The heat of his hand around mine, comforting when we'd made the hike here, now felt like a trap. I pulled my hand free. "Selene's in love with you."

"That's not true." His voice went quiet.

"It is true," I insisted. "She might not tell you outright, because she hates it when people have power over her, but I know her, and she's—"

"Selene likes to toy with me," he said, interrupting my little diatribe. "That's who she is. She's used her sexuality all her life to get what she wants, and it's driving her crazy that I won't give in to it."

"But you—I mean—" I stopped, not wanting to reveal the stories Selene had told me in confidence. She wasn't the type to share all the details, but I knew they'd messed around.

He sighed, like he didn't want to explain, but had no choice. "Selene is damaged. It's part of my spiritual path to help her, to counsel her, but it's not *love* between us. At least, not the sort of love you're talking about. We're friends, coworkers, but that's all we'll ever be."

I stared at him, trying to gauge his sincerity. In the moonlight, his skin had a slightly blue tinge, a monochromatic flatness that made his expression hard to read.

"You, on the other hand." His eyebrows slanted in a vulnerable, pleading way, a look I'd never seen on him before. "You're different. From the first second I saw you, I was mesmerized."

I stood, veering perilously close to the edge of the cliff. Rob stood too, reaching out to pull me toward him. I stepped sideways, out of his grasp but away from the edge, and gripped my forehead with one hand, feeling light-headed.

"That's not—" I started, then closed my mouth, unsure of what I meant to say. "I could never—I mean, Selene would—"

He stood and put a finger to my lips. "Shhh. I know, I know."

"You don't know, or you wouldn't be—"

"Okay." He ran a hand over my hair, smoothing it. Then he pulled me in, encasing me in his strong arms.

It felt good, in spite of everything. The softness of his linen shirt against the side of my face, the feeling of being held tightly. Even the aroma of weed clinging to him was comforting—the smell of my father.

"I'm sorry," he murmured into my hair.

After a moment, I pulled back and peered up at him. "I mean, you're married, Rob."

He made a face like I was a very young child and he was about to break the sad truth to me about Santa Claus. "Karla and I are partners, not lovers. We made an agreement to support one another on our spiritual quest, but we're not connected in that way—intimately, I mean. We're more like brother and sister."

Even at twenty, this sounded dubious to me. "So why get married, then?"

"Karla has a very fragile ego." He tilted his head back and studied the stars, as if the words he needed were written there. "She needs to feel secure. Marriage gave her that security, so I agreed. I'm starting to think that arrangement has run its course, though. I'm leaving the community to pursue my own path."

I stepped out of his embrace and held my hands up in front of me. "We don't really know each other, so none of this is any of my business. All I wanted to say is—"

"We do know each other," he said with simple conviction.

I suppressed an impatient sigh. "We've never even talked outside work before now."

He stepped closer. "When two souls recognize one another, that connection is instant. The second I saw you, I knew you. I've been biding my time all summer, waiting for the right moment."

"The right moment for what?" I couldn't hide my confusion.

"To come together." He gripped my shoulders hard and pulled me to him, closing his mouth over mine.

For a long moment, I was too shocked to move. I was a deer in the headlights, frozen to the spot. Rob moved to deepen the kiss, parting my lips and probing my mouth with his tongue. I wrenched myself out of his arms and held him away from me, palms flat against his chest.

"I could never do this to Selene." My voice shook. "She's my best friend."

He smiled tightly. "Maybe you should think about yourself for once, Tansy. What do you want? What do you need?"

"I—this is not—" Again I hesitated, flustered. Rob had a way of twisting everything around. My heart was pounding; I couldn't tell if it was excitement or fear that had my pulse racing. Maybe a little of both.

Rob was attractive, yes. I'd always thought he had a certain mystique, roaring in to work on that motorcycle, peeling off his jacket to reveal hard, sculpted brown muscles. He strutted around

The Springs like a reigning prince, his posture regal. But before Selene brought it up tonight, I'd never even considered getting together with him. I wanted to make sure he didn't destroy Selene. I'd always sensed his intentions were half-hearted, and that scared me, because it was clear Selene's were anything but. All I wanted was to wrangle a promise from Rob that he wouldn't decimate my friend.

I took a deep breath and gathered my thoughts. "Selene comes off as tough, but she's got a soft side, too. If you're not in love with her, fine. You can't help that. But I want you to promise me you'll let her down easy."

He nodded, all compassion. "Of course. We don't want to hurt her."

It took me a second to see he'd intentionally misunderstood me. "*We're* not going to do anything. I'm talking about how *you* handle things."

"I'm not going to tell her about us, if that's what you're worried about." He reached out and tried to pull me close again, but I pushed him away.

"Rob, Jesus," I huffed. "There is no us. There never will be."

"You don't mean that."

"This"—I waved a hand between our bodies, stepping back to emphasize my point—"is not happening."

"Sometimes, when feelings are this intense, people use words as a smokescreen." He tried to close the distance between us, but I kept my hands out, backing away again.

He kept coming. There was a new hardness to his face now, a sour determination.

I swallowed around the lump in my throat. My mouth felt dry, and I didn't think it was just the wine. Some animal part of me understood the tide had turned.

"I'm heading back to the party." I tried to make it sound light, casual, but it came out high and squeaky.

With unexpected speed and agility, Rob seized my wrist. It took me a second to understand he was yanking me toward the flat rock we'd been sitting on earlier.

Nothing in my life had prepared me for this moment. I'd never been shoved the way Rob shoved me as he bent me over the rock and pulled up my dress. Though some voice at the back of my brain kept shouting *run!* I was too stunned to follow that command.

Nothing had prepared me for it, yet at the same time, everything had prepared me for it: lewd comments shouted from car windows as I walked down the street; long, lingering looks from men old enough to be my grandfather; boys in high school who carved *hippie slut* into my locker. It shouldn't have been so shocking when all that longing and rage culminated in action.

Rob pinned me with his hips, forcing my pelvis against the jagged edge of the rock. With his free hand he yanked my panties to my knees. That's when something snapped inside me, my animal instincts finally kicking in. I twisted my body around and tried to knee him in the balls. It almost worked. Rob was strong, though, and years of martial arts had trained him to see an attack long before it landed. He sidestepped my clumsy attempt at defense and spun me around again, this time pulling my hair so hard I cried out.

He leaned over me, pinning me with the full weight of his body. Still gripping my hair, he whispered into my ear, "Do not fight me, Tansy. You want this. I know you do."

"Goddammit," I grunted, my voice hoarse with tears. "Get off me!"

"You can't hide how much you want me." His breath smelled acrid. He fondled my bare ass and yanked harder on my hair, pulling my head up toward him. My scalp burned.

All at once the fight went out of me. I played dead. It wasn't a decision so much as an instinct. Wriggling and struggling only aroused him, so I let my muscles go limp. I felt myself zoning out.

Years later, I learned the word for this: dissociation. At the time, I just felt the numbness creep over me, a resigned blankness; I regarded my own plight with clinical distance, like a dream where you're at once the actor and the observer.

The next thing I remember is blurred motion out of the corner of my eye. Something tore free of the darkness and hurtled toward us, moving fast. Rob grunted in surprise and then his weight lifted off of me. I heard him call out—not in words, but in strange, guttural sounds that got louder and then dwindled into nothing.

I turned and saw Selene standing at the edge of the cliff, her hair blowing wild like an avenging angel. Her red dress was startling in the moonlight.

With painful slowness, I eased myself off the rock and tried to stand. My hands shook as I pulled my panties up from my ankles. It struck me that it was probably less than an hour ago that I'd peed in the woods. Such a short time, yet everything had changed.

My knees turned to jelly. I collapsed into a sitting position on the ground, curling into a protective ball. After a moment that seemed to last forever, Selene came and sat beside me, saying nothing.

"Man," she said into the silence. "I could really use a cigarette right now."

I heard a peal of hysterical laughter that seemed to rise all the way to the treetops. It took me a second to realize it had come from me.

As soon as the laughter stopped, I started to shiver—violent, whole-body shivers that made my teeth chatter. The night was still warm, as far as I could tell—the rock against my back still held the summer heat—but I was freezing.

Selene wrapped an arm around me. I curled into the warmth of her body, craving her heat.

"We can never talk about this to anyone." Her voice was low, almost soothing, but there was an edge of warning trapped inside it.

I nodded, unable to speak through my chattering teeth.

"Never," she whispered.

I turned and met her gaze. Her eyes were luminous, fierce.

"Can we go back to the dome?" I sounded broken, pitiful.

She stood and helped me up. "Of course. I'll take you to my truck. Then I'll go back to the party and say our goodbyes, so nobody will think it's strange."

It was so unlike Selene to worry about what people thought. Then the word sprang into my head from out of nowhere: *alibi.*

The truth started to seep into me, a new wave of cold spreading like a tide through my blood. Shock had done its job until that moment, cushioning me from reality, but now the facts started to line up and I was afraid I might be sick. I thought about the cliff, about Rob and me peering over its edge, the way it made my stomach tingle with vertigo. Then I pictured Rob's body splayed at the bottom, his legs and arms akimbo, his skull crushed, his blood soaking into the dry earth.

"Come on," Selene said, her words brisk and businesslike. "We need to get you home."

I stared at her, unable to articulate the questions clustered at the base of my throat, trying to break free.

She pushed her hair out of her face. "Please don't look at me like that."

I shook my head, though I had no idea what I was denying.

"I mean it, Tansy." A muscle twitched in her jaw as she regarded me. "Don't."

Finally, a question broke free from my lips.

"Did you have to kill him?"

Her reply was immediate and sharp. "Did you have to wander into the woods with the guy like fucking Bambi?"

I recoiled.

She put a hand on my arm. "I'm sorry. Just—"

"I wasn't—I didn't know he was going to—"

"You have to be more careful, is all I'm saying." She frowned. "Didn't I teach you to watch your six?"

It was her favorite piece of advice. She said it whenever we parted, instead of goodbye. Another question bubbled up. "How did you even find us?"

She pulled her hair into a messy knot. "I saw you wander into the grove, and when you didn't come back right away, I checked on you."

I bristled a little at her choice of words. Had I really "wandered" into the grove? No. I went there with a purpose. She made me sound like a clueless fawn stumbling around on spindly legs. "So you followed us here?"

She nodded. "I figured this is where you were heading. It's Rob's favorite spot."

"You heard us, then?" I asked. "Our conversation?"

"Not much." Her lips pressed together into a hard, flat line, and I saw what she would look like many years later—the parentheses framing her mouth, the sharpness of her cheekbones. She seemed much older than ever before, her eyes ancient in the moonlight.

She seized my arm and started pulling me back toward the trail. "We can talk about this later."

I let myself be led for a few steps, but then I stopped, planting my feet.

She turned back to me, annoyed. "I mean it. We have to—"

"Don't you feel . . . ?" I trailed off, unsure of how to finish.

"Don't I feel what?" she snapped.

"Anything?"

She fixed me with a withering look. "I feel everything, Tansy. More than you'll ever know. But now is not the time for feelings. Now is the time to act."

*   *   *

By the time I finish my story, Tim and I have walked down the Embarcadero all the way to Aquatic Park. We stand at the end of the pier, staring out at the calm water as fog drifts around us. A little man with a face as wrinkled as a shriveled apple casts his line out into the bay. A couple pushing a baby carriage laugh at something the man says as they pass.

"Christ," Tim says. "I had no idea."

"You're the first person I've told," I say. "Ever."

He leans against the railing, his face pensive. "Not even a therapist?"

I pick at a patch of lichen, not wanting to look at him. "I didn't know if it was safe. I mean, there's confidentiality, but something this serious? I didn't want to risk it."

Tim wraps an arm around me. "You didn't do anything wrong, Tansy."

"I covered up a murder." My voice breaks on the last word.

"It was self-defense, and you weren't even the one who pushed him."

"I know," I mumble. "But still. I didn't report it. Doesn't that make me an accessory or something?"

"Technically . . . ," he concedes. When he sees my expression he adds, "But you were under duress."

We stare out at the water in silence for a long moment. Tim's arm wrapped around my shoulders feels good. Telling him was scary but also a relief, like finally putting down a heavy burden I'd carried for almost twenty years. Now I feel drained and curiously light.

Tim pulls me closer. "How long before they found the body?"

"It took a few weeks. He and his wife were breaking up, so she figured he was staying with friends." I swallow around the thickness in my throat. "Work didn't notice, because he'd already planned on taking time off to move out. It was a pretty isolated spot. A hiker found him eventually."

"Were you or Selene ever questioned?"

I shake my head. "They ruled it a suicide. I guess he suffered from pretty serious depression, and he'd been hospitalized for an overdose years before, so nobody considered it suspicious."

Tim grimaces. "I know it might sound cold, but I'm not going to shed a tear. If he weren't already dead, I'd have to kill him."

I don't respond. A part of me agrees. It's complicated, though. The anger I felt for Rob that night, the impotent humiliation of being bent over that rock, had gotten so mixed up with my guilt, it was impossible to separate. In some ways, I longed for pure, white hot rage. It seemed simple and honest compared to the muddy swamp of culpability I slogged through.

When I moved to Santa Cruz a week later, I stuffed it all away into a trunk, locked it tight, and threw away the key. I had nightmares—horrible, graphic nightmares—but the change of scene and the distraction of all new friends helped me divorce myself from that night. It seemed more like a movie, like a book I'd read long ago, than an actual experience I'd lived through. Survived.

Until now. Ever since Selene ambushed me at my office ten days ago, the memories have come springing back to life with vivid animation.

As if reading my mind, Tim says, "Did Selene ever try to contact you after you moved to Santa Cruz?"

"Yeah." I remember the terrible, middle-of-the-night phone calls, Selene slurring her words, speaking in riddles. The night she showed up and surprised me in my apartment was even worse—bad enough to make me move in with Marius just to ensure it would never happen again. We were just friends at that point, but I felt safer at his place. I don't have the energy to go into all that now. "She was pretty messed up."

"What about you?" He squeezes my shoulder. "Must have been tough for you, too."

"It was easier for me. I mean, she was in love with the guy." I sigh, imagining how alone she must have felt, how bereft and abandoned. "She still worked at The Springs, where all the memories were. I was off in my new life. It was simpler for me to pretend it had never happened."

In wordless agreement, we turn away from the railing and start the long walk back to the Ferry Building. After we've passed a man throwing sticks into the bay for his golden retriever, I say, "She tried to kill herself, you know."

Tim stops walking. "What?"

"Selene." I pull my hair back to keep it from flying into my eyes. "She got wasted and drove her car into oncoming traffic. She called me right before and told me she was going to do it."

"Jesus," he breathes. "Was she hurt?"

"By some miracle, she survived with barely a scratch." Now, looking back, it occurs to me she must have been pregnant with Jupiter at the time. The thought makes the whole incident that much more horrific.

Tim fixes me with a sympathetic look. "You can't blame yourself. You know that."

My eyes sting, and then tears are running down my face. "Maybe I shouldn't have cut her off like that."

He takes a step toward me and grabs my hand. "Oh, Tans."

"It might be the worst thing I've ever done."

His arms close around me, holding me tight, and I can smell the citrusy tang of his aftershave, feel the soft cashmere of his coat against my face. I cry harder into his shoulder, grateful that the beach is mostly abandoned, that the fog makes it feel almost private.

"Sweetheart," he says into my hair, "you were twenty years old."

"But she needed me." I pull back and look into his kind brown eyes. "She only did it to protect me, and how did I repay her? I stopped taking her calls. What kind of shitty human being—?"

"Shhh," he soothes, clutching me tighter and speaking into my hair. "You did the best you could."

6

THE FOLLOWING WEDNESDAY, I'm halfway through my lunch and skimming my emails when Jupiter appears in my office doorway.

"Hey," I say, surprise making my voice high and squeaky. I reach for a napkin and wipe my mouth. "I wasn't expecting you. Did you—?"

"Sorry. I don't have an appointment. If it's a bad time . . ."

"No, no, it's fine." I gesture to the chair in front of my desk. Normally, being interrupted during my lunch break would annoy me, but in this case, curiosity trumps irritation. I've had Rathbones on my mind for days; seeing one of them in the flesh startles me, as if a character from a movie stepped out of the screen and into my office.

"Thanks. I had a class downstairs and just had this sudden urge to stop by." She keeps hovering in the doorway, looking uncertain. She has on a teal minidress with bell sleeves, thick brown tights, and knee-high boots.

"Cute dress," I say.

"Colton got it for me." She tries to hide her shy smile as she tucks her umbrella into the little stand I keep near the door. "I saw it online and he noticed I kept going back to it."

She saunters in, looking around my office as she did last time. It's as if she sees something in my world she likes, and she's trying to memorize the details so she can re-create it. There's something flattering about that, but also something unnerving. She looks at everything with an avaricious gleam in her eyes. I doubt she's lusting after my file cabinets or framed prints, so there must be some mood here she wants to get her hands on.

I stand and close the door she left open, giving her a moment to examine the space. She reminds me of a cat, sniffing the corners and rubbing up against doorways before she finally settles in.

Outside, a storm has descended, lashing rain against the windows. I take a seat again behind my desk, putting the lid back on my container of soup. "How are things going?"

"Not bad." The gray, rainy light through my windows illuminates her peach-like complexion. She really is one of the most beautiful young women I've ever seen.

When she doesn't elaborate, I add, "Is there some reason in particular you wanted to see me?"

She looks at her lap. "Is it okay to talk to you about . . . relationship stuff?"

"Of course." Thinking I should be up front, I elaborate. "I'm not a mental health counselor, so I can recommend you to a colleague if you prefer, but I'm happy to listen if you just feel like talking."

Her eyes widen a little at this. "I don't think I need a mental health counselor."

I give her what I hope is a reassuring smile. "Most of us just need a safe space where we can talk things through. If that's what you're after, you've come to the right place. Anything you tell me won't leave this room."

I try to ignore the nagging conviction that Selene is bound to show up soon, demanding a report on my meetings with Jupiter. Well, she can ask, but she won't get the answers she's looking for. I do have some integrity.

"Okay." Her hand goes to the delicate gold necklace she wore last time.

In my gentlest, most inviting voice, I ask, "What's going on in your relationship?"

She sighs so deeply, her whole body visibly deflates. Outside, the rain taps at the window in a steady rhythm, a lull between gusts.

Jupiter speaks in such a small, childlike voice, I almost can't hear her over the rain. "We've been fighting."

"What about?"

"Everything." She meets my eye with an ironic little smile. "And nothing."

"Is this new? Have the fights become more frequent since you moved in together?"

"Yes and no." Her gaze roams the ceiling as she thinks about it. "Colton goes through these phases where nothing I do is right."

I nod. "So he gets overly critical?"

Her hand goes to a tiny braid she's woven into her long blonde hair. "Yeah. Like his dad."

"Sometimes we unconsciously mimic what our parents modeled for us," I say.

She breathes out a bitter laugh. "God, I hope I don't do that. The last person I want to become is my mom."

I work to keep my expression neutral. Is it a breach of her confidence, not telling her I have history with her mother? Would she feel completely betrayed? Probably. But I can do real good here, giving her a chance to unburden herself with someone outside her inner circle. I wonder if she has any close friends. Somehow, I suspect she doesn't, though I'm not sure where this idea stems from.

Leaving the comment about her mom untouched, I turn the conversation back to her boyfriend. "Can you give me an example? What kinds of things do you fight about?"

"Honestly? Sometimes I think he just doesn't like me very much."

"Why do you say that?"

She shrugs. "I guess he's just stressed about law school. I mean, he's under a lot of pressure. Yesterday, I knew he had a big exam, so I looked up a recipe for braised short ribs. I remember him saying he loved ribs, and I'd never made them, so I thought it would be a nice way to celebrate him getting through this big test, you know?"

The rain gets louder. Jupiter pauses in her story, nibbling her lower lip.

"How did it go?" I prompt.

"Not good." Tears glimmer in her eyes as she stares at the edge of my desk. "He said they were too dry and threw his plate on the floor."

I try not to react, though inside I'm screaming. This guy sounds like a classic abuser. If he's not violent with her now, it's only a matter of time before he starts. Plus, he sounds like a spoiled dick, frankly. But nobody wants to hear that about her boyfriend, and saying it outright will only shame her, so I go with the classic therapist response.

"How did that make you feel?"

A tear spills down her cheek. I push the box of Kleenex closer, and she snatches one, dabbing at her face. "Like shit. I mean yeah, maybe they *were* a little dry, and he didn't do well on his test, so I guess he was already in a shitty mood, but still."

"How did you react, when he threw his plate?"

She darts a quick look at me. "When he does that kind of stuff, I just—I don't know. I kind of freeze, you know? In one of my classes we were talking about the fight or flight reaction. But for some reason, when I get my feelings hurt like that, I just kind of unplug. I don't fight back, I don't run away, I just sort of play dead. Is that weird?"

For a second, I flash on my body bent over that rock, limp and motionless. I push the image aside and focus on Jupiter.

"Have you heard of dissociation?" I ask.

She looks blank and shakes her head.

"It's a coping mechanism, a way of disconnecting. Sometimes, when we find ourselves in a situation that's uncomfortable—maybe one that triggers earlier trauma—we 'unplug,' as you say." I choose my words carefully, eager to reassure her that she didn't do anything wrong. "It's quite common. Our psyche likes to protect us from trauma, and dissociation allows us to distance ourselves from whatever's happening in the present."

Her fingers work the tissue in her lap, rolling it into a ball. "Is it bad?"

"Not at all. Like all coping mechanisms, it's there to protect us." I pause. "It can interfere with our ability to function, though. It's like our brains are computers, and dissociation means that computer freezes, needing to restart before it can get on with everyday tasks."

"How do you restart yourself?" She looks curious.

"You could keep a journal and start identifying your triggers. Breathing exercises sometimes help too, or yoga. Some people keep a 'rescue box' in their house."

Her brows knit together in confusion. "What's a rescue box?"

"It's a box filled with things that help you snap out of your trance, like calming essential oils, little pieces of candy or mints so you can focus on taste, stuff like that. When you tune back in to your senses, that can help bring you back to the present."

I want to get back to the issue of her boyfriend. It's one thing to counsel her on how to stop dissociating, but if she's in real physical danger, all the breathing exercises and rescue boxes in the world won't keep her safe.

"Tell me more about these fights you're having with Colton," I say gently. "Does he often do that sort of thing—throw his dinner on the floor?"

She squirms a little in her chair, a guarded look coming into her eyes. "I mean, not *often* . . ."

"You said you'd been together for seven months?"

Her voice rises in surprise. "Wow. Good memory."

For a second I worry she suspects I have a special interest in her. I've played over the conversation we had last week far more obsessively than I would any normal session. I quickly dismiss this notion as paranoid. Everyone likes to be heard, right?

"So, over the course of seven months, how often would you say he's lashed out like that—thrown something, broken something, that sort of thing?" I work hard to keep my tone bland as milk, as if petulant man-boys flinging their dinner around is something everyone deals with on a regular basis. Making Jupiter feel judged right now would be the kiss of death.

She looks out the window, a slightly glazed look on her pretty face. The rain hammers at the glass, a growl of thunder barely audible in the distance. Is she trying to come up with an acceptable answer? Is she remembering scenes much worse than a sulky boyfriend throwing his dinner?

A sharp knock on my office door startles us both. It's so rare for me to be interrupted when I'm with a student. Gabby knows not to give me messages until I'm between appointments. With a quick, apologetic look at Jupiter, I rise and am halfway to the door when it flies open. This is even more startling; knocks mid-session are rare, but someone barging in is unheard of.

I stop and take in the young man filling my doorway. He's wearing an expensive-looking raincoat and jeans. He's not especially big, but he's got classic alpha-male posture, standing tall and taking up as much space as possible as his raincoat drips onto the carpet. His gray-blue eyes regard me with haughty disdain, as if I'm the one interrupting him.

"We're in the middle of—" I begin, but Jupiter cuts me off.

"Colton," she squeaks, standing so quickly her bag falls to the floor. "What are you—?"

"We were supposed to meet Dad at Little Rome five minutes ago." His nostrils flare as he works to keep his anger in check. "Did you forget?"

Jupiter's hand covers her mouth. "Oh my God! Is it one already? How did you find me?"

"I tracked your phone." He says this like it's the most normal thing in the world. I know a lot of young people do that, but to me it seems incredibly invasive.

Colton shoots me a quick, annoyed look, like this is somehow my fault.

Taking the high road, I offer him my hand. "You must be Colton. I'm Tansy Elliot, Jupiter's guidance counselor."

With visible effort, he manages to squelch his impatience and takes my hand. His fingers feel clammy, and he shakes with a firmer-than-necessary grip. I watch his face go from raw frustration to calculated charm.

"Great to meet you, Tansy. So sorry for the interruption." He shoots Jupiter a mock-scolding look with real heat simmering just below the surface. "My girlfriend here obviously forgot we have a lunch date."

Jupiter scrambles to gather the things that tumbled out of her bag when she dropped it: hand sanitizer, a tube of lipstick, a prescription bottle, a pen. When she straightens again, her face has gone red and her eyes are feverish with panic.

"We better hurry," Colton says, giving her a meaningful look.

While his barely concealed ire is focused on her, I take the opportunity to study him more closely. He's got a military bearing, with dark blond hair gelled into a perfectly coiffed flat-top. His face is clean-shaven and tanned. I can see his thick, dark eyebrows working hard not to furrow into a deep scowl. There's an old-money, frat-boy prettiness to his bone structure; the high cheekbones, flawless complexion, and full lips give him an all-American look, the natural by-product of generations of powerful men choosing physically flaw-less women to mother their offspring.

"I'm so sorry." Jupiter's eyes dart between her boyfriend and me. She looks smaller, somehow, since Colton appeared, as if she's shrunk to make more room for him. Or to disappear. "I don't know how I forgot."

Colton tosses me a tight, condescending smile, as if to say, *You see what I put up with?*

"Don't worry about it," I say to Jupiter. "I'll have Gabby reach out to reschedule, okay?"

She nods, flashing me a quick, apologetic look before the two of them hurry down the hallway. I can hear Colton talking to her in a low, terse voice while she trots along behind him, struggling to keep up with his determined strides.

It's not until they're out the door that my gaze falls on Jupiter's umbrella. It's a nice one, a vivid red with a sturdy wooden handle.

Seizing it, I hurry after them, ignoring the slow elevator and jogging to the stairs, where I'm pretty sure they were headed. I hustle down the steps, but stop when I hear Colton's voice echoing in the deserted stairwell one flight below me.

"What the hell were you telling her, anyway? You're still pissed about last night, aren't you?"

There's a murmur from Jupiter, too low to decipher.

"Dammit, Jupiter, if you'd just keep your mouth shut for once we wouldn't have these problems. Nobody needs to know what's going on with us, okay? Not your crazy mom, not your overpro-tective uncle, and certainly not some judgy bitch in the goddamn counseling department."

I have to quell my urge to storm down there and whack this entitled little shit upside the head with the umbrella. Interrupting their heated conversation will only infuriate Colton and mortify Jupiter. The cutting edge of his voice tells me she'll suffer for this enough as it is.

Still feeling torn, I creep back up the stairs and tell Gabby to
schedule an appointment with Jupiter as soon as possible.

I wanted to keep my distance from this tangled Rathbone
drama, but I can feel myself getting drawn into it more every day.

* * *

As I walk through campus that evening, my cross-body bag slung
over my chest and my raincoat flapping in the stiff breeze, a silhouette peels away from Jack London Hall and slinks toward me.
She's carrying an umbrella, one of those clear bubble kinds five-
year-olds favor. Somehow, she makes it look like a futuristic fashion statement. Her rubber boots splash through the puddles as she
darts to my side, her hair pulled into a thick black braid down her
back.

"How's it going?" she asks, chirpy and bright.

I don't reply, just walk quickly, hiding my face deep inside the
hood of my raincoat.

"I know you've been seeing her," she says, and her voice is hard
to read. Is that gratitude, or smugness?

"She's a good kid," I reply, walking faster. "I enjoy talking to
her."

"You see what I mean, right? About the boyfriend?" She grips
her umbrella more tightly as a heavy gust pushes the rain sideways.

"I can't talk about that," I say, keeping my voice crisp and
businesslike.

There's a charged pause. She says, "Let me buy you a drink."

"No, thanks. There's somewhere I've got to be."

"Where? Alone at home with a glass of merlot?" One eyebrow
shoots upward, a sardonic taunt. Then she softens her voice to a
husky sweetness. "Come on, I'll get dinner, too. It's payday. I'm
flush."

I stop. "I'm not doing your bidding, Selene. I'm just letting her
talk. If you think I'm going to tell you a single thing about what

we discuss—well, it's not happening. It's unethical. I have to draw the line."

"Did you know I'm working at The Springs again?" Her eyes are bright and friendly, like I haven't even spoken.

With an annoyed sigh, I start walking again. The rain's hammering down on us harder than ever. My boots are soaked. The toes of my socks are squishy and damp. I don't need this right now, at the end of a long day, with so much on my mind. The fact that I do, in fact, hate Jupiter's boyfriend changes nothing. Confidentiality is confidentiality. I told Jupiter I'd keep whatever she said a secret, and I intend to keep that promise, no matter what.

Selene bringing up The Springs is a calculated ploy to break my defenses down. She knows I'm curious. I decide to let myself be distracted.

"What's it like working there again?" I ask.

She laughs. "Oh my God, Tansy, it's so great. Gerhold still works in the bath house. Remember him? The German guy with the long white beard? God, he was ancient when we worked there, and he looks *exactly* the same. I think he might be immortal."

I can't help laughing a little, in spite of myself.

"And Roger still owns the place. He has a new, younger wife, though. Her name's actually Bambi."

"It is not!" I say, covering my mouth.

She nods emphatically. "For real! Fake tits, twenty-nine, the whole clichéd bullshit trophy wife thing."

"Ew! Roger should know better."

"I know, right?" She laughs. We've ducked into the arched corridors that line Fox Hall, which provide some shelter as we walk. The sound of her laughter reverberates against the cold, wet stone.

We hear footsteps slamming through the puddles behind us and turn to see a huddled shape in a khaki raincoat hurdling toward us. His hood is up, but I recognize him anyway. Zack.

Great. Within the last five hours, I've officially been ambushed by every Rathbone in a fifty-mile radius.

When Zack reaches us, he falls into step beside me, flanking my other side and talking around me to his sister. He begins without greeting or preamble, as if in mid-conversation. "Selene, we talked about this."

"This has nothing to do with you." Selene scowls at him. I can see the bossy older sister in that look.

Zack glances at me in exasperation. "She's trying to lure you to some happy hour, isn't she?"

I open my mouth to answer, but Selene gets there first. "Tansy and I are old friends. There's nothing wrong with us going for a—"

"You need to stop," Zack barks, wiping rain from his face with one hand. "If you try to influence Tansy, you'll piss Jupiter off even more than you already have, and then she won't trust or listen to *any* of us. Is that what you want?"

"How is Jupiter going to know about two old friends going for a—?"

"That's not the point," he insists. "Tansy can't tell you anything, okay? It's against the ethics of our profession."

I can't decide if Zack arguing in my defense is endearing or annoying. Does he assume I would have given in to his sister's manipulation if he hadn't intervened? Though this puts me on the defensive, I have to admit he has reason to worry. So far, I've played right into her hands, albeit with my own rules in place—namely, that I won't tell her anything Jupiter's revealed. Of course, he doesn't know why I've been so easy to break. Without knowledge of the shared criminal past she holds over me, I must look pretty weak.

Since I haven't managed to get a word in edgewise, I'm relegated to the sidelines of this conversation, my head swiveling side to side as the siblings bicker. By now, we've reached the edge of the corridor offering shelter. My car is about twenty yards away, in the parking lot just beyond.

I make an executive decision.

"Let's get a drink."

They both look at me.

"To talk about Jupiter." I narrow my eyes at Selene. "But not anything told to me in confidence."

We all look out at the rain.

"O'Brien's?" Zack suggests.

I race to my car, calling over my shoulder, "See you there in five minutes."

*   *   *

O'Brien's is an Irish pub with a crackling fireplace and a convivial vibe. Even though it's a Wednesday night, the rain seems to have drawn people in. There's a guy who looks like an ancient Druid playing a dulcimer on a small stage at the back, and the din of conversation, punctuated by laughter, fills the air. The lighting is a warm gold as the windows fog with body heat. Our timing is good enough to score a booth, where we huddle with pints of ale between us and a couple of baskets of fish and chips.

"It's not that I like the kid," Zack says, spearing a fry into a silver cup of tartar sauce. "It's just that I think Jupiter has a right to make her own mistakes."

Selene shakes her head and smiles at the ceiling, like every word out of his mouth is trying her patience. I've stayed mostly quiet, letting the siblings talk, trying to get a handle on their dynamic.

"You don't understand, Zack." Selene's smile is condescending. "You're not a woman."

Zack takes a swig of ale. He grimaces and reaches for another fry. "That's so patronizing."

"I'm just saying." Selene seizes a fry, salts it, and rips it in half with her teeth. "Bad boys can be very alluring."

I know her glance is coming before it lands. There it is, that little *we're in this together, sister* grin.

My glance bounces off of hers and lands in my lap. Is she talking about Rob? Is that the bad boy she thinks we share? I recall his taught, brown shoulders as he peeled his leather jacket off. Rob *was* a bad boy, albeit decades past real boyhood, and yes, he was alluring. But I don't want to think about him now—not in this warm, cozy pub. I don't want to see her standing on the edge of that cliff, her hair whipping around like a sorceress.

"There are bad boys, and then there are predators," I say.

"Exactly." Selene points a fry at me. "Jupiter sees the bad boy, but we know he's a predator."

Zack looks unconvinced. "You don't know that. At this point, he could turn out to be either a spoiled brat or a serious threat. The jury's still out."

Selene frowns. "For you, maybe. My jury delivered the verdict months ago."

"What Selene and I disagree on," Zack says, ignoring his sister's comment, "is how we navigate the situation if Colton really is dangerous. She thinks you can orchestrate a breakup. I say that's bound to backfire. If Jupiter finds out you two know each other, she'd lose her shit. It's clear she's—"

"You talk like she's *your* kid," Selene spits at him, bitterness in her voice.

"She basically was my kid for three years, so I think I have a say." His tone is even, but his eyes spark with anger.

It occurs to me that Selene is jealous of the period Zack spent parenting Jupiter. She messed up, missed some crucial years, and now she sees him as lording it over her, assuming he has a say in how Jupiter should be parented.

I motion to the waitress for another round.

"We need to focus on how we can help Jupiter." I reach for a fry and wind it through a bowl of ketchup. "That's all that matters."

Selene turns to me with a look of such warmth, it takes my breath away.

"What does she need from us right now?" I say, surprised by the slight catch in my voice. "How can we help?"

Zack sits up straighter and points at me, addressing his sister. "This is what healthy people sound like."

"Shut up." Selene throws her napkin at him. "Of course we all want the best for her. We just disagree about what that is."

"Selene thinks we should control her from afar via you." Zack raises his eyebrows at me, as if inviting me to chime in.

I oblige. "Which is a really bad idea."

Zack gestures at me, turning again to his sister. "You see? This is what normal people say."

"Stop with the 'healthy, normal people' shit." Selene's tone is light, but when she punctuates it with a swig of beer so deep she finishes the pint, I know she's being serious. Selene has never liked being compared to "normal." She bristles at the very mention of the word. She spits on normal. Normal is the enemy. Zack must know this. Is he goading her?

"All I'm saying is we should check our egos at the door." I gesture expansively, feeling the beer more than I should. I snatch a piece of fish and dip it in tartar sauce. "We shouldn't let our personal agendas get in the way of helping Jupiter."

"Hear hear!" Zack raises his beer with enthusiasm before finishing it off.

The waitress appears with a fresh round of pints, gathering the empty glasses. She's young and buxom, with a low-cut shirt that shows plenty of cleavage. I notice she gives Zack a flirty little smile when she asks, "Anything else I can get you?"

"We're good for now, thanks." Zack returns her smile, though his is decidedly bland.

When the waitress is gone, Selene leans back in the booth, eyeing us both. The warmth I saw in her face minutes ago is gone, replaced now with a suspicious stillness. When she speaks, she addresses me. "So, what? You've met her twice for like five minutes, and now you're an expert on what she needs?"

"I'm not saying I'm an expert."

"Sure sounds like it." She throws a quick, annoyed look at her brother. "God knows this guy thinks he is."

Zack puts a hand on hers. "You're her mom. You'll always be her mom. But at a certain point—"

"I have to let go," she finishes, slipping her hand out from under his and wrapping it around her pint glass. "I know, you've told me a thousand times. If Jupiter were in a burning building right now, you'd say, 'Hey, she's an adult, she'll find her way out.'"

"She's not in a burning building, Selene." Zack works to make his voice calm.

I can tell this is an argument they've had so many times the grooves run deep. There's history here. They're not used to having a third voice in the conversation, and Selene doesn't like that everything I've said so far lines up with her brother's laissez-faire attitude. She feels outnumbered, and it's putting her in a dangerous mood.

Selene's gaze slides back to me, her hazel eyes sparking with irritation. "I'm floored, honestly. I thought another woman would get it, but apparently I was wrong."

"I'm not taking anyone's side. I'm the outsider here," I say. "That's my strength."

Zack nods, but Selene looks at me like she's waiting for more. The dulcimer drones on in the background, a sleepy plucking. Somebody at the bar unleashes a ridiculous, braying laugh.

I choose my words carefully, holding Selene's gaze. "People go to therapists and counselors because they offer a perspective that's different from everyone else in their life—an objective one, free of judgment. It's essential that I *stay* objective."

"You haven't seen what I've seen." Selene's eyes burn with frustration. "Colton Blake is a monster."

I try again. "I believe you. But the only way to get Jupiter away from him is to get *her* to see that. And the only way that's going to happen is if we give her the time and space to figure it out on her own."

"Time is the one thing we don't have." Selene runs a hand through her hair, a look of disgust twisting her lips into a sneer. "He's isolating her. Don't you see that? He's cutting her off from everyone who cares about her."

"I agree," I say. "All the more reason to keep my interactions with her purely professional. If Colton sees me as a threat, he might order Jupiter to stay away."

I recall the conversation I overheard in the stairwell—the biting tone in Colton's voice when he accused Jupiter of telling everyone about their private business. It's a classic pattern in abusive relationships: isolate the victim so she doesn't have anyone to run to when things get bad.

With an uncomfortable twinge, I note that Colton's behavior is a lot like Selene's own MO in relationships—at least, it used to be. During the two years of our friendship, the people around me grew increasingly suspicious of Selene. My dad thought it was weird I chose to spend all my time with someone ten years older; my brother accused me of joining a cult built for two. Within weeks of meeting Selene, my old high school friendships died off. Selene never told me to stop hanging out with other people, but the frosty way she acted whenever I did sent the message loud and clear. My other friends didn't fit inside the insular bubble we built around ourselves, so they drifted away, and I barely even noticed.

I wonder if Selene did the same with Jupiter, raising her in a private, intimate world, dismissing outsiders as average, small-minded people who couldn't understand their unique way of life. Jupiter said they moved around a lot. That probably kept her from forming lasting bonds with other kids. I can just imagine the thrift store outfits, the funky homes, Selene shaming Jupiter for wanting to fit in. Maybe Colton feels familiar to Jupiter in that way. On the outside he looks like the opposite of her mother—stable, wealthy, ambitious, deeply conventional—but in many ways, she's traded the tyranny of her mother for the tyranny of Colton. For someone like Selene, losing that control would be intolerable.

Of course, I don't say any of this, but Selene narrows her eyes at me as if she's read my mind. "You don't get it. She's not going to leave him unless we do something drastic."

"If we do something drastic, that will only push her away." Zack sounds weary.

"So, what do you suggest?" Selene snaps. "We just sit back, do nothing, and hope she comes to her senses? I love her too much to wait until it's too late."

Zack sighs. "The best thing you can do for Jupiter is start dealing with your own issues."

Selene glares at him. "Let's leave 'my issues' out of it."

"You know I'm right." He speaks so quietly, it's hard to hear him over the din of the pub. "The reason Jupiter wants nothing to do with you is—"

Selene pushes out of the booth and stands, suddenly furious, stopping Zack mid-sentence. "Spare me the psychoanalysis." She yanks her coat on, glowering at both of us. "While you two sit here doing nothing, going on about what my daughter needs, she's getting buried alive by that prick."

"Don't go." Zack sounds too tired and resigned to give the words much conviction.

Selene fixes me with a look so cold and disdainful it's chilling. "I thought you would be different. I thought you'd understand."

"I do understand," I assure her. "That doesn't mean I'm going to compromise my professional ethics."

She makes a sound of disgust in her throat. "You two make the perfect pair."

"We're only trying to—" Zack begins, but she cuts him off.

"Go right ahead, enjoy yourselves. Drink beer and wallow in your psychobabble all night. Meanwhile, I'm going to figure out a way to save my daughter. Alone. As usual." With that, she strides through the crowded pub and out the door.

An awkward silence settles over us. The dulcimer player starts a new song, something plucky and upbeat, just as the dart players in the back room let out a raucous cheer.

Zack's eyes are sad when they meet mine. "Sorry we dragged you into this."

I eat another fry, not sure what to say. Am I sorry? I'm no longer sure. Selene scares me for so many reasons. It feels dangerous, edging closer to her, getting to know the people she loves. I can't deny the very real connection I've forged with Jupiter, though—a bond that's somehow deeper and more meaningful than our two short conversations warrant. I see so much of myself in her, especially her struggle to free herself of Selene's stranglehold. Maybe this is a chance for me to come to terms with that messy chapter of my past—to finally deal with the festering fear and guilt I've tried to ignore until now.

"I'm happy to have another person telling Selene she needs to back off." Zack looks around the pub, his face anything but happy. "Unfortunately, all she can see is two people she cares about ganging up on her. That's a thing for her—it's part of her illness. Everything is a test of loyalty for Selene."

A flutter of nerves assails me, in spite of the thin layer of numbness the beer provides. I don't want to think about what Selene might do if she feels betrayed. This might be a chance for me to heal old wounds, but it's hard to ignore the very real stakes involved—not just my emotional well-being, but my freedom. Selene holds a weighty secret from our past, one she wields like a grenade. If she decides to blow up my world, there will be no repairing it. Maybe I should have placated her more tonight. I think of the determined set of her shoulders when she bolted just now, the hardness in her face, and repress a shudder.

Zack studies me. "You're afraid of her, aren't you?"

What is it with these Rathbones? Am I that transparent, or do they have a special ability to see through me?

"I'm afraid of what she's capable of," I admit, my voice soft.

He leans closer. "You should be. She's my sister, but I'll be the first to tell you she's dangerous. All the same, we can't let her get what she wants through bullying and intimidation. She's done that all her life, and it's got to end somewhere."

I nod. He's right, of course. Still, he has no idea what's at stake for me.

"You said something happened when you were friends. Something . . . what's the word you used?" He searches the air, finds it. "Irreversible. I'm not trying to pry, but I'd really like you to tell me what that is."

"Why?" I avoid looking at him, fiddling with the paper napkin in front of me.

He takes a moment before answering. "It will help me understand what's at play here. Maybe it's not as bad as you think."

I breathe out an incredulous little laugh. "It's bad. Take my word for it."

"Is it . . . something sexual?"

My gaze snaps up in surprise. "Excuse me?"

He shrugs. "Selene's been with women before." Is it my imagination, or is he blushing? "It's nothing to be ashamed of. I know it might feel really private, but if that's—"

"It's not that." Now I'm blushing, goddammit. "I'm not homophobic. If that was all it was, I'd be fine with that."

"Then what?" His eyes scan my face, searching every inch of my expression. I'm scared of what my eyes might reveal.

I turn my attention back to the napkin, folding and refolding it like my life depends on it. "I don't think you really want to know."

"I do." He spreads his hands out. "Of course I do."

"You work for the FBI, right?" It's out before I can stop myself.

He looks a little taken aback. "I've consulted on a few of their cases, sure, but I'm not an agent or anything."

I exhale loudly, feeling defeated. I've come this far, I might as well spell out what I've already implied. "Selene and I committed a crime together, okay? If you knew about it, you might not turn us in, but it's not a fair position to put you in. It's my mistake, and I have to live with it. Selene knows I'm eaten up with guilt about it, and she's threatened to tell the cops if I don't do what she wants. I'm trying to placate her without making anything worse for Jupiter or compromising my professional integrity."

He scowls in thought, taking in this new information. "You two haven't even been in touch for—what? Twenty years? Surely the statute of limitations—"

"Not in this case." The second it's out, I know I've said too much. I'm no legal expert, but I'm pretty sure there are only a handful of crimes with no statute of limitations.

"Wow." He swallows hard, taking this in. "Okay."

I dig in my purse, pull out some money, and slap it on the table. If I stay here any longer, who knows what confessions this man will pull from me? I can't risk it. Besides, it's getting late, and I have to be up early tomorrow for work. Just the thought makes me feel bone tired.

Zack waves my money away. He looks distracted, still running through the implications of what I've just said. "I'll get it. Don't worry about it."

"It's fine," I say, leaving the money and pulling my raincoat on.

"Look, just because I've worked for the feds, doesn't mean—"

"You don't need to know," I snap. "It's not going to help—in fact, it will almost definitely make things worse."

"It's blackmail, what she's doing." He grips his beer so tightly I can see his knuckles turning white. "You're playing into her hands."

"You're right," I admit.

"So break the cycle, then. Tell me what it is, and we can make a plan."

I offer him a wan, tired smile. "You can't fix this, Zack. I've got to go."

"Tansy," he says, but I'm already walking away, pushing through the swinging doors and out into the rainy night.

When I get to my car, I see a message written in red lipstick across my window. In the rain, the words have smeared—rivulets of deep red dripping down the driver's side. The little hairs prickle on the back of my neck when I see what it says.

Watch Your 6.

CHAPTER

7

I WAKE AT TWO in the morning the following Tuesday to the insistent vibration of my phone. My hand grabs it before my mind kicks into gear. The room is cold, the woodburning stove having gone out hours ago. I pull the phone under my fluffy duvet and squint at the screen.

It's Jupiter.

Yesterday, when she didn't show for her appointment, I broke down and did something I've never done. I pulled her number from her student file and texted her.

Just checking in. Call me if you feel like talking.

It was supposed to come off as breezy and professional. As soon as I'd sent it, I worried I'd gone too far. I kept hearing Colton's voice in the stairwell. *Nobody needs to know what's going on with us, okay? Not your crazy mom, not your overprotective uncle, and certainly not some judgy bitch in the goddamn counseling department.* For two days, I obsessed over whether he was keeping her from me. When she didn't get back to me, I fretted over what her silence meant. Had I crossed a line? Did she suspect I knew her mother? How would she know?

I push the green button and hear a loud sniffle.

"Jupiter? Is that you?"

She's crying—hard, broken sobs, the kind that wrack your whole body. My chest tightens in sympathy. My heart starts to race, adrenaline kicking in.

I sit up in bed, clutching my duvet. "Where are you? I can come get you."

Some deep breathing, like she might be hyperventilating.

"Jupiter? Sweetheart, where are you?"

After a gasp and another wracking sob, she chokes out, "Denny's."

"Can I meet you there?"

She splutters something I can't make out.

"What's that? I didn't—?"

"Thank you," she manages, her voice trembling.

*   *   *

I see her from across the room. In the glaring light of Denny's, her golden hair glows like a beacon—a bright, natural thing in the midst of tired vinyl and plastic.

She stands as I approach the table. Her eyes are red and puffy from crying. She wears a huge fisherman sweater over jeans. There's a small cut on her lip.

"I'm so sorry for dragging you here." She won't meet my eye.

"Hey." I squeeze her hand, wait for her to look up. "It's fine. I'm happy to help."

Tears spill over her red, raw lids and stream down her face.

"It's okay," I murmur. "Really. I'm starving, anyway. I could use a waffle or two."

"Only the finest dining here at Denny's." She smirks.

"Exactly. You're just a convenient excuse. I'm here for the sugar, carbs, and bacon." I scoot into the booth.

She sits across from me, but all the way in the corner, as if tucking herself into the deepest crevice. I notice she's chosen the booth farthest from the windows. The waitress comes over right away, a tall, dark-eyed woman with stooped shoulders and short red hair. She looks like someone who's done time. I don't know what makes me think that—maybe the stick-and-poke tattoo of a cross on her wrist, or the defensive posture, like she's expecting to take a punch at any moment.

I order waffles with a side of bacon and a hot chocolate. When the waitress looks at Jupiter, she just wraps a hand around her steaming cup of coffee and says, "I'm good."

"You sure you don't want something to eat?" I ask.

Jupiter shakes her head, her long hair falling around her face like a curtain.

When the waitress leaves, I let the silence settle around us before I break it. "Looks like you've had a rough night."

She lets out a thin laugh, like that's an understatement. I scan her face and neck for bruises, but aside from the cut lip, which looks like it might have been done by her own teeth, she's as flawless as ever.

"You want to talk about it?"

Her eyes stay glued to her coffee cup. "I thought I did, but now that you're here, I don't know where to start."

"That's okay. Take your time."

She looks up. Tears pool in her eyes. "Why are you so nice to me?"

For a second, my pulse quickens. *Because your mother asked me to meddle in your personal life.* I can see it in her wide-set crystalline eyes, simple and sad: this girl isn't used to anyone taking such an interest in her—not without an ulterior motive. The deeper I get into this, the more betrayed Jupiter will feel if she learns the truth.

"I like you," I say simply. "You remind me of myself twenty years ago."

One corner of her mouth curves up a little at that—a bashful smile that makes her look like a child. I try to imagine her as a little girl, wearing secondhand dresses and shoes that don't quite fit. Was Selene a fun mom, in some ways? Probably. I bet they had some good times, singing along to the radio as they moved from town to town, having impromptu picnics like Selene and I used to have in the tea houses at the spa. Selene has a way of making ordinary days magical, of wrapping old scarves around tired, dusty lamps and transforming a dingy room into a fortune teller's lair. I bet she wove a story for Jupiter of them against the world, a couple of free spirits dancing from one adventure to the next. It would have been an exciting life, at times.

But Jupiter's tired of adventure now. She craves normal. The problem is, her system isn't wired for normal. The internal compass Selene gave her leads straight to trouble.

"I bet your life wasn't as messed up as mine, even back then." Jupiter cradles her coffee cup like she's trying to draw its warmth inside her.

I remember how cold I was the night Rob died. The way my teeth chattered so hard I worried they might break. Even when Selene drew me a hot bath and eased me into it, I went on shivering; the cold wouldn't leave my bones. What is it about trauma that sucks all the heat from our bodies? Why does our internal fire go out just when we need it most?

"I had my share of problems," I assure her.

She surprises me with a question. "Like what?"

I hesitate. This is not how counseling works; it's not supposed to be about me. Then again, counselors don't show up at two thirty AM at Denny's, either. I've already crossed the line. I crossed it when I texted her. She wants to know who I am, what I've lost, what I've survived. If it will help her to open up, then who am I to deny her?

"Once, when I was about your age, I was almost raped." It surprises me a little, hearing the words out loud. "It took me a long time to get over it, to trust people again."

She takes this in, her forehead crinkling with empathy, and something else—confusion, a question she's afraid to ask.

"What?" I say, inviting her to voice it.

She pulls her coffee cup closer, takes a sip. "You said 'almost.' How did you stop it?"

"I didn't." My voice comes out thick. I see myself unmoving, lying limp against the rock, my eyes vacant. I clear my throat. "Somebody else did."

She nods. For a moment I'm afraid she'll ask more questions, but she licks her lips and says, "When I first met Colton, I thought he was heroic—the kind of guy who saves you from all the shit that's wrong with the world."

The waitress returns with my hot chocolate. I thank her and take a sip, silently willing her to go away so Jupiter will keep talking.

"How did you meet?" I ask.

She smiles, and I can see in some ways she's still smitten with him, still feeling lucky that he chose her. "I was at a party at my friend Julia's house. Some jerk kept hitting on me. He was drunk—really drunk. No matter how many times I told him I wasn't interested, he kept coming back. Colton warned him to leave me alone. When the guy ignored him, Colton punched him in the face."

I watch her, noting the pride in her voice, the warmth in her eyes. I don't tell her what I'm thinking: that people who punch assholes in the face might seem like heroes in the moment, but it's only a matter of time before they turn those fists on you.

She must sense what I'm not saying, because when she meets my eyes she backpedals a little. "I guess that should have been a red flag, in a way, but I couldn't help it. I fell for him right then and there. After that, we were just . . . together. It was like finding someone I'd known forever, you know? Like we already knew everything about each other, somehow."

"That can be very seductive," I say.

"Have you ever heard that quote?" She purses her lips in concentration, looks at the ceiling. "Something like 'your friends will know you better in the first seconds you meet than your acquaintances will know you in a thousand years'?"

"Richard Bach," I say, my voice quiet.

She laughs in delight. "Exactly! How did you know?"

I shrug and hide behind another sip of hot chocolate. The whipped cream has mostly melted, leaving a thick white sugary sludge. Selene told me that the first day we met. We left our creative writing class and huddled in her pickup truck for hours, the rain hammering on the metal roof as she spun stories about her days in New Orleans, her adventures in Seattle, weaving a spell as only Selene could. By the time she dropped me off at my car, I was convinced I'd made the friend I'd been waiting for all my life—someone who could open me up to a vast, sparkling world. I felt like the luckiest girl alive.

"And now?" I say, nudging the conversation gently toward the present. "Do you still feel like you understand Colton?"

Her blue eyes darken and she looks past me, her smile fading. "Sometimes. Other times he's a total stranger—like somebody else takes over, and I have no idea what that person will do."

The waitress returns balancing an enormous waffle and a side of bacon. There's a scoop of butter in the middle of the waffle, balanced atop the ridges, melting at the edges. I pour syrup from the tiny glass pitcher and spread the butter with my knife.

Pushing the bacon toward Jupiter I say, "Have some. Bacon's good for bad nights."

She tears a tiny piece of it with her small, delicate fingers and nibbles at it with rabbity bites. I notice how pronounced her collarbones are, the way they jut out from the neckline of her oversized sweater, and I wonder if she eats enough. She's talked about cooking, but always for Colton. Does she starve herself and feed him? I remember her saying he works out for hours every day. He seems like the type to make a girl self-conscious about her weight.

I finish my bite and wipe my mouth with a napkin. "Do you want to tell me what happened tonight?"

She balances the bacon on the rim of her saucer. It was an inch-long strip, and she's hardly made a dent in it. "Yes. No. I don't know how."

"Start at the beginning," I suggest. "Did you have a fight?"

She nods. Her nostrils flare and the tears well up in her eyes again. She doesn't say anything for a long moment. The waffle's not that good, but I keep eating it, just to give my hands something to do while I wait for her to gather her thoughts.

"He gets mad when I tell people things." Her voice is so quiet, I have to lean a little closer to hear. ABBA's singing about a dancing queen through a speaker overhead, and even though it's only a low burble of innocuous sound, I wish they'd turn it off so I can catch every word.

"What do you mean?"

"Like, if he hears me talking to my uncle." She sighs, rotates her coffee cup in its saucer once, twice, like she's a curator adjusting a sculpture. "Colton thinks whatever I say to Uncle Zack, he'll end up telling my mom. We have a restraining order against my mom because she attacked Colton."

"She attacked him?" I try to recall the way Selene described the events leading up to the restraining order. I'm pretty sure she admitted to pushing Colton as she tried to get past him, which is a lot milder than "attack."

"It's a long story." Jupiter looks tired, her eyes rimmed with shadows. "My family's screwed up. Not my uncle, though. I trust him, and he knows my mom can be crazy."

I trail a bite of waffle through a puddle of syrup. "Has Colton always disliked your mother? Were things okay between them before she attacked him?"

"He says she's insane." She glances at me quickly, turns her attention back to her coffee. "She is, I guess. But everyone's a little crazy, right?"

"We all have issues," I hedge. The last thing I want to do is advise Jupiter on whether or not she should communicate with her mom. I cut Selene out of my life with a scalpel so sharp and deep she tried to kill herself. No, that's not fair; I can't assume it was my abandonment that led her to drive her car into oncoming traffic. Even though she blamed me at the time, it was her own despair and loneliness that made her do it.

I force myself not to get lost in my own memories. Right now I'm here for Jupiter, and I'm going to give her my full attention.

"Is it just your family you and Colton fight about? Does he encourage you to stay close to other people?" I wait, and when she doesn't answer right away, I say, "What about your friends? Do you still hang out with them?"

Her mouth tightens, and for a second I'm sure she'll start crying again. "I don't really have any friends."

"Even before you started seeing Colton?"

She nods, her neck flushing with little pink splotches. "We moved so much when I was little. Our houses were always weird, so I didn't want to have people over—and even when I did, my mom wasn't into it. I guess I got used to being alone."

"You said the night you met Colton you were at a friend's party. Julia?"

She grimaces. "Not a friend, really. An acquaintance. And anyway, Julia used to date Colton, so it would be awkward now."

I eat a piece of bacon, thinking hard before I try to articulate what I'm about to say. "Sometimes, when you're in love, it's easy to isolate, just focus on each other in your own little bubble. Some of that's natural, especially at first, but in the long run, we need other people, you know? They remind us of our other interests, the parts of ourselves that might not be encouraged by our partner. No two people can be everything to one another. It puts too much pressure on the relationship, putting it in a vacuum like that."

She picks up her bacon and takes a minuscule bite. Her eyes fall on my left hand. "Are you married?"

The question takes me by surprise. "No."

"Divorced?"

I put my fork down. Again with the questions. My counseling instinct makes me want to change the subject, but this is something different and we both know it. She doesn't want a counselor. She wants an older, wiser friend. Just like I did when I met Selene.

"No, I've never been married. I was with someone for almost eleven years, a guy I met in college, but it didn't work out. His name's Marius. We're still close friends—I live on his property, in fact."

"Why didn't it work out?" Her innocent blue eyes are full of guileless curiosity.

I think of Scottie. For the second time that night, I tell her something I've hardly told anyone. "We were in a band together—Marius, me, and this guy named Scottie. The three of us were really close, but then Scottie died. After that, Marius and I couldn't seem to get along. It was like Scottie was the glue keeping us together."

"How did he die?" It comes out barely more than a whisper.

I meet her gaze. "Overdose. He had a problem with heroin. I don't think it was suicide, but I guess we'll never know."

She nods, and there's something about the gesture that tells me she knows a little something about drugs and what it's like to live with an addict. Selene was pretty careful about drugs after she got clean; she drank too much, but when I knew her she stayed away from the hard stuff. She's always had dangerous taste in men, though. I shudder to imagine the kinds of domestic arrangements Jupiter might have endured.

This time, I do change the subject back to her. I want her to trust me, and being honest with her about my past—or parts of it, anyway—seems essential for that to happen. But that doesn't change the fact that I'm here in this sad Denny's in the middle of the night because of her distress call, not mine. I need to find out if she's safe and what I can do to help.

"Do you need a place to stay tonight?" Before I can overthink it, I add, "You can stay with me, if you like. My place isn't big, but it's cozy."

She finally polishes off her mouse-sized portion of bacon. I push the plate toward her again, but she shakes her head. "I can go back. He'll be apologetic for a while."

Alarm bells go off in my head. "Apologetic for a while" sounds like another red flag, a textbook example of the cycle of abuse. The tension builds, the abuser explodes, followed by a period of prolonged apology and sweetness. The more I hear, the more obvious it becomes that Selene's instincts about Colton might be right. My stomach turns at the thought. The sickly sweet waffle feels heavy inside me.

"I'm going to ask you a question, and I want you to tell me the truth."

She holds my gaze, gives an almost imperceptible nod.

"Does Colton ever hurt you?"

The song switches from ABBA to Elton John's "Candle in the Wind." She doesn't answer for a long time.

When she finally does, her voice is reedy and thin. "This is the first time he's hit me. Before tonight, he'd do other stuff—throw things, punch walls. He just gets so mad, it's like he can't stop himself, you know?"

"Are you hurt?"

"He punched me in the stomach." She stares at the table. With one hand, she continues to caress the coffee cup. Her voice has gone flat, distant. "It knocked the wind out of me, but nothing else. I'll be fine."

I sigh. "I don't want to tell you what to do, Jupiter. You're smart. I'm confident you can figure this out on your own. Still, you should know that men who hit women don't stop. It's a pattern of violence. No matter how much he promises it will never happen again, chances are it will. You deserve better than that."

Her eyes fill with tears. She swipes at her face and then wipes her nose with a napkin. She nods, still not meeting my eye.

"If you don't want to stay with me, I could pay for a hotel."

She shakes her head. "You don't have to do that. I'd feel terrible."

"It's no big deal," I assure her.

"Can you give me a ride to my uncle's?" She stares at her lap. "He's cool. He won't ask a lot of questions. I keep a toothbrush there, just in case."

"Of course." An image of a sleepy Zack stumbling to the door in his boxers flashes through my mind. I push it aside and focus on the other part of her statement. "How did you get here, if you didn't drive?"

She makes an embarrassed little snorting sound. "I walked. I don't have a car. I like to walk at night, anyway. It clears my head."

I take some money from my purse and wave Jupiter away when she offers to pay for her coffee. Once I've settled with the waitress, we step out into the cool night and make our way across the parking lot to my car. It's almost three thirty. The air smells of fog and something sweet—maybe fresh donuts from the little bakery across the street. I get behind the wheel and wait for Jupiter to buckle herself in.

"Ready?" I ask.

"As I'll ever be." She sounds tired, but I think I hear a note of something else in her voice, too. I'm hoping it's determination.

* * *

For the second time that night, I fumble for my vibrating phone in the darkness to find a Rathbone speaking directly into my ear. This time it's Zack.

"Oh my God, what happened?" He sounds gruff and bewildered.

I got home an hour ago, but I'm not sleeping. My body is so exhausted it's close to hijacking my mind, but it hasn't yet managed it completely. I'm just lying in the dark, staring out my skylight at the stars.

When I dropped Jupiter at Zack's house, I offered to walk her to the door, but she insisted she didn't need an escort. I waited until Zack let her in, but he was little more than a shadowy figure in the doorway, so I couldn't gauge his reaction to her unexpected appearance. In a way, it was a relief, avoiding an interaction with Zack in front of Jupiter. I was a little worried Zack might be too groggy and disoriented to pretend we don't know each other; if that happened, Jupiter would no doubt suspect I'm more embedded in her family than I've let on.

I feel a nagging guilt about my deception. I keep seeing Jupiter's face, the way her flawless complexion, even pink with tears, was so beautiful, but her eyes so sad. They were like deep pools, so luminous and trusting. When Zack calls, I'm happy for the distraction.

"Can you be more specific?" I ask.

He clears his throat, and I picture him in his boxers, his torso broad and sloping in the moonlight. "I'm sorry to call you at this hour."

"*Now* you remember your manners?" It comes out with more sass than I'd intended. There's something weirdly intimate about lying here with his voice penetrating my ear at four in the morning. It reminds me of high school boyfriends, all that uncertainty and yearning.

"Rathbones are moody bastards," he says, his voice a scratchy whisper. "We've established that. I just need to know: what's going on with Jupiter?"

I hesitate. It's not like our conversation at Denny's was an official counseling session. Still, I *am* Jupiter's counselor. Do professional ethics dictate I keep everything to myself, even with Zack, who I'm pretty sure has her best interest at heart?

He must hear the hesitation, because he sighs and softens his tone. "Sorry, I'm being a dick. I'm tired and I'm worried, is all."

"What did she tell you?" I ask.

"She said you met her at Denny's because she was upset." He pauses. "And you're easy to talk to."

I squint into the darkness, trying to decide how betrayed she'll feel if I reveal the part about Colton hitting her. "She didn't say anything about Colton?"

"We kind of have a deal." There's a rustling sound on his end, and then I detect the clink of ice falling into a glass. "I don't ask her too many questions."

I smile. "Yeah, she mentioned something about that."

"Selene can be a real ball buster, as you probably know." The ice clinks again, and I wonder what he's having. He strikes me as a whiskey man. "When we were growing up, I nicknamed my sister The Inquisitor. If she senses you're holding back, she's like a dog with a bone."

"I'm familiar with that aspect of her personality," I say.

He chuckles. "Jupiter really hates that about her mom, so when she lived with me, we made a deal: I'd trust her to tell me anything important, and I'd never grill her or invade her privacy in any way."

"Wasn't she, like, three?"

"She was young, yeah." I can hear the smile in his voice. "You think that's weird? Toddlers need privacy, too."

"Good point."

"Right now, though, that deal is pretty damn inconvenient. I feel like something really bad is happening here, and looking the other way won't cut it."

"What do you want to know?" I'm still not sure how much I should tell him, but I figure getting the question out there will help me decide.

"Did he hurt her?" His voice is tight, like he's speaking through clenched teeth.

I don't give myself any time to think about it. Sometimes it's best to throw your training aside and follow your instincts. "Yes."

He swears.

"Yeah," I say. "Pretty much my reaction, too."

"Are we talking about a slap, a punch, what?" I can hear the pain and fury in his voice.

"She said he punched her in the stomach." The image hits me with fresh horror, lying there in the dark. My abs recoil in sympathy.

There's a long silence. More tinkling ice. "What do you think we should do?"

"I know it's hard, but I still think we can't force anything." Outside, a fox yelps in the night, the sound hoarse and otherworldly. I snuggle more deeply under the covers. "I'd love to drag her out of there, kicking and screaming, but it won't work. She'll just go back to him. She's in love."

He opens a door and I imagine him stepping onto a back porch, staring at the rain that's just started falling softly against my skylight.

"I hate that you're right," he murmurs.

"I hate that I'm right, too," I admit. "She's a smart girl, though. We can make—no, not make—*help* her see how wrong this is. How much staying with him will damage her. We just have to guide her toward that conclusion, as quickly as we can."

He lets a breath out. "Can't we kidnap and deprogram her? You know, like they do with cult members?"

"You're not serious right now," I say, concerned.

"Yes. No. I don't know." There are footsteps on his end, and I picture him pacing the length of a back porch. The rain's coming faster now, tapping against my roof in a jaunty rhythm. "Damn, this is exactly the kind of crazy shit Selene would dream up— kidnapping Jupiter. She wants him dead, you know."

"Colton?" Something in me slithers with cold, wet unease. I reach out, find Diego's warm body in the dark, and stroke his fur. "Selene told you that?"

"Yeah. Pretty much."

I run a hand along my cool, soft sheets. I just changed them yesterday and they smell divine, like lavender. "Did she actually say that, or are you interpreting?"

"Her words were, 'If that little shit doesn't leave my daughter alone, I'm going to slit his goddamn throat.'"

My gasp is involuntary. "That's pretty clear, then."

He makes a sound somewhere between a cough and a laugh. "I'm scared, Tansy."

"Of what?" My throat aches with tenderness.

"I'm scared Jupiter will stay with this douchebag and he'll beat the shit out of her." His voice breaks. He gets even quieter. "I'm scared Selene will kill the bastard and go to jail for it."

"Neither of those things is going to happen," I assure him.

He groans. "How can you know that?"

"I just do," I say, with more certainty than I feel. "We won't let them."

"It's so weird." His breath down the line sends shivers along the length of my arms.

"What is?"

He drops his voice again. "Having someone on my team."

I can't think of a snappy retort. There's a warm tingle in my chest, like I'm the one drinking whiskey.

"Thank you, Tansy." I hear him swallow. "For everything."

I've just opened my mouth, searching for words, when I realize he's dropped the call. After staring at the dark screen a few seconds, I set my phone down on my bedside table and pull Diego close, ignoring the indignant sound he makes in his sleep. I breathe in his scent and run my hand over his velvety fur again.

The situation with Jupiter is getting way too complicated, way too quickly. Suddenly I'm occupying this weird space in her life between therapist and older sister. I've landed a leading role in this Rathbone drama, like it or not. Maybe it's time to stop fighting the inevitable, and just accept that they're in my life. I care about Jupiter. She's sweet, and smart, and funny, and she deserves so much better than Colton Blake.

Then there's Zack. He's intriguing, though I know getting close to him will mean Selene's in my life more than ever. In spite of my efforts to keep my distance, there's a definite attraction there, something smoldering between us that no amount of good sense can put out. That glow Tim noticed last weekend is alive and well as I lie in bed, replaying the cadence and swell of his voice. My cheeks feel hot as I run a hand down the length of my body, rolling around in the memory of his final words.

When I think of Selene again, my fizzy warmth goes flat. She said she wants to slit Colton's throat. It's such a violent image, one I can imagine all too easily. I see her blue-black hair in motion as she yanks him backward and slashes a knife across his jugular. It's a graphic, terrifying mental picture, in full color. I can see the profusion of blood as it fountains from his throat. Most of all, though, I see the victorious, feral sparkle in her eyes as she does it, the same one she had the night she stood at the edge of that cliff.

*   *   *

I try to get back to sleep, but it's no use. Just before the sun comes up, I finally give in to the insomnia and drag myself out of bed, navigating the loft stairs carefully. The moonlight coming through the skylights and the wall of windows is just enough to illuminate my Martin hanging on the wall. It calls to me, its pale wood gleaming, its curves faintly outlined in the gloom. I unhook it from its wall mount and carry it to the couch, tuning up quickly before strumming a few chords, the sound bright and airy, heightened by the acoustics of my high, A-frame ceilings. I start to reach for the lamp beside the couch, but decide to stay in the dark. Something about the moonlight and the deep quiet of predawn feels delicate, as if I'm wrapped in a silvery bubble that lamplight might break.

For the first time in years, I manage to pluck a melody from the ether. It's a simple chord progression—nothing fancy—but it feels right. Before I know what's happening, lyrics are tumbling out of me, my voice soaring toward the ceiling, resonant and deep.

It's a song about that long-ago summer, but it's also about Jupiter and Zack—all the Rathbones who haunt me. Without forcing it, the words spring up unbidden, just like they used to. No, that's not exactly right. When I was younger, I would tease the lyrics out like tugging at a ball of string, unraveling each line with careful patience. This time, the song has a force of its own, rising like something long buried finally floating to the surface of a deep lake, something heavy but buoyant that refuses to remain submerged.

*   *   *

The next evening when I get home from work, I see Selene's car, this time not hidden up the road, but sitting right there in front of my house, gleaming in the dying light with an inky, self-satisfied glow. I'm so not in the mood for Selene right now.

After getting about four hours of sleep last night due to the Denny's escapade and my late-night chat with Zack, my eyes ache with exhaustion. My vision kept blurring as I drove myself home, making me roll down the window to stay awake. The very last thing I want right now is to spar with Selene. I feel too naked and raw in this grimy, sleep-deprived mood. She'll shred me like a tiger pouncing on a child, and I'll just flop around limply while she does it, too weak with fatigue to put up a fight. With a sigh, I grab my bag and head into my house.

She's out on the deck again, a bottle of Dos Equis in her hand. On the funky outdoor coffee table there's a bowl of guacamole, another of pico de gallo, and a platter covered in nachos. They're just the way she used to make them for me, smothered in cheddar cheese and tiny cubes of avocado, with sour cream and salsa sitting on top like the peak of a snowy mountain. My mouth waters in spite of the nervousness blossoming in my belly.

"Welcome home, honey." She swigs from her bottle of beer and plucks another from the cooler at her feet, popping off the top before handing it to me.

It's icy cold under my fingers, sweating so much it feels slippery. "Thanks."

"I made your favorite." She nods at the nachos.

I can't help smiling. This whole situation is weird and messed up in at least nine different ways, but who doesn't like to come home to a cold beer and nachos? I chide myself for being so shallow. Still, I take a long pull from my beer and then grab one of the cheesiest chips, swooping it through the chunky, homemade guacamole and cramming it into my mouth. Hot cheese liquefies on my tongue. I can't help groaning in appreciation.

"Right?" she says, looking smug.

"You are the nacho champion of the world," I concede. "But what are you doing here?"

She leans back against the cushions of the outdoor couch, beer bottle cradled between her thighs. "Do you plan to go on hating me forever?"

"I don't hate you," I say automatically.

"What then?" She's very still, waiting for my reply.

I drink more beer, stalling for time. What do I feel for Selene? The room where I've kept my memories of her has been locked for so long, I'm not sure I know how to enter and take stock. There's so much in there: the closeness that sprang up between us and became my whole world for a while; the darkness of that night in the woods; the self-preservation that made me shut her out when I moved to Santa Cruz, barely letting her anguish touch me, even when she tried to kill herself. It's been so much easier to keep it all in a secret compartment, to move on without looking back. Until now.

"What I feel for you is complicated," I say finally. "I haven't really processed everything that happened between us."

"Do you have plans to process it any time soon?" She reaches over and grabs a nacho. "Because I did give you plenty of space to get over it. Twenty years, in fact."

I'm surprised to hear myself say, "Do you ever think about him?"

She finishes chewing, swallows, and washes it down with a swig of beer. This is the first time we've referred to that night in anything but oblique references. "Of course I do."

"Do you regret . . . ?" I can't quite manage the words "killing him" so I start again. "Do you have any regrets?"

Her gaze moves to the middle distance. There's something pensive and brooding in her eyes. "I don't regret protecting you."

She's sidestepping the real issue here, and we both know it. She could have stopped Rob from raping me without *killing* him. He didn't have a weapon. It would have been us against him. If she'd just pulled him off me we could have gotten away. Even in my nightmares, Rob was never a bloodthirsty maniac, just a troubled man. Was it jealous rage that made Selene push him over that cliff, or did it really seem like the only way to stop him?

"Anyway," I say, changing the subject, "our friendship isn't really the issue here, is it?"

Her eyes narrow as she watches me. "No? What is the issue, then?"

"You didn't barge back into my life to resuscitate our bond." I try to keep my voice even, steady, like I'm in charge of this conversation, even though it feels like a runaway train I'm barely holding on to. "You came to me because you wanted something."

A couple of ravens fly overhead, making clicking sounds in their throats. She looks up, following their progress in the twilight. "Is that what I'm doing? 'Barging in'?"

"I'm not sure you're aware of this," I say carefully, "but most people don't rekindle a friendship by breaking into each other's homes and making demands."

She chuckles, but it's a tight sound, and there's a tension in her face I don't like. "I haven't made any demands. All I made was nachos."

I don't have the energy to push back, so I try to focus on what matters. "I like Jupiter. She's got a lot going for her."

Her eyes meet mine. "And . . . ?"

I shrug. "I'm doing what I can. You're right about Colton—he's dangerous—but I still think she's the one who has to decide that. Nobody can force them apart."

She picks at the label on her beer. "She's stubborn. No idea where she got that."

"She's in love. You have to let that run its course."

With her free hand, she sweeps her hair into a cascade that falls over one shoulder. "I don't know, Tansy. I'm not sure I have the patience for that. She could marry the bastard. They could have kids. She'd be trapped, locked inside his prison forever."

"I think she's smarter than that." Even as I say it, though, I'm not so sure. Love has a way of trumping intelligence. Jupiter is young, and Colton offers all the things her childhood must have lacked: financial security, a sense of belonging, the thrill of being chosen by someone society deems worthy. Will she get away from him? Right now, I'd put the odds at fifty-fifty.

Selene hisses out a breath, sadness filling her face until her eyes go glassy with tears. "It's so hard, having a daughter out there in the world. It's like your own heart sprouted legs and arms and decided to make the stupidest goddamn choices in the world."

"You must have done something right," I say. "Because she's lovely."

She looks at me with such gratitude and vulnerability, like she'd been waiting for someone to tell her that for years. "I don't think I can take credit for that, but thank you."

We sit in silence, drinking beer and eating nachos. Though it's a little twisted, I can't help savoring the camaraderie. Normally, it's just Diego and me from the time I get home until I leave for work the next morning. I've always treasured my solitude, but lately I've noticed how isolated I've become. From a distance, we probably look like two normal friends enjoying the rain-washed night, listening to the crickets and the babble of the creek in the distance. Nobody would guess we're fugitives, running from our past into a dangerous, unknown future.

8

SATURDAY MORNING, I'M lingering in bed with a good book, enjoying my laziness, when a knock on my front door startles me. Surely it's not Selene. She was just here Wednesday night, and anyway, it's more her style to sneak in through the back door and give me a heart attack. I get up and glance at myself in the mirror: old pink pajama pants and a sleep-rumpled camisole. My phone tells me it's after nine o'clock. Well, whoever it is, I'm not changing my clothes for them. This is my lazy weekend, dammit, and if they're going to interrupt they can just deal with me in pjs.

When I open the door, Jessica's standing there, looking impossibly fresh and perky. Her long brown hair is styled in luxurious, shiny waves, and her olive skin seems to glow. In one hand, she carries a basket filled with vegetables: kale, cauliflower, bok choy, eggplant, and tomatoes. She's wearing a cropped hoodie that shows off her tiny baby bump, which draws my eye like a beacon.

"Hey, Jessica." I rub my arms as the cold October air creeps into my warm little house. "What's up?"

She proffers the basket with a smile so big it looks like she might strain a muscle. "Autumn harvest."

"Oh, hey, that's so nice of you." As I take it from her, Diego saunters past me and rubs against Jessica's ankles. "This is gorgeous. Those little Japanese eggplants are so cute."

She reaches down and scratches Diego between the ears. "Hey, kitty."

"You want to come in?" I don't really want her inside my house—what I want most is to crawl back into bed with tea, toast, and my book—but it feels rude taking her basket and closing the door.

To my enormous relief, she shakes her head. "I've got to film like seven more yoga videos—I'm way behind. I've got an actual film crew now; did I tell you? We're trying to get as many in as possible before I'm enormous." She reaches down and strokes her exposed baby bump.

I nod. "That's right, Marius said you're pregnant. Congratulations."

"Thank you." She nods, running her fingers through her hair, not quite meeting my eye. "We're so happy."

"Very exciting. Well, thanks so much. Have fun with your videos." I start to close the door.

"Actually," she says, smiling even wider. "Do you have a minute? There's something we've been meaning to bring up."

The royal "We." This can't be good. Her enormous, forced grin and the manic brightness in her dark eyes don't bode well either. I grip the basket of vegetables tighter, until I can feel the stiff wicker poking into the soft inner flesh of my forearm.

"Sure. What's up?" Even I can hear the slight quaver in my voice, the premonition of something I don't want to hear. For a second, I fantasize about slamming the door in her face, running back upstairs, and diving under the duvet. Instead, I stand there, leaning against the doorjamb, trying not to stare at her exposed, nut-brown belly or her deranged smile.

"Marius was supposed to say something, but I think he's scared." She winces a little, and I can't help but notice that her face remains taut no matter what expression she makes.

I rub my forehead, feeling haggard next to her. "He said you guys are having a baby and getting married."

"Right. Well, because of that, our situation has changed." She purses her lips in a pout, though I see no evidence in her shining eyes that she's actually sad about what she's going to tell me. "I know Marius has been renting this place to you for almost nothing, but we can't afford to do that anymore."

Interesting sentence structure, I note. It starts with Marius as the subject, but switches post-conjunction into the mighty "We."

Then it hits me. This woman is jacking my rent up. A rush of anger pushes through me, leaving a bitter, acidic taste in my throat.

"We'd love to, but we can't." She does that little girl, scuff one toe against the ground and look up sideways thing. It's such a calculated move, I'm sure she practiced it in a mirror. "You're paying fifteen hundred?"

I nod, swallowing hard against the fear tightening my vocal chords.

"See, that's way too low." She shrugs one shoulder, like it's out of her hands. "We've got to double it."

"Double it?" I echo, tilting forward a little. A tomato escapes from where it lies wedged between an eggplant and some bok choy, tumbling toward the ground in a death plunge. It splatters on the flagstone walkway in a violent burst, seeds flying up to freckle the hem of my pajama bottoms.

"Oh, too bad." She stares at the mess with a regretful frown.

"You're going to charge me three thousand dollars?" I can't keep the edge of panic from my voice.

"Believe me, we wouldn't if we had any choice." She does that face again, half wincing and wrinkling her nose, like she smells something rank. "With the baby coming, though, we've got to be smarter about money."

Marius, the goddamn coward, was supposed to tell me this three weeks ago when he caught a ride down the driveway and helped me with my groceries. That's definitely what happened. I feel sick. It would have been bad, coming from him, but not this bad. Jessica, glowing with health and flashing smiles that could blind you, rubbing her baby bump like it's a magic lamp, is the worst person to hear this from. I wish to God I'd never answered the door.

"It's nothing personal." She smiles, her eyes seeking approval.

Seriously? It's not enough for her to rob me of my home, I'm supposed to make her feel okay about it? An unruly burst of anger makes me want to hurl the entire basket of vegetables at her head.

I take a deep breath, gathering my thoughts.

She's already starting to back up, though, hands still wrapped around her belly protectively. "Okay, well, great. You can just leave my basket on the porch when you're done with it."

"Jessica, I can't pay three thousand. It's not—I can't."

"Actually, that's still way under the going rate." She treats me to an apologetic smile.

I can hear my voice getting too loud, desperate. "I'd have to move."

"Honestly, Tansy?" She takes a step back toward me, lowering her voice like what she's about to say is confidential. "Maybe it's time to think about moving on. I'm not sure living here is really *serving* you anymore."

What the hell does that mean, "serving" me?

The bitch wants me out. Forget hurling the basket, I long to take one of the overripe tomatoes (she always gives me the ones so far gone their skin ruptures at the slightest touch) and smash it into her superior, compassionate little yoga goddess face.

I resist the urge to slam the door so hard it rocks in its hinges. Instead, I manage a polite goodbye, pull it firmly closed, and stagger to my kitchen, dazed. I can't believe this is happening. Rental prices in this area are unreal. There's no way I'll ever find something as stylish and perfect as this in my price range—not even close.

I can't believe Marius would do this to me. His girlfriend basically told me to pack my things and skedaddle. She always did resent my presence here. Now that she's knocked up, she must feel empowered to lay down the law. No wonder Marius couldn't tell me. He could never look me in the eye and kick me off the property we've shared for years.

With a sigh, I heave the basket onto the counter, glaring at it. But then a faint, timid voice in the back of my head suggests Jessica might be right. Maybe it's creepy to hang around after your ex has a wife and a kid. Pathetic. She may have a point about me needing to move on. Still, I'm furious with both of them about the way it went down, forcing me to confront imminent homelessness and Marius's betrayal, all before I've had my first cup of tea.

I pop a couple of pieces of bread into the toaster, absently pulling the butter from the breadbox and flipping on the electric kettle. Is it possible there could be a place out there that would represent a new start? I've lived here seven years. Maybe it would be exciting, finding new digs, someplace funky and charming close to downtown. I could walk to the movies, ride my bike to get groceries or a cup of coffee. After ages spent at the end of a winding dirt road, the thought of walking somewhere to buy pastries or Chinese food seems exotic. A place in town. Small, but cozy. A mother-in-law unit, or a garage apartment. Maybe there will be exposed brick walls involved.

The water boils, and I make myself a cup of tea. Slathering butter on my toast, I shove a bite into my mouth. It's comforting. Then Jessica's news comes back to me, and I feel the room spinning. This is so unreal. I'm at home here, more than any place I've ever lived since childhood. It's so *me*. I can't picture myself coming home to some other place, blank walls and shag carpet, depressing blinds. The smell of other people's cooking rising up the stairwell. It sounds appalling.

No, I can't give in to that despair. I have to believe there's a place that will check all the boxes and feel like a fresh start. It's a tall order, but if I don't cling to it, I might sprint down the driveway and tackle Jessica to the ground. Not a good look, considering she's "with child." God, did she have to rub her belly every single second? You'd think she *invented* pregnancy.

Okay, clearly the wound is too fresh. I need to give myself at least a day to feel pissed off about this, and then I should start looking, see what's out there. The rental market might not be as bleak as I imagine. God, maybe I should even think about buying a house. I don't have much in savings, but I've heard there are great loans out there for first-time buyers. Tim's been nagging me to invest in real estate for ages, and I know he and Jay would lend me the down payment, though I'd rather not have to ask. Maybe, once I'm done feeling hurt and angry, I'll see this as a gentle push from the universe, guiding me away from the past and into my future.

*   *   *

That evening, I realize my pantry's pretty bare, and I'm starving. Even though a part of me wants to keep hiding away in my house, I know I'll feel better if I go to the store and make myself a proper meal. I take a shower and put on a little makeup just to feel human again. When I survey myself in the mirror, I have to admit it's a vast improvement.

The only semi-productive thing I've done today is play my new song over and over. It feels great making music again, like rediscovering a part of myself I thought I'd lost. The thrum of my guitar against my chest and the burn of the strings under my fingers has done wonders for my mood. The anxiety Jessica's bombshell planted in my belly this morning isn't gone, but the situation no longer seems insurmountable. I know my brother won't let me go homeless, and I have a decent job, even if my salary isn't lavish. I remind myself things could be a lot worse.

I start driving toward Safeway, but halfway there I decide I'm in the mood for something a little more upscale, so I head for Whole Foods instead. Their dark chocolate sea salt caramels are life-changing. Getting out of my car, I stretch and feel my spine loosen with a satisfying pop. October is well underway, and though we've had glimpses of winter, today the weather has gone warm again, balmy and mild with a gentle breeze. I turn my face to the sun, enjoying the feel of it on my face as I cross the parking lot.

My cart only has a few random things in it when I cruise down the ice cream aisle and spot Jupiter gazing intently at the selection of Ben & Jerry's. Her hair's piled on her head in a messy topknot, and she's got on a pair of faded denim overalls that make her look like a little girl. Though she's not smiling, there's something relaxed and uncomplicated about her expression that reassures me.

Zack texted to let me know she's been staying at his place the last few nights, ever since I dropped her off there early Wednesday morning. When I texted back asking if she plans to break up with Colton, he sent the shrug emoji with the words *I'm not allowed to ask tough questions, remember?* Though I can see why Zack's *don't ask* policy makes a certain amount of sense, I can also see why Selene gets so impatient with his passivity. I'm the one who keeps insisting Jupiter has to decide for herself, but there's a part of me that wants Zack to hold her hostage until she sees her boyfriend for the piece of shit he is.

I put a hand on Jupiter's arm and she jerks around so fast I step back a little. Immediately, I realize my mistake. She might look relaxed and childlike in her cute little overalls, but Jupiter's been through a terrible ordeal this week. It was stupid to sneak up on her like that, even though surprising her wasn't my intent.

"Sorry. I didn't mean to startle you," I say.

She puts a hand to her chest and laughs, her expression losing its skittishness as soon as she recognizes me. "Oh my God, Tansy, you freaked me out."

"My bad, really. How are you? I've been thinking about you all week."

She blushes, her cheeks turning a pretty pink. "I'm okay. Better than when I saw you last."

Zack swings around the corner with a cart, heading toward us, and my heart does a tiny involuntary flip. He's wearing a blue button-down shirt and jeans, his hair damp as if he recently showered. There's something about the sight of him performing an everyday domestic chore that does something funny to my insides.

When our eyes meet, his grin is warm but also a little worried. Jupiter doesn't know we're acquainted, so the situation presents a bit of a quandary. Zack and I are colleagues, and it's a small town, so it makes sense we could have crossed paths, but I have no idea if he's told Jupiter we know each other. I didn't admit to knowing Zack when Jupiter asked me to drop her off at his house, and with a last name like Rathbone, it doesn't seem believable that I'd remain clueless about their connection if we'd already met.

This is why I hate lying—even by omission. It gets tangled into a Celtic knot before you know it.

Jupiter's head swivels back and forth as she looks from her uncle to me and back again. Then she gets a wicked little gleam in her eye, like she's up to something. "Tansy, this is my Uncle Zack." She looks back at her uncle and tells him, "This is Tansy, the counselor I told you about."

Zack holds out his hand for me to shake. I take my cue from him and place my hand in his, though it makes me a little sick to perform this charade for a girl who's given me her trust.

Jupiter's face lights up suddenly and she claps her hands together once like she's just had an amazing idea. "What are you doing right now, Tansy?"

I'd like to say I have glamorous plans that will make me sound alluring, but one lie is enough for this conversation. "Just stocking up on groceries to hang out at home."

"You should totally come with us." She reaches into the freezer for a pint of Ben & Jerry's Chocolate Chip Cookie Dough and deposits it in her uncle's cart. "We're going to a barbecue at Uncle Chet's."

I can feel my brow furrowing in confusion. "You have another uncle?" Immediately, I realize my mistake. How would I know how many uncles she has? She could have ten uncles if I didn't know Selene only has one brother.

"He's not my *real* uncle," she clarifies, apparently oblivious to my little slip. "He's Uncle Zack's best friend, and I've known him my whole life, so I just call him that."

"Got it." I glance at Zack. "Well, thanks for the invitation, but I don't want to impose."

Zack looks a little uncertain, so I'm about to say my goodbyes and wheel my cart away when he surprises me by adding, "Chet does a mean barbecue. You'd be more than welcome—no pressure, though."

I study him, trying to decide if he really wants me to come, or if he's just being polite because Jupiter put him on the spot. It's hard to tell; his expression doesn't give much away. Jupiter's face, by contrast, is incandescent with hope. I find her enthusiasm both touching and tempting. Zack may have a *don't ask hard questions* policy with her, but I don't. Maybe if I tag along she and I will have a chance to talk about Colton, and I can help her see that she deserves so much more than a man who hits her.

"Sure," I say before I can overthink it. "Why not? Sounds fun."

Jupiter lets out a little squeal of excitement and pounces on me, wrapping me in a big hug. Over her shoulder, Zack and I exchange a quick look; I can see he's pleased, but I can't tell if it's because Jupiter's happy I'm joining them, or because he is too.

Zack taps the top of the ice cream in his cart pointedly. "We'd better get a move on, or this is going to melt before we get there."

"Should I follow you?" I ask.

"You can ride with us, if you want." Zack looks at what I've got in my cart: two bottles of wine, some pasta, and the dark chocolate sea salt caramels. The Single Girl's Comfort Kit. "That stuff will be okay in your car until later. We can drop you back here after the party. Did you need to do any more shopping?"

"No, I'm good." I'm still starving, but a barbecue sounds like an excellent place to solve that problem.

Jupiter strides toward the registers, leading the way, casting quick looks back over her shoulder at me like she's worried I might try to escape. It occurs to me that she could be attempting a little matchmaking here. Maybe that's why she's so excited. The thought is both nerve-racking and flattering. I know she thinks the world of her uncle, so if she considers me worthy of him, that's a big compliment. At the same time, I've told myself over and over that getting involved with Selene's brother is a big mistake. Somewhere along the way, that resolve has started to wear thin, along with my determination to stay away from all Rathbones and their complicated issues. Maybe everyone is complicated, and jumping into their mess is the price you pay if you don't want to be alone.

Zack pushes his cart beside mine and asks in a low voice, "You okay with this?"

"Yeah." I keep my tone light as I glance at him from the corner of my eye. "You?"

"More than okay." A little grin tugs at the corner of his mouth, and I feel my resolve getting flimsier every second.

*　*　*

The party is in full swing when we get there. Chet's yard is green and expansive, with fragrant clumps of lavender rimming its borders and a circular stone patio taking up center stage. A dozen chairs are arranged around a big fire pit, and there's a huge trampoline where little kids bounce, their laughter and screams of delight filling the air. The scent of grilled meat floats on the breeze, mixing with the aroma of the lavender and the perfume of dead leaves. The backyard is surrounded by vineyards, their leaves now gold and red; starlings swoop and dive in elaborate formations, hunting for the last of the grapes. Most of the adults are either gathered around the barbecue or sitting around the fire pit, drinking wine or beer, munching on hot dogs and burgers. It's a warm, convivial scene, and though I feel a little flutter of nervousness about meeting Zack's friends, I'm also glad I came along.

Zack introduces me to Chet, a big, affable guy with a red beard and a hearty laugh. His wife, whose name I immediately forget, is his exact opposite: a tiny, birdlike woman with short dark hair and a brittle, nervous laugh. I don't miss the covert thumbs-up Chet gives Zack when he thinks I'm not looking, and I can't help but wonder if Zack usually shows up at Chet's parties alone. The thumbs-up could be a blanket endorsement of Zack bringing *any* woman along, or it could be a specific endorsement of me. Either way, I'll take it. It beats a thumbs-down, anyway.

After the three of us have polished off our share of burgers, coleslaw, and potato salad, Zack gets pulled into a conversation by the grill with Chet and a pretty redhead who seems to be chatting him up, flipping her hair and touching his arm for emphasis. Jupiter and I sit near the firepit as dusk deepens and a string of lights festooned around the patio blinks on. There's a small gaggle of girls in their teens who have made brief appearances before disappearing back into the house, their phones cupped in their hands, but Jupiter didn't show any sign of interest in or familiarity with them. They're probably too young to draw her eye. Jupiter seems at once younger and older than her eighteen years. Socially, she seems a little behind the curve, probably because of her nomadic upbringing. But every once in a while, when I catch her staring into the fire with a pensive sadness, she looks much more world-weary than her fresh-out-of-high-school peers.

I search my mind for a question I can ask that won't be too invasive. "Have you been staying at your uncle's this week?"

Jupiter tears her gaze away from the fire, but there's something a little guarded in her eyes when they meet mine. "Yeah. It's been good."

"Any new thoughts about Colton?"

She sighs. "I haven't been taking his calls. I need a little space."

I want to tell her a guy who punches you in the stomach deserves permanent exile, not "a little space," but I can tell from the tension in her shoulders and the tightness in her voice that this is no time for a lecture. "That makes sense. Zack seems like the kind of guy who would listen if you want to talk."

She jumps on the opportunity to change the subject. "What do you think of my uncle, anyway?"

"Which one?" I shoot back, playing dumb. My earlier suspicion that Jupiter's playing matchmaker is confirmed by her secretive tone and the glee in her eyes.

I cast a quick look at the grill, just as Zack meets my gaze and holds it just a beat longer than usual. The redhead, who's still laughing uproariously at something he said, doesn't seem to notice. Something warms me from the inside, and I don't think it's just the wine.

Jupiter gives an impatient little shake of her head. "Duh! Zack, the *single* one. He's cute, right?"

I give a noncommittal half-shrug, but she just laughs off my attempt at coyness.

"You two are like *made* for each other." She leans closer, her silky blonde hair falling forward. "Don't even try to deny it."

I give her a dubious look. "What makes you say that?"

"He has a serious weak spot for chick singers," Jupiter says. "You do sing, right? I know you said you were in a band with your ex."

I nod. "I play guitar, mostly—but yeah, I sing."

"Ooh, guitar, really?" She rubs her hands together, excited. "Even better. Every girlfriend he's ever had was a singer—opera, church choir, one time a backup singer for Beyoncé. But a guitar adds something extra special."

"Really?" I'm trying not to reveal too much interest in this topic, but I can't help feeling a little intrigued. Zack and I have never talked about music—or girlfriends—so this is all new to me.

Jupiter squirms in her seat, barely able to contain her delight. "Pretty soon, Uncle Chet will break out his guitar. He loves to play, though honestly, he's not that good. You sing one song, and don't butcher it? Zack is all yours."

I chuckle at her overly confident assessment of the situation. "What makes you so sure I want him to be 'all mine'?"

She raises her eyebrows at me in a *you can't fool me* face that almost makes me spit out my wine with laughter.

As if on cue, half an hour later Chet produces a guitar and settles before the fire. He plays the opening bars to "American Pie," and a few of the folks nearby clap and cheer. Chet belts out the lyrics in a gruff but enthusiastic baritone, mostly in tune, but even when he's off key, he sings with gusto. This is obviously a familiar ritual, and all the guests sing along whenever he reaches the chorus, even the kids, who have grown bored with the trampoline and are now preparing to roast marshmallows. Chet's wife is setting out the ingredients for s'mores, and the kids circle her like a brood of ducklings.

After Chet's done a few campfire favorites, Jupiter says, loud enough for everyone to hear, "Uncle Chet, did you know Tansy was in a band?"

Several people turn to stare at me as I shoot Jupiter a dirty look. She, in turn, casts her eyes in the direction of Zack to check his reaction, looking incredibly pleased when he halts his conversation with the pretty redhead.

"I *didn't* know that." Chet appraises me with renewed interest. "What band?"

I clear my throat, suddenly nervous. "The Insatiables? We broke up a long time ago, so I'm sure you've never—"

"Get out of town!" Chet roars, his pink face lighting up with delight. "You were in The Insatiables? That's incredible. Didn't you guys open for Jo-Jo Sloan one time?"

I can't stop the proud smile that spreads across my face. "Yeah, we did."

"I *saw* you guys," Chet says. "You were unbelievable."

Chet's booming voice and his obvious excitement has drawn the attention of people scattered around the yard. They edge closer, pausing their conversations to observe our exchange.

Jupiter smiles winningly at Chet. "Can she play your guitar?"

"Of course." Chet stands and holds his gorgeous old Gibson out to me. I've been admiring it from across the fire pit; it's a vintage J-45 with a sunburst finish, probably worth at least five or six thousand dollars. Every time a spark broke free and floated anywhere near it, I found myself holding my breath.

"I couldn't," I demur. "I'm sure you don't want a stranger playing your beautiful—"

"Nonsense!" Chet says, cutting me off. He's clearly had a few, and I worry as he dangles the Gibson in one hand while gesturing expansively with the other. "First of all, you're not a stranger. You're here with my man, Zack—my children's godfather, my best friend ever—so you're practically family. Second, everyone here is sick of my two-bit covers. Let's hear one of your originals. If I remember correctly, you guys wrote some damn good stuff."

I hesitate, unsure, but when Chet practically shoves the Gibson into my arms, I realize it would be bad form to say no. It's been years since I've played for anyone but my brother and Jay, so I feel a pang of stage fright. I strum a few chords, checking out the feel of the stately old guitar. As I suspected, she's a beauty, with brand new strings and warm, buttery tones only vintage guitars seem to pull off.

After a moment's thought, I play "Feckless," the only Insatiables song that ever made it to the radio. It's upbeat and bright, a real crowd pleaser that always gets people dancing, and tonight is no exception. A couple of hipsters I saw sharing a joint earlier climb onto the trampoline and dance like people possessed. I keep half-expecting Marius and Scottie to join me on the chorus, doing our signature three-part harmonies. Their absence makes me a little sad, but I realize it sounds pretty good solo, too.

When I've finished, the whole crowd hoots and hollers their approval, making me blush. Jupiter's beaming at me like a maniac. I shoot her an *I'll deal with you later* side-eye. I don't dare look at Zack or the redhead who—last I checked—had scooted her chair even closer to his with a possessive air.

I try to hand Chet's guitar back to him, but he waves me off.

"Come on," he says. "Play us another. This is the best thing to happen at my backyard barbecue in forever."

Again, I hesitate. I can't deny this feels good—not *good*, fucking amazing—playing for an audience for the first time in seven years. Sure, it's no more than thirty or forty people scattered around a fire pit, but that does nothing to diminish the joy flaring inside me like a match. I spent my twenties chasing this feeling—the delicious high that only comes from making music for people who want to listen. It feels different now, but delicious all the same.

I realize with a burst of gratitude what a gift it is to suddenly find myself in this yard, under the stars, with a bunch of eager faces staring back at me, their smiles bathed in firelight. Something comes over me, and I decide to just go for it.

I play the song I wrote the other night. I don't know if Jupiter or Zack recognize themselves in the lyrics. If I think about that too much, I know I'll mess it up, so I just close my eyes and belt it out, feeling my whole body expand, making room for the song and all the emotions that go with it.

When I finish the final note, I open my eyes and find myself staring right at Zack. For a long moment, the rest of the guests disappear, dissolving into the night, and we're the only ones here, sharing a moment so intimate it almost hurts. He raises his beer in a toast, and the spell breaks, leaving me awash in the sweetest sound in the world: a screaming, clapping crowd barely audible beneath the sound of my own thundering heart.

*　*　*

Zack and I are walking through the vineyards later, navigating the rows of deep red foliage. Our exit did not go unnoticed by Jupiter, who laughed a little too knowingly when Zack offered to "show me around." That's when the attractive redhead left the party, looking like she'd just bitten into a lemon, and I can't say I was sorry to see her go. Now a thin sliver of moon hangs lazily above a low, creeping fog bank, and the smell of harvest hangs in the air, heavy and ripe. Chet's booming voice can be heard in the distance; he's belting out the lyrics to "Yellow Submarine," and I feel a warm rush of affection for him, even though I've only known him a couple of hours.

"Chet's really great," I say. "You guys seem pretty tight."

"Man, you made that guy so happy tonight. He loves good music. That's how we met, actually—at a Neil Young show thirty years ago." Zack casts me a sideways glance. "Your song was . . . wow. When did you write that?"

"A couple nights ago." Butterflies flutter in my belly as I add, "After I got off the phone with you."

His fingers brush against mine as we walk side by side. "I don't think anyone's ever put me in a song before."

"I find that hard to believe."

He does a slight double-take. "Why do you say that?"

"Jupiter says you have a thing for 'chick singers,'" I say.

His laughter is loud and infectious. I find myself giggling, too.

"You know she's trying to set us up, right?" I bump him with my shoulder.

"She's not exactly subtle, so yes, I picked up on that."

"What do you think she's going to do about Colton?" I ask. "I tried to bring it up earlier, but she seemed eager to change the subject."

"Yeah, she's the master of deflection." He squints into the distance. "She seems so much happier away from him—like her old self, you know?"

I haven't known Jupiter long enough to assess the accuracy of this, but I have noticed how much more carefree and vivacious she seems tonight than any of my previous encounters with her.

"She's definitely bubblier than usual," I offer.

"Right? I'm just hoping she'll keep her distance long enough to see she's better off without him." Zack sounds optimistic, but also a touch wary, like he's afraid of getting his hopes up.

At the edge of the vineyard, there's a tiny treehouse perched in the upper branches of a sprawling old oak. I pause to admire it, trying to make out its details. A sturdy-looking rope ladder dangles almost to the ground.

"Cute treehouse," I say.

Zack follows my gaze. "Chet and I built that when his kids were little. Mostly me, if I'm being honest. Chet's pretty useless with a hammer."

"That was nice of you." A breeze carries with it the scent of dry, golden hills, fermented grapes, and fog. "I love treehouses."

He shrugs. "Yeah, I always wanted one growing up, so it was fun making one for someone else."

"Is it still pretty sturdy?" I reach out to grab the rope ladder and tug on it a couple of times.

"Of course. I may not be a master carpenter, but the stuff I make is built to last." His voice is full of pride that's only half joking. He looks at me, a boyish grin lighting up his face. "You want to check it out?"

I bite my lip and nod. We clamber up the ladder, him in the lead, and soon we're standing inside the cutest little playhouse I've ever seen. There's a dark green carpet remnant covering most of the floor, a big window facing west, a bright yellow bean-bag chair, and a tiny table strewn with random objects: an abalone shell filled with acorns, a couple of plastic dinosaurs, and a Barbie who looks like she's seen better days. It smells a little musty, but not in a bad way. I walk to the window and gaze out over the rolling vineyards. When I turn back around, Zack's standing directly behind me.

The look in his eyes is a cross between asking permission and taking charge. His gaze moves from my lips to my eyes and back again several times before he lowers his mouth to mine and kisses me. My whole body melts into him, my skin tingling with a giddy effervescence. He pulls back and looks at me again, his breath catching a little as he runs a hand through my hair. When he kisses me again, there's nothing tentative about it. His mouth is full of promises, his hands moving into the pockets of my jeans to cup my ass. I feel my body going liquid in his arms—liquid but also electric, like a sea churning with phosphorescence.

After a long moment of surrendering to pure bliss, I pull away and look at him. All the doubts I've harbored about the wisdom of falling for Zack suddenly reassert themselves. "This is a bad idea, isn't it?"

"What?" he whispers, his face inches from mine. "Making out in a rickety little treehouse I built for my godchildren? I take it you're not impressed."

I snort with laughter. "No, us. This. Getting involved."

He squints at me, scanning my face for clues. "Because of Selene?"

"Yeah." I'm too electric with longing to think straight, let alone articulate the hazy swirl of fears I've sequestered at the back of my brain.

He gives me a peculiar look. "She's not the boss of you, Tansy."

"I know that." I lift my chin, a tiny spike of defensiveness shooting up out of nowhere.

"What are you afraid of?" His question is gentle, his eyes kind.

I pull away, leaning back on the windowsill in an effort to think more clearly. There was definitely a reason this was a bad idea three minutes ago; now, though, I'm struggling to remember what that was.

It feels safe to think aloud, so I open my mouth and let the unedited thoughts tumble out. "Selene and I have all kinds of history, and because some of it was bad—really bad—I cut myself off from her for a long time."

He nods, listening intently. I realize with a start that I'm expecting him to interrupt with something dismissive, the way Marius used to whenever we got into emotional territory he felt ill equipped to handle. Zack doesn't, though. He just looks at me, waiting for me to go on.

"Now I feel myself getting all tangled up in her family, and it scares me." I pause, trying to gather my thoughts. "You said yourself she suffers from borderline personality disorder. I didn't even know that term, back when we were close, but looking back, it fits. She's obsessed with who's loyal to her and who's not. You saw how she reacted that night at the pub—she stormed out because you and I agreed on how to handle Jupiter and our opinions didn't happen to concur with hers. She saw us as disloyal, and for her that's the worst crime in the world."

I keep my next thought to myself, though it's one of the most pressing reasons Selene and her impulse for vengeance scare me. I've always suspected Selene pushed Rob off that cliff not to protect me, but to punish him for abandoning her. It's a fear I've always harbored, but never gave voice to. It's one of the many reasons I've refused to think about that night for the last eighteen years.

Again, Zack surprises me by refusing to dismiss or shoot down anything I've said. Instead, he looks out the window, running a finger down the glass. "You're right. Selene doesn't deal well with the slightest betrayal—real or imagined."

"How do you navigate that?" It occurs to me that Zack has way more experience with Selene than I do. Maybe he has tools for defusing her mood swings I never knew existed.

He breathes out a helpless sound that tells me he doesn't have any easy answers. "It's a minefield, let me tell you. That's one thing you, Jupiter, and I have in common. We know what it's like to tiptoe around Selene."

"How did Selene react to your previous girlfriends?" I ask.

There's a pause as he stares at the floor, and when he meets my eye again I know it wasn't good. "She's never welcomed them into the family, that's for sure. There was a woman I dated while Jupiter was living with me. Selene was in a bad place back then, barely able to keep herself together, but she managed to make life a living hell for Katie. That was partly because Jupiter liked her."

I raise my eyebrows. "That doesn't bode well, given our current situation."

"True. Jupiter liked Katie, but she loves you." Something in my expression makes him reach out and squeeze my hand. "I realize I'm giving you every reason to run as far away from me as you can."

I don't answer, too distracted by the warm pressure of his hand cupping mine.

"Maybe I'm being selfish, but Selene will always be my sister, and I'm not willing to be alone forever just because she gets weird when I date someone." He sighs. "Correction: weird*er*. She's unstable. That's who she is. I love her, but I can't let that instability control me."

"Why did you move here?" I ask, watching him.

"What do you mean?"

"Sounds like you had a great job at Cal, and living in the Bay Area gave you some distance from Selene's drama." I tilt my head to the side, watching him carefully. "Why uproot yourself and complicate your life by moving right into the center of it all?"

He lets out a slow, thoughtful breath. "Jupiter and Selene are the only family I have left. They're no walk in the park, but I needed to be close to them. After Mom died last year, Selene went downhill. Maybe it's unhealthy to feel so responsible for her—for both of them, really—but there have been times in the past when I wasn't around, and I still have trouble forgiving myself for that."

I think of Selene's late-night phone calls after I moved to Santa Cruz—the way I came to dread the sound of the phone waking me from my troubled dreams. The slur of her words as she'd mumble dark, lost things. *You're the only one who knows me, and now you've left . . . I just want to die, Tansy.* I think of the accusations she screamed at me when she tracked me down in Santa Cruz, calling me a cold, selfish bitch who has no idea what it means to really love someone. After she drove into oncoming traffic, I told myself again and again that it wasn't my fault, but I never truly believed it. I understand the guilt that can fester like an infected wound when Selene decides you've failed her.

Zack uses his thumb to smooth the crease between my furrowed brow. "Please don't feel pressured, Tansy. I can see you have doubts about all of us Rathbones, and I don't blame you. We're not easy."

"I'm not looking for easy," I say automatically.

"What are you looking for?" His hand cups my neck, pulling me closer.

I think about this. "Something real."

He kisses me again, and this time I don't let my doubts get in the way. I wrap my arms around his neck and kiss him back, losing myself in the sweetness of the moment.

CHAPTER

9

THE FOLLOWING TUESDAY, Zack finds me in my office at lunchtime and holds up a bulky-looking plastic bag. "Sushi and tempura with miso soup. You interested?"

I stand, smoothing my dress, glad I decided to put on something a little nicer than usual this morning. His eyes slide over me in a slow, appreciative scan that makes my skin tingle against the silk of my new lingerie. On Sunday, I went shopping and spent a fortune on exorbitant underwear. Today I'm wearing a kelly green wool sheath dress with a matching blazer and knee-high boots. I've even got on lipstick—candy apple red, just for the hell of it. Underneath: Agent Provocateur black lace balconette with matching panties.

I feel indestructible.

"I'm ravenous," I say, smiling. "Come in."

He gestures at the exit. "I have someplace I'd love to take you, if you can get away."

I glance at my computer and see I don't have another appointment for almost two hours. "I'm all yours."

Zack leads me across campus to the science building. High clouds cast the day in a gray gloom. A light breeze whispers through the majestic oaks that line the walkway, the Spanish moss stirring like old lace. I look up to see a woodpecker hammering away at a sturdy old pine, his beak moving so fast it's a blur, the sound amplified as it bounces off the buildings.

Zack's expression is inscrutable when a gaggle of pretty girls in tight jeans walks by giggling. I catch myself studying his profile for the telltale movement of hungry eyes taking in young skin and gleaming hair. Then I scold myself for being so paranoid. Still, it's gratifying that he doesn't even seem to notice them.

When he unlocks a door at the end of a long corridor, I squint into the darkness of what looks like a large lecture hall. I don't venture into this building often, so I don't recognize the room.

"Does lunch come with a lecture?" I ask, a little baffled.

He takes my hand and leads me into the dark hush of the empty seats. We trail up a carpeted aisle with tiny recessed lights built into the steps.

"There'll be a quiz, so pay attention." His voice is low and conspiratorial, as if we're breaking in.

Once I'm settled into a seat he hurries up the steps, taking them two at a time.

"Wait, where are you going?" I ask, more confused than ever.

"Give me two seconds," he calls over his shoulder, sounding like a little boy.

I lean back into the cushy, adjustable chair and close my eyes. The smell of tempura, sushi, and miso drifts from the bag tucked into the seat beside me. My stomach grumbles. I didn't have time for breakfast this morning, and I'm hungry enough to eat an entire truckload of sushi.

There's a muffled clicking sound from the back of the room, and then the whole ceiling, a massive dome, becomes a sea of stars. I gasp in surprise. There's a galaxy up there, sparkling gems wrapping up and over me, pulsing with light.

"Oh my God!" I cry in delight. "It's beautiful."

After a moment, Zack reclines in the chair next to mine, smiling proudly. "I figured our first date was kind of unconventional, so I'd keep on trend."

I laugh. I can't remember the last time I felt *courted* by someone. In a world full of people who swipe right and call it romance, the concept is anachronistic and charming.

He reaches into the bag on his lap, pulls out a tray of sushi, and hands it to me. Then he digs around some more, locates a pair of wooden chopsticks in a thin paper sleeve, followed by a cardboard container filled with miso soup.

"Careful with this one, it's hot," he says.

I love that he cares about feeding people. There's a warm, solicitous air about him as he doles out the meal, making sure I've got what I need. I'm not naturally nurturing in this way, and I can't help smiling at his instinctive attention to other people's needs.

Balancing the unopened sushi on my lap, I peel the lid off the soup and blow on it, watching the seaweed and broth swirl. I take a careful sip. It's delicious.

"You bring all your chick singers here?" I tease.

He laughs, holding a fist in front of his mouth. "What is it with the chick singers?"

"Jupiter said you have a thing for them," I remind him. "It's okay. We all have our fetishes."

"Yeah?" He raises an eyebrow. "What are yours?"

"Psych professors with unhinged sisters and achingly beautiful nieces."

"How unfortunate for you." His gaze slides down my body again. "You look amazing, by the way."

I nod in acknowledgment. "I thought about you while I got dressed."

"Yeah?" He puts his food down and traces a line from my chin to the hollow at the base of my throat.

"I did." I put my food down too, suddenly done with it. I bite my lip. *No need to confess how much you spent on lingerie.* "I was hoping I'd see you."

He cups my face with his hands and plants a slow, silky kiss on me. I want him so badly I have to fight the urge to tear my clothes off and climb on top of him. I remind myself we're in a public building—a place where we happen to work. I need to get hold of myself.

As we pull away, I clear my throat to stop the tiny moan of pleasure trying to escape. This is out of control. I have to get us back on track. I pick up my sushi again, glad the dark room conceals the heat flooding my cheeks. "How's Jupiter?"

If he's thrown by my abrupt return to conversation, he doesn't show it. "She's hanging in there. Colton's been texting and calling incessantly, but so far she's keeping her distance." He pulls apart his chopsticks and seizes a California roll with one deft movement. "She's been staying with me almost a week now, and I've made it clear I want her to move in. So far, she's noncommittal, but I think we're making progress."

I recall Colton's efforts to seem polished and polite the day he cornered Jupiter in my office. In spite of his obvious irritation, he struck me as the kind of guy who can launch a formidable charm offensive when he puts his mind to it. That can't be easy for Jupiter to resist.

"Has he tried to see her?" I ask.

Zack's lips curve into a rueful grin as he chews and swallows. "He wouldn't dare show up at my place. He knows I'm not his biggest fan. I'm sure he's probably cornered her on campus, but Jupiter hasn't mentioned it. He sent a big-ass bouquet of red roses, though, which I was *this close* to throwing in the trash."

I smile, imagining his moral dilemma. "I take it you resisted the urge?"

"Barely." He sips his miso soup. "It's pretty distracting, worrying about her all the time but trying to pretend like everything's cool so she won't feel scrutinized. It's kind of driving me crazy. My lecture made no sense this morning. I might as well have been speaking in tongues."

I flash him a sympathetic frown. "Does Selene know she's staying with you?"

He makes a sound in his throat. "Yes, but I'm trying not to 'be her bitch,' as Jupiter says. That's my other balancing act: feeding Selene just enough information to calm her down, but not anything that will violate Jupiter's privacy. They're keeping me on my toes, I'll tell you that much." He eats another roll and shakes his head suddenly like a dog climbing out of water. "Man, that wasabi's intense. I think my nasal cavity just exploded."

"I love that feeling." I spear a smoked salmon roll and trail it through a puddle of soy sauce laced with wasabi.

We eat in companionable silence for a while. The underwater light of the spectacular, starry sky overhead casts his features in pale blue. I sneak glances at him, trying to read the shifting expressions on his face. There's worry there, a touch of exhaustion. But there's also hope—the kind of hope you feel when the sun comes up and you sense its warmth on your face for the first time in what feels like forever.

Being Selene's baby brother has been hard on Zack. It's been a full-time job lately, safeguarding Jupiter and keeping Selene from doing something stupid. I put my food down again and slip my hand between the headrest and his neck, massaging gently.

"You're a very giving person," I tell him. "An amazing brother."

"Selene might take issue with that statement." He puts his food down and tilts his head a little in my direction, his smile coy and bashful. "I do try, though. Thanks for noticing."

"You're also a stellar uncle," I add.

He bangs his armrest decisively. "*That* I will take full credit for."

"As you should," I agree.

With a flip of his torso, he lies on his side, facing me. "I don't want to brag, but I'm told I make a pretty fucking wonderful boyfriend."

"'Fucking wonderful,' huh?" I trace a finger down the line of his nose. "Is that a direct quote from one of your reviews?"

"It's more like the general consensus." He strokes my hip with his palm.

"Well, are you going to sell me on it?" I ask, mock serious.

He grins impishly. "You want the hard sell or the soft sell?"

"The hard sell, for sure."

His hand glides up my body, tracing my waist and my ribcage before finally cupping my breast. "I can lock the door."

"Oh my God, are you serious?" I widen my eyes at him.

He looks alarmed. "What?"

"We're going to have sex in the planetarium on our lunch hour?"

His brow furrows. "Too much too soon?"

"You have a condom?" I whisper, feeling like a naughty schoolgirl.

With one hand, he reaches into his pocket and produces a Trojan. His expression lands somewhere between proud and sheepish.

I widen my eyes at him. "You really *do* bring your chick singers here, don't you?"

"Every one of them," he taunts, stopping my giggles with a long, torturous kiss. When he pulls away, he fixes me with a serious look. "Really, though, we don't have to if you're not—"

"Oh, so now you're chickening out?" I catch his earlobe between my teeth, one hand stroking the fly of his jeans, and he lets out a soft groan. "You can't throw down a dare like that and not deliver."

His voice is strained as I plant a trail of tiny kisses down the side of his neck. "It's just that Jupiter's staying at my place and ever since Saturday I can't stop thinking about—"

"Me too."

"Just so you know," he says as I unbutton the top few buttons of his shirt and kiss my way down his chest. "This isn't my *fetish*, as you so charmingly put it—sex in public places. I'm just as happy in a bed. Though I think I could get used to—"

"You better lock the door before I change my mind," I warn.

With a wicked grin he crosses the room, flips the deadbolt, and strides back to me. His mouth closes over mine and suddenly we're making out like teenagers—long, delicious, hungry kisses. My shoes tumble to the floor with a clatter.

After some awkward negotiations with the armrests, I straddle him, my knees digging into the upholstery. His hands slide up under my wool skirt and toy with the edge of my silk panties. I gasp when he finds my center.

He shoots me a look of adorable surprise. "You're so wet."

I throw back my head and laugh. "If you must know, I've been thinking about this long before Saturday."

"Really?" He quirks an eyebrow, one finger reaching inside me, bolder now, making me catch my breath. "How long have you been thinking about it?"

"Since the day you—" I have to stop talking as he circles my clit with his thumb.

He grins, enjoying my incoherent sounds of pleasure. "Since the day I . . . ?"

"Accosted me outside the faculty meeting."

"I didn't *accost* you," he protests, but he shuts up the second I unzip his fly.

When he slides inside me, I can't bite back my groan of pleasure. I feel torn apart and made whole all at once.

I look down just in time to catch the expression of wonder on his face.

"How can you be so beautiful?" he whispers.

* * *

The next day, I'm still awash in the glow left over from lunch with Zack when a visitor shows up at my office I don't recognize. He's in his mid-fifties, with short, grayish-blonde hair. He's wearing a suit that looks expensive, dark wool that accentuates his trim, athletic physique.

"Hello," I say, looking away from my computer and giving a little start of surprise. His imposing silhouette fills my doorway, though I never heard footsteps. "Can I help you?"

"I'm looking for Tansy Elliot."

I stand. "That's me."

He crosses the room in two long strides and holds out a hand the color of boiled ham. "Henry Blake. I believe you know my son, Colton."

"Oh." It comes out a croak, so I clear my throat twice. "You're Colton's dad."

"Guilty as charged." He holds up his hands and leans back, like a stand-up comedian delivering his punch line.

"How can I help you?" My mind's spinning. Jupiter came to see me yesterday, and I feel optimistic about her state of mind. She's still staying at Zack's, thank God, and though she's cagey on the topic of Colton, we have every reason to believe she's getting ready to break up with him for good.

Henry Blake gestures expansively at the visitor's chair. "Mind if I sit?"

"Please." I return to my seat, feeling a cold prickle of dread along my back.

"I understand you're Jupiter Rathbone's counselor."

I nod in mute agreement, not trusting my voice.

He smiles. He has the kind of face that makes a smile look like work. "According to Colton, you two have been seeing a lot of each other lately."

"I can't really discuss that." I wonder how Colton could have known Jupiter's spent time with me. Is Jupiter really avoiding his calls and texts, as she's led us to believe? Maybe Colton's been following her. I recall the day he showed up here after tracking her phone. Does he still have the ability to do that? "Why do you ask?"

"I didn't ask." His beady eyes study me with a hint of disdain. "I made a statement. I know you've been in touch with her, and that she hasn't been home in over a week."

I find my voice, and I'm surprised to hear how calm it sounds, smooth as butter. "She might not feel safe going home right—"

"And why might that be?" His tone is frosty now, all the bonhomie gone.

I blink at him. "Mr. Blake, this is entirely inappropriate."

"Let me tell you something." He leans forward, lowering his voice to a hiss. "My son is not violent."

My eyebrows raise involuntarily.

His cheeks flush with anger. "I don't care what that lowlife little girl says, Colton would never hurt anyone."

This time, I have to work to keep the fury from my voice. "If you think Jupiter's such a 'lowlife,' why are you so upset they're breaking up?"

"My son—" He stops, pressing his lips together with what looks like sincere grief. The forced joviality he put on earlier has now vanished. With one hand, he fishes in his pocket and jingles what sounds like a fistful of coins.

"Your son . . . ?" I prompt.

His hand shakes as he puts it on my desk. "My son loves that girl. And he's . . . well, he hasn't had it easy. He's just bouncing back from a bad drug problem, if you want to know the truth. I'm not proud of it, but there it is. He can't take a breakup, not right now."

Colton is an addict? This does complicate things. It explains the mood swings Jupiter described to me. If he's coming down off hard drugs, some of his erratic behavior makes sense. People can get mean as rattlesnakes when they're trying to kick. Henry Blake looks pretty straight, in his starched white shirt and bespoke wool suit, but I don't think he's talking about a little weed and pills. Colton's addiction had to get pretty harrowing for a man this proud to admit something like that to the likes of me, a perfect stranger, within minutes of meeting me.

But if Colton's a newly recovering addict, how could Jupiter not mention this? Is she ashamed of it? Or does she somehow not know?

"You're afraid if they break up Colton will start using again?"

He nods, his expression clouding. "I know for a fact that's what will happen."

I'm not sure I believe him. I tilt my head sideways and give him a dubious look.

"We've been through hell and back with that boy, my wife and I." He grips the arms of the chair so tightly his knuckles turn white. "I have to do whatever I can to keep him clean and sober. He's my son."

"I understand."

He shakes his head, like my empathy is infuriating. "You can't possibly understand until you've—"

"I've been through it." Scottie's laughing face streaks through my mind. "Believe me."

"Then you should understand why it's essential Colton not be alone right now."

I sigh. "If Jupiter doesn't feel safe around your son, that's my main concern."

He looks incredulous. "You think I feel safe knowing my son could overdose any day now? Every single night she's gone, he gets a little closer to breaking down."

"I'm sorry. I know that's hard."

"No you don't," he spits through clenched teeth, "or you wouldn't be doing this."

"I'm not *doing* anything, Mr. Blake. Jupiter is an adult. She makes her own choices."

He squints at me, his all-American good looks going pinched and twitchy. "You're telling her to break up with him, aren't you?"

"That wouldn't be my place," I say, holding up my hands.

"Do you know I'm on the board of trustees?" He leans back in the chair, knees splayed.

This change of subject is so startling, all I can do is stare at him for a long moment. Finally, I choke out, "For VMU?"

He nods. "Small world, huh?"

I offer a tight smile in response.

"I'm also district attorney, so I'm not a good enemy to make." He yanks his phone from his pocket and glowers at it. "I've got to get going, Ms. Elliot. I trust I've made my point."

After he's gone, I sit at my desk for at least three minutes, twirling back and forth in my chair, trying to recover. I can't decide who's more toxic, the father or the son. Most likely, Colton learned his violent tendencies from his father. The man oozed menace. Colton's addiction does shed new light on his behavior, but it's not a game changer. If anything, it makes me more convinced than ever that Jupiter's got to stay away from him.

I don't have tenure, though. Making an enemy on the board is not a good idea. Not just some random guy from the community, either—the DA. If Henry Blake wants to make my life difficult, I have no doubt he has the power and sway to do it.

Why do all these people assume I can influence Jupiter's life choices? She's her own person. All I do is listen. She's the one figuring things out.

I pick up my phone and call Zack. He's the only person I can think of who will know how to handle this situation.

* * *

"He actually threatened you?" Zack is incredulous.

We're standing in Zack's kitchen while he makes stew. I've been inside his house once before, giving Jupiter a ride home after our end-of-the-day counseling session. Though Zack and I haven't officially admitted we're dating, Jupiter loves to tease me about my "boyfriend." Unfortunately, my relationship with Zack hasn't progressed past our one steamy encounter in the planetarium, which feels so high school. It's too weird to think of having sex at his place while Jupiter's sleeping right next door, though, and staying at my place isn't an option, since we don't want to leave Jupiter alone until things with Colton settle down. As a result, all week I've been in a state of feverish longing. It's excruciating but also kind of fun.

Zack's stew smells divine, a rich aroma of browning onions, garlic, and beef filling the warm, cozy kitchen. He owns a two-bedroom house downtown, a short walk from the plaza. It's a quaint, pale green Tudor with ivy creeping around the mullioned windows. His kitchen is the color of butter and a Bluetooth speaker is playing Motown. Aretha Franklin's singing about respect as Zack moves around the kitchen with fluency and ease. He likes to cook, I can tell.

"He didn't *openly* threaten me, but the subtext was pretty obvious. He let me know I'm in danger—like a predator baring its teeth." I shudder at the memory.

Zack stirs the stew with a wooden spoon, sprinkling it with a dash of salt. He's not a measurer, I've noticed. "So let me get this straight. Basically, he's saying his son has a drug problem, and if said son doesn't get to keep his girlfriend, he might go back to the junk?"

"Pretty much," I say. "Colton's drug habit must have been bad. His dad seemed authentically terrified he would OD."

Zack shakes his head. "That is *so* not our problem."

"I feel for him, and I'm sorry Colton's struggling, but you're right." I sip my wine, appreciating the cherry and vanilla in every sip. It's the best Syrah I've had in ages. I hold the glass up to the light and swirl it around, "Good God, what is this? It's so good."

He grins. "You like it? My buddy Chet makes it."

God, I love California.

"Delicious. Go, Chet." I pull my cardigan open a little, feeling hot. Underneath, I'm wearing a camisole, so I'd feel too naked taking off my sweater. The heat of the wine in my blood has turned my cheeks pink, I'm sure. Jupiter's not home yet, so we have the place to ourselves. A part of me wants to drag him off to the bedroom, but I resist. She could come home any second.

I lean forward onto the butcher block kitchen island. "What am I supposed to do, though? This bastard could cost me my job."

"That's tough." He rubs his chin with one hand. "We can't tell her to go back to the douchebag just because his dad says he'll kill himself if she doesn't. That's crazy."

I nod, rotating my wine glass as I consider the problem from every angle. "I guess if he wants to get me fired, he'll get me fired. He might as well find a reason to lock me up too. Otherwise, I'll be homeless."

"What would he lock you up for?" Zack asks, looking at me sharply.

"I'm joking," I say too quickly. There's an awkward silence; just as it's starting to blossom, I hurry to fill it. "How's it going with Jupiter?"

"Good." He nods and pours a mason jar full of what looks like homemade canned tomatoes into the soup. "I'm my usual noninvasive Uncle Chill. She appreciates how supremely incurious I am."

I study him. "So, are you talking?"

"Yeah, sure. Mostly about books and movies and bands, but we talk all the time." He chuckles. "The other day I started telling her about a book I'm reading with an abusive relationship in it, and she quickly changed the subject to *Hellboy*."

The music transitions from Aretha to Nina Simone. I sip more wine, wondering if he'll think it's weird if I take off my sweater. What the hell, I tell myself. You're overheating here. Live dangerously.

I shuck off my sweater, throwing caution to the wind. Zack's head swivels toward me so fast I let out a bashful laugh.

"Sorry. It's hot in here, and my sweater's really—"

"Not a problem." Zack's face goes red. "That was lame, I just—you caught me off guard."

I take a step closer. I can feel my body pulsing with the wine and the delicious aromas.

"That's a pretty color." He closes the distance between us and reaches out to touch the spaghetti strap. It's a vintage buttercup yellow camisole, and I happen to know it looks good on me.

With one finger, he slides the strap slowly—so slowly—off my shoulder. Our eyes catch for a long, suspended moment. Nina Simone croons about putting a spell on someone. I can feel my hair curling in the steam.

His hand reaches out and strokes my cheek, his fingers warm against my skin.

"Hey!" The word is drawn out into two syllables, friendly and teasing from the doorway.

We spring apart and turn to face Jupiter, me sweating with embarrassment as I pull my strap back into place.

"Hey, Jupes." Zack picks up the wooden spoon and goes back to stirring, angling away from her. I'm jealous he has an excuse to hide his face.

"How's it going, Jupiter?" I say, trying to keep the mortification from my voice.

She widens her eyes at me like we're girlfriends bonding over the cute date I just walked in with. As her uncle turns to look over his shoulder, though, she ditches the expression, going for blank and clueless.

"Fine. Dandy, actually." She seems so chipper, so happy. She's been moody all week, so the change is both refreshing and unnerving.

I watch her carefully, trying to read what's happening in her face. "Yeah? What's going on?"

She shrugs. "I had a great day, is all."

"Okay."

She yanks the heavy book bag back onto one shoulder. "Now I'm going to pay for it, though. I have to write like seven hundred essays and study for a thousand exams."

"That sounds intense." I still can't decide what's different about her. She's glowing with some sort of light I don't trust, a luminosity in her eyes that reminds me of her mother.

She grabs a banana from a bowl of fruit on the counter and takes a step toward the hallway. "Better get started."

"Stew in about fifteen minutes," Zack calls over his shoulder. I can't help admiring the muscles of his back as they flex under his T-shirt.

"You two eat without me," Jupiter flashes me a sly, knowing grin and I shoo her away.

"I'm making this for you." He points the spoon at the big copper pot on the stove. "This is your family history in here."

"I know, I know, Mhamo Rathbone's secret recipe." She saunters down the hall, sniggering. A moment later, music blares from her room, some kind of hip-hop.

Zack turns to me. "Busted."

"So busted." I snatch a piece of carrot from his cutting board and crunch it between my teeth. I consider putting my sweater back on, but decide against it.

He steps closer and runs a hand down my bare arm. "You are irresistible."

I mouth the words, *You are.*

His head slumps forward with a soft groan. "It's very inconvenient, being an uncle right now."

"What would you do if you weren't?"

"I can't talk about that." There's a smile in his voice as I trail my finger under the waistband of his jeans, just a little, studying the gap between his hipbone and his belly.

Our conversation is interrupted by Jupiter's reappearance in the doorway, her backpack slung over one shoulder. "I'm heading out."

We both turn to her in surprise.

"Where are you going?" Zack's tone is cautious. I can tell he's trying not to sound worried, but it's audible just the same.

"Home." She smiles brightly. There's that glow again, the curious radiance I don't trust. She's put on a pretty, deep violet blouse that brings out the purplish hues of her vivid blue eyes.

Zack turns the heat down on the stove and takes a step toward her. "What's going on, Jupes?"

"Colton and I made up." She holds up a hand to ward off anything we might try to say. Her gaze darts to me, then back to her uncle. "I know what you're thinking, but he really is different now. People change. They have to, right? Otherwise, what's the point of working on yourself?"

I bite my tongue, feeling my stomach sour at her words. Is this youthful naïveté, or something deeper? I hate to think Jupiter's the sort of woman who accepts violence as something normal and expected. I haven't had a chance to ask her yet about Colton's alleged drug problem. It's still not clear if she even knows about that. I'm not sure if it's my place to bring it up.

Zack gives an exasperated sigh. "People do change, but it's been less than two weeks since your big fight. Maybe you should give it more time."

"What fight?" She blinks at him, her expression going cold. "I never said we had a fight."

He looks wrong-footed, but recovers quickly. "I kind of assumed, since you showed up in the middle of the night and you'd been crying."

Jupiter's face is guarded now, an angry flush creeping up her neck. Her eyes move from him to me and back again, her jaw tightening. When her gaze finally lands on me, the cornflower blue goes two shades darker. "You told him, didn't you?"

I open my mouth, but no words come out.

"Jesus Christ, Tansy—"

Zack steps between us. "Hey now, let's not take it out on Tansy. I begged her to let me know if Colton was hurting you, okay? That's all. She didn't divulge any details."

Jupiter's having none of it. She sidesteps Zack and fixes me with an accusing scowl. "I thought I could trust you."

"I was worried," I say, but it sounds weak and ineffectual. "You needed backup. I'm sorry."

She shakes her head, her lip curling like I disgust her. "Colton's right. You just want to break us up."

"Come on, Jupiter, let's talk about this." Zack tries again to step between us, but Jupiter spins on her heel and hurries toward the door. I hear a stifled sob on her way out. From the street, a jaunty car horn tells us Colton's out there, waiting for her. She slams the front door behind her.

"Shit." I cup my forehead, feeling overwhelmed. "This isn't good."

"No." Zack stares at the ceiling, looking as devastated as I feel.

"She hates me."

He looks at me. "She's eighteen years old. Her psyche is subject to tropical storms that move through quickly. Two things both the Rathbone women have in spades: moodiness and resiliency. Jupiter will be over this before you've even had time to figure out what you did wrong."

"She feels betrayed." I rub my arms, suddenly cold, and cross the kitchen to pull on my sweater. "I don't blame her. I shouldn't have told you."

"You had to tell me. I'm her uncle." He says it like I had no choice.

I shrug. "I'm her counselor. Whatever she tells me is supposed to be confidential. You know that."

"You're more than her counselor."

"I crossed a line." I stare at the floor, feeling waves of guilt as I remember Jupiter's accusing glare.

He cocks his head. "If you did, you crossed it for the right reasons."

I hoist my leather tote onto my shoulder and take a step toward the hall. Minutes ago, I was ready to drag him off to the bedroom, but now all I feel is cold and lost.

"I think I should go," I say, inching toward the doorway.

"Why?" His face is unreadable. "I made all this stew."

I gesture toward the door. "It's just . . . I feel like I failed her."

"Tansy," he says, gripping my arms and making me face him. "Rathbonology Rule Number One: Do not take it personally."

I can feel tears stinging at my eyes. "You saw her face. She blames me. How can I not take that personally?"

He pulls me into a hug abruptly, and I surprise myself by snuggling into him, drinking in the warmth of his body.

"We're moody bastards," he murmurs into my hair. "I told you that. It's the Irish in us. Please stay. Mhamo Rathbone's magical stew can cure anything."

I blink away tears. "It's like I drove her right into Colton's arms."

"It's not your fault." He lifts my chin with one finger. "Really. Jupiter's going to follow her heart, no matter what any of us say or do. We just have to let her know we're still here for her when she needs a place to land."

10

TWO DAYS LATER, I've replayed my last conversation with Jupiter so many times, it's like a film reel on a loop. She won't answer my texts, which is making me crazy. For the first time, I think I understand a little something about Selene's state of mind the day she came to see me. Being cut off like this without warning is maddening.

According to Zack, Jupiter's giving him the silent treatment as well. When he tried to go see her at home, she refused to come to the door, and Colton politely informed Zack that if he didn't leave immediately, he would find himself with a restraining order just like Selene. Zack said he seriously wanted to punch the smug bastard, but he knew this would only make everything a thousand times worse.

Friday evening, I decide to go to a drop-in yoga class on campus after work. I could use the exercise, but my real motivation is the slim possibility I might run into Jupiter. One of the things Jupiter and I worked on during our counseling sessions was finding healthy ways to manage stress. She mentioned taking a yoga class on campus a few times, and though I have no idea which one, I figure it's worth a shot. Of course, as her counselor I could bring up her schedule and show up outside one of her classes, but this feels a little too invasive as a first move. The whole reason she's shut me out in the first place is that I blurred the boundaries I promised to respect. I doubt she'd talk to me if she knew I was there specifically to check up on her.

The yoga class is a bust—no Jupiter. I try to do the class anyway, but find I can't concentrate. My anxiety about Jupiter's situation feels like a hive of bees crawling under my skin. When the teacher invites us to do yet another downward dog, I flash her an apologetic smile and slip out the back door.

In the faculty locker room, I run into a few other counselors who have just finished Zumba. We chat for a few minutes, then I take a quick shower, even though I barely broke a sweat. The hot water feels good. When I head back to my locker wrapped in a fluffy white towel, I feel refreshed, if not exactly relaxed. Zack and I are meeting for dinner in a little over an hour. I pull my makeup bag from my locker, trying to concentrate on my excitement about seeing Zack rather than my disappointment about failing to track down Jupiter.

When I close my locker, Selene's standing right there, less than a foot away. I let out a yelp of surprise.

One of the counselors I ran into earlier calls from a couple rows over, "Tansy? Everything okay?"

"Fine," I call back automatically. "My friend just startled me."

Selene's lips curve in a slow, sardonic grin. "Oh, I'm your *friend* now, huh?"

Selene's a mess. Her normally olive-toned skin is so pale and drawn, she looks a little ghoulish. I smell something sharp on her breath, possibly vodka. She's wearing a strange mélange of clothing: black leather pants that have seen better days, a plaid flannel shirt two sizes too big, and a bright green beanie that conceals her hair. Selene always had a knack for putting together eccentric, unexpected outfits, but this feels different—like she threw on whatever she could find with zero regard for how it looks. If I saw her on the street, I might even think she was homeless.

"You know this is a faculty locker room, right?" It comes out a little bitchy, even sotto voce, but my pulse is still racing after the jump-scare, and it's making me prickly.

She chuckles. "What are you going to do? Call security?"

"How did you find me?"

"Let's just say you're not very stealthy. I followed you here and waited. Easy-peasy lemon squeezy." She slurs this last bit, confirming my suspicion that she's drunk.

"I hope you didn't drive."

She smirks. "Why's that?"

"Come on, Selene. You smell like a distillery." I pull on my panties under my towel and turn away from her as I put on my bra. Nothing about this conversation bodes well, and having it while naked only makes me feel more vulnerable.

She shakes her head in disgust. "So easy to judge when your life's not falling apart."

"What's up?" I ask as I button my blouse.

"What do you mean, 'What's up?'" She repeats my words with a mocking lilt that gets my hackles up. This whole situation is reminding me way too much of the night she ambushed me at my place in Santa Cruz. She was drunk then too, and it didn't end well.

I pull on my pants and buckle my belt. *That was then, this is now. You're a grown-ass woman, Tansy, not a frightened twenty-year-old with PTSD.*

"Well," I say, keeping my voice calm, almost clinical, "you went to the trouble of following me here, so I'm assuming you have something to tell me."

Her eyes look a little unfocused. She sits on the bench behind her, but misjudges it and almost falls on her butt. "She's marrying him. That power-hungry shit-for-brains."

"*What?*" I stop buttoning my blouse to gawk at her stupidly. Selene nods, apparently pleased by my shock. "Jupiter's engaged. You happy now? Is this what you and 'Uncle Chill' had in mind?"

I sit beside her. "How do you know?"

"Little thing called Instagram." She burps softly. "I can't go anywhere near my baby, but I can see her life online. She's got a very expensive engagement ring."

I cup my face in my hands. "Goddammit."

"Yep. Pretty much."

"I'm so sorry, Selene." I put a hand on her arm. "That's terrible news."

She yanks off her hat, and I gasp. Selene's head is shaved bald. For all the years I've known her, she's worn it long enough to reach her waist. Now her exposed scalp shines in the fluorescent lights of the locker room, pale and hairless as an egg.

"Christ, Selene!"

Her smile is mean and joyless. "You like my new look?"

"Why would you—?"

"Military chic." She laughs like this is hilarious, then stops abruptly, fixing me with her gaze. "You know what this means, right?"

I just blink at her, not sure where she's going with this. "What, your haircut?"

"Not my *hair*. Fuck my hair. I don't give a shit about my *hair*." She's getting louder, and I can't help but think about my colleagues two rows down overhearing us.

"Listen." I touch her shoulder, trying to calm her down. "I'm meeting Zack tonight for dinner. Why don't you come, and we'll talk strategy. There has to be a way to stop this."

"There's only one way to stop it," she growls.

The laughter two rows down has faded. My heart's hammering so hard in my chest it feels like it's spasming. I use my stern-but-not-angry emergency voice, the one I use to talk down hysterical students. "You need to lower your voice."

She puts her fingers to her lips in a pantomime of shushing. Then she whispers, "You know these guys. He thinks he *owns* her now. This won't end until someone ends it."

"Jesus, Selene," I whisper. "You're hardly making sense. Whatever you have in mind, it's not the answer."

"Oh, yeah?" She narrows her eyes at me, raising her voice again. "Then tell me, what is the answer?"

I shake my head, at a loss.

"That's what I thought." She jumps up and strides away from me, surprisingly steady on her feet, making a beeline for the exit.

"Wait!" I call.

She doesn't even turn around.

I shove my workout clothes and makeup bag into my duffle as quickly as possible, but by the time I dash outside, ignoring my coworkers' worried looks, Selene is gone.

*   *   *

"What the hell is she thinking?" Zack scowls at his pasta, his face stormy.

The busy restaurant bustles around us. We're perched at a table before the plate-glass windows, our entrees and salads virtually untouched. The waitress has checked in twice to make sure our food is okay, since we've barely made a dent in it. A baby keeps crying at a nearby table—long siren wails that echo my own distress.

After I filled Zack in on my encounter with Selene, we drove around for over an hour, checking at her yurt and all her favorite haunts. We finally gave up and came here for dinner, though neither of us has much of an appetite.

"She's out of her mind with worry. Not to mention drunk." I take a bite of bread, but it tastes like paste. "Maybe we should drive around again, see if we can—"

"Not Selene," Zack snaps, cutting me off. "Jupiter. Why would she agree to marry that frat-boy dickhead two weeks after he punched her in the stomach?"

I pick at my ravioli, a little taken aback by his sharp tone. First, Selene shows up acting like this turn of events is my fault, now Zack's tone implies I've missed the point.

"Selene's got every right to be pissed off at me." Zack swigs his wine, looking grim. "I should have done more."

I swallow a bite of ravioli, trying to read his mood. This is a side of Zack I've never seen. Until now, he's stayed true to his original position that Jupiter needs support, not manipulation or ultimatums. I've always agreed with that approach, but after my run-in with Selene, my convictions about how to handle this have started to erode. I keep hearing her words echoing in my head: *You happy now? Is this what you and 'Uncle Chill' had in mind?* I was hoping Zack would convince me that Jupiter's engagement isn't our fault. Instead, he seems to be wavering just when I need his reassurance the most.

"What could you have done differently?" I try to keep my voice calm and reasonable, though the baby's high-pitched screams force me to say it louder than I would otherwise.

Zack grimaces and leans back in his chair. "For starters, I should never have let Selene take Jupiter back. I should have adopted her when I had the chance."

I don't know what I was expecting him to say, but this wasn't it. Until now, it never occurred to me that Zack considered raising Jupiter indefinitely on his own.

"Selene dragged that girl around like she was just another cardboard box filled with crystals and tarot cards." Zack glowers at the ceiling. "You can't raise a kid like that. God only knows what kind of men she was exposed to. If I'd insisted on keeping her, raising her, she might not have such a twisted view of love."

I choose my next words carefully. "I didn't know you considered adopting Jupiter."

"Of course I did," he says, his tone gruff, as if this should be obvious. "Selene was a mess. I knew that. She'd cleaned up a little, but she still wasn't a fit mother—not really. I should have fought for permanent custody."

His tone stings a little, though logically I know he's not angry with me. He's pissed at his inability to fix this. I share that frustration, but it bothers me that he's treating me more like an annoying bystander who doesn't get it rather than a partner who's also invested in Jupiter's fate.

I take a sip of water and try to nudge the conversation in a more productive direction. "We all have our regrets. The question is, what do we do now? Is there any way we can stop her from marrying him?"

Zack grips his wine and stares out the window, distant and brooding. "I'm starting to think Selene's right."

My stomach drops, like when you're driving too fast and the road dips unexpectedly. "Right about what, exactly?"

He keeps his gaze fixed out the window. A muscle in his jaw flutters. "Maybe the only way to keep Jupiter safe is . . . something drastic."

My mouth has gone dry, and what little food I've managed to eat roils in my stomach. "Like what?"

When he doesn't answer, I press the point, unwilling to let it drop. "Selene said, 'This won't end until someone ends it.' I know what that means, in Selene-speak. Tell me you're not saying you agree with her."

"Come on, Tansy." He shoots me a quick, sideways glance before staring out at the street again. "You know how these guys work. This is just the beginning. Before long, Jupiter will get pregnant, she'll drop out of college, he'll probably take her away somewhere so she's even more isolated. She might as well be facing a prison sentence, because Colton's going to keep her under lock and key."

The baby at the next table howls with renewed vigor, the sound slicing through the din of conversation and drawing dirty looks. I massage my temples, fighting a headache. "Jupiter might come to her senses any day. This is not a done deal. Lots of women get away from their—"

"No." Zack slaps his hand on the table, making me flinch. "That's the wishful thinking that got us into this mess."

"Well, I hate to break it to you," I say, my tone matching his. "But in spite of what you and your sister seem to think, you can't just go around killing people because they're assholes."

He blinks at me a couple times, like a man waking from a dream. His expression softens for the first time since I told him about my conversation with Selene. "You're right. I'm sorry."

"Jupiter's an adult," I remind him. "We can't make her choices for her."

He nods. The aggressive posture he showed seconds ago deflates into one of defeat. "I know. I'm not thinking straight. I just—" His words catch in his throat, and he starts again. "I love Jupiter so much, you know? It kills me to see this happening to her. And Selene?" He runs a hand through his hair and breathes out a long, ragged breath. "I just know she's going to do something crazy. A part of me thinks I should do it for her just to—" He breaks off.

I put my hand on his, my anger instantly dissolving. "I know."

"I feel so powerless." Tears glitter in his eyes. He swallows hard, gripping my hand like a lifeline. "I need my girls to be safe."

I nod, aware that nothing I say can stop the wave of helplessness washing over him now. I feel it too, though it's probably so much worse for him.

Selene's bare face and shaved head flash through my mind. She looked raw and deranged, like someone who had severed all ties to normalcy. I want to contradict Zack, assure him Selene will sleep it off and wake up tomorrow ready to strategize, but this would be an empty promise. Zack and I both know she's out there somewhere, fierce and ready for anything.

I push my plate aside. "Let's go look for her again. We can drive around town one more time, cruise past her place, then park near Colton's just in case she shows up there."

His smile is sad but grateful. "I guess you're right. It's not doing us any good pushing food around our plates."

"I'll ask for a couple of boxes and the check." I try to sound brisk and efficient, though the pain in his eyes is killing me.

He stares out the window while I summon the waitress and tell her we've got to go. When he turns to face me again, I can't quite read his expression.

"What?" I ask gently.

It takes him a couple of beats to respond; when he does, his voice is thick with emotion. "I'm just so used to doing this alone. Worrying about them. Trying to ward off disaster. I can't tell you what it means, having you here."

I reach for his hand again, covering it with mine. "I'm not going anywhere. You guys are stuck with me."

It catches me off guard to realize just how much I mean it.

* * *

My eyes fly open, heart pounding, trying to swim to the surface of consciousness from the depths of a disturbing nightmare. Rob had a kitten, which he cradled lovingly at first, but then he became Colton, and threw the kitten hard against a wall, leaving a smear of blood as it fell lifeless to the floor.

I shudder at the memory, blinking hard to clear my head. That's when I notice I'm not in my bed. A surge of panic flutters through me like a trapped bird before I remember I'm at Zack's.

It's been a week since our tense dinner at the Italian restaurant, and it feels like we've both been holding our breath, waiting for the storm to break. In spite of our efforts to find Selene, she's remained MIA. Zack and I managed to track down the guy who owns the yurt she's renting outside of town, but he hasn't seen her for at least a week. Jupiter has continued to evade us as well. Even when I broke down and looked up her class schedule, I wasn't able to intercept her on campus. It's as if both Jupiter and Selene have disappeared into thin air.

I reach over in the darkness and touch Zack's smooth, muscular back. Still sleeping, he turns over and pulls me close, enveloping me in warmth. I snuggle in, loving the feel of his bare skin against mine, his smell filling me with a narcotic blend of pleasure and peace.

That's when I hear a loud banging sound downstairs. Someone's hammering on Zack's front door.

Zack's gentle snores stop abruptly and he sits up, rubbing his face. "Did you hear something?"

"Yeah." My voice comes out thick with sleep. "Someone's at your door, I think." I'm mentally cataloging the possibilities: Jupiter? Colton? Selene?

I fumble around in the dark until I find my phone on the bedside table. It's three fifteen in the morning. There's a click, and the room floods with light from Zack's bedside lamp. He's already up and out of bed, pulling on a pair of sweats.

"Who do you think—?" I begin, but he cuts me off.

"Maybe Jupiter's back." He looks hopeful. "She has her own key, but she's always losing it."

I find my clothes strewn around the room and hurry to put them on.

"It's okay," he says. "You can stay in bed."

I wonder for a moment if he's trying to keep me hidden from whoever's out there.

He must read something in my face, because his brow smooths and he offers me a warm smile. "Or not. If it is Jupes, she might feel more comfortable talking to you."

I scoff. "I doubt it, given the way she's been ghosting me."

He looks at me as he pulls on his sweatshirt. "You can stay here or come with, whichever you prefer. I just want you to know, you're not a secret."

I can't help smiling at the way he's read my mind. I'm jolted out of my moment of pleasure by another barrage of angry knocks downstairs. Whoever's out there is either angry or in a hurry or both. Exchanging a glance, we make our way along the hall, down the stairs, through the living room, to the front door, Zack turning on lights as we go.

Zack wrenches the door open just as another hailstorm of knocks begins. Selene's standing there, wild-eyed. She's wearing a turquoise silk kimono over a white tank top and black yoga pants. Her face is as white as her shirt. Her hair's grown just enough to cover her scalp in dark stubble. Jupiter's right behind her, crying and shivering, hugging herself and hunched over like she's in pain. Selene's MG is parked along the sidewalk, one wheel up on the curb, canting the little car at a crazy angle.

When Selene's gaze slides from Zack to me, something changes in her expression, but it's hard to read the exact emotion there. I pull my hoodie a little tighter around me, the chill of the October night breathing through the open door, the smell of dead leaves and wet pavement filling my head.

Zack wraps a protective arm around each of them and pulls them inside. Once they're in the brightly lit living room, I see Jupiter's face is covered in fresh bruises. Her blouse is torn at the neckline, exposing the edge of her white lace bra.

"Oh my God, Jupiter," I gasp. "You're hurt."

Zack examines her in the light, swearing under his breath.

Selene massages her temples. "I killed him."

"Mom, no," Jupiter murmurs. "Please don't."

"You *what?*" Zack spins around, his voice an incredulous croak.

"I did. I wanted him dead, and I floored it." Selene's gaze ping-pongs between Zack and me, manic, waiting for our response. "I hit him with my car and drove off."

Everyone starts talking at once. Zack holds up a hand, his voice cutting through the noise, his question aimed at Selene. "Are you sure he's dead? Should we call an ambulance?"

Selene's answer is flat and final. "I'm sure."

Zack walks Jupiter over to the couch. I run to the kitchen to get some ice, wrapping it in a clean tea towel. When I get back to the living room, Selene still looks like she's in shock. Her complexion has regained some of its color, but there's something alternately vacant and frenzied in her eyes, like she has an internal switch that keeps flipping on and off.

"You've got to turn yourself in," Zack's saying.

Selene gives him an arch look. "You know how many hit-and-runs are solved every year?"

Zack runs a hand over his face, blinking with exhaustion.

"Eight percent." Selene leans back in her chair, retying the sash of her kimono. "I read that in one of my 'trashy thrillers' you're always making fun of. That means I have a ninety-two percent chance of getting away with it."

Jupiter says, in the smallest voice possible, "I can't believe he's dead."

She's sitting alone in the leather club chair near the gas fire, which Zack has turned on. I hurry to her, perching on the arm of the chair and pressing ice to her bruised face. She flinches away from me at first, but then our eyes catch, and she surrenders to my ministrations.

"What happened?" I ask, looking from Jupiter to Selene.

Selene plucks a silver flask from the pocket of her kimono, unscrews the cap, and takes a generous pull from it. "He beat the shit out of her, is what happened."

"Colton did this?" I examine the bruises on Jupiter's face and throat more carefully. There's a necklace of purple bruises forming around her throat, and for a second, I'm glad he's dead.

"No, Tansy, the Easter Bunny did it." Selene's voice is hard and sarcastic. She's not pleased that I'm here, for a number of reasons, that much is clear.

I look away from her, concentrating again on Jupiter, moving the ice from the blue, raised bump blossoming on her forehead to the cinnamon-colored scratch along her cheek. Her teeth are chattering. I remember that feeling all too well.

Zack paces by the fire, shaking his head. "I don't care if you *can* get away with it, telling the cops is still the right thing to do."

"Really?" Selene studies him, her eyebrows high. "For me, or for you?"

"For Jupiter," he answers immediately.

"Yeah?" Selene turns to her daughter, hunched in the chair a few feet away, her shoulders slumped in defeat. "You think she'll be better off if her mother's in prison?"

"They'll work with you, if you come forward." Zack's voice goes gentle. "It's involuntary manslaughter. Maybe two years, tops, less if you're good."

"It wasn't involuntary," Selene hisses.

Jupiter groans. I pull the ice away, thinking I've applied too much pressure, but she glares at her mother and I see the groan is directed at Selene. "Mom, please."

"Involuntary manslaughter." Zack nods, agreeing with himself. "It will definitely fly, especially if you turn yourself in. Look, I know I already asked, but are you one hundred percent sure he was—?"

"He was dead." Selene's eyes are feverish. "His head was caved in."

Jupiter cups her hand to her mouth and runs from the room. She makes it the bathroom—just in time, it sounds like.

Zack's brow is furrowed, trying to work out the puzzle before him. "Are there cameras at Colton's?"

The question is directed at Selene, but she turns to Jupiter, who is just limping back into the room. "Are there?"

"What?" Jupiter wipes her mouth with the back of her hand.

"Cameras at Colton's place," Zack explains gently.

Jupiter considers a moment, then shakes her head. "Not that I know of."

Zack starts looking for his keys. "We need to get Jupiter to the hospital. Selene, you're coming too. You can both give a statement to the cops there."

Selene throws her flask at the wall so hard, the plaster cracks. The room goes silent, all three of us gaping at this strange, bald woman with the feral eyes.

"No cops. No hospital." Selene's voice is quiet but full of menace.

Zack looks like he wants to protest, but he turns away from his sister and focuses on Jupiter instead. "Sweetheart, I'm going to take you to the hospital, get you checked out, okay?"

Jupiter shakes her head, her gaze darting back and forth between her mom and her uncle like a trapped animal.

"Just to be sure nothing's broken," I add, wading into the fray. "A quick exam. You probably won't have to stay there long."

Jupiter's lip quivers. "I'm okay. Really."

"You don't know that," Zack says. "You might have a concussion, or internal injuries. It's not always easy to—"

"She said no!" Selene barks. "For God's sake, it's her body, leave her alone."

Zack and I look at each other. This is clearly not a battle we're going to win, at least not right now.

"Maybe we should get you up to bed," I say, standing and taking Jupiter's arm. She looks ready to wilt to the floor any second. Zack nods. "Do you mind? She needs to lie down, at least."

"Let's go." I guide her toward the staircase. "You've had enough trauma for one night."

She allows herself to be led. When Selene calls to her, my hand is on her back, and I feel her whole body go rigid, her spine taut as a steel cable.

"I did it to protect you, Jupiter." Selene's voice is an odd mixture of honey and menace.

Jupiter resumes her slow, shuffling progress up the stairs. I grip her elbow, trying to assess her injuries without crowding her. She blinks away tears, her jaw working like she's grinding her teeth.

*   *   *

Jupiter takes a long, hot shower. When she comes out of the bathroom, her hair damp and parted in the middle, she looks like a little girl. She's wearing an old T-shirt of Zack's with the scabby remnants of a Cal logo across the chest. I pull back the covers and she climbs into bed, wincing a little at her injuries. After a moment's hesitation, I sit by her side and tentatively touch her wet hair. I don't know how she feels about me right now, given her silence over the past couple of weeks, but leaving her alone up here feels wrong, so I linger.

"You're sure you don't want to go to the hospital?" I ask again.

She shakes her head. "I'm fine. Just a few bruises."

"How are you feeling?" I ask in a whisper.

She blinks a couple of times, her blue eyes almost violet in the dim lamplight. "Messed up."

"Do you want to talk about it?" Dimly, I'm aware of Selene's and Zack's raised voices downstairs. I wonder what they're talking about. Is he still trying to convince her to turn herself in? They're too far away to make out any specific words.

Jupiter starts to cry—silent, pretty tears that slide down her temples toward her golden hair. "Not really."

"You want me to hang out for a bit?" I whisper.

"That's okay." She blinks up at me, her eyes full of a bottomless sorrow. "Thanks, though."

"Try to get some sleep." I stand and turn out the light. "Everything will seem less chaotic in the morning."

"You promise?" Her voice is soft and childish, a kid making a wish.

"I promise."

I only hope my vow isn't an empty one.

*　*　*

"Is she going to turn herself in?" My voice sounds too loud in the darkness.

Zack squirms, trying to get comfortable between the sheets. "I don't know. I tried my best to convince her, but she's on a different planet right now."

I rest my hand on his chest. His skin feels hot, almost feverish. "You tried."

"Maybe I should just call the cops myself." He sighs. "I don't think I can do that, though. She'd never forgive me. How's Jupiter?"

"Still in shock," I say. "They both are, probably. I don't think any of her injuries are that bad, but it's hard to be sure. He could have killed her, Zack. Those bruises around her neck look like he choked her."

Zack makes a sound in his throat, part growl, part groan.

I hesitate before I pose my next question, unsure of how he'll react. "Are you positive Selene should confess?"

His head turns toward me, surprised. "You don't think she should?"

"Colton's dad is the DA," I remind him. "They're going to throw the book at her."

"It happened a couple blocks from downtown," he reminds me. "There were probably witnesses. It's going to be worse for Selene if she doesn't offer herself up."

"But it was like three in the morning," I counter.

"On a Friday night. All it takes is one person coming home from the bars, or watching TV, glancing out a window." He sits up, fluffs his pillow, and lies back down again, restless. "Maybe it's because I've worked with the feds, but even a bastard like Colton deserves some kind of justice, don't you think?"

I'm quiet, curled against him so he can't see my face. It's the question I've asked myself about Rob all these years, wondering if Selene and I should have paid for his death.

Zack doesn't ask the question again, thank God, because I don't have an answer. Instead, he cups his hands behind his head and sighs. "Maybe it's my duty to tell them what I know."

"It's better if it comes from her," I murmur into his shoulder.

He wraps an arm around me, his words falling gently into my ear. "I'm so glad you're here right now."

"Yeah?" I look up at him, his face lit by the moonlight streaming through his mullioned windows. "Selene wasn't happy to see me."

"She's ashamed." He falls silent, thinking.

I sit up on an elbow, studying his face, sensing there's something he hasn't told me yet. "What are you thinking?"

"She did promise to turn herself in if suspicion falls on Jupiter." He watches me, his eyebrows tilting. "And that's pretty much inevitable."

Though I hate the thought of anyone going to jail over the death of the bastard who did that to Jupiter, it's better for Selene to pay the price than her. I picture the ring of bruises around Jupiter's delicate, pale neck and shudder.

"How are you doing?" He scans my face.

I nod. "I'm okay. It was hard to see Jupiter like that."

He swallows and nods. It's got to be tougher for him, seeing his niece beat to a pulp.

"Physically, I'm sure she'll bounce back," I assure him.

"The blessing and the curse of youth," he says, with a mirthless chuckle. "Resiliency."

I lie back down and snuggle in, trying to soak up his warmth. "I still have so many questions, but it seemed cruel to quiz Jupiter. How do you think Selene ended up at Colton's apartment, anyway? Do you think Jupiter called her?"

"Maybe. Or Selene could have been staking the place out."

"But the restraining order," I remind him.

He scoffs. "My sister doesn't have a lot of respect for law and order, in case you haven't noticed."

We lie there in silence for a long moment. The wind pushes through the trees outside, rattling their branches. A dog barks somewhere in the distance, then falls silent.

"If Jupiter did phone her mom, why do you think she'd call Selene instead of us?" I ask.

Zack shifts under the covers, his hand reaching out to rest on my hip. He takes so long to answer I wonder for a moment if he's fallen asleep. "Sometimes a girl needs her mom, I guess. There's a lot of love there, it's just . . . messy."

His words swim through my head as I drift off to sleep, wondering if all love is messy in its own way.

CHAPTER

11

"TANSY. WAKE UP."

My eyes pop open, and I find myself staring into Selene's face. She looks older, her face haggard and her eyes shadowy in the dim predawn light. In my groggy delirium, I think for a moment that we're back in her geodesic dome and it's the morning after Rob died. She woke me early that day too, whispering my name, her face hovering over mine in the gray light creeping through the skylight, her blue-black hair hanging around her face like a shroud.

I blink at my surroundings, disoriented. Zack's fast asleep beside me, his body turned away from me and his head buried underneath a pillow. He goes on snoring softly, oblivious to his sister's presence.

Selene glances at him, then locks her eyes on mine again. She's kneeling beside the bed, keeping her voice low. "I need to wash my car."

I sit up, rubbing my eyes and yawning. "Now?"

"Yes, now." She's agitated, high strung, in spite of her obvious exhaustion. I wonder if she slept at all. "Before anyone sees it."

"What time is it?" I run my fingers through my hair, trying to wake up.

"Just after five. If an early morning jogger notices my car, I'm screwed." She keeps casting nervous glances at Zack, like she doesn't want to wake him.

I look out the windows. The sky is still dark. "You need my help?"

She nods. "Can we do it at your house? I can't take a chance with a carwash, and my yurt has too many neighbors. You're out in the country where nobody will notice."

"Jessica and Marius might," I point out.

"Still, it's the best option we've got." Selene bites her lip and darts another nervous look at her brother.

I study her. "You don't want Zack to know?"

She shakes her head. "He wants me to turn myself in."

"But you're not going to?"

Her head tilts to the side like she's trying to decide if I'm being serious. "You know me, Tansy. Do you really think 'surrender' is in my playbook?"

Zack stirs in his sleep, one arm reaching out to hug the pillow more tightly over his head.

Selene gestures toward the door, whispering, "Come on. Let's go."

I hesitate. The thought of Zack waking up to find Selene and me MIA makes me nervous.

As if reading my mind, she says, "You can leave him a note. If we get out of here now, there's a chance we could get it washed and come back before either Zack or Jupiter have woken up."

I'm hesitant to help Selene, even though a part of me thinks what she did was justifiable. The words *accessory to the crime* flash through my mind, bringing with them the usual flutter of fear. There's always that line with Selene, the one she didn't have to cross but did anyway. I've spent the last eighteen years of my life eaten up with guilt over Rob's death. He was a rapist who took advantage of my naïveté for his own sick pleasure, but did he really deserve to die? Colton was an entitled, screwed-up mess—violent, controlling—but getting run down in the street still seems extreme. It's like Selene and I are caught in this recurring cycle of revenge, some kind of karmic loop where we keep playing similar roles in different dramas.

Again, she must read my mind, because she lowers her voice even more, her words coming out in an urgent hiss. "You owe me, Tansy."

It's the wrong move. I sit up straighter and look her in the eye. "Fuck that, Selene. I don't owe you anything."

She looks a little stunned, her eyebrows floating toward her hairline.

"You made your choices," I say, my voice low but steady. "It's not my place to say if what you did was right or wrong, but they're just that—*your choices.*"

"And what about you?" She folds her arms. "What do you choose? Where do your loyalties lie?"

I remember the way Selene helped me that terrible night so many summers ago. She got me away from The Springs without anyone noticing. She drew me a hot bath and sat with me while I shivered in the steamy water, waiting for the heat to worm its way into my bones. Later, when we went to bed, she sang me Bob Dylan songs until I fell asleep. In the morning, she made us breakfast and insisted I try to eat some. My own mother was little more than a shadow flickering around the edges of my life, so maybe I'm not the best judge; looking back, though, Selene did all the things I'd want my mother to do, guiding me through my shock and grief with a steady, gentle hand.

More than anything, though, Selene bought me time that night to figure out what would happen next. Sure, she insisted we could never tell anyone about Rob, but she also didn't try to stop me when I moved away a week later. Whether she meant to or not, she bought me my ticket out of that nightmare; without her help,

I would have been snared in the aftermath of Rob's assault. If he'd raped me, I would have been weighed down by that, whether or not I'd pressed charges. If she'd insisted we go to the cops about Rob's death, that would have opened up a legal maze that would have made it impossible for me to keep going with my education, at least for a while. It could have completely derailed my life, sending me on another trajectory entirely. Though Selene resented my choice to cut her out of my life, she's the one who gave me that freedom when she took charge and helped me through my dark night of the soul.

I still don't know if I agree with Zack about Selene needing to turn herself in. If suspicion falls on Jupiter, then yes, she needs to come clean. Morally, though, I'm not sure if Selene's obligated to confess if Jupiter's in the clear. Colton was vicious enough with Jupiter last night to justify almost anything Selene did to stop him. Even Zack himself hinted at taking drastic measures to keep his niece safe. Surely he can't condemn his sister for following those same instincts.

What I do know is this: Right now, I have a chance to buy Selene some time. If her car is discovered in its current state, she won't have any choice in the matter. Eighteen years ago, she carved out a safe space for me to figure out my next steps when I was too rattled to think. Now Selene's the one reeling in the aftermath of a brutal, life-changing night. The least I can do is give her the breathing room to make a choice she can live with.

All at once, I know I'm going to help her, but more importantly, I know why. "Fine. Let's do this. But I want to be clear: I'm not helping because I 'owe' you. I'm doing it because I love you."

* * *

Selene always was an unnerving driver, teetering between adept and reckless. When I was younger, I accepted the fear that came with riding shotgun in her little pickup truck, knowing it was all part of the heady danger she offered. This morning, though, as we navigate the dark, autumn landscape of empty predawn streets, I can tell she's holding back. She disciplines herself with meticulous caution, surprising me with her self-control.

"So, what's going on with Zack?" She asks it casually, but there's an edge beneath her words.

I stare out the window, taking my time before I answer. "I don't know. It's all really new."

My eyes stay glued to the scenery, the silhouettes of houses looming in the darkness. Halloween decorations festoon the porches, witches and jack-o-lanterns grinning from the gloom. A memory of carving pumpkins with Selene the first month we were friends comes back to me in vivid detail. I was no older than Jupiter. I can smell the pulpy innards as we scooped the contents out with our bare hands, salvaging the seeds so we could bake them. We gathered sage wands, crystals, candles, flowers, and did a ceremony under the full moon. She said the end of October is when the veils between worlds grows thinnest, and you can communicate with those who have passed to the other side. We sat cross-legged and invoked every moon goddess we could think of: Diana, Hecate, and of course Selene, the goddess for whom Selene named herself. Her birth name was Jennifer, but she ditched that long before I met her. That's so like her, to shrug off the plain, pedestrian moniker she was given at birth like an old T-shirt, replacing it with the name of a lunar goddess without an ounce of self-consciousness or regret.

"You didn't waste much time," she says now, bringing me back from my reverie.

"I don't know what that means," I say, my tone flat.

"Do you love him?"

"Like I said, it's just starting, and I'm not sure it's any of your business." My words come out sharp, defensive.

"Well, he is my brother." She takes a left turn through an intersection, handling the wheel with such deliberate movements she might be taking a driving test. "And you were once my best friend."

Her words linger in the air between us, like a scent that brings back a barrage of memories. I see us drinking wine in her cozy little dome, listening to *Blood on the Tracks*; I picture the little tea houses where we would spread our picnics on a massage table, smearing hummus and avocado onto rice cakes, eating strawberries so ripe and sweet they exploded in juicy, sugary tartness on our tongues. Some of my favorite memories are with Selene. I never had a female friend like her before or after—not even close. I wonder what would have happened if I hadn't cut her out of my life that fall, blocking her number and ignoring her letters. She must have had Jupiter not long after. I might have been like an aunt to her. Zack and I would have met earlier, too, and who knows where that might have led. The thought makes me suddenly sad for all those lost years. Then again, Selene always comes with plenty of drama, and I'm not sure I could have endured it for long.

"Like you said, maybe it's none of my business, but if you want my honest opinion—apparently you don't, but I'm going to give it to you anyway—I think it could work." She keeps her eyes fixed on the road, turning onto the highway with care.

I study her, trying to figure out her game. "You think Zack and I could work?"

She nods. "I do. You might not remember this about me, but I actually have killer intuition about these things."

I can't help smiling. She always did claim to have a witchy sixth sense when it comes to couples, something about seeing people's auras and how they blend or repel.

I change the subject without really meaning to. The question just pops out. "Who is Jupiter's father?"

Her fingers tighten around the wheel. She doesn't answer.

"You must have gotten pregnant not long after that summer, right?" I watch her carefully. "Or was it earlier?"

I know she and Rob never slept together, but she was pretty obsessed with him back then. It's hard to imagine there was some-one else, but Selene could be strangely secretive about her sex life, answering direct questions with cryptic riddles.

She flashes me a sideways, sphinx-like smile. "I'm not sure that's any of your business," she says, throwing my words back at me.

"Fair enough," I concede. "Is he in the picture at all? Jupiter told me she's never met him, but are you still—?"

"No," she says, cutting me off before I have time to finish my question, her tone sharp.

We ride in silence the rest of the way to my house, watching as the sky goes from navy blue to a frosty gray.

* * *

I'm glad the light is still dim when I examine Selene's front bumper and wheels. There's blood splattered all over the grill. Bits of gore cling to the front wheel on the driver's side, smearing its worn treads. I shudder to imagine what's stuck to the undercarriage. All at once, Colton's death feels real to me in a way it didn't last night. I think of my promise to Jupiter that things would be less chaotic in the morning. At least she doesn't have to be here for this grisly task.

"We'll need some rags and sponges, some kind of soap—dishwashing liquid is fine—and bleach." Selene snaps into survival mode as she examines the car with clinical detachment.

I open my mouth to answer, but nothing comes out.

She peers at me in the early morning gloom, assessing my silence. "Do you have a hose that will reach over here, or should I park somewhere else?"

I nod. "It will reach."

She sighs. "You don't have to help if you don't want. I thought you were eager to get back to Zack, though."

The thought of Zack sleeping soundly in his bed, warm within the sheets, makes me long to slip silently into place beside him, curling into his envelope of body heat. She's right, of course, I don't have to help her. This is the moment to decide: am I in, or am I out? Just bringing her here indicates I'm in, but now, with *accessory to murder* swimming around in my brain once again, with blood splatter on her grill and God knows what stuck to her tires, I'm starting to have second thoughts.

It's a familiar feeling, going along with the plan Selene's got mapped out. That's one of the qualities that drew me to her in the very beginning: her instinct for survival. On the worst night of my life, Selene's bossy kindness guided me, that odd mixture of compassion and cruelty that made me trust she knew exactly how to handle everything.

Not until later, when I fully absorbed the ramifications of what we'd done, did I question why I went along with it all like a passenger riding shotgun. It was my life, too. Why did I accept everything she told me? What made me trust her so much in that moment, when mere weeks later I found her so toxic and dangerous I was determined to shut her out of my life forever?

It's impossible to be sure what drove me back then. Survival instinct, I suppose. When the Harvest Moon Ball took everything from me, I was too depleted to question her tenacious will. Later, when I had a chance to start a new life and distance myself from the horror she was inextricably intertwined with, I jumped at the chance. Both times, I was acting out of survival. Maybe it was cruel, but self-preservation is strong, and apparently I had more of it than I'd realized.

Maybe it's time to forgive myself for everything that happened back then. I did the best I could. As Tim pointed out, I was twenty years old. I was dealing with shit women twice that age would be challenged by.

The question is, what do I want to do now? I'm faced with a similar choice. Do I help Selene cover up a crime she committed in the name of love? This time, I'm not a scared, violated young girl. I'm a woman who's learned a thing or two about what matters.

The image of those bruises around Jupiter's slender neck comes back to me. I take a deep breath. "I'll get us everything we need."

She flashes me a tired smile. "Thank you, Tansy."

Once I've come back with rags, sponges, dish detergent, and bleach, I turn on the hose and douse the car with water. The spray is cold, and just holding the hose turns my fingers numb with the October morning chill. The sun's starting to rise in the east, spreading its fingers through the valley and up into the hills. Jessica and Marius's rooster crows with energetic verve, his shrill greeting ringing through the silence. As we scrub, Diego comes trotting over, his whole body radiating indignation.

"Oh, cutie," I say, scratching under his chin. He has an automatic feeder that drops food twice a day, so I know he didn't go hungry, but he gets cranky when I'm out all night. "Are you lonely, handsome? I'm sorry. Don't be mad."

He sniffs at the pinkish water in the bucket. Horrified, I shoo him away. Can he smell the blood? My stomach fizzes with queasiness at the thought.

Selene's cleaning the tires and the undercarriage while I concentrate on the chrome grill and the front bumper. I know she's given me the easy job, and I'm not complaining. There's a slight dent in the bumper just below the headlight that worries me. Will the cops inspect Selene's car? Will this damage give them reason to test for traces of blood? Maybe they'll do that regardless.

"Sorry I shut you down earlier," she says. "Force of habit."

"When I asked about Jupiter's dad?"

"Yes." Selene's words come out on a breath, barely audible. "I want you to know the truth."

I pause and glance at her. She's crouched on the ground, her yoga pants speckled with dirt. "What changed your mind?"

"In case Jupiter ever wants to know, and I'm not around."

"Why would you—?" My words are squeaky and shrill. I take a breath and lower my register, forcing myself to stay calm. "Why would you not be around?"

She shrugs. "I said *in case*."

"Okay." I'm a little puzzled by this change of heart, but I try not to read too much into it. The rooster crows again, his call so frantic it sounds like a warning.

Selene goes back to scrubbing, her hands working hard at the bloody tire. "If Jupiter ever asks, her father was Rob Marsden."

I swallow hard, shivers dancing up my spine. "I thought you said you two never—"

"I lied." She says it without apology or regret, a simple statement of fact. "I know the exact moment when she was conceived, two nights before the Harvest Moon Ball, in the springs. You can tell her that too, if she wants to know."

"Did you tell him you were pregnant?" I ask.

She shakes her head. "It would only have made things worse. He was so tormented—half easy rider, half Buddhist monk. If he knew I was pregnant with his child, it would have pushed him over the edge."

I think of her standing on that cliff top, her eyes fierce, and feel a little sick at her unintentional pun.

All at once, I can see the resemblance. I remember the first day I met Jupiter, the preternatural self-possession and poise in spite of her youth. She has Rob's calm, his wordless intensity. Her eyes, too—those enormous pools of crystal blue. Those are Rob's eyes, refashioned, like sapphires plucked from one setting and placed into another.

"How bizarre," I whisper.

She turns to me. "What?"

"She looks like him—those eyes—but I never made the connection." I roll my shoulders, conscious that they've been slowly tightening throughout this conversation.

"We see what we want to see," she says, not looking at me.

I dip my rag into the soapy water and scrub harder at the grill, trying not to think about the pulpy substance coming free as I dig into its crevices. "Do you think about him much?"

She rakes her fingers through her hair. "Only when I'm drunk."

"Sounds like an excellent reason to stop drinking." I keep my voice light in spite of the dread in my belly.

Her eyes find mine. "I know you probably think of him as a monster, but I really did love him. Jupiter was born from that, thank God."

I don't say what I'm thinking: that Rob was a rapist, and that Jupiter has the unfortunate distinction of being born to a mother who killed her own father. It's an ominous origin story.

"Does Jupiter ask about him?"

Selene cocks her head to the side, considering. "When she was little and first started noticing most kids have dads, she asked. I snapped at her, and after that the questions stopped."

"I'm surprised you didn't just make something up." I don't mean it as an insult, but her eyes snap to mine with a rebuke.

"I wouldn't do that to her." She wrings out the rag she's using and returns to her work. "I have a code of honor, even if it is twisted."

I'm focused on dissolving an especially stubborn streak of blood lodged between the tines of the grill; when I hear Selene release a quick, strangled sob, it catches me off guard. I look over to where she's kneeling in the dirt, her forehead pressed against the side of the car, her body shaking. I toss my rag into the bucket of water and go to her, putting a hand on her back. She doesn't look up.

"Hey." Gently, I tug her to her feet and pull her into my arms. "It's okay. Let it out."

She clings to me, sobbing into my sweatshirt, her shoulders heaving. For a long moment, I just hold her, rubbing her back and letting her cry.

When she's gotten the worst of it out of her system, she pulls back and looks at me. "He wasn't going to let her walk away."

It takes me a second to realize she's talking about Colton now, not Rob.

"I know you think I'm crazy," she says, her hazel eyes still streaming tears, "and maybe I am. But I can't sit back and watch the people I love get hurt. It brings out something fierce in me, and once I turn that corner, I can't stop myself."

I fold her back into my arms, holding her tight. After a long moment, she pulls free, wiping her eyes and trying to compose herself.

"Shit. Sorry." She plucks a rag from one of the buckets and gets back to work, embarrassed.

"Selene?" I stare at her until she looks up and meets my gaze. "I'm sorry I cut you out of my life. I was young and confused and I didn't know how to deal with what we'd done. I was trying to protect myself by moving on. I'm sorry I abandoned you."

She holds my gaze for a long moment. "You did the best you could. You weren't equipped to deal with my particular brand of crazy."

"Can you forgive me?" Hot tears roll down my cheeks. I wipe them away with one hand.

There's a surprisingly tender smile on her lips. "I forgave you a long time ago."

We turn our attention back to cleaning. I feel a little lighter, but the buckets filling with pinkish blood are a sober reminder: We have bigger problems now than the ones buried in our troubled past.

* * *

When the car is clean we climb back inside and I see my phone's been blowing up: three missed texts from Zack, two from Jupiter, all wanting to know where Selene and I are. They sound worried and a little pissed off. It was too much to hope they would sleep through our absence.

I make a decision to be as transparent as possible with both of them. Sending a text about where we are and what we've done is too risky, but when we get back to Zack's, I'm not hiding anything. I made my choice to help Selene, and this time I'm taking responsibility for that decision. Long ago, my frightened twenty-year-old self stumbled through the aftermath of Selene's violence. I can forgive myself for that, but I'm no longer that girl. This time, I'm not ready to condone Selene's crime, but I can understand it.

As we head back to Zack's, I send them both texts saying we'll be back soon. When we pull up in front of his Tudor, Zack's framed in the arched doorway. I feel a warm ache as I see him there in jeans and an old fisherman knit sweater. Everything is happening so quickly, blurring together—Selene and Jupiter showing up in the wee hours, the story they told, the raw remorse and tenderness I felt as Selene and I scrubbed away Colton's blood. There's a niggling voice in the back of my mind insisting it's an ominous start to a relationship. Zack and I have been dating less than two weeks, and within that time, all hell has broken loose. I don't want to be superstitious, but the thought is there just the same.

Zack eyes Selene's MG as it sparkles in the morning sunlight. The rain of last night has blown through, and it's turning into one of those unseasonably warm October days, complete with a lemony sunshine that feels totally out of sync with my mood.

"You washed it?" Zack's jaw is tight. He's got one arm up as he leans against the frame of the stucco archway, and though the pose should come off as casual, he looks anything but.

Selene breezes past him into the house. "We had to."

"And you helped her." Angry lines form at the corners of his mouth. I've never seen that look on him before, and it stops me in my tracks.

I stay out on the porch with him, pulling myself up to my full height. "I know it might not make sense to you, but I had my reasons."

"Care to share them?" He doesn't raise his voice, which somehow makes his fury even more intimidating. He has every right to be angry, but I don't appreciate the way he's looking at me, like suddenly I'm the enemy.

I sigh, overwhelmed at the challenge of articulating the complex web of reasons that led to this moment. "A long time ago, Selene gave me the space to make some hard choices. If we left her car on the street the way it was, she wouldn't have a choice—it would be made for her. I wanted her to have the power and the space to choose. It's what she would have done for me—what she *did* for me."

His expression remains hard and impassive, unmoved by my words.

"I wanted to do this for her. I needed to." I step closer, even though his body language is anything but inviting. "I know you don't agree, but there's a lot of backstory here you're missing."

He turns his head, a cynical smile drifting across his lips. "You think a little car wash is going to help her? If they're looking—and they will look—they're going to find it. A single hair, the dust of a crushed tooth. I've worked with these guys. I know what an investigation looks like."

"You worked with the FBI," I remind him. "This is a hit and run in a small town."

"It's the DA's son." He barks the words at me, then looks around to see if anyone's heard.

I back up, flustered by his anger. "I'm aware of that. And you might want to keep your voice down."

"You're helping her cover it up." He lowers his voice to a soft, menacing rasp. "The boy is dead, Tansy. Does that mean nothing to you?"

"Does it mean nothing to you that your sister could go to jail? And for what? For killing the sadistic bastard who strangled your niece?"

He looks away, squinting into the distance.

I step closer and speak softly. "You even said it yourself: Doing something drastic was the only way to keep Jupiter safe."

"If I'd chosen that road, I would face up to it," he says through gritted teeth.

"Good for you. Except you know what? That's theoretical. Right now, Selene's facing real consequences." I'm a little breathless, so I take a moment, trying to gather my thoughts. "I didn't help her so she could get away with it. I just wanted to buy her a little time."

"This is what she does." Zack sounds distant, remote, as if he's already retreated from the conversation. "She blows shit up and gets other people to clean up the mess."

I study my fingernails. "Have you called the cops yet?"

He doesn't reply. I know this means he hasn't.

"Why not?" My tone is getting a little belligerent in spite of my effort to stay calm.

"Failing to report a crime and actively concealing it are two different charges." His eyebrows arch. "I don't think I have to tell you which one is more serious in the eyes of the law."

"Maybe you're right." I feel tired, suddenly. Exhausted. "Maybe I did something really stupid. All I can tell you is I did it out of love."

"I'm sure that will be very comforting when the two of you are sharing a prison cell." He rubs a hand over his face, looking as tired as I feel.

I shrug, not backing down. "I made a choice, okay? It seemed like the right one in the moment. If I regret it later, you can say 'I told you so.'"

He spits out every syllable. "I don't want to say 'I told you so.' That is exactly what I don't want. Can't you see that?"

I shake my head, not sure I understand his point.

His expression goes distant, as if he's remembering something. "Once you decide to help her, you can't turn around. You find yourself doing worse and worse things just to cover her tracks."

Jupiter appears in the doorway, her face taut with panic. "It's on the news."

Together, we head into the house, just in time to read the headline scrolling across the bottom of the TV screen: *District Attorney's Son Killed in Hit-and-Run.*

* * *

Henry Blake holds a press conference later that morning. He looks ten years older than he did in my office less than two weeks ago. He's wearing a suit, and his white shirt looks starched and ironed, his burgundy tie knotted in a perfect triangle at his throat. In spite of his impeccable grooming, there's a hollow exhaustion in his eyes and his complexion looks waxy. He stands at a podium, lightbulbs flashing, addressing the cameras with a solemn air. Just behind him, in a tasteful black dress and pearls, stands a woman with silvery blonde hair and red-rimmed eyes. She must be Colton's mother. I study her, fascinated, my heart aching as I think about what they must be going through, the terrible pain they'll have to endure for the rest of their lives.

Jupiter and Selene stare fixedly at the screen on Zack's living room wall. Jupiter's on the couch, huddled under a down throw with a mug of tea in her hands. Her bruises look worse than they did last night, sickly purples and greens covering half her face, one eye almost swollen shut. The garland of bruises around her neck is lurid in the morning light. Selene paces the room, her face drawn. Zack and I stand at the edge of the couch, mesmerized.

"Today, at approximately four AM, my son, Colton Blake, was discovered on West Spain Street, near his apartment." Mr. Blake looks at his notes, clears this throat, and continues. "He was the victim of a fatal hit-and-run."

As a frenzy of lightbulbs flash, Blake takes a moment, blinking slowly and licking his lips. "I urge anyone with information about this tragedy to come forward immediately." His voice breaks on the last word, just as a hotline number flashes across the screen.

Selene jabs at the remote and the screen goes black. The sudden quiet is startling. I don't know where to look or what to do with my hands. Jupiter's expression is stunned. She pulls the blanket up to her chin and huddles in the corner of Zack's couch, sipping from her mug. Selene goes on pacing, a manic energy lighting her from within. The gas fire glows in the hearth, radiating warmth, but the room still feels cold somehow. The silence falls around us like snow.

Zack speaks quietly, staring at the rug. "I know I'm in the minority here, but I still think we should talk about our options before it's too late."

"What's done is done," Selene says.

"As I told you last night, you're going to come through this much more easily if you turn yourself in right away." Zack's working hard to keep his voice soft and even, I can tell. "Chances are, somebody's going to come forward with information."

Jupiter makes a soft whimpering noise and puts down her mug with a clunk on the coffee table. She curls herself into a ball. I go to her and sit beside her, trying to give her space while still letting her know I'm here if she needs me.

Zack gestures at Jupiter. "I mean, look at her. He obviously beat the shit out of her. If we can get in front of this, we can shape the narrative, rather than running scared like fugitives."

"Mexico." Selene stops pacing suddenly, and looks around the room like someone just waking from a dream. "I can go to Mexico."

Zack massages his neck with a tired sigh. "You're not going to Mexico."

Selene ignores him. "Remember Berto? I bet he's still in Cabo. I could drive there in a couple of days, easy. He can help get me a job in one of the spas."

"Selene, please," Zack says.

She pivots to face him, her body bristling with anger. "Excuse me if turning myself in doesn't exactly sound like an awesome plan, Zack."

"You're making all of us accessories," he says, losing patience. "You do realize that, right?"

Her laugh is harsh as a slap. "That's the real issue, isn't it? You're worried about saving face with the feds. You want to prove how upstanding and righteous you are by turning in your own sister."

"I haven't turned you in," he says, dropping his voice again. "Though I have to admit I'm tempted."

Selene glares at him. "Is that a threat?"

I get to my feet, angling my body between them. It feels like stepping into the line of fire, but I can't just sit back and watch them snipe at each other. "I'm not sure this is helping anyone."

"It's not," Jupiter grouses. "And it's making my headache worse."

My attention goes to her again. "Do you want to go to the hospital? I still think we need to get you checked out."

Zack nods. "I agree. She needs a doctor."

"I don't need a doctor," Jupiter says, her tone truculent. "It's just a little headache."

"It could be a concussion," I say.

Suddenly a musical ringtone blares through the room. Jupiter pulls out her phone and her face goes white as a sheet.

"Who is it?" Selene asks, her words a hesitant croak.

Jupiter looks at her mom, then at me, finally landing on her uncle. "It's Colton."

12

Z ACK PULLS THE phone from Jupiter's hand and answers with
a terse, "Yes?"

He listens for a moment, then says in a cold, professional tone,
"I'm afraid she's not available right now. Can I take a message?"

After another interminable pause, during which we all strain
to make out the tinny buzz of words coming through the phone,
Zack shoves a hand through his hair and says, "This is her uncle,
Dr. Zack Rathbone."

I've never heard him pull rank like that, dragging out his
doctorate like a cowboy casually opening his jacket to reveal a
holstered gun. Under less terrifying circumstances, it might be
sexy.

"I appreciate your call, Detective Clayfield, and we'll be happy
to do whatever we can to help."

Another pause as Zack listens intently to whatever the detective
is saying. Jupiter stares at her uncle with wide eyes, her lips thin
and tense, like she's holding back a sob.

"Jupiter would be happy to speak with you. Just to be on the
safe side, I'm going to recommend she do so in the presence of her
lawyer."

Jupiter shrinks back into the couch, looking half her age as she cowers under the blanket. I sit beside her again, tempted to wrap an arm around her, but afraid this might be overstepping. Selene is so agitated she'll probably accuse me of trying to mother her. The last thing we need is more conflict in this room.

"Let me get back to you," Zack says, his tone polite. "We'll be happy to answer your questions."

Once he's ended the call, he looks around the room, blinking with exhaustion. "Looks like we're going to need a lawyer."

I pull out my phone. "Leave it to me."

*　*　*

"So, let me get this straight," Tim says, looking from Selene to Jupiter and back again. "After this kid nearly killed you, your mom was about to get you out of there, but she ran him over instead."

We're gathered around Zack's kitchen table, which is small and round, with a tiny couch against the wall and three mismatched chairs crowded around the other side. I'm squished into the little couch with Tim. There's a window to my right, and though the warmth feels good, the sun is far too bright for my taste. I wish it would rain again; maybe that would wash away the grime coating everything today.

Tim looks down at the legal pad he's been scribbling on, then back up at Jupiter. I'm not sure why he's so tuned in to her. It's Selene who committed the murder—manslaughter, self-defense, whatever we're calling it. Somehow, though, Tim's gaze keeps wandering back to Jupiter, searching for something in her face.

"I want to remind you," he says, looking back and forth between Selene and Jupiter. "You can tell me anything. I'm bound by law to keep it to myself."

Jupiter's gaze darts to her mother's face. Selene gives her daughter a serene smile and wraps her brown, ringed fingers over hers.

"We understand attorney–client privilege," Selene assures my brother. "That's how it happened."

"Sorry," Tim says, studying her carefully. "I just can't shake the feeling you're leaving something out."

The lines around Selene's mouth deepen. "Are you digging for dirt? I thought lawyers are supposed to take clients at their word."

"Lawyers are supposed to provide a rigorous defense." Tim's eyes never leave hers. "There's a range of approaches, but in my opinion, you can't parry an attack you don't see coming."

There's a long, tense silence. Selene and Jupiter exchange a complicated look I can't quite read.

When Jupiter speaks, her voice is barely audible. "Colton didn't just beat me up. He raped me."

Zack looks like he wants to hit something, his hands balling into fists. Selene reaches out and strokes her daughter's hair, obviously unsurprised by this confession. A fresh explosion of fury erupts inside me, mixing with the ache I feel for Jupiter.

Tim's expression stays calm, his eyes full of empathy. "Thank you for sharing that, Jupiter. I know this must be a nightmare for you, but you're being very brave. The more you tell me, the better equipped I am to help you."

"Well, there you go." Selene's tone is decisive and final. "Those are the facts."

Tim's gaze searches the ceiling, thinking. He makes another note on his legal pad.

Selene cocks her head. "You have a plan?"

"I do." Tim glances at me, then at Zack. "I don't want to be presumptuous, but can somebody make coffee? This is going to take some caffeine."

Zack jumps up. He's been quiet since Tim got here, just hanging back and listening to the conversation. Of course, all the questions have been directed at Selene and Jupiter so far. Tim has grilled them about every detail, and I'm proud of the kind, sensitive way he pulls the story from them. It occurs to me that our jobs aren't so different—at least, this part, anyway. Tim and I both draw people out of their shells, then help them map out a plan.

As Zack puts the kettle on for coffee, Tim scribbles notes, a determined look on his face. His energy is endearing, but more than that, it's comforting. If Tim doesn't think this is insurmountable, then maybe it's not.

Selene leans back in her chair, the flannel shirt she borrowed from Zack hanging loose on her small frame. "Do you think I should turn myself in?"

"God, no." He winces. "Why would you do that?"

"See?" Selene says to Zack.

Zack uses a sponge to wipe up some jam from the counter. "I have this weird thing about obeying the law."

"No, I see that," Tim says, gesturing at Zack with one hand. "Sometimes it makes sense. And that's an option. If we decide to go that way, we can get you a pretty good deal, I think, but you'll probably do time."

A vein in Selene's temple throbs. "I'd rather not, if it's all the same to you."

Tim nods and turns back to Zack again. "Less than eight percent of hit-and-runs get solved."

Selene slaps the table. "Exactly! What did I tell you, Zack?"

"I know Blake by reputation," Tim continues. "He's very image conscious. If we start talking about his son's drug habit, the fact that he nearly killed his young girlfriend"—again, his gaze darts to Jupiter—"he's not going to like that one bit."

"The man just lost a son, though," I point out. "He's probably more fixated on getting revenge than saving his reputation."

Tim rubs his chin, which is sprouting auburn stubble. "I wouldn't be so sure. It's an election year. Someone like Henry Blake is never going to forget people are watching."

That rings true for the man I saw in my office ten days ago. The man I watched this morning on TV, though—he looked too broken to care. I feel a dull ache thinking about how awful this must be for him and his wife. First the drugs, and now this. They must be in excruciating pain.

"So what do we tell the cops?" Zack's electric kettle comes to a boil, and he grinds the beans for French press coffee. "We need to meet with them soon, and we all have to tell the same story."

"True." Tim nods, reviewing his notes.

"I think everyone should tell the truth, right up until the hit-and-run," I say.

Tim wraps an arm around my shoulder. "My thoughts exactly. Rule number one in the liar's playbook: stick to the truth as closely as you can."

Jupiter chews at a fingernail, looking sick. She hasn't said much since Tim got here. Like Zack and me, she's been hanging back, letting her mom do most of the talking. "Do I have to tell them about . . . ?" She hesitates.

"The sexual assault?" Tim says it very gently. "I'm afraid so. I know that's asking a lot."

Jupiter's eyes go hard. "I can do it. They need to know what he did to me."

"Exactly." Tim tips his head to the side and gives her a sad smile. "That part of your story is essential. They'll probably have you talk to a woman. They won't be dicks about it, and I'll be there to set them straight if they're out of line. It's like being on a witness stand. You answer the question, nothing more. Don't narrate."

Zack pushes the plunger on the French press and I find some coffee mugs to hand out. Zack goes around pouring everyone the strong black brew and I put creamer on the table with a bowl of sugar. It's a weirdly domestic moment, like this is our house and we're serving our guests.

My mind returns to our argument out on the porch earlier. Though we've both brushed it aside to deal with more pressing issues, I can feel the unresolved tension crackling between us.

"What are we supposed to say about last night?" Zack asks, once we're settled again at the table.

Tim sips his coffee. "You tell them exactly what happened, minus the hit-and-run. Jupiter was assaulted, she called her mom, they came here, and the three of you found out about Colton's death on the news like everyone else."

Zack glances at me, then back at Tim. "What about the car?"

Tim shakes his head, perplexed. "What do you mean?"

"Selene and Tansy took it somewhere and washed it." I can't read Zack's tone. "Should they admit to that?"

Tim looks at me, his expression turning uneasy. "You didn't take it to a carwash, did you?"

"No, of course not." I can't help shooting Zack an annoyed look. "We took it to my place. I don't think anyone saw us."

"Okay, but traffic cameras probably did somewhere along the way." I can see wheels turning behind Tim's eyes. He taps his pen against the table a couple of times. "If it comes up, you and Selene went there to grab something—let's just decide what that is. It needs to be something you couldn't get from a store."

"Painkillers," I say, and everyone looks at me. "For Jupiter. It makes sense. I have some left over from my root canal. They're in my purse, so if they need to see them I can show them."

"Perfect." Tim grins at me. "You're a little too good at this."

Selene looks at her hands, nervously twisting a couple of her rings. "I have to ask, even though I don't want to . . ."

Before she can get the question out, Tim holds up a hand. "You're my sister's friend. I'm not going to charge you. Getting you out of this mess will be reward enough."

I rest my head on his shoulder, so grateful I could cry. I know Tim isn't exactly Selene's number one fan. He's waiving his usual three-hundred-and-fifty-dollars-an-hour fee for me.

"Thank you," Selene and Jupiter say at once.

"Don't worry about it." Tim turns his attention to Zack. "There is one more thing we need to resolve, though."

Again, an awkward silence descends.

Zack clears his throat. "You want to know if I'm willing to lie?"

"Lie is such a strong word." Tim's half-joking, but there's a seriousness under his words. "I prefer to think of it as editing. You're obviously of the opinion that Selene should confess. Are you willing to go along with this plan?"

Zack grips his mug so tightly his knuckles blanch. He looks at each one of us in turn, then lets out a long, defeated sigh. "I'm obviously outnumbered. So yes."

Selene mouths *thank you*, but he just looks out the window, his expression brooding.

*   *   *

Josh Clayfield is an almost cartoonish man, his square jaw, barrel chest, and broad shoulders so perfectly fitting the image of a detective I have to suppress a nervous giggle when I see him marching up Zack's walkway toward the house. His partner, on the other hand, Aanya Patel, is barely five feet tall and looks a bit like a girl playing dress-up in her matching navy blazer and slacks. They arrive in the afternoon. When Tim called to set up the interview with Jupiter, he explained that all of us are willing to answer questions if needed. They said that would be helpful, and they'll want to interview each of us separately.

On the doorstep, Tim introduces himself and tells them he's representing the whole family, which makes them exchange a cryptic look. I feel so thankful Tim is here, a beacon of familiarity.

When the detectives catch sight of Jupiter, with the bruises still fresh and her right eye nearly swollen shut, the ring of greenish blue around her neck looking like a ghastly choker, they exchange another unreadable glance, but offer no comment. Jupiter is the

first person they want to interview, and Zack shows them to his
office before coming back downstairs to the living room, where
the three of us perch nervously on his large gray sectional, sipping
coffee and avoiding one another's eyes. It's a huge relief knowing
Tim's up there, but I still feel afraid for Jupiter, who's barely more
than a child, really. Thinking of all the pressure heaped on her
narrow shoulders so soon after what has to be the most traumatic
night of her life—it just seems unfair. I remember the way her
voice shook when she asked Tim if she would need to tell them
about Colton raping her. I try to imagine what it would have been
like, if I'd had to face a similar inquiry the morning after Rob
died.

Then I think of Henry Blake and his wife, the terrible grief
they must be going through, the shock and horror of their only
son crushed beneath the wheels of a car.

I look at Selene, who's staring out the window, her face a mask.

"Tim's really good," I say to her. "He won't let her say anything she shouldn't."

Selene's eyes dart to meet mine, then return to the window. A
bunch of finches have gathered around a hanging bird feeder in
the yard, pecking at the seeds and grousing at one another as they
try to force their way into better position. There are a couple of
Japanese maples out there, one with dark red leaves and another
that's bright yellow. Some of the finches settle amid the fall foliage, cleaning themselves and chirping amiably in the dappled
sunshine.

Zack sits a couple of feet from me, elbows propped on his
knees, face cupped in his hands. He looks more exhausted and
stressed than I've ever seen him.

Selene's gaze slides over to her brother, then back out the window. "Go ahead. Say it."

Zack shakes his head slightly, like someone trying to wake
himself up. "I've already said everything I need to say."

"I can *feel* you judging me," Selene murmurs, her voice tired but also dangerously coiled, like a snake getting ready to strike. "Just like you judged Auntie Maeve."

Zack's head snaps around so fast I flinch. He looks at his sister with cold bewilderment. "How is bringing that up going to—?"

"Did he tell you about that?" Selene cuts him off and turns to face me, though I have a feeling she's still speaking to her brother. "About Maeve?"

I look from Selene to Zack and back again, shaking my head in mute reply. The birds are still chirping happily outside, at stark odds with the new tension in the room.

"Maeve was an addict, like pretty much everyone in our family. She was a mess, but we loved her." Selene's smile goes fond at the memory. "She was almost ten years younger than our mom, so she was more like an older sister."

I glance at Zack, feeling uncertain and awkward. Zack obviously doesn't want his sister telling this story, but I don't know how to stop her. Also, there's a part of me that wants to hear it. I know precious little about their shared childhood. Back when we were friends, Selene touched on her years in Vermont only briefly—quick, cursory sketches of the dark, tangled family she escaped from, her brother the only bright spot in that whole landscape. Most of her stories were about dancing in the seedy clubs of New Orleans or helping Danny, her husband, plan his bank robberies. She knew I loved those dark fairy tales, and I could see she needed to tell them, painting herself as a wild, powerful vixen in a gritty world of sex and violence. My innocence and her worldliness were a potent combination, the force that drew us together magnetically and bound us for two memorable years.

Even if I tried to stop her from finishing this story, I can tell by her expression it wouldn't work. She's got a determined fire in her eyes, and it's obvious that attempting to derail her now would be as effective as stepping in front of a train.

"Unlike our mother, who never liked to leave her bed if she didn't have to, Auntie Maeve was ambitious." Selene licks her lips, checking her brother's reaction, before continuing.

"Mom got migraines," Zack says, barely audible.

"Mom was a lazy, fat, manipulative bitch." Selene's tone is harsh, devoid of compassion.

Zack winces and stares at the floor. A muscle in his jaw flutters, then goes still.

Selene leans back against the cushions, savoring her role as storyteller. "So, Auntie Maeve, who was only in her twenties at the time, lived with us and made sure we had what we needed."

"She supported you?" I ask, drawn into the tale in spite of myself.

"She tried." Selene pauses, her gaze returning to me slowly as if she'd forgotten I was there. "In her own way. She hooked up with this lowlife sleaze bag known in town simply as 'Troll.' He was short, with a long white beard and a snake tattoo on his neck. Anyway, Troll got Maeve to sell drugs to high school students, since she could blend in more easily around the schools and down at the mall, not being quite so obvious as Troll, who was notorious."

Selene sips her coffee and stares out the window again at the golden leaves fluttering to the lawn. "When Zack was in high school, his best friend, Jeff Mayberry, got hooked on oxy. Pills were big back then—heroin, if you could get it, but mostly pills."

Zack massages his temples, his expression pained.

Selene continues, noting her brother's discomfort but plowing on anyway. "Maeve was selling to Jeff, who was from a good, upstanding family. What was his dad, Zack? A doctor or something?"

"Psychiatrist," Zack mumbles, his tone flat and airless.

"Psychiatrist," Selene echoes, her voice spiking with amusement. "That's right. It made the whole thing that much more scandalous. Dr. Mayberry's son, strung out on pills."

Zack stands, walking to the fireplace and gazing into it, his back to us.

Selene leans closer, lowering her voice, though it's still loud enough for Zack to hear. "Jeff ODed. Very sad. And you know what my righteous, upstanding baby brother decided to do?"

I look at Zack, whose shoulders have gone rigid beneath his sweater, his hands stuffed into the pockets of his jeans.

"He told the cops everything—about Maeve and Troll and everyone else in that shitty little town who was dealing. He gave the cops all the details they'd need to catch Maeve red-handed." Selene's eyebrows arch, a cruel twist to her lips. "Our aunt, the only adult who gave a shit about us, got fifteen years. Troll, of course, got off on a technicality. That's justice for you."

Zack spins around, staring down his sister, nostrils flared and hands still shoved inside his pockets like he doesn't trust himself to set them free. "Does it make you feel better, dragging me down into your misery? Because there's really no need. I'm already plenty miserable, thanks very much."

At his words, I feel a pang of guilt about my own contribution to his misery. Our argument from this morning still hangs over us like a dark cloud, no doubt adding to his sense of isolation.

Just then, Detective Patel sticks her head around the corner and we all turn to her in surprise. She must have drifted down the stairs and the hallway as silent as a ghost. She takes us in with a tight, knowing smile, as if our jumpiness confirms something she suspected all along.

"Who's next?" she asks.

I stand. "I'll go."

Zack's in no state to answer questions, and God only knows what Selene will say, given her mood. It seems only right I should take my turn, give the two of them time to cool down.

*　　*　　*

I pass Jupiter in the hallway as she makes her way back toward the stairs. Her good eye is bloodshot, the other one having puffed up so much it's sealed shut. She looks wretched.

Patel hovers at a discreet distance, discouraging a long conversation but otherwise giving us at least the illusion of privacy. The detective checks her phone with a preoccupied frown, though I suspect she's listening to every word.

Grabbing Jupiter's hand, I examine her face, trying to read her expression. "How do you feel?"

"I've been better." She tries for a smile, but abandons it. "You're next?"

I nod.

Jupiter cuts her eyes to Patel and gives me a look I'm having trouble deciphering. I think it translates to something like, *Be careful of that one.* I nod, hoping I read her message correctly.

Inside Zack's office, the walls are a deep teal and the furnishings are fairly minimal. There are teak filing cabinets taking up most of one wall, an expansive desk with a Mac on one side and a bell jar housing a white and purple orchid on the other. A large picture window lets in dappled light. In addition to the desk chair, several others have been brought in and placed on either side of the desk: one next to the desk chair itself, two on the other side. I can't help smiling when I notice that Tim has taken the desk chair and is now gesturing for me to sit beside him. He's chosen what I can't help but think of as the power side of the desk, reminding the detectives that they're visitors here, and he is ultimately in charge. It's a strong move, and I want to hug my brother once again for being here.

I take a seat beside Tim as Patel shuts the door and joins her colleague in one of the rickety folding chairs. Another calculated Tim choice, I'm willing to bet. No need for either of them to get too comfortable. I can't resist squeezing Tim's hand where they can't see, behind the desk. He flashes me a reassuring smile.

Clayfield watches me, his brown eyes studying my every move. I give him what I hope is a friendly, open look, but his expression remains impassive. Beside him, Patel scrutinizes me, her posture and attitude panther-like—sleek and casually dangerous.

Patel takes a notepad and pen from the pocket of her blazer. In the deep quiet, I almost flinch at the sound of her jabbing the ballpoint into position, but I manage to catch myself. Even though it's reassuring having Tim here, I still feel edgy and vulnerable, desperate to say all the right things and—more importantly— none of the wrong ones.

"So, Ms. Elliot, I understand you're a friend of the Rathbones, is that correct?"

"Yes." I nod. "I've known Selene a long time."

Patel squints. "And now you're dating her brother, Zack. Is that right?"

I hesitate, glancing at Tim. He gives an almost imperceptible nod.

"Um, sort of," I say. "We just started seeing each other."

"When?" Clayfield asks.

I blink at him. "When, what?"

"When exactly did you two start dating?"

I clear my throat. "A few weeks ago, I guess."

Tim, picking up on my discomfort, leans forward, propping his elbows on the desk. "I'm reasonably sure Tansy's love life isn't the focus of your investigation. I know you're just getting the lay of the land, but we've still got two more of my clients to interview."

Patel flashes him a polite smile and turns her attention back to me. "Tell us about last night."

"Um, okay." I lick my lips, feeling how dry my mouth has gone. "Starting from where?"

"What time did you arrive here at the house?" Clayfield demands.

I close my eyes, trying to picture that far back. It feels like a lifetime ago. "After work, around six, I think."

"Had you been here before?" Patel leans back in her chair and then, clearly annoyed at the lack of comfort offered by its flimsy backrest, sits up straight again.

"Yes." I recall Tim's earlier advice to stick to the facts and squelch my urge to babble.

Patel's dark eyes study me intently. "And then?"

"We had dinner." I clear my throat again, wishing desperately I had something to drink to wash away the taste of fear coating my tongue. "We talked. Eventually we went to bed."

"Together." Though her tone is matter-of-fact, Patel's mouth curves down at the corners.

I hope to God she wasn't this snide with Jupiter. If she brought even an ounce of this tartness to the retelling of Jupiter's nightmare, I'll kill her.

Since murdering a detective is generally frowned upon, I take a breath and try to let out my frustration so it's not obvious when I reply. "That's right, Detective. Together."

Clayfield jumps in. "And what happened later? Can you tell us about that?"

I glance at Tim, and he gives me another nod. I launch into my account—Jupiter and Selene showing up a little after three, Jupiter injured, both of them upset. I tell them everything I can remember, aside from the pesky little detail about Selene telling us she killed Colton.

When I'm finished, Patel looks at me like I'm a moldy piece of cheese she's considering tossing. "You say you're the one who took Jupiter upstairs?"

"Yes." Something in my gut twists.

"Why was that?"

I stare at her, confused. "I'm sorry, I don't understand."

"Here's this young girl, obviously injured—she nearly died, in fact, according to her story—and yet nobody offers to take her to the hospital?"

"We did offer," I say, "but she refused to go."

"Why is that?"

I frown. "Nothing was broken, she wasn't in much pain, she didn't need stitches."

"But wouldn't you want her to get checked out, anyway?"

I nod. "We did—I did—but I wasn't going to take her against her will. She's an adult, after all. Not everybody has health insurance, and sometimes going to the hospital doesn't seem worth it."

Patel leans forward, warming to this line of inquiry. "The question still remains, why were *you* the one to take her upstairs?"

Again I flounder, trying to understand where she's going with this. "Why *not* me?"

"She had her mother and her uncle right there, but it's you— her uncle's brand-new girlfriend—who offers comfort after this deeply personal, traumatizing event?" Patel shakes her head, glancing at Clayfield in a quizzical way, as if looking to him for answers. "That doesn't make sense to me."

"I'm her counselor at VMU," I say. "She likes me. We get along."

My mind starts racing at a hundred miles an hour. Should I say that's how I met Zack—through his niece? Jupiter thinks she introduced us, so if it came up in her interview that's what she no doubt told them. But what if Zack or Selene contradicts that? I already mentioned I've known Selene for years. A headache starts to pound in my temples, making it hard to think straight. I decide to play it safe and offer nothing on this topic.

Patel arches an eyebrow. "So you're her counselor."

I nod, not trusting my voice.

"Is that how you met Jupiter's family?" she asks, her tone casual.

My gaze swivels to Tim. He nods, and I take this to mean, *stick to the truth*.

"Like I said, Selene and I were friends a long time ago. I met Zack recently, at work."

Patel's eyes narrow. "You were friends with Selene a long time ago—but not anymore?"

"We haven't been close for a number of years." I keep my voice soft and even, though images from the past are cartwheeling through my brain: Selene driving too fast to the Harvest Moon Ball, Rob's leering face, Selene standing at the edge of the cliff, her muscles coiled.

"And why is that?" Patel's words come out almost a purr, her feline stealth making the little hairs on the back of my neck stand at attention.

Tim steps in. "I'm sorry, but is this relevant? What does Tansy's friendship with Selene have to do with what happened last night?"

"I don't know." Patel's eyes stay locked on mine. "You tell me."

"I went away to college." My voice sounds too loud in the small room. "That's it. We lost touch."

"You see?" Patel's smile is slow and superior. "Was that so hard?"

Clayfield steps in, his big fingers thumbing through his notes. "I thought Jupiter said she introduced you to Mr. Rathbone."

My heart sinks. "That's . . . yes, that's what she thinks."

Patel's eyes light up. "That's what she *thinks*?"

"I knew Selene from years ago and I met Zack recently. He's a coworker at VMU." I can feel myself talking too fast, over-explaining. "When Jupiter came to me for counseling, I didn't see any reason to mention I already knew her family."

"Really?" Patel's tone is downright bitchy now. "Isn't that against a professional counselor's code of ethics? Don't you have to disclose—?"

"To be clear, I'm an academic counselor," I say, cutting her off. "Not a therapist. But Jupiter needed someone to talk to. I knew she'd feel more comfortable discussing her issues if she had no fear of me sharing those details with her family."

Patel seizes on this. "And yet you did, didn't you?"

I stop talking, a wave of adrenaline flooding my system, making it hard to breathe.

Patel glances at Tim, perhaps wondering if he'll let her continue, then says, "You told Mr. Rathbone that Colton Blake punched Jupiter in the stomach, didn't you?"

Again, my mouth refuses to open. I just stare back at her, feeling pinned by her steady, searching gaze.

"That's why Jupiter left her uncle's house on"—she consults her notes—"October thirteenth, isn't it? She was angry when she realized you'd told her uncle about the abuse." Patel looks smug, her whole body telegraphing victory.

Tim says, "I think we're getting off track here. What could any of this possibly have to do with last night's hit-and-run?"

Patel flashes him a condescending smile. "Just getting the lay of the land."

When her gaze slides back to me, I feel a cold chill down my spine.

13

TIM RETURNS TO the city that evening, just as the sun is sinking low in the west. A coastal fog has rolled in, smelling of the ocean, and I'm grateful that the weather at least matches my mood now—still and ominous.

I walk my brother out to his car, a spotless white Volvo. For a second, I long to climb inside, take refuge in his heated leather seats, hide away in his adorable guest room in the city, let him shelter me from all this angst. It feels like once he's gone all the dangers of the world will crash down on us, drown us in the repercussions of what Selene has done.

"Hey," Tim says, his voice gentle, "don't look so down. You did great."

We stand on the sidewalk, feeling the cool fog on our skin. I'm trying to decide if the kind, optimistic expression he's wearing is sincere, or if it's for my benefit, an effort to keep me from the despair I feel rising all around me like a dark tide.

"Be honest with me." I look down at my hands, which are fidgeting with the zipper of my hoodie. "What do you think is going to happen?"

He gazes past me, his brown eyes running calculations. "It's hard to say. Under normal circumstances, hit-and-runs are notoriously difficult to prove. You could be right about the DA, though. He might throw a lot of muscle at this, which could make things tricky."

I can't stop zipping and unzipping the hoodie. My body feels heavy with exhaustion, but the fear and adrenaline snaking through my veins have me itchy with nerves. Tim reaches out and cups my hands in his, forcing me to be still.

"This has got to be hard for you," he murmurs, his glance darting to the house.

I turn and follow his gaze just in time to see the curtains twitch closed. "It feels like déjà vu. Except this time, I'm trying to make real choices—adult choices—not just get pulled along by the current."

"Selene's a powerful character." Tim's eyes are sympathetic.

"She's got me dancing on a string, as you can tell."

"What do you mean?"

He grins. "Pro bono? Me? You think that's normal?"

I smile, knowing he's trying to make me feel like I don't owe him for this, which I totally do.

His hands rub up and down my arms like he's trying to warm me. "I can hardly fault you for falling under her spell when you were barely more than a kid. She's got serious charisma, something few people can resist."

"I wish she had a little more self-control. I mean it's crazy, right? This is the *second* time she's . . ." I trail off, unwilling to finish that sentence. "Zack thinks we're going about this all wrong."

"He's a real law and order type." Tim says, his expression thoughtful.

I nod.

Tim's eyes sparkle as his expression shifts to a teasing smirk. "He's also super hot."

I shove him off the sidewalk, feeling a blush rising to my cheeks.

"You really like him," he says, his tone going more serious. "Don't you?"

I sigh, starting to run my hand through my hair but giving up as my fingers snarl in the tangled craziness of my curls.

"It's a hell of a way to start a relationship," I say.

Tim shrugs. "Crisis reveals character. I like him, tell you the truth. He's got integrity."

My eyebrows arch at that. "Wait a second, you're saying you actually *like* someone I'm dating?"

"Don't get me wrong. Nobody's good enough for my little sister." He cups his hands behind his head, eyes dancing. "But I can tell he's crazy about you, and that goes a long way with me."

I can't deny the warm glow that sparks in my chest. Glancing back at the house, I catch the curtains fluttering again, this time in one of the upstairs rooms. I turn back to my brother. "What do you think of Jupiter?"

Tim considers my question for a long moment. "She's kind of fascinating."

"I know, right?"

"Even with all those bruises, it's obvious she's gorgeous, but it's more than that." He watches the house, considering his words carefully. "She's the kind of girl people underestimate. She's so delicate and waifish, that's all some people ever see. But I have a feeling she's tougher than she looks."

"Yeah," I say. "Me too."

His expression darkens. "She's going to need plenty of grit to get through this."

My mood sours again as his words sink in. I pull him into a hug. "Thank you. For everything."

"Chin up." He pulls away and examines me before folding me into another hug, this one even tighter. "We're going to figure this out, okay? Together."

There are tears stinging at my eyes. I just nod, not trusting my voice, and blow him a kiss as he gets in the car and drives away.

*   *   *

Zack makes a delicious dinner that night—salmon, roasted vegetables, and a big green salad. We all pick at our food in silence, the mood in the house a prickly combination of anxiety and suspicion. Part of me wants to grill each one of them about their interviews with the detectives, but I'm limp with exhaustion and wrung out by the intense effort it took to keep my guard up all day.

The tension between Selene and Zack continues to simmer, and I can't help dwelling on the story Selene dragged out earlier about their aunt. It underlined just how deep their past goes, how much more history they have together than I have with either one of them. Zack and Selene have been stuck in these roles since childhood—the law-abiding baby brother and the outlaw older sister. Though I'm curious about that dynamic and how it will play out here, I know better than to bring it up directly, especially when we're all so tired and threadbare. It's a hornet's nest I don't dare poke at, swarming with family secrets and ancient resentments.

Selene drinks too much wine, and Jupiter covertly scrolls through her phone under the table. Zack flashes me a smile that I think is meant to be reassuring, but it only serves to highlight his discomfort. I wonder if he longs to kick us all out so he can be alone with his frustration. He's angry that nobody is doing what he thinks is right, that we've all ignored his advice and spent the day building a tower of deceit. It's obvious this whole situation is pushing old buttons for him—family buttons, which are the deepest and most dangerous. It's pushing old buttons for me, too. Rob feels like a fourth presence at the dinner table, wafting like a bad smell, morphing with Colton, just like he did in my nightmare.

When Selene pours herself yet another glass of merlot, Zack says, "You've had too much to drive. You guys should stay in the guest house tonight."

"I'm fine." Selene drains her glass, watching him over the rim, eyes defiant.

He grimaces. "Another DUI is the last thing you need right now."

"I *said* I'm fine." Selene wipes her mouth with the back of her hand and stands.

"You're not fine." Zack's tone is hard, unyielding. "Don't be an idiot, Selene."

She laughs, a mean-spirited cackle that grates on my nerves. Nothing good comes from a laugh like that. "Oh, so *now* you care about me? If you had your way, I'd be sitting in a jail cell right now."

"You're drunk," he says, his words clipped and terse. "You're staying here."

"Fuck you." She stalks away from the table, weaving slightly. It takes her a moment to find her purse, but when she does she seizes it and heads for the door.

Jupiter shoots me an imploring look, but I don't know what she expects me to do. Zack doesn't move; he stares at his plate, his face stony.

There's a crashing sound from the front room. I stand and follow the noise. Selene's standing by the open front door. A smashed vase lies in broken shards at her feet. She's digging through her purse, clawing at its contents like a wild animal.

When she spots me standing there, she glares at me accusingly, her eyes not quite focusing properly. She must be drunker than I thought. Her spine goes ramrod straight in the exaggerated manner of wasted people who are trying to convince everyone they're sober.

"What the hell did you do with my keys?" she demands, slurring her words.

I shake my head. "I didn't do—"

"Zack!" she roars, cutting me off and pushing past me, marching back into the kitchen, teetering unsteadily in her boots.

I go to the door she left hanging open and close it. Then I follow her back to the kitchen, though a big part of me just wants to slip out, climb into my car, and escape all this drama. They're not my family, after all. I'm the outsider here, the interloper. Maybe they're all wondering what I'm even still doing here, waiting for me to leave so they can finally relax.

When I get back to the kitchen, Selene's glowering at Zack with fresh intensity. She runs her hands over her buzzed head. "Give them back, you asshole."

"I'm not giving them back until you're sober."

"What the hell?" Selene glances around at Jupiter, then at me, as if searching for support. "You're not my goddamn babysitter, Zack."

"Really? Because I kind of feel like it right now."

Selene grabs his sweater, balling it in her fists and trying to shake him, though Zack stays perfectly still. "Give me my fucking keys."

"No."

"Selene," I say, "calm down. You don't need to—"

"Shut up!" She wheels around, shooting me a poisonous glare. "Just because you're fucking him, you're going to take his side? I've known you twenty years, and you two have known each other, what? Five minutes?"

Jupiter's eyes widen. "Wait, you two have known each other twenty years?"

I meet Jupiter's shocked stare, feeling overwhelmed. "We used to be friends, yeah."

"I made her meet with you," Selene says, her words tripping over each other in her hurry to get them out. "I wanted her to get you away from Colton. Guess that plan backfired."

Jupiter stands, gaping at me in mute betrayal.

"That's not—she's misrepresenting—" I start, but Selene cuts me off.

"That's the only reason she's even here," Selene tells her daughter, talking about me in the third person like I'm not even worth addressing. "I forced her to get involved. I threatened her. She didn't even want to meet you. Now look at her, acting like she's part of the family."

"Jesus, Selene," I say, losing my temper. "I'm a human being, okay? I make my own choices. You're not the puppet master here."

She barks out another mean, aggressive laugh. "That's what you think."

"Enough." Zack stands and glares at his sister, yanking his phone from his pocket. "I'm giving you two choices: you can go to the guest house right now and cool down, or I'm calling you an Uber."

"No, you're giving me my—"

"Those are your options." He enunciates each word clearly and pauses after each one like a father addressing his unruly teenager.

She glares at him with pure loathing, then hurries out the back door. We watch as she stalks along the edge of the pool, illuminated by the lights in the garden, throws open the door to the guest house, then slams it behind her.

I turn to Jupiter, my heart pounding. "It's true that your mom suggested we meet, okay? But I never agreed to influence you in any way. I just wanted you to have someone who would listen, that's all."

Jupiter gives me a mutinous look, her battered face flushed with anger. She grabs her coat and starts toward the door.

"Where are you going?" Zack calls after her, his voice tired and exasperated.

"Anywhere but here." She storms out, leaving behind a thick, deafening silence.

* * *

After a moment, Zack stands and starts clearing up the dishes, carrying them to the kitchen and slotting them into his stainless steel dishwasher. I pick up my plate and follow him.

"Do you think we should go after her?"

"Which one?" He sounds so lost and deflated I want to hug him, but I'm not sure that would be welcome. There's something about the way he's moving, stiff and a little mechanical, that makes me think he needs his space.

"Jupiter." I rub my neck, trying to work out the tension knotting my muscles.

He shakes his head. "She'll be fine. She does this sometimes—goes on walks when she needs to clear her head."

"I wish she didn't have to learn about my history with Selene right this second. It's bad timing."

He rinses a dish, his back to me, steam rising to kiss the window before him. "That's the thing about lies. Once you start telling them, it's hard to keep them all straight."

I blink at him, feeling stung. Earlier today, with everyone gathered around the kitchen table drinking coffee, we were a makeshift family. Sure, it was a dysfunctional one—we were plotting how to get away with murder, basically—but it felt like we were all on the same team. Now that togetherness has dissipated, sending us all scattering in opposite directions like the shards of an explosion.

"I know you don't approve of what's happening here," I say, "but we're all doing the best we can."

"Are we though?" The glass he's washing slips from his hands and shatters in the sink. He swears, rushing to pick up the pieces, and his hand comes away bloody.

I hurry to his side, trying to get a good look at the cut. "Hey, slow down. Let me—"

"I don't understand why you're okay with this." He says it very quietly, angling away from me as I reach out to examine his hand, shoving his fingers under the stream of water. The dark red blood turns pink as it mixes with the suds and circles the drain.

How do I answer that? Do I tell him this isn't the first time I've helped Selene cover up a murder? I don't think that's going to help my case here—*I'm doing this because I've done it before.* That sounds weak, even to me.

Maybe Selene was right that night at the pub when she implied men can never understand the double-edged allure of "bad boys." They draw you in, and by the time their charm turns toxic, it's too late. When you've gone from independent, carefree girl having a great time at a party to helpless victim bent over a rock, you recognize what it means to feel trapped and impotent. We're taught that we have power, that we make our own choices. We're not prepared for the sheer animal ferocity of a man's rage until we find ourselves powerless before it. Jupiter survived a night like that with Colton. Selene's choice to kill him for what he did, for what he threatened to do in the future, was rash and misguided and morally questionable. I see that. But Jupiter's the person who matters most in this equation. She's the survivor who must not be broken by this experience, because she's young and full of promise, and in the last twenty-four hours she's suffered the most.

"I don't think Jupiter will benefit right now from watching her mother go to jail." I risk a look up at him.

Anger radiates from his whole body. He yanks a paper towel from a roll of them and wraps it around his bloody fingers. "Selene can't keep doing this."

I freeze. "What do you mean, 'keep doing this'?"

He looks at me. His eyebrows slant upward, his expression forlorn. "This isn't the first time."

"The first time for what?" My stomach feels like we just crested the hill of a roller-coaster. I'm looking down at a steep vertical drop.

Zack glances around, as if making sure we're alone. "It's not the first time she's killed someone."

*　　*　　*

Like me, Zack needs to move when he tells a hard story. I think of my walk with Tim along the Embarcadero, the way the fog wrapped us in our own private world, muffling the words to keep them secret. The lightness I felt afterward was intoxicating. Unburdening myself felt magical and dangerous, like a spell I'd conjured and set loose upon the world. Or maybe I was being set free of a spell, the one Selene kept me under, thinking I had to keep our secret forever.

For Zack, this story has a similar weightiness, I suspect. He finds me a wool pea coat and a knit beanie before wrapping himself in a similar getup. Outside, night has fallen. The windows of his neighbors' houses are lozenges of gold, and the sharp tang of woodsmoke hangs in the frosty air. We walk north, toward downtown, our hands shoved deep into our pockets and our breath hanging in clouds before our lips like speech bubbles.

"When did this happen?" I ask.

He stares at the sparkling sidewalk in concentration. "I was fourteen, and she was seventeen. Just a little younger than Jupiter."

I want to ask him a thousand questions, hammer the story out of him fact by fact, but I know it doesn't work like that. That day on the Embarcadero, Tim gave me room to find the memory, let me unspool the story in my own time. I vow to give Zack the same space, even though a big part of me longs to tear the truth from him like ripping off a Band-Aid.

We walk half a block in silence, and I keep myself from blurting out questions by admiring the neighbors' jack-o-lanterns, the

gauzy ghosts dangling from the branches of an elm. One crafts-
man bungalow has littered its lawn with fake tombstones. The
next house, a towering Victorian, has a row of seven carved pumpkins on its expansive porch. I stare at the windows of the Victorian,
watching the vague shapes of people moving behind the curtains
in rooms that glow with the underwater blue of a flickering TV.

Zack clears his throat. "Selene was seeing this guy, Danny
Wanicki. He was older than her—early twenties—and even
though he was from out of town, it didn't take long for everyone
to figure out he was trouble. He thought he was James Dean, with
this badass motorcycle and dark, greasy hair. The first time I met
him, I thought he was the coolest human I'd ever seen outside the
movies. He gave me a pocketknife. Never seen the guy in my life,
and he hands over this beautiful knife with real mother-of-pearl
inlay in the handle. Said he didn't need it anymore, that I should
keep it safe until he did."

He's silent for a long moment. We hang a right at the next corner, and before long a park comes into view, its jungle gyms and
monkey bars looming out of the fog like skeletal monsters.

"Danny was her husband, right?" Selene told me countless stories about him, all of them bittersweet and laced with longing.

Zack turns and squints at me. "Selene's never been married."

I feel my brow scrunching up in confusion. "That can't be
right. She told me she married Danny. They split up right before
he went to jail for bank robbery."

"She's never been married," Zack repeats, shoving his hand
into his hair and looking away.

I hesitate. "Why would she—?"

"One of the hallmarks of borderline personality disorder is
pathological lying." His eyes meet mine, and I think I see a
flicker of pity there for my naïveté. "Danny's dead. He died that
winter."

"What winter?" I feel sick. The salmon Zack lovingly broiled writhes inside me like it's coming back to life.

"The winter I'm talking about. When Selene was seventeen."

I swallow hard, trying to absorb this. Zack takes my hand and leads me toward a swing set. We trudge through the sand pit and take a seat on the strips of rubber dangling from chains.

He twists toward me on his swing, studying my face. Streetlights tinge the fog a sickly yellow. "Selene was madly in love with Danny. They dated for . . . I don't know . . . maybe two months? Then she caught him with another girl, and she lost her mind."

"What did she do?" I whisper.

"They were at this spot she and Danny used to go to—we called it Twisty Woods. Selene saw them there, lying on a blanket in a clearing, and she freaked out. She got back in her car and floored it, mowed them both down. Just like Colton."

I put my hand to my mouth, bile rising in the back of my throat. "Are you sure?"

"Yeah, I'm sure." He breathes out a harsh, unhappy laugh. "I helped her clean her car, just like you did this morning."

"Oh my God."

"That's why she didn't ask me." He looks up at the sky just as a curl of fog wraps around the moon, darkening his face. "She knew better than to call in that favor twice."

I curl forward on the swing, my stomach churning as I clutch at it. Jesus Christ. Her entire marriage to Danny was pure fiction, the product of a pathological imagination. The details she shared about their life together were so vivid, though, so *real*. It gives me vertigo, looking back on those stories and realizing she made every one of them up. Why? What was the point? But I'm trained enough to know lying isn't logical when it's pathological. The rest of us might lie to cover our asses, to get out of something or into something or away from someone. Pathological liars weave stories because they can, because it gives them power and pleasure. Understanding spreads through me like the first chills of a fever.

Zack's tone becomes apologetic. "I probably overreacted this morning when you helped wash her car. I just hate to think of you living with the shame I've dealt with all these years."

If only you knew, I think.

"Was she a suspect?" I ask.

Zack shakes his head. "There wasn't much of an investigation. The spot was pretty remote. Danny and the girl he was with were both drifters from out of town, criminals, so they disappeared pretty frequently. There was a heavy snowfall that night. By the time they were found the following spring, everyone just assumed they got too high, passed out, and died of exposure."

"She got away with it," I say, my voice faint.

Zack puts his hand on my shoulder. "I know it's a lot to take in."

I nod, wondering if I should tell him about Rob. Will it make him feel better, knowing he's not the only one keeping her secrets? I worry it will only cause him more pain.

He swings a little, dragging his feet in the sand. "This is why I can't justify Colton's death as a freak, heat-of-the-moment, once-in-a-lifetime crime of passion. Selene isn't getting better, and she might be getting worse. I've been cleaning up her messes all my life. I'm starting to wonder if I'm really just enabling her to keep doing this." His expression is so regretful, so full of anguish.

I go to him and take his hands, tugging him up out of the swing. I wrap my arms around his neck. "You're a good brother, Zack."

He sucks his teeth and looks away, unconvinced.

"You are." I pull his head back so he has to meet my eye. "She's a hard person to love, but you do it beautifully."

His eyes search mine. "What should I do?"

"I know this probably isn't what you want to hear, but I think we should let Tim do his thing."

He hangs his head.

"I'm thinking about Jupiter here." I slip my hands inside his coat, feeling the warmth of his body through his shirt. "She's going to suffer more than anyone if there's a huge, messy trial. Can you imagine what that would do to her? Taking the stand, talking about Colton raping her? She shouldn't have to go through that. And if Selene is convicted, I'm not sure she can handle that on top of everything else."

"There might be a trial no matter what we do," he murmurs.

I nod. "But Tim will do his best to keep it from going that far. He knows Jupiter's future is what matters most here. He gets it. If he thinks Selene needs to turn herself in to make things easier on Jupiter, that's what he'll tell her to do."

"Good luck telling Selene to do anything."

"Yeah." I cringe. "True."

He leans down and kisses me. When we pull apart, he says, deadpan, "It's usually months before I introduce my girlfriend to the family. You and I navigated that hurdle, huh?"

I laugh. "Is that what I am? Your girlfriend?"

"Is that too juvenile?" His gaze searches mine, his eyes still sparking with humor. "Do you prefer 'partner'?"

"No. Girlfriend's much better."

His tone stays light, but there's something serious in his face when he says. "So? Will you be my girlfriend?"

"I will," I say, smiling.

We walk out of the park and down the street, holding hands. All the while, the story of Rob burns inside me. Why am I not telling him? Because I hate reliving that moment of sheer powerlessness? Because I don't want to worry him even more? I suspect the biggest reason is I'm afraid it will tip him over the edge, force him to turn Selene in, and I'm not sure that's the best choice for anyone.

As we walk, I can feel the past taunting me. The neighbors' jack-o-lanterns glow like demons in the fog. In their sinister grins, I see one face again and again: Selene as she stood on that clifftop, her face ablaze with righteous fury.

CHAPTER

14

THE FOLLOWING THURSDAY, I'm in my office with a student when there's a sharp knock on my door. When I open it, Jupiter is standing there. She's wearing a scarf that covers half of her bruised face and a knit cap, but I can see she's been crying. I usher the student out and push the button on my electric kettle for tea.

"What's going on?" I ask.

Jupiter tears off her scarf and perches on the seat across from my desk, then immediately gets up again, too agitated to sit still. "A witness came forward. One of my neighbors."

My pulse races. "And?"

"She didn't see everything. Not the actual . . . accident." She seems to stumble over this last word.

I breathe out a sigh of relief. "That's good, right? What *did* she see?"

"She could tell it was a dark sports car, maybe a convertible."

I wince. "But she didn't get a license plate?"

"Right, no plates." She paces, rubbing her hands together like she's trying to warm them. "She said she saw two women, one outside the car and one inside. Arguing."

I raise my eyebrows. "You were arguing?"

"A little." Jupiter looks sheepish.

"What about?"

She sighs. "Mom showed up kind of drunk after I called her. She's already gotten one DUI. I didn't want her to get another."

"So what did you do?" I ask.

"I had to get away from Colton, so I got in."

"Do you know how to drive?" My kettle button pops. I lift it from its base and pour water over a tea bag. "Do you want tea?"

"Yes, please." She sits again.

"Chai?"

"Sure," she says, toying with the buttons of her coat.

I rip open a bag of Tazo and douse the teabag with hot water. This conversation is so unnerving, doing something simple grounds me. "So, do you drive?"

"More or less." Her fingers tug at a thread on her coat sleeve, and she looks preoccupied. She sits again, avoiding my gaze. I get the feeling she's carrying on a complicated conversation with herself that has little to do with the one we're having.

"Hey." I pour soy milk into her tea. "Are you okay?"

"No, I'm not okay," she goggles at me, indignant.

"You're worried this witness will seal the deal for your mom?"

"They took her car," she says in a hoarse rasp. "They're going to do a full-on forensic analysis. Uncle Zack says they're bound to find something."

"Oh my God. Why am I just now hearing about this?" I look around for my phone, but it's not on my desk where I usually keep it.

"Tim and Zack have both been trying to reach you," she says, irritated.

I finally locate my phone at the bottom of my messenger bag. Sure enough, there are several missed calls from Tim and Zack. I must have silenced it for my appointment and forgotten to check it.

The thought of a forensics team examining Selene's car hits me like a punch to the gut. It felt like we were being thorough at the time, but Zack's right. No way could we have gotten every hair, every bone chip. I picture somebody in a hazmat suit using a pair of tweezers to pluck a speck of brain tissue from the grill. The banana nut muffin I had this morning threatens to make a second appearance.

"What does Tim say?" I ask, my voice shaking.

She looks down. "He's looking into it, but he suggested Mom might want to confess. She doesn't want to do it, but it's looking more and more like they'll have a solid case against her."

I hand her the mug of tea and wait until she meets my gaze. "What do you want her to do?"

Tears stream down her face, long dark rivulets of mascara. "I don't *know*. I wish I knew."

"Tim's pretty smart." I put my hand on her shoulder. "You can trust his advice. If he says it's time, it's time."

She nods, raises her mug to her lips, and blows, sending wafts of steam snaking into the air. "I just can't see her in prison."

"It would probably be low-security and not for very long."

Her eyebrows tilt at sharp angles. "My mom can't live in captivity. She's like a wild animal. If you put her in a cage, she'll die."

"Don't say that." I try not to reveal that I've had the same thought myself. "Human beings are adaptable. Your mom's resilient. Like you."

She looks like she's going to cry again, but blinks hard and grabs a tissue, dabbing at her damp face. "Is it true you only talked to me because my mom made you?"

Here it is. I wondered if we'd get around to that question. This is the first time I've seen her since she fled Zack's kitchen last weekend. I've been hoping for a chance to explain myself, and now she's giving me exactly that.

I take a deep breath. "Your mom and I hadn't seen each other in years. She showed up here in my office and demanded I pay her back for a favor she did me a long time ago."

"What favor?" Jupiter looks intrigued.

I grab my mug and walk back over to my side of the desk, take a seat, and sip my tea. It's too hot, so I put it down on my desk. "She saved me from a terrible situation. I think I told you that story. She was the person who saved me."

She looks impressed. "My mom? How did she save you?"

"She pulled the guy off me." I look away. "We're getting off topic, though. The point is, she felt like I owed her, which I kind of did, and she came here to collect on that debt. She was worried about you, so she asked me to meet with you."

Jupiter's eyes narrow to slits. "She told you to break us up."

"She did." I raise a finger. "But I told her I'd never do that."

"But you *did* meet with me." She's still wary, unconvinced.

"Because I wanted you to have someone to talk to." I blow on my tea. "As soon as I met you, I adored you. I wanted you to feel safe and listened to by somebody with no agenda."

"You totally had an agenda," she says, her face full of accusation. "You're basically Mom's bitch."

"I'm not her bitch." It comes out louder than I intended. With a paranoid glance at the door, I lower my voice. "I sincerely wanted to help you. But yes, I met with you initially because I felt like I owed your mom after what she did for me."

It's a sanitized version of the truth, but nothing in it is a lie.

Jupiter scans my face, gauging my sincerity. Finally, she sips her chai and says, "I guess that makes sense."

"The important thing is," I say, leaning closer, "now we're friends. I'm not going anywhere. I want to be there for you, and that's the truth."

She raises an eyebrow. "And Zack?"

To my annoyance, I can feel my cheeks flaming. "What about him?"

"What's going on there? Are you in love?" Her eyes sparkle in a way I haven't seen them do in days.

I'm shocked to find my lips have almost formed the word *yes*. What the hell is this? Me, in love with Zack Rathbone? It's *way* too soon. It makes no sense.

I look down, wrestling with my thoughts. "I think it's a little early for 'love.'"

"Zack always says, *when you know, you know.*" She flashes me an impish grin. "You know, huh?"

There's a knock at the door, and we both look at it, startled.

"It's Grand Central in here today." I open the door to see Zack, his face pinched with worry. He looks gorgeous in a dark green cashmere coat, jeans, and a navy blue sweater.

"Did you get my messages?" he asks.

"No, I just—" I stop, flustered. "Jupiter's here."

He steps into my office and closes the door behind him. "Did she tell you about the witness?"

I nod. "What does Selene want to do?"

"She's not inclined to turn herself in, though your brother says it's her best chance at a light sentence." He shakes his head, and I can see a vein at his temple throbbing. "I was afraid she'd do this."

My stomach ties itself into knots. "Can we convince her?"

"I'm trying." He cups his jaw in his hands and pops his neck. "It's not easy, though. You know that."

"Have *you* tried?" I ask, turning to Jupiter. It seems to me if anyone can get Selene to do the right thing, it's her daughter.

Jupiter squirms. "I'm not good at convincing her."

"That's not true," Zack says, his brow furrowing.

Jupiter looks uncomfortable. "Maybe Tansy can do it."

I take a step back. "She won't listen to me."

"You can try." Zack throws a stern look at Jupiter, then trans-
fers it to me. "We can all try. This could be the difference between
a year in prison versus five or even ten. That's how important this
is. We need her to strike a deal so we can get her in and out of
there as soon as possible."

Jupiter nibbles her lower lip. "You really think she'd survive
in prison?"

"Your mom?" He raises an eyebrow. "She's tough. In a year,
she'd be running the place."

*   *   *

Selene's at my house when I get home that night. I'm not surprised, but my stomach does a little swan dive at the sight of her
there on my porch. The cops still have her car, so the MG doesn't
give me my usual warning. She must have gotten a ride out here.

I spot her in profile through the windows, leaning back in the
Adirondack chair, her gaze distant and pensive. The solar string
lights I hung around my porch last summer twinkle brightly in the
darkness, casting faint golden light on her face. The crease between
her brows and the glazed look in her eyes tells me she's lost in
thought. She whips around when she hears me open the back door.

"Finally. I've almost polished off this bottle of wine." She
grins, her eyes not meeting mine.

I toss down my bag and collapse into the couch. "God, pour
me some. I need it."

"You okay?" She picks up the bottle of red and pours me a
glass, hands it to me.

I kick my shoes off, rubbing my stockinged foot. "I heard about
the witness, and the cops searching your car. Everyone thinks you
should turn yourself in."

"Oh, 'everyone thinks,' huh?" She shakes her head and makes
a sound in her throat. "You know me, Tansy. I'm a gambler. It's in
my blood. My people have always been gamblers."

"Zack wants you to do it," I say quietly.

"Zack!" She lets out a cry of laughter. "Of course he does. He's so predictable. If he had his way, I would have turned myself in the first time this happened."

That knocks the wind out of me. *The first time this happened.* She's never implied something like this happened before. Does she know Zack told me? Is that why she's bringing it up? I drink my wine, turning her words over in my head, deciding my next move.

"What do you mean, 'the first time'?" My words come out faint and thin.

"The first time." She hits each syllable hard, like I might be stupid. "Back in high school. He told you, so don't pretend, okay?"

I don't respond.

She leans back in her chair again, considering me. With one lazy hand, she reaches over, grabs her wine glass, pulls it to her lips, and drinks. The sparkle of the reflected string lights bobs along the rim of her glass.

"Did you tell him about Rob?" Half her face is draped in shadow, and when she looks at me the moonlight turns the whites of her eyes a milky blue.

"No," I say. "Should I?"

She bursts out laughing.

I recoil, alarmed. "What's so funny?"

"I don't care, Tansy. Tell him, don't tell him." She flashes a savage grin at me, running a hand over her buzzed head. "I'm beyond all that now. It's like my hair, you know? One day I woke up and I was like *why am I carrying all this weight around? I don't give a shit about any of it.*"

There's definitely something off about Selene tonight, something reckless and at the same time resigned. I used to think I was good at reading her moods, sensing the stormy weather that ruled her. Now, though, I have to wonder if I ever knew Selene at all. An eerie prickle tingles along my skin as I think about all the lies she must have told me over the years. I think of Danny, who was so real to me—the way he whisked her out of Vermont and rented them an apartment in New Orleans, an old flat on the third floor just a block away from Bourbon Street, with a wrought iron balcony and a velvet fainting couch and a mirrored drinks cabinet and a spiral staircase going up to the loft. Everything about their life together was so detailed, so vivid, a movie full of characters I believed in and cared about. But none of it ever existed. It was the product of Selene's fevered imagination, the life she'd wanted with him, and all the while he was nothing more than bones.

"Listen," she says, her voice going serious. "I came here tonight to tell you the truth."

"The truth," I echo, thinking, *what a riddle.*

She nods, her brow creasing. "Of course you doubt me. Why wouldn't you? But tonight, for once in my life, I'm going to arm you and only you with the truth, the whole truth, and nothing but the truth."

I scoff at her dramatic phrasing.

"I mean it," she insists. "You're the Keeper of Rathbone Secrets, after all."

The phrase circles around in my brain. Is that what I am?

"We all tell you the truth, for some reason." Her voice goes low and husky. "What you choose to do with it is entirely up to you."

This feels familiar, but it takes me a moment to realize why. Selene used to do this all the time when we were close: build me up so I'd feel important. Weave a story peppered with words like Fate and Destiny and The Keeper of Secrets, casting me as the brave heroine. She wants something from me, that much is clear.

A silence falls over us. I listen to the crickets and bullfrogs and gaze up at the carpet of stars. It occurs to me that I should be frightened, sitting there with a cold-blooded killer, but I still can't think of her like that. Instead, I tell myself, *I will always remember this night.* It's not a happy thought, but it's tinged with that weird sense of reverse nostalgia, when you know a moment will be a memory before it's whisked away. Selene always made me feel that way, when we were close—like every moment was a Polaroid snapshot I'd want to take out later and pore over. Just about everybody else I know spends their days like they're killing time, waiting in line for the big event. With Selene, every moment is ripe and bursting with meaning. It's addictive, even if it's all built on lies.

"Tomorrow's my birthday," she says. "Did you know that?"

With a jolt of surprise, I realize she's right. I've never been good at remembering birthdays, but I do remember hers: October twenty-ninth. Two days before Halloween. Well, I remember now that she's reminded me.

She makes a sound that's part laugh, part sigh. "Last year of my forties. Who would have thought I'd make it this far? I fully intended to be dead by twenty-seven like Janis Joplin and Jimi Hendrix."

"And Amy Winehouse," I add. "Don't forget her."

"You, on the other hand." She slides me a sly, knowing look. "You're going to be a wise old woman someday."

Another silence blossoms between us, softened only by the babble of the creek in the distance, swollen with rain, and the ever-present chorus of crickets.

"Are you going to turn yourself in?" I ask, my voice quiet.

She gives me a stern frown. "That's not what I'm here to talk about. I have something I want to tell you, and I refuse to be sidetracked. All that legal shit just gives me a headache."

"Okay." I have to admit—to myself, at least—I'm curious.

Her gaze falls to her glass. She swirls her wine like a fortune teller studying her crystal ball. "I want you to know what really happened."

I'm not entirely sure what she's talking about. I say nothing, waiting for her to continue.

She pauses, looking at me. With her hair gone, her eyes have a new gravity. They look huge and solemn. "I'm not the one who killed Colton."

Though I've lost what little faith I had in my ability to suss out her lies, something in her voice is so cut-the-shit honest, it sends chills right up my spine. I recall the moment earlier today in my office when Jupiter was trying to tell me about their argument over who would drive. I wasn't really listening, distracted by the news of the witness coming forward and the forensics team examining Selene's car.

"Jupiter." I can barely speak around the lump in my throat.

Selene nods, her expression somber. "She called me for a ride, but when I got there, she knew I'd been drinking. I let her get behind the wheel—I didn't want to, but she insisted, and I was ready to do anything just to get us out of there."

An owl calls from one of the trees, low and mournful. I sit motionless, watching her, picturing the scene.

"Then Colton came out. He had a baseball bat, and he was ready to use it—I could see it in his eyes." She drinks more wine, taking a big swig and swallowing hard, her throat working. "He took a few steps toward me, the bat raised, headlights shining in his eyes. I turned to Jupiter and screamed, 'Go! Drive!'"

She pauses again, looking up at the oaks as a gust of wind stirs their branches.

"Instead of pulling into the road, swerving away from him, she put her foot down on the gas and drove straight at him." She licks her lips, glances at me, then turns her attention to the stars. "I saw the look on her face when she decided to do it. You can only push a girl so far before she snaps."

I don't know what to say, so I hold my silence. Anything I might utter seems too trivial for the moment.

Selene puts her wine down and leans her elbows on her knees. "I'm telling you this because I want you to understand what she's been through."

I let my breath out, long and slow.

"You've got to be there for her, Tansy. No matter what."

"Of course, I plan to—" I say, but she interrupts like I'm missing her point.

"You're the only one who will ever know what really happened." She gives each word its own weight, like bricks she's laying down one at a time. "Jupiter's going to need that. Someone who gets it—gets *her*."

"Why did you tell me and not Zack?"

She flashes a melancholy smile at the sky. "I love my baby brother, and he tries—God knows he tries. But he's a man. He'll never understand what Jupiter went through that night. Not really."

I recall the flash of fury I felt for Zack that morning when we got back from washing Selene's car. When he questioned me, accused me of incriminating myself, it wasn't just defensiveness that made me push back. I was angry at him for not understanding what it's like to be a woman enduring a night that's stripped you of all your power.

"Are you going to take the fall?" I don't even know if that's the right thing to do anymore.

Selene holds my gaze. "I'd do anything to keep her safe. You know that."

"Zack and Tim say the sooner the better." I pull out my phone. "We can call Tim right now, make a plan."

"Not yet." She sips her wine. "I need tonight. You can give me that much, right?"

It seems churlish to rush her, when she's obviously resigned. I put my phone back in my pocket.

"I'm worried about her." Selene's words are shaky with tears. "I'm scared she's like me."

I feel a tear slip down my cheek, hot against my cool skin. My instinct is to say something reassuring, but no words come.

Selene pins me with her eyes. "Keep an eye on her, okay? I want you to teach her to be more like you, less like me."

"I'm not sure that's—"

"Please." She goes on staring at me with her huge, moss-green eyes. "I want you to take care of them both."

The little hairs on the back of my neck stand at attention. I've got a bad feeling about this. "What do you mean?"

"Jupiter and Zack." She sighs. "Promise you'll watch over them, make sure they're okay."

I study her, but her face tells me nothing. "Even if you have to serve time, Selene, it's not going to be for—"

"Just promise me," she repeats. It's the closest I've ever seen her come to begging.

"I promise." I know it's more than a promise—it's a vow.

She smiles again, her white teeth glowing in the moonlight. "You're the Keeper of Rathbone Secrets, like it or not. Use your power for good."

I return her smile, though mine's a little uneasy.

"Listen, can I stay here tonight?" Her face looks vulnerable, her eyebrows tilting this way and that as if unsure of where to settle.

I'm surprised. This is the third time she's ambushed me, and she's never asked to stay. Then I remember she doesn't have a car. With a sickening lurch, I picture the forensic experts examining every speck, every hair, every fiber. We should have scrubbed harder. Can they tell we tried to cover our tracks?

"How did you get here?" I ask, stalling for time. Can I handle her staying here? It's so much like old times, those long summer nights in her dome.

She ignores my question, her jaw tightening. "If you don't want me to stay, I can get a ride."

"Of course you can stay." It's out of my mouth before I can think better of it. "The couch converts into a bed. It's pretty comfortable."

Her mouth goes from a tense pout to that radiant smile of hers, grateful and warm. "Thank you. I didn't want to wake up alone on my birthday."

We fall silent again. I can smell the apples in Marius's orchard, the perfume of autumn on the air.

"Play me a song, Tansy." The smile is still there in her voice. "You haven't done that in ages."

As I stand to get my guitar, we both look up just in time to see a dying star streak across the sky.

* * *

The next morning, I lie in bed for a long moment, listening. The house is quiet. Selene must still be asleep. I heard her puttering around downstairs most of the night, so it's no wonder she needs her rest. I move as quietly as I can, showering and getting dressed in stealth mode, like a burglar.

I make her a breakfast burrito, her favorite. It's got bacon, cheddar cheese, scrambled egg, avocado, and salsa. It's amazing, if I do say so myself. I want her to feel loved, and since I hadn't thought about it being Selene's birthday until she brought it up last night, I have to make do with homemade offerings. I know she won't mind. They're the kind of gifts she likes best.

Slipping outside to my garden, I cut a handful of deep violet chrysanthemums, enough to make a pretty bouquet. I know she'll like these, and it's a miracle they're still blooming this late in the season. My yard has mostly gone to seed. Violet is Selene's favorite color. She should have something pretty today.

As I shake the dew off the chrysanthemums and arrange them, I think of Jupiter's deep purple top the night she went back to Colton's. A twinge of guilt shoots through me, remembering how angry Jupiter was with me, but I remind myself she was getting back with Colton anyway. It's not like I drove her into his arms.

Still, it makes me sad to think about. If only she'd stayed at Zack's, broken up with Colton, none of this would have happened. I feel a deep, sudden yearning for a total do-over. What I wouldn't give to turn back the clock and make Jupiter stay away from him.

Stop that, I admonish myself. *What's done is done.* Selene will turn herself in, taking the rap for Jupiter. It will be hard, but Tim will get her through it.

I hear Jupiter's words from yesterday. *My mom can't live in captivity. She's like a wild animal. If you put her in a cage, she'll die.*

Please don't let that be true, I think, praying vaguely to anyone who might be listening. She needs to get through this. We need to get through this together.

I carry the flowers back inside, moving quietly so as not to wake her. I deposit them in a lemon yellow vase and fill it with water, tying a large white satin ribbon around its neck before putting it on the counter. Then I gently transfer the burrito onto a plate and arrange it near the flowers. Against the vase I prop up a note on a piece of lavender origami paper with tiny silver cherry blossoms. On the white side I write: *Happy Birthday to my oldest and most complicated friend. You are a mystery to me, but I do love trying to unravel you. Please, please, please, do whatever Tim suggests and get this over with quickly. Sorry, it's your birthday, don't want to nag, I just . . .*

I've nearly run out of room, and it seems tacky to add another square of paper. I resolve to wrap up quickly, in the scant square inch or two left. I write, *I love you and I want what's best for you.*

I want to add *and Jupiter*, but there's no room. Not to mention Zack, who I get the feeling hasn't breathed properly all week. He's so tense about all this, he's like a grenade. I doubt he'll rest until Selene comes clean and gets her plea deal; no other solution makes sense, in his mind, and it's killing him to stay quiet.

I add a Post-it note to the edge of the plate saying "Bon Appétit! xo." There's a steaming carafe of French press coffee, fresh fruit, orange juice. She's got everything she needs for her birthday breakfast. I only wish I could stay here and enjoy it with her. Honestly, though, the thought of food right now makes me want to retch. Even the smell of the bacon I cooked this morning made me nauseous.

If bacon doesn't smell good, something is deeply wrong.

When I get to work, the atmosphere's harried and everyone seems to be running late. By noon, I'm so hopelessly behind, half my afternoon appointments will need to be rescheduled. There's a softball-sized migraine blossoming at the back of my skull, so when I get Zack's call I'm tense as a coiled spring.

"Hey," I say, breathless. "How are you?"

"She's gone." Zack's voice sounds hollow, dazed.

"Who?"

"Selene." The single word shoots down the line. "I think she's probably in Mexico."

I feel dizzy and sit down, almost missing my chair. "That's impossible. She stayed at my place last night. She was asleep this morning. Are you sure she's not just curled up on my couch?"

His voice rises in surprise. "She stayed at your house last night?"

"Yeah. She was there when I got home from work." I rub my eyes, then stop, knowing I'll smudge my mascara. "She said she didn't want to wake up alone on her birthday."

He hisses out a breath, frustrated. "I came home for lunch, and there was a note here. She's left the country."

"Oh my God."

I hear a rustling sound on his end, like he's flipping through papers. "She left a signed confession, 'in case we need it.'"

"Confessing to the hit and run?" I massage my temples, the headache getting stronger every second.

He grunts in the affirmative, then lets out a growl of frustration. "I should have seen this coming."

"Are you going to show her confession to the cops?"

"I don't know." He swears, and I hear something fall on his end; it sounds like he's dropped something heavy. "This is—why does she always do this?"

"Do what?" I ask gently. His voice sounds more agitated than I've ever heard it before, and the oil slick that's been lurking in my stomach all day feels deeper and darker than ever.

"Fuck everything up and leave me behind to clean her mess." He pauses, and I can almost hear him gathering himself, pushing down his anger and frustration so he can focus on what needs to be done. "I have class in an hour. I'm going to her place to see if this is real. I know where she keeps her passport and emergency cash. If they're gone, then I guess we have to take her at her word."

I nod, then realize he can't see me and murmur, "That sounds like a good plan. Do you want me to come with you?"

It's an offer I can't really afford to make, given that I'm already behind on appointments, but I make it anyway.

"No, you're at work, right?" I hear footsteps, then a car door slamming through the phone. "Don't worry about it. I just wanted to let you know."

"Have you told Jupiter?" I ask.

If Zack shows the cops Selene's confession, that's it—she can never come home, or if she does, she'll be looking at doing serious time. Cops don't like it when their prime suspect leaves the country, and it won't help that her number one enemy is the DA.

I hear his car starting up. "No. Let's wait, figure out what's really going on before we sound the alarm."

"Okay. Keep me posted."

We end the call, and I sit there, trying to make sense of this new twist. Why would she want to sleep at my place if she knew she'd be leaving the country the next morning? She doesn't even have a car, and Uber isn't always easy to summon from my place—cell reception's not even a given. Was this a spontaneous decision? Does somebody really start a brand new life in Mexico without any planning at all? Selene can be impulsive, sure, but that's pretty extreme, even for her. I picture her on a plane, adding two mini bottles of vodka to her Coke, smiling at the prospect of a new adventure. It makes sense, in a way. Selene's moved more times than I can count. It's always her first instinct, when things go wrong—to pick up and start fresh someplace new. Something about the picture won't come into focus, though. When I try to imagine her on a plane, Jackie-O sunglasses masking half her face, a secret smile on her lips, the image keeps fuzzing out, like an old TV with bad reception.

Is this dark feeling in my gut a premonition, or just too much caffeine? I try to concentrate on work, seeing students one after another, helping them sign up for spring classes and talking them through their ed plans. When Zack texts me with a simple message—*Passport and money are gone. I guess Selene is, too*—I tell myself, *That's that.*

Still, I keep hearing her voice as she sat there on my porch last night: *I want you to take care of them.* Did she know she was leaving the country the next day, that she might never return? The heavy feeling weighing me down tells me there's more to it than that. Selene has more surprises up her sleeve. I'm sure of it.

15

I GET HOME EARLIER than usual that evening. It's a little before five, and the sun is a massive yellow lozenge at the edge of the western hills. It's warm again today, which bothers me. I prefer gloomy weather most of the time—mist, rain, snow—I'll take any of that over the balmy, dry weather we're having today. The rain hasn't yet greened up the hills. They're the golden brown of lion fur, and they look as tired as I feel. It's fire season, something everyone around here is skittish about after the record number of infernos we've seen. Even the traffic on my way home is a tinderbox, people honking and speeding more than usual, everyone wired for conflict.

It should be a relief when I get home, but for some reason the sight of my cozy little A-frame makes something inside me tremble. What do I think is going to happen? Selene's left the country. She can't hurt me anymore. I want to feel relieved about that, but what I feel instead is enormous sadness.

When I walk into my house, the stillness feels oppressive. I stand for a long moment near the front door, sniffing the air, trying to detect what's different. The house seems to be holding its breath. I put my bag down in the kitchen and do a slow, full rotation, drinking in the walls and furniture, looking for signs. Something is definitely different here than it was when I left this morning. I can't put my finger on it, but it's distinct. Potent.

My eyes fall on a piece of paper lying on the counter. It's plain, unlined computer paper, and I recognize her looping cursive right away. My stomach lurches as I reach for it. With a pounding heart, I touch the letter to my lips, readying myself for whatever I'm about to learn. The paper smells of amber, Selene's signature scent. It's another one of those Polaroid moments, a mental snapshot I know I'll hold on to forever. I also know this one will always be accompanied by a stab of pain, because what I'm about to read can't be good.

Beneath the letter there are seven postcards from various parts of the world: Berlin, Paris, Morocco, Amsterdam, Shanghai, Tokyo, and Bangkok. Each one has a simple message—just a couple of lines, signed with love from Selene. I flip through them, my mind reeling. Then I read the letter addressed to me.

\ * * *

Dear Tansy,

By the time you read this, I'll already be dead.
(I always wanted to write that.)

You know it's not my style to apologize, but I actually am sorry it has to be like this. I chose you to be the keeper of this letter because you're stronger than anyone I know. Only you can handle what I'm about to throw at you.

The downside to being strong and deeply capable? You get all the worst jobs. Congratulations! You're amazing at absolutely everything. Now you get to clean up everybody's messes.

That's what Zack always says about me—that I leave him to clean up my messes. He's not wrong. This time, though, I choose you.

Know that I have the utmost faith you can pull this off better than anyone.

First question: Do you know how fucking hard it is to dig a grave? Answer: Incredibly so. It took me seven hours, and it's not even all that deep. Sorry about that. It's about three and a half feet, which is actually pretty standard, in spite of the common belief that it's six. The things you learn from Google when you're about to kill yourself.

Because I have killed myself, as you've no doubt guessed. Don't worry, though, I'm not in your house. I wouldn't do that to you. No, I literally dug my own grave. Now I plan to lie down inside it, swallow a bottle of sleeping pills, and wash those down with a shaker of ice-cold dirty martini. Classy touch, right? Shaken, not stirred. I expect it will be a pleasant way to go. I was going to slit my wrists as well, just to be safe, but I wanted to spare you the sight of the blood. I know that's not your thing. Remember when I cut my finger at the dome when we were making guacamole? You almost passed out. Don't worry, you delicate flower. If all goes as planned, I should look just like Sleeping Beauty—assuming I don't vomit all over myself. That would be disgusting. Apologies in advance if that happens.

All you have to do is find me and bury me. I'm quite deep in the woods. I've drawn a map on the back of this letter. Give yourself a good twenty minutes to hike there. Once you find me, you'll see a shovel propped against a craggy oak. Just take it and fill in my hole. That's it. Easy peasy.

Except it won't be. I know that. I'm not a monster. I know I'm asking you to do the hardest thing you'll probably ever do in your life. I'm not even asking, really—I'm demanding. Please forgive me for this, Tanzanita. Please forgive me for everything.

If it weren't for you, I could never take this option. But now that I know you're going to be there for Zack and Jupiter, I feel free to move on down the road. Don't rest too easy, though, because I doubt I'll truly be gone. You'll see me in the Spanish moss and the sun on the river; you'll see me in the morning dew and the full harvest moon. I'll be everywhere, and because I love you and you love me, you'll feel me. I think that's how it works. It's a mystery, where I'm going or what it will be like, but I know in my bones that a part of me will be here with you, lingering. I'll be with you and Jupiter and Zack, always.

Selene

P.S. Please let Zack and Jupiter believe I've gotten away, at least for a little while. Let them imagine me on a beach somewhere in a string bikini getting ogled by seventy-year-old playboys and drinking fruity drinks full of cherries and umbrellas. Tell them I'm in Shanghai or Paris or Morocco. Let them hope. Will you do me this one last totally undeserved favor? I've included some pre-written postcards from various corners of the world in case you want to mail them for this purpose. You're a clever girl. You can figure out how to fake the postmark.

I know I always ask too much.

If, when the shock wears off, you think the truth would help them move on, I authorize you to tell them. You're the Keeper of Rathbone Secrets, like it or not. Use your power for good, and watch your six.

I don't know I'm crying until I see my tears smearing the ink. I gasp like somebody breaking the surface after staying under water too long, sucking in a greedy lungful of air. The letter falls to the counter and I lean against it for support, trying to slow my breathing.

She can't ask this of me. She's right. It's too much.

I'm not doing this. There's no way.

I look at the windows. There's barely an hour of daylight left.

Shit.

* * *

It takes me thirty minutes to hike to the spot. She's drawn me a primitive but workable map. It leads me past the goats grazing in the pasture, past the chickens and the orchards. About a quarter mile down the dirt road, I take a deer path off to the right no wider than my hips. Blackberry bushes crowd the sides of the trail. I wade through them as the path gets narrower and narrower. By the time I arrive, the beginnings of an apricot sunset streak across the sky to the west in messy smudges like a child's fingerpainting.

I see the shovel first. It's propped against the biggest oak, its handle cradled in the Y shape of the branches. I don't recognize it. She must have brought it with her. That's when I know this is real—that this is actually happening.

As I come around a bend, I notice the earth piled up in a semicircle around a deep oval hole. I creep toward it, my breath coming fast, partly from the exertion of the walk, partly from fear. I'm almost panting as I inch toward the edge, willing myself to look down, to take in what I know will be there. My heart feels like a ticking bomb inside me, a delicate mechanism apt to explode at any second.

When I finally find the courage to look down, my breath catches in my throat. It's hard to make out the details of her face. The sun has sunk below the western hills, leaving only an orange glow and the deep blue of twilight. The hole is deep enough to cast most of her body in shadow. I can see the pale contours of her bare feet. They look so vulnerable there, so childlike. Her shoes are down there with her. She must have taken them off before she took the pills. The thought sends a stab through me, sharp as a knife. I can imagine her so clearly, taking off those hiking boots like someone getting ready for bed.

For a moment, I consider clambering down there, checking for a pulse. I don't know when she left her note. Maybe she's still alive. I pull a flashlight from my pocket and shine it into the hole, bracing myself. I move the beam up the lines of her body. Beside her, I spot a silver cocktail shaker and a martini glass. Trembling, I focus the light on her face. That's when I see her eyes. They're wide open, staring at the sky. My heart clenches inside me like a fist. I let out a strangled sob and turn away.

She must have known she was going to do this last night when she extracted that promise—that vow—from me. Her claim that she wouldn't have done this if not for me makes me squirm. Does she know how much that hurts? Is it more of her usual MO, to make everyone around her as miserable as she is?

I don't think so. I suspect she considered it a kindness. It's like she's willed her family to me, put them in my care. The truth is, nothing she could do would tear me away from them, now that I've found them. She doesn't have to worry about me reneging on our bargain. When it comes to the Rathbones, I'm all in.

With a racing heart, I go to the edge again and peer down into the shadows. She's wearing the red dress—the one she wore to the Harvest Moon Ball. Of all the dresses she could have chosen, why that one? I mean, yes, it looks amazing on her—I marvel at how it still fits her curves exactly, just as it did eighteen years ago. She knew I'd be the only person to see her in it, though. Why would she want to remind me of that night?

Then I think of her letter. *You'll see me in the Spanish moss and the sun on the river; you'll see me in the morning dew and the full harvest moon.* Maybe she wants to remind me of that summer: skinny dipping in the hot springs late at night, eating fruit popsicles, giggling in the tea houses. And yes, maybe she wants me to think of that night, the way she rushed out of the trees like

an avenging angel and pushed my would-be rapist to his death.
Maybe she wants me to remember it all.

Darkness is starting to gather, casting long shadows from the
massive oaks standing sentinel. I consider my options. I could dial
911 and let the police take over. I could call Zack and tell him
everything. Or I could do what she asked in her letter—honor her
dying wishes.

Would it be a kindness, letting them think she's gotten away,
started a new life somewhere? Did Selene choose this option
because she sensed Jupiter wavering, getting ready to turn herself
in rather than let her mother take the fall?

Maybe. She did say I could tell them later, if I think it will
help them move on. I picture Jupiter, her face still mottled with
bruises, those morning glory eyes full of innocence and hope. She's
been through so much in the last week. How can the news of her
mother's suicide be anything but a fatal blow to that innocence? If
I can shield her from that, even for a few days, it's worth it.

I grab the shovel and get to work.

*   *   *

I've just passed the goats cavorting in the moonlight when I
hear a flicking sound in the darkness. It's different from the
countless animal sounds I've encountered on the walk back,
rustling in the bushes, wings overhead. The moon is ripe and
full, a golden orb hanging low over the eastern hills, silvering
the trees. It's bright enough to illuminate the figure skulking
near the barn, a man-sized silhouette that makes my heart jump
into my throat.

My body freezes. I feel exposed and vulnerable, standing in the
middle of the road, my limbs still coated in sweat and grime from
my exertions. With a quaver in my voice I call, "Who's there?"

The figure emerges from the shadows, moving slowly, almost
lazily. Then a flicker of flame from a lighter appears, illuminating

his face. Marius. Lighting a joint. The smell of smoke drifts over to me.

"What's up, Tansy?" His voice is low and smooth, like a late-night DJ.

I let out the breath I didn't realize I was holding and rest the tip of the shovel in the dirt, feeling self-conscious. What the hell am I going to tell him? I can't admit I just a buried a body on his property. Christ, he'd freak.

I recall Tim's advice from the other day. *Rule number one in the liar's playbook: stick to the truth as closely as you can.*

"I'm having a shitty night," I admit. "How about you?"

"Can't complain." He comes closer, taking another drag off the joint. "What the hell are you doing wandering around in the dark with a shovel? You're not burying any bodies, are you?"

A sound escapes me, explosive and slightly hysterical. At first it sounds like a laugh, but then it turns into a keening sob. Fuck, I'm really bad at this.

"Whoa," he says, putting a hand on my shoulder. "Easy there. What's going on?"

"I had to bury a cat," I blurt, grabbing at the first explanation that pops into my brain.

He squeezes my shoulder. "Oh no. Not Diego?"

"No, a different cat." My mind races ahead, trying to find a viable explanation. "There was a stray that kept coming around, and I started feeding it."

"I told you not to do that," he scolds, but his voice is gentle.

I nod. "I'm a softie when it comes to kittens, you know that."

"How did it die?"

Shaking my head, I try to get my tears under control, wiping at my eyes, smearing dirt across my face. "I'm not sure. Maybe a rattlesnake? He was really sick this morning, and then when I got home tonight he was dead."

Marius's brow furrows. "Where did you bury him?"

I gesture vaguely toward the east, away from where Selene now lies. I picture her body beneath all that dirt, the worms starting to feast on her flesh, and I think I might be sick. *Please, Marius, don't go looking for her.* I pray it's far enough away that he won't happen upon the spot until long after the relentless blackberries have grown over it. Anyone would be able to see at a glance that grave is way too big for a cat.

"Why didn't you just bury it over by your place?" he asks.

I shrug. "It was too sad. I didn't want the reminder right there in my yard."

He nods, and offers me his joint. I shake my head. That's all I need right now, to get high and spend all night poring over my questionable life choices.

"Hey, I saw someone at your place this morning," he says, his tone casual but curious. "Some chick with a buzz cut?"

I will myself to sound normal. Of course, as always happens when I'm desperate for "normal," I no longer have any idea what that sounds like. "Oh. Yeah. Selene."

"*The* Selene?" he asks, surprised.

I just nod, not trusting my voice.

"What was she doing at your place?" I can't tell if he's insinuating something or if I'm being paranoid.

"She needed a place to stay. Just for the night." I realize with something like wonder that the songs I played her last night were the last songs she'd ever hear.

He studies me, his bloodshot eyes unreadable. "Huh."

Eager to change the subject, I cast around for something to say. It occurs to me that he's pretty far from his house, at least a five-minute walk down the road. "What are you doing all the way down here, anyway?"

In the moonlight, I can just make out his sheepish grin. "Jessica doesn't want me getting high anymore."

Laughter erupts from me, catching me off guard. Half an hour ago, I felt like I'd never laugh again. "Has she noticed what you do for a living?"

"Right? Got to sample the goods." He takes one last drag off the roach, which is quite stubby by now, before tossing it into the dirt and grinding it under his boot.

With a sick little flip in my stomach, I recall Jessica's recent visit to inform me they're doubling my rent. Under normal circumstances, I'd be obsessed with that life-changing announcement, but the drama of the last few weeks has totally eclipsed my ability to worry about anything not Rathbone related.

As if feeling the shift in my thoughts, Marius coughs and looks at his shoes. "Jess told me she, um, broke the news. About your rent?"

"Which you were supposed to break weeks ago." I can't resist scolding him.

He hangs his head. "I just hate the whole situation. I feel terrible."

With sparkling clarity, I know it's time for me to move on. Jessica was right. Living here isn't really "serving" me anymore. I need to get on with my life, and living on my ex-lover's property isn't helping anyone.

"It's okay," I say, my voice going gentle. "She's right. I get it. It's time."

He locks eyes with me. "I'm going to miss you, Tansy."

I squeeze his arm. "I'm going to miss you, too."

We stand there for a long moment, studying each other.

An owl hoots gently overhead. We both look up, finding its white wings easily against the dark sky. It's flying toward the spot where I buried Selene, gliding over the oaks with silent, ghostly grace. She always did love owls. Maybe it will watch over her tonight.

A deep, overwhelming sadness sweeps through me, and suddenly all I want is my bed. I start walking backward, away from Marius. "I'll start looking soon, okay? Let Jessica know I'm working on it."

"Take your time. No rush." He flashes me his crooked grin.

I turn and stride down the road in the direction of my house. Not really *my* house, I remind myself. It's just on loan. I'm going to need a new life. The breeze stirs the trees lining the drive, the silvery leaves dancing and sighing.

"Tansy?" Marius calls.

I turn back around, heaving the shovel over my shoulder. "Yeah?"

"You're going to land on your feet." He chuckles. "You always do—just like a cat."

"I've got nine lives," I shoot back. "Let's just hope I haven't used too many of them."

As I walk the rest of the way, the breeze carries a whiff of woodsmoke and the pungent aroma of rotting apples. It's the smell of fall slipping gently into winter. By spring, I'll be someplace new, watching over Zack and Jupiter, whether they want me to or not. I made a vow, and I plan to keep it.

* * *

Colton's funeral is held a week later. It's at the St. Francis Solano church, just a few blocks away from where he died. Jupiter has gone back and forth about whether or not she should attend. Saturday morning, though, when we all gather at Zack's house, she comes out of her room dressed in a black sweater dress and a plum-colored scarf.

"I can't not go," she says.

Her bruises have faded, and she's used makeup to cover the last, yellowish remnants. Seeing her there, I'm struck by how much her bone structure resembles Rob's. Those eyes, too—a violet blue so vivid and unique it's a wonder I didn't see it right away. After so many years of trying to forget his face, I guess my brain rejected the resemblance. The sight of her standing tall, with the proud posture of her father, doesn't fill me with revulsion; instead, I feel proud of her courage.

"If you're going, we all go," Zack replies, his tone decisive.

I nod, and when I catch Jupiter's eye she offers a sad, brave smile. I know better than anyone how much this decision must cost her. I try to keep my expression neutral. She'll tell me about that night if she wants to. Until then, I have to keep her secret to myself.

As the three of us walk into the packed church, I can't help glancing at Jupiter every few seconds to gauge how she's doing.

She leans close and whispers, "I'm fine. Stop looking at me like I'm a bomb about to go off."

"I'm not—"

"You are too." Her fingers squeeze mine, one quick, tiny pulse. "Really. I've got this."

We squeeze into a pew near the back. It's cold out, one of those windy, clear days when the sun is glaring and the trees toss in a restless dance, shedding the last of their dead leaves. Inside the church, though, people have shrugged off their winter coats, the humid warmth of all those bodies mingling with the faint perfume of incense.

As we listen to the priest speak about the tragic loss of someone so young and full of promise, I peer down the aisle to the front row, where Henry Blake keeps a protective arm around his wife. Though I can only see slivers of their faces in profile when they turn toward the priest, I feel a sharp pang of empathy mixed with guilt. I can't imagine what they must be going through. How could I have thought, even in passing, that I was glad their son was dead?

Then I think of what he did to Jupiter, his brutality that night. I remember the determined optimism in her young, pretty face when she stood in Zack's kitchen, her backpack slung over one shoulder, her eyes shining. *People change. They have to, right? Otherwise, what's the point of working on yourself?*

As the priest brings his eulogy to a close, Henry looks around the church, and our eyes catch for a moment. His expression goes from tired to livid as his gaze slides over to Jupiter. Instinctively, I wrap an arm around her, wanting to shield her from the naked hostility in his bloodshot eyes. He whispers something into his wife's ear, and she twists a little in her seat to peer back at us. While Henry's expression is easy to read, hers is less easily decoded. Her face has that disturbing frozen quality of someone who's had a lot of plastic surgery. There's something vacant and medicated about her stare, hollow and broken. It makes my heart contract inside me.

I glance at Zack, who sits on the other side of Jupiter. As our eyes meet over her head, I see my own anxiety mirrored in his.

"How you doing?" I whisper into Jupiter's ear.

She nods vaguely and paws through her bag until she produces a crumpled Kleenex. I reach into my pocket and offer her a fresh packet of tissues, which she takes from me with a murmured, "Thanks."

As the service draws to a close, Colton's family forms a line near the door to thank people for coming. Colton's younger sisters are blonde, slender girls in black, fitted dresses who look like they're probably still in high school. They flank their mother in a protective way that makes her look even more fragile. I wonder what they're going through, how their brother's death has altered their young psyches. They both wear heavy makeup that renders their faces expressionless masks.

Zack and I take a few steps toward the exit, but Jupiter dithers, casting furtive glances at the Blakes, plucking at her sweater dress.

"Jupes," Zack says, his voice low and gentle, "maybe we should just—"

"I need to offer my condolences." Her words are quiet but determined. She looks to me as if seeking approval.

I give a little shrug, wondering how I would have felt if I'd gone to Rob's funeral. Would I have been able to face his family? I honestly don't know.

Not for the first time, my own inadequacy as a surrogate mother—aunt?—whatever I am, slaps me in the face. I don't know how to guide Jupiter. She's not a child, though. I hear Selene's voice in my head: *I want you to teach her to be more like you, less like me.*

My fingers find hers, lacing together. "Do you want us to go with you?"

Her eyes sparkle with gratitude. "Would you?"

Zack looks grim, but he nods his agreement and follows us into the long line of well-wishers. *Colton obviously had some fans,* I think as I survey the hordes of young people lining up. There are older people too, but more than half of the mourners are young and beautiful—college students decked out in elegant black designer clothes, all of them radiating health and privilege. I suspect Colton was the kind of guy who served as class president, captain of the football team. He would have been the first to do a keg stand at a party, to bring out the baggie of coke, but it wouldn't have stopped him from showing up bright and early to his law school classes, demonstrating the tireless work-hard-play-hard YOLO machismo his generation worships. These friends probably never saw the side of Colton that wrapped his hands around Jupiter's throat.

I notice some of the kids in line casting quick, uncomfortable glances at Jupiter. They greet one another with hugs and tears, but nobody says anything to her. Jupiter stares straight ahead, lips tight, nostrils flared, and I ache for her. She looks like a boxer psyching herself up for the next round. The courage it must take for her to stand here, knowing what she knows, feeling their suspicious eyes giving her the once-over. I wonder what sort of narrative they're spinning on their insidious social media, what kinds of accusations are flying around the church even now via text. Do they blame her for Colton's death?

Though Jupiter took a couple of days off from school after that terrible night, she went back midweek, her bruises still showing in spite of her best efforts with makeup. How did her injuries factor into the stories and rumors they told each other, if at all? I doubt they accepted Jupiter even before all of this. Maybe her crime, in their eyes, has nothing to do with Colton's death and everything to do with her inability to belong.

We reach the two younger sisters first. They refuse to look at us, fixing their gazes instead on the people behind us like we're invisible. As we shuffle along uncomfortably toward Mr. and Mrs. Blake, it looks like they'll do the same. I can't decide if I'm relieved or appalled. Maybe this is the best we can hope for, given the situation. Perhaps they're showing us a kindness, though it feels cold beyond reason, being denied the basic human connection of eye contact.

Just as we're getting ready to head toward the door, Mrs. Blake fixes her hollow, medicated eyes on Jupiter and something moves behind her Botox mask. It's unsettling, the way the anger pierces her serene exterior, like a shark surfacing from placid water.

Jupiter looks her in the eye. "I'm so sorry, Mrs. Blake. For everything."

Mrs. Blake's face freezes in shock. Then something in her softens, and I wonder if deep down she understands what Jupiter went through. Her husband was obviously in denial about his son's abusive tendencies, but in this moment, I suspect she saw her son more clearly. Maybe she sees the remnants of Jupiter's bruises and recognizes their kinship.

She doesn't speak, but her almost imperceptible nod implies an understanding.

We leave the church together. I grip Jupiter's hand in mine, holding tight.

One Year Later

JUPITER AND I go shopping for Halloween costumes at the Goodwill. Selene and I used to shop at thrift stores a lot when we were friends. She's the one who introduced me to the joys of pawing through other people's castoffs, hunting for treasures amid the dusty figurines and scuffed shoes. The minute we walk through the door, that familiar smell washes over me: musty old clothes, sunlight, desperation.

"What are you going to be?" Jupiter's wearing ripped jeans and a lavender sweater. In the past year, she's had a few can't-get-out-of-bed days and scattered panic attacks, but overall she's been weathering the storm with admirable resiliency.

I sort through a rack of dresses, pausing to inspect a bright orange monstrosity with rhinestones clinging like scabs to the bodice. "Don't know. I'm looking for inspiration. What are you going to be?"

"I'm torn between slutty nurse and slutty policewoman."

I turn to look at her.

"Kidding," she says with a smirk. "You should have seen your face."

"Doesn't really seem like your style."

She scoffs. "I hate those costumes. Seriously, what *is* that? The one night when you get to be anything you can dream up and you choose the just-add-slutty route? I mean, I've got nothing against sexy, but those cookie-cutter basic bitch costumes are the hallmark of a starved imagination."

"Totally," I say, hiding my smile. This is one of the things I like best about Jupiter, a side of her I'm seeing more of lately: the hyper-opinionated mini-rants that come out of nowhere, complete with indignant irritation at everything the world's getting wrong. It's good to see her planting a flag in ideological soil, taking a stand on things.

My eye catches on a floor-length midnight blue velvet gown. "Oooh, look at this."

"Love!" Jupiter reaches out and pets the velvet. "That would look so good on you."

I check the tag to see what size it is. It might be a little big, but it's in the right ballpark. It's got a sweetheart neckline and a fitted waist. I hold it up to myself, assessing the length. The hem dangles right around my ankles. It might be perfect.

"What would I be, though?" I muse, looking for stains. "Middle-aged woman trying too hard in pretty blue dress?"

Jupiter tilts her head, thinking. "I know! You could cover it in twinkly lights or glitter stars and call yourself the Night Sky. Add a star-studded crown, maybe? That would be beautiful."

"I like that idea." I picture myself in the finished product and feel a little prickle of pleasure at the thought of Zack seeing me in it.

"Oh my God, look at this!" Jupiter holds up a silver sequined cocktail dress. "You could be the stars and I could be the moon."

My breath hitches at the unexpected compliment. Jupiter wants us to have matching costumes. The sense of belonging pumps through my veins like a drug. It's still early days, I know, but I haven't felt this since the years I spent touring with The Insatiables. I'm inching my way into this strange little makeshift family we're forming; until now, I haven't let myself admit how much I miss being a part of something bigger than myself.

The pause has lingered too long, and Jupiter looks at me, confused. "What? You don't like it?"

"I love it," I gush. "Sorry, I'm just flattered that you want to do matching costumes."

She shoots me a funny look. "Why wouldn't I?"

There it is, the sweet, uncomplicated acceptance Jupiter has granted me from the beginning. I swallow the lump in my throat and focus on the dress.

"It's got a little tear here, but we could mend that easily." I finger a gap along the seam near the waist.

Later, once we've purchased our dresses, a couple of picture frames, and a suede bag Jupiter plans to turn into a throw pillow, we pile our bags into my car and climb into the front seat. It's sunny out, but a stiff breeze from the coast has kept the temperature pretty low all day. The front seat of my Subaru has grown toasty in the sun. We tuck ourselves into the pocket of warmth, enjoying the heat after the nippiness outside.

I'm just about to start the car when I notice the look on Jupiter's face. She's been chirpy and bright all morning, but I'm starting to recognize how the very air shifts with her mood swings, as distinct as a change in the weather.

I pull my keys from the ignition and turn toward her, watching her face for clues. "You okay?"

Tears sparkle in her eyes. "My mom loves Halloween. Except she always called it Samhain."

"I know." I recall my own celebrations with Selene, the jack-o-lanterns and our makeshift pagan rituals.

Jupiter sneaks a look at me before fixing her gaze on her lap. "It's my fault she had to leave."

"No," I say, "that's not true. None of this is your fault."

"It is." There's something in the way she says it that adds gravitas to the two words.

I pick a piece of lint from the sleeve of her sweater. "I know you miss her, but the last thing you should feel is guilt for—"

"It was me, Tansy." Her face crumples into tears and she squeezes her eyes shut. "I did it."

Whatever I was about to say dies on my lips. "What do you mean?"

"I was the one driving." She risks another quick glance at me, but she can't meet my eye for more than a second. "I killed Colton."

Jupiter lets out a quick, stifled sob and hangs her head, her golden hair falling forward and shielding her face. "I was so angry—beyond angry. All the rage I kept pushing down just exploded."

With one hand, I brush her hair back so I can see her face. She looks at me, her eyes red, tears streaming down her face. I can see a question in the angle of her eyebrows, the vulnerable shape her pretty mouth makes as she searches for my reaction.

"He could have killed you," I whisper. "Your fury is understandable."

She covers her face, crying harder. I pull her into my arms and let her sob, rubbing her back and murmuring soothing sounds, stroking her hair.

After a while, she pulls away, trying to mop up her tears with the sleeve of her sweater. I reach behind my seat and find a crumpled box of tissues, yank a few out and hand them to her.

When the worst of her sobs have passed, she blows her nose and tries to compose herself. "So now you know. I'm a terrible person. Colton's parents are never going to recover, Mom had to leave the country. It's all my fault—everything."

"Hey," I say, my voice deep and decisive. "That's not true. You're not a terrible person."

"I killed my boyfriend, Tansy." She wipes her tears with a tissue. "And I meant to do it. That's not something a good person does."

I clear my throat, choosing my words carefully. "Sometimes good people do bad things in order to survive."

Jupiter stares out the windshield, her brow furrowed in worry. "Mom's never coming back, is she?"

I don't know what to say. If I confirm this, will she guess the truth? Is that such a bad thing? But then I remember my promise to Selene—to let Jupiter and Zack have hope, at least until they're through the worst of it.

"Your mom loves you so much." I run my fingers through her hair. "Nothing will ever change that."

"She sacrificed everything for me." Her eyes fill with tears again. "Maybe I should turn myself in so she can come home."

"No." It comes out more forceful than I intended.

Her head turns to face me, surprised. "But—"

"One thing I know for sure," I say, looking her in the eye. "Your mom wants you to live a rich, full, beautiful life. You hear me?"

She nods, but I can see the doubt in her face.

"The best thing you can do for your mom is move on. I'm not going to say 'Forget this ever happened,' because that's not possible, but you do have to move past it." I take a deep breath, trying to find the right words, the ones Selene would want me to say. "You're fierce and magnificent, a force of nature. Your mom made this sacrifice because the thing she wants more than anything is to see you thrive. If you want to make it up to her, turn your life into a dazzling masterpiece."

She nods, taking this in. After a long moment, she says, "You love her too, huh?"

I smile, feeling the sting of tears. "I love all you Rathbones. Madly."

"Poor you." She laughs.

"Lucky me," I say.

* * *

It's Halloween, but the weather feels like summer. Zack's pool is a shimmering turquoise gem as I lounge on a lawn chair, watching through heavy-lidded eyes as he flips burgers on the grill. Jupiter's got friends over—Sarah and Lexie, a couple of girls she met at school and has grown close to. They're lying on blow-up loungers in the pool, talking in animated voices about some movie they saw this afternoon. Occasionally, Jupiter's laughter lifts off the water and floats like a butterfly across the lawn, as free and light as the breeze.

In May, on Jupiter's birthday, I slipped one of the postcards Selene gave me, the one from Paris, into Zack's mailbox. Jupiter squealed with delight, speculating for hours that night about the adventures her mom must be having, how happy she must be to finally see the world, just like she always wanted. Zack acted equally pleased, but when he didn't know I was looking his smile looked uneasy. Was my painstakingly forged postmark not convincing? When our eyes met, though, he just grinned and said, "That's great, Jupes. Paris! I can't think of anyplace more perfect for your mom."

Will I tell them someday? I don't know.

Several times I've been so close to telling Zack the truth. But then something always comes along to break the spell. I'll get a call from my brother I have to take, or Jupiter will burst through the door, or Diego will jump onto our laps, and the opportunity will slip through my fingers. Is it crazy to think Selene's spirit has something to do with that, pulling the strings of the people she loves, even from the Great Beyond?

Diego and I moved in with Zack in April, right before Jessica had her baby. Jupiter lives in the guest house, where more often than not Diego can be found curled up on the sunny expanse of her bed. He's a finicky cat, but he apparently has a thing for Rathbones. I was worried he would rebel when I moved him away from the only home he's ever known. To my surprise, he's taken up residence in the fine old Tudor with a dignified, proprietary air, as if this was the life he was born to lead.

A sweating beer from the cooler appears before me, dripping icy droplets onto my bare stomach. I sit up and take it from Zack's outstretched hand.

"How you doing?" He collapses onto the lawn chair next to mine, wiping sweat from his brow with his forearm. "You getting hungry?"

"I'm starving." I smile. "It smells amazing."

"The meat's done. I'm just waiting for the corn. Should we make a quick salad?"

"Sure." I take a sip of beer and try to find the energy to hoist myself out of the chair.

"Tansy?" I turn my head to see Zack staring at me intently.

"Yeah?"

He looks down, picks lint off his shorts, and raises his eyes to mine. "You think she's ever coming back?"

My throat suddenly feels dry. I take another sip of beer. This is definitely *not* the moment—not with Jupiter and her friends a few yards away and dinner imminent. I wonder if the timing will ever be right, or if I'll continue slipping the postcards into his mailbox, keeping up my deception forever.

"I don't know," I say quietly. "I don't think so."

"Neither do I." It's hard to tell how he feels about that. There's sadness in his voice, but also the barest hint of relief.

We stare at each other for a long moment, drinking in each other's loss, and also our mutual gratitude for what we have: this house, Jupiter, Diego, each other. We've formed a ragtag little family, and though I'm sad Selene can't be here with us, a part of me knows her instinct for destruction would never allow this sweetness to last. She was her own worst enemy, driven by forces nobody—least of all her—understood.

Jupiter laughs at something, pulling our attention. The sound is so girlish, so carefree, I know I can't pierce the bubble of joy she inhabits. Maybe it's wrong to deceive the people you love best, but I'd like to think we're all allowed a few secrets.

"Let's make that salad," I say, standing.

He gets to his feet and together we go inside.

Enjoyed the read?

We'd love to hear your thoughts!

crookedlanebooks.com/feedback

ACKNOWLEDGMENTS

M Y DEEPEST THANKS go out to the creativity, support, and hard work of all the people who helped make this book a reality.

First and foremost, I thank my lucky stars for my agent, Jill Marr, who is always in my corner. James Bock and Jessica Renheim, my perceptive and brilliant editors at Crooked Lane Books, pushed me to make this novel so much sharper and more vivid. A big thanks to everyone at CLB for your tireless work on my behalf, especially Melissa Rechter, Rebecca Nelson, and Madeline Rathle. Special thanks to Kara Klontz for her inspired cover design.

Lisa Rosenstreich, thank you for all of our therapeutic walks, for reading my first draft, and for encouraging me to find the story I needed to tell. You suffered through my long, meandering monologues as I tried to pinpoint who these characters are and where their journeys might lead.

To my family, thank you so much for your ongoing love and support. Thanks to the Big Moon Music crew, especially Rose Bell, Stacey Sheldon, and Alicia Bales for putting me back in touch with my singer-songwriter self. Wendy James and Kate Morein, thanks for squealing over cover designs and helping me see the big picture when I get stuck. Ellen Weed, you are a gem among friends and an inspiration.

Last but far from least, my gratitude goes out to David Wolf. You're the only person on the planet who can make lockdown not just tolerable but kind of fun. Let's make music together until we die. I love you.

Read an excerpt from

THE
PROTÉGÉ

the next

NOVEL

by JODY GEHRMAN

available soon in hardcover from
Crooked Lane Books

CROOKED
LANE

NEW YORK

1

Hannah

I'M SITTING ON the stage, contemplating Mick Lynch's skull.
It's nicely formed, as craniums go. He's bald—shaved skinhead naked, not just buzzed—so it's easy to observe its shape. The parietal bone forms one long, elegant curve from the top of his head to his occipital bun. The frontal bone, with its pronounced brow and sharp zygomatic curvature, gives his face a strong, intimidating look. We find a strong frontal bone appealing in males because of its ability to resist blunt force trauma—to survive a falling limb, a spear, a tire iron. We crave signs of strength; it means our offspring have a better chance at passing on our genes. Mick Lynch's cranium screams safety, warmth, security. Genetic success.

But what really catches my eye is his zygomatic arch—that tender, gently curved place just behind the ear. His seems to be . . . flexing. Not the bone itself, of course, but the temporalis muscles; they're hypnotically active. I watch them move as he addresses the crowd, arms outstretched like an evangelical preacher. Though I know this is scientifically inaccurate, it gives the impression his brain is too active to be caged within his skull. It's mesmerizing.

He's mesmerizing. I hate the son of a bitch, but I have to admit, he knows how to work a room.

A quick scan of the packed lecture hall confirms my suspicions. The audience can't take their eyes off him. Some of the men sit canted forward in their seats, faces eager. Others lean back, contemplating each word. The women wear faint, dreamy smiles; some flex their frontalis muscles, resulting in furrowed brows. On closer inspection, I suspect the frowners react differently to sexual stimuli than their starry-eyed sisters. The smilers enjoy the way his voice caresses them. The frowners know better.

Do I know better?

The question emerges from the dark underbelly of my mind, blindsiding me.

Of course I know better. Jesus. The guy's a first-class narcissist. He's in love with the sound of his own voice.

Granted, it does have a compelling cadence—part gospel minister, part Steve Jobs.

I force myself to focus on his lecture. I've been so fixated on Lynch's cranium, I've barely heard a word. Lynch whisks away a red velvet cloth, revealing a humanoid robot as a chorus of gasps erupts from the audience. Cheap magic tricks. Lynch is an old-time charlatan pedaling snake-oil and virility charms.

As if sensing my eyes on it, the robot whips its head around and gazes in my direction. I flinch. It has a realistic face that looks a little like my uncle Jack's—humble, unassuming, wrinkled. Designed to be disarming. It flashes me a feral grin; then it turns back to face the audience with a placid expression.

"Many people ask me, 'What if they get smarter than us and take over the planet?'" Just as Lynch poses the rhetorical question, the robot does a double take, not unlike a ventriloquist's dummy.

THE PROTÉGÉ   293

The audience lets out a nervous laugh.

Lynch scans the crowd, his face open, inviting. I try to pinpoint which muscles communicate that microscopic shift from stern to curious. Is it the gentle rise in the orbicularis oculi? A barely perceived tightening of the corrugator supercilii?

Lynch takes a step closer to the edge of the stage. He's a man soothing a spooked horse, reaching out a hand, meeting his audience halfway. He doesn't come on too strong. There's empathy there, a human connection; he makes each listener feel like he's speaking only to her.

He glances sideways, and our eyes meet. Is it my imagination, or is there a pulse of challenge there, a flash of hubris? When I spoke earlier, as part of the panel, I didn't inspire rapt attention. I delivered a mini-lecture on the culture of identity and bioethics in an emergent scientific discipline like AI. Eyes glazed over. I deliver information, not theatrics. Mick Lynch can work the room all he likes; it's not my strong suit, and I know it.

He turns away from me, and his gaze locks on the audience again. His volume drops to a low, confiding tone. "It's a primal fear—the lifeblood of science fiction. And yes, it's a valid question. An essential question, in fact."

The tension in the room is so palpable you can taste it. The air simmers with the electric tang of a coming storm. I can't help but wonder how the hell he does it. What is charisma, exactly? Is there a genetic predisposition for it? Can it be measured? I don't like mysteries that can't be solved. Amorphous qualities we sense but cannot quantify make me itch. Bones can be measured, weighed. Many studies indicate we can even compute beauty after adjusting for cultural norms. There's a distinct symmetry of features the majority of homo sapiens find aesthetically appealing, a specific ratio between waist and hips most men find sexually attractive. But charisma? The chemistry between speaker and audience?

Watching him, it's undeniably there—the charged, almost sexual electricity between this strange bald man and his mesmerized spectators.

"The answer is not simple, but it is definitive." Lynch beckons to his robot, who hurries to its master's side with a meek, pliable air. "We are the creators. We must remember that. We don't need to fear Roger here anymore than we fear our phones or our computers or our toasters."

Lynch gestures, and Roger instantly falls to his knees, bowing his head in a gesture of submission.

"We are the masters of this brave new world. We must find the courage to banish our irrational fears so that we may inhabit the future." He pauses, gazing out into the rapt auditorium, his blue eyes sparkling. "Thank you."

The audience explodes into applause. It's like a volatile liquid suddenly escaping, a soda shaken hard and released. They jump to their feet. I gape, unable to contain my amazement. I've delivered hundreds—maybe even thousands—of lectures. Never, in the history of my career have I inspired a standing ovation.

A queasy feeling stirs in my belly. It takes me a moment to name it.

Envy.

* * *

Winter

She's so smug. I watch her sitting there on stage, her body as motionless as a statue. She looks pretty good for forty; I'll give her that. Her shoulder-length auburn hair is shiny and well cut. The long white neck hasn't yet turned into a disgusting turkey wattle. She's skinny enough. Like most of the professors in this Nor Cal backwater think tank, she wears hardly any makeup, and her clothes are expensive but boring. I've never seen her in heels. She's big on army green and khaki, like she expects to take off on safari at any second. Tonight she's wearing knee-high boots that probably cost more than my yearly stipend, army-green fitted slacks, and a camel-colored sweater. She's totally married to her job. Everything about her screams *leading forensic anthropologist*.

I don't even know what she's doing on this panel. It's clear the robot freaks her out. When it turned and looked at her, she flinched like she expected it to spit in her face. I can't help but notice her eyes following Lynch everywhere, though. Oh, Lord, tell me she doesn't have a crush. That would be too hilarious. God, I think she does. I can't decide if that's sickening or sweet. If the two of them had a kid, it would be a total abomination, an uber genius baby with a massive brain, a Rhodes scholar by the time it hit kindergarten. Yeah, she's definitely hot for him. The way she watches him—there's something there I haven't seen before. Normally, she's cool, calculating. She's got as much warmth and humor as a crocodile. When she looks at Lynch, though, her eyes light up with pale green fire.

This is good. I can use this.

It's easy to see why Lynch has got even Dr. B lusting after him; he's sexy in a bald, sweaty, old-guy sort of way. He's got a definite Bruce Willis circa *Die Hard* appeal. He's way more fit than most of the guys on campus, young or old. You can see he's cut, even in a suit. That's another thing that sets him apart; he dresses like a man. Guess that's the UCLA influence lingering, even though he's been here since fall semester. He hasn't yet gotten the memo that Mad River University men are filthy hippies across the board, from their nasty dreads to their socks-and-Birkenstock toes. It's not just Lynch's action figure body or his suit that make him hot, though. It's his game. Every woman in this auditorium is ready to drop her panties for him. Some guys are just like that. They're tigers in a field of gazelles.

I sit back in my chair, enjoying the show. The AI is cool—whatever, boys and their toys. The real entertainment is watching Dr. B devour Lynch with her cool green eyes.

My mind wanders, dreaming up the many ways this information might prove useful in the days to come.

2

Hannah

MAD RIVER UNIVERSITY is a peculiar little campus, tucked into the wild hills above the sea, three hundred miles north of San Francisco. It was built by wunderkind architect Liam Dubois. Though the school was founded and constructed just ten years ago, Dubois has a thing for the collegiate gothic style, so it looks at least a hundred years old. An article in *Architectural Digest* described the main building, Thorn Hall, as "a cross between Hogwarts and Neuschwanstein." There are towers, finials, stone facades as intricate as lace; lancet windows, spires, and turrets give it a vaguely medieval look. Now, climbing the stone steps of Thorn Hall as the sky turns indigo, I can't help sighing with pleasure. This place is over the top, but I love it. Cantankerous gargoyles crouch on either side of the entrance, wings half extended, teeth bared.

It's a building every bit as anachronistic, guarded, and gloomy as me—and that's no small feat.

There's a catered party in Thorn Hall after Lynch's AI display. I despise these things—social gatherings in general give me heart palpitations—but my boss, Dr. Eli Balderstone, didn't give me much choice but to attend. Compulsory merrymaking. Mad River was founded by mavericks looking for an academic home that would be less mired in bureaucracy than the universities they fled. Private schools require funding, though, which means donors must be dazzled and pandered to. This shindig promises to be crawling with major donors looking to rub elbows with the brainiacs they fund. Thank God Lynch's performance ensures they'll swarm him and leave the dry academic types like myself to languish amid the canapés and bacon-wrapped figs.

Joe catches up with me just as I pass through the great stone arches of Thorn Hall. Joe's my friend, colleague, and downstairs tenant. He just moved in a few months ago, after a two-year campaign. He finally convinced me that living all alone in the woods was making me even more of a social outcast. He has a point. I do tend to isolate more than I should. Besides, the house I bought five years ago came with a self-contained apartment downstairs, complete with its own kitchen, two bedrooms, and a bathroom. It was decadent and wasteful, leaving it unoccupied.

All the same, he's living there on a trial basis. I value my solitude. Joe's presence downstairs is sometimes comforting, but it's also a little distracting. He's a musician. Two days after he moved in, I invested in an economy-sized pack of earplugs.

"Hey, Hannah." He puts a hand on my back. "Sorry, my lesson went late."

"I doubt the demo would have interested you much anyway." We continue together up the stairs toward the study, a cozy if slightly pretentious room on the second floor. Administration likes to hold parties there, especially ones involving generous benefactors.

Joe brushes a bit of lint from his blazer. "Really? Sounded kind of cool. Mr. Robot didn't impress you, huh?"

I shrug. "He's an alpha-male with delusions of grandeur. Dime a dozen."

"What about his robots, though?"

"Robot—singular." I pull a face. "It's anthropomorphic, which just seems wrong. Gives me the creeps."

He shoots me a mock-appalled look. "Dr. Bryers! I'm shocked."

"That's sarcasm. I can tell because of the movement in your orbicularis oculi."

He grins. It's a long-standing joke between us, my inability to detect subtle social nuances like sarcasm. "You seem like the last person to fall prey to base superstitions."

"I'm an anthropologist for a reason. 'Anthro' is all about man— the kind made of blood, sinew, and bones. That's my world. I'm just as susceptible to instinctive revulsion about pseudo humans as the next guy."

By now, we've reached the entrance to the study, a long, elegant room with a massive fireplace at one end. It's a gas fire— Mad River is fanatical about the environment—but it gives off a warm, golden glow just the same. Richly hued oriental rugs cover the oak floors. Oxblood leather chairs and moss-green velvet sofas abound, many of them already occupied by guests. Iron chandeliers and wall sconces add to the flattering light provided by the fireplace. In spite of my pronounced social anxiety, I can't help but feel lucky. There's a subtle glow that ignites inside me, knowing I'm welcome within this privileged space, the inner circle of an institution I consider home.

A waiter darts past with a tray. I start to reach for a glass, but he's moving too quickly and doesn't even see my outstretched hand. A huff of irritation escapes me as I spot the object of his attention. Isabella Lynch, Mick Lynch's ex-swimsuit-model wife, stands in a circle of male admirers. I recognize a couple colleagues among them: Gil Matheson from Engineering and my boss, Eli Balderstone. Isabella's wearing a dress the color of blood. Her velvety brown skin, lush black hair, and plunging neckline have drawn a crowd of men, all of whom vie for her attention like hummingbirds swooping around a trumpet vine. As the waiter arrives, several of her fans practically lunge for the chance to hand her a drink first.

Mrs. Lynch appears to enjoy the attention. Human social nuances are not my specialty, but I base my hypothesis on the way she flicks her hair over one shoulder and laughs, throwing her head back to expose her long, vulnerable neck. She's displaying typical mating ritual signifiers. I have learned these do not necessarily indicate imminent plans to copulate, unlike in the animal kingdom. They do, however, comprise the ritual we refer to as "flirtation." We humans go to great lengths to prove our ability to attract potential sexual partners, without having any serious mating intentions; that's just one of the many reasons I find human behavior fascinating and mystifying.

Joe's managed to secure two flutes of champagne. He hands one to me and follows my gaze. "Isn't that Mrs. Robot?"

"Mm. Your moniker is amusing."

"Remember that thing we talked about?"

I pull my eyes away from the spectacle of Isabella and focus on Joe. "What thing?"

"If you find something funny, it's best to . . . you know, chuckle, chortle, snort, giggle—"

"Ah, right. Don't just remark on its amusing qualities, indicate amusement with a sound or facial expression."

"Even a hearty smile will work." He grins. I grin back.

Joe sometimes refers to himself as my "trainer." He says being friends with me is a full-time job, but somebody's got to do it. Once, I heard him telling a lab tech to think of me as a brilliant but clueless alien, one who must be introduced to the customs of earthlings in a patient, methodical fashion. It doesn't escape me that my greatest strength as an anthropologist—my ability to view humans with clear-eyed objectivity—is also my greatest weakness as a friend and teacher. It's not something I worry about, though. It's just the way I'm made.

I approach the art of socializing the way others approach unpleasant but obligatory tasks such as cleaning the toilet or suffering through a root canal; I avoid it whenever possible but strive to be brave and endure it with dignity when no alternative makes itself available.

"Lester's over there. I better schmooze." Joe nods in the direction of Lester Wang, the chair of the Music Department. Joe teaches guitar and music theory at Mad River part-time. I deduce he wants to get chummy with Lester in the hopes of adding more sections, a social ritual that at least results in monetary gain.

"Go ahead."

He glances at me. "You sure you're okay on your own?"

I give him a wry look. "I'm not afraid to be left alone. You know that. I'll just blend with the natives, indulge in some participant observation."

"Become one with the wallpaper?" His eyes smile down at me, the crow's feet crinkling in that old familiar way.

"There's no wallpaper." I'm being deliberately literal this time to amuse him.

It works. He guffaws. "Be right back."

I know from experience this is a lie. Joe thrives at a party; he feeds on the energy of a buzzing room. He excels at flitting from one conversation to another, with the effortless grace of a pollinating insect. Me, I tend to stake out one corner and observe. I could blame my observation tactics on my profession, but it would be more accurate to say I chose my profession because this has always been my way. My dad says I did it even as a baby—retreated from crowds. I was so silent and watchful, others in the room invariably forgot I was there. Once, when I was two, my Aunt Ellen actually sat on me.

"Dr. Bryers." I recognize the voice immediately—that tone, warm and rich as hot chocolate. He's standing right behind me.

I force myself to take a deep breath as I turn to face him. "Dr. Lynch."

"Thanks again for agreeing to sit on the panel."

"Accurate verb choice."

One of his eyebrows arches—the corrugated supercilii muscle, I note automatically. "Sorry, not sure I—"

"Lots of sitting. Not much talking. You obviously had that covered. But you're welcome."

He takes a step back, assessing me. Though he joined the faculty back in September—six months ago now—we've never had a proper conversation, just the two of us. I'm acutely aware of his smell. I detect something citrusy, probably an expensive after-shave. That's not what catches my attention, though. Underneath that layer of artifice, there's a scent that's pure animal—sweat and musk and salt.

I can see him considering his next words carefully. I'm a respected faculty member, one who's been here seven years. He cannot afford to alienate me. But he's also not a man accustomed to backing away from a challenge.

"It's unfortunate we didn't get to hear from you more." He's testing the waters, trying to figure out my game. "I'm sure you have valuable insights to share."

"I doubt my insights would concur with yours." Even I recognize the bitchiness in my tone.

"How interesting."

I squint at him, hunting for signs of condescension. To my surprise, he looks curious. It's that same look he gave the audience earlier—the open, childlike expression that says, *Tell me more.* I know the difference between someone putting on an interested expression and someone who's sincere. It's in the eyes. People can do all kinds of deceptive things with their mouths, their foreheads, even their brows, but the eyes never lie.

He takes a minute step closer, peering at me. "What specifically do you disagree with? My theories, or the way I present them?"

"I find your presentation theatrical but effective. The audience responds well—that's obvious."

"And you find that suspect?"

"Of course."

"Why 'of course'?" One corner of his mouth curls upward, amused.

"It's natural to feel instinctive revulsion when one is being manipulated."

"And yet, as you say, the audience responds."

"Most people run on pure pathos. They're slaves to their emotions, as much as they'd like to think otherwise. They're too busy being seduced by your charisma to question your ethics or the soundness of your hypotheses."

"But not you." He says it softly. I can't tell if he's mocking me.

"No. I'm driven by logos." I meet his gaze head-on. "Logic tells me you're dangerous."

Instead of looking defensive, he lets out a laugh so loud and genuine, I flinch. Several people nearby turn to look, including—I can't help but notice—his wife.

"Dangerous," he repeats. "It's not the first time I've been called that, but it's never sounded so much like a compliment."

"It's not a compliment or an epithet. It's a fact."

Isabella glides toward us, a glass of wine in her hand. It's a deep, plummy red; it matches her dress, her lipstick, and her ruby earrings. My limbic cortex recognizes danger; the fight-or-flight instinct flares inside me, poised to move. Her dark eyes scan me before fixing on my face with a pleasant smile. Her mouth says "friend," but her eyes say "foe."

"Have you met my wife?" Mick reaches out a hand as she approaches, and pulls her close. "Isabella, this is Dr. Bryers."

"Yes. From the panel." She has a husky, lightly accented voice.

"Are you from Peru?" I enjoy trying to place accents. I have an excellent ear for languages.

Her eyes flash with irritation, and she glances at Mick. "Venezuela. I have been here for many years, but I never seem to lose my accent."

"It's beautiful." I'm being sincere. I hope she can tell. People say I don't express emotion well—that I have a flat, unreadable affect. Maybe that's why I like accents, especially South American ones; they always sound so expressive, the polar opposite of my colorless monotone.

Mick smiles down at her in a way most people would read as reassuring. To me it looks condescending, but I'm hypersensitive, so I could be wrong. Nothing spikes my pulse faster than a patronizing man in power, and not in a good way.

Isabella turns back to me. Her shiny dark hair swings forward as she moves, nearly covering one eye. The effect is alluring, I'm sure, but all I can think about is how a couple strands have adhered to her thickly glossed lips. I can never stand to have my hair in my face; I usually pull mine back.

"You are a professor here, yes?"

I nod. "Yes. I've been here since right after the college was founded seven years ago."

"You must have been very young." She's trying to flatter me. Personally, I've never understood why looking young is so important. It's indicative of a culture that values physical beauty and prowess over wisdom and experience. While I'm trained not to judge the prevailing values of a culture, I can't help but prefer the value systems of the Hopi or the Koreans, where the elders are treated with the reverence we Americans reserve for rock stars and super models.

"I was thirty-three," I say simply.

Isabella blinks her thickly mascaraed lashes and forms a pleasant little smile, but I can tell she's only being polite. The eyes again, telling the truth in spite of all the other facial muscles conspiring to feign interest. She is interested, but not in my academic career. She wants to know one thing: if I'm a threat to her marriage. I wish I could just tell her how baseless her fears are. Of all the women in this room, I'm the least likely to fall prey to her husband's charms.

This is why parties exhaust me. All the social niceties contrast sharply with the body language tells. My brain races, trying to make sense of the contradictions.

A waiter carrying a tray of miniature meatballs offers them to us. Isabella and Mick both take one, but I stick to my champagne. I find conversation challenging enough without adding the effort required to masticate and swallow, all while guarding against the social faux pas of talking with your mouth full.

Isabella takes a delicate bite and somehow manages not to mar her lip gloss. When she swallows, her throat moves. I find myself fixating on her sternocleidomastoid; I have to drag myself back to hear her question.

"You are teaching the robotics, like Mick?"

Lynch breathes out a little laugh. "No, Dr. Bryers is a forensic anthropologist. She studies cultural artifacts—"

"Not artifacts," I interrupt, correcting him. "Human remains."

"Dead bodies?" Isabella looks uneasy.

I focus my attention on her. "Whatever's left of the corpse, I examine to reconstruct the cause and approximate time of death. I specialize in forensic taphonomy—or, in simpler terms, decomposition. After just a day or two, the internal organs start to break down; soon after, the body bloats, emitting blood-containing foam from the mouth and nose."

She puts down her meatball with a moue of distaste.

"Of course, anthropoid colonization affects the decomposition process—"

"Anthropoid?" she echoes, her brow furrowed.

"Bugs," Lynch clarifies. He looks like he's trying not to laugh, which I find perplexing. There's nothing especially humorous about anthropoids.

I continue my explanation, holding her gaze, though she looks increasingly queasy. "Various carrion insects are attracted to the biological and chemical changes a carcass undergoes as it decays. I examine this as well, though that's more the purview of my entomologist colleagues."

Joe finally returns from his strategic wooing of Lester Wang. He looks bright-eyed and flushed, the way he always does at a party. A quartet of stringed instruments has started playing. Joe's always in his element when there's music, booze, and beautiful people filling a room.

"Uh-oh," he says by way of greeting. He nods at Isabella. "I know that look. Is Hannah regaling you with tales of rotting flesh?"

"She asked about my work." I know I sound defensive, but I don't care. Joe has a habit of turning me into a joke to make me appear more sympathetic. I find it either charming or infuriating, depending on my mood.

Isabella laughs, and her relief is evident. Heat creeps up my neck and spreads across my face. Joe's saved these two helpless captives from my awkward social efforts. He can now translate the behavior of the alien for the puzzled earthlings.

Lynch catches my eye. I'm not sure I understand his expression, but something about his steady gaze calms me.

Joe extends a hand to Lynch, then to Isabella. "Joe Shepley."

"You are Dr. Bryers's husband?"

"No! We're friends," I say, my tone sharp.

Joe looks wounded. He recovers quickly, though, flashing a self-deprecating grin. "I'm just the dude who lives in her basement."

"It's not a basement," I correct. "He has an apartment on the first floor of my home. He just calls it a basement because he thinks it sounds amusing."

"Sorry I missed the presentation." Joe changes the subject smoothly, addressing Lynch. "I hear it was riveting."

Lynch flicks a quick look at me, then turns to Joe. "Not according to Dr. Bryers, but I don't mind. It's refreshing, talking to someone so honest."

Joe pats my arm. "Hannah's nothing if not honest."

*   *   *

Winter

One of the things I like best about grad school is how temporary it is. Sure, there are losers who work on their doctoral dissertations so long they become part of the landscape—scared Peter Pans cowering in the libraries, unwilling to move on—but for most of us, it's a stepping-stone. We uprooted our lives and drove U-Haul trucks to this God forsaken forest several hundred miles from civilization. We flocked here from all over the world to be mentored by these elusive geniuses, professors who are giants in their fields—never mind that outside their field nobody gives a shit. In their specialized sphere, these professors are celebrities. We came here to apprentice with the best and the brightest.

It's a lot like joining the circus. You pitch your tent for a few years, study hard, and party harder. Then, when it's all over, you tear down your tent and move on.

I like that. Temporary works for me.

Where I come from, everyone's been there forever. Nobody in Apalachicola ever leaves or returns. They're born in that sad little outpost on the edge of a humid, primeval swamp. They eat there, work there, mate there; they have ugly, wrinkled little babies, and their babies have babies; and then they die. Those people exist like trees, rooted to one spot, doomed to see the same humdrum shit day after day. It makes them boring and bored.

If there's one thing I've learned in my twenty-three years, it's that boredom breeds evil.

The other great thing about the temporary nature of grad school is that even boyfriends come with an expiration date. I wasn't planning to hook up with anyone, but Cameron makes an excellent camouflage boyfriend. He's so trustworthy and respected, he makes me disappear beside him. For my purposes, this is ideal. The day I met him, I decided to make him mine because being his girlfriend makes my mission here that much easier.

I list here—in no particular order—the main reasons he provides amazing camo:

1. He's freakishly attractive. Though I'm pretty enough, when I walk into a room with him, he's the one everyone notices first. He's four inches taller than me; since I'm five eleven, this is a definite perk. He's got dark hair, dark eyes, five o'clock shadow, and an impish, crooked grin that's just dirty enough to offset his crisp button-down shirts and trendy jeans. Most dudes in this part of the world are fugly hippies who smell like bong, so even if he's a little preppy for my taste, it's way better than the alternative.
2. Cameron went to Yale for undergrad. People remember that way more than my forgettable alma mater.
3. He can play the violin. Serious violin.
4. He's rich (see numbers two and three).
5. He's smart. Not just ace-your-GREs smart, but actually smart.
6. Luckily, he's not smart enough to know when I'm lying.

Cameron annoys me at least as often as he entertains me, but that's because of how I'm wired. I've got a very low tolerance for people's flaws. Nobody else finds him the slightest bit irritating, but I'm funny that way. Even saints could try my patience. Most of the time, I'm able to hide this. See number six. The truth is, Cameron has no idea who I am. I'm very careful not to reveal much. He knows I grew up in Florida, but he thinks I was an only child in a happy family. He knows my parents died in a car crash, but he thinks this happened right after I left for college. Whenever possible, I avoid talking about anything that transpired before the day I met him. I never discuss ex-boyfriends. Like most guys, he's happier believing I sprang into existence the moment he laid eyes on me. It makes things easier for both of us. *Suppressio veri*—concealment of truth. It's win–win.

After Lynch's AI lecture, Cameron and I walk through the gathering gloom toward downtown. The campus sits on a dramatic bluff above the ocean. Salt Gulch was barely more than a gas station and a post office before MRU, from what I've heard. Now it's hardly a bustling metropolis, but it's grown. Since its whole raison d'être is the university, all of the businesses are just a short walk from campus. There's a pub, a bakery, a café, a Thai restaurant, a taco joint, a few boutiques that specialize in high-end pot princess chic. There's a market called the Salt Gulch Bazaar that sells everything from bamboo T-shirts to artisanal bacon. Between these meager offerings and Amazon, we get by.

"What did you think of Lynch's demo?" Cameron's all amped. He's got that earnest, fired-up look. Whenever we go to these things, he likes to sort through the ideas afterward like a kid poring over his prize collection of baseball cards.

Sometimes, I find it a bit much. Tonight, I'm in an indulgent mood, though. Getting a glimpse of Dr. B's crush has made me generous. "He's a great speaker."

"Amazing, right? I'm dying to take one of his classes."

I snort. "Good luck with that. They fill up months in advance. Anyway, Dr. Bryers would shit a brick."

"You think?" He looks at me, eyebrows rising. "Because it's outside our program?"

"And she thinks AI is the devil."

"Really?" Cameron looks intrigued. Behind him, in the distance, the ocean churns in the twilight, glowing a luminous blue. "It's not like her to be biased about a field with so much potential."

I want to tell him he has no idea what she's capable of.

Cameron idolizes Bryers. It's one of his most irritating traits. We're both her star students, but there's a huge difference between us. He worships her; I study her. We're in our second year of the PhD program, with two more to go. I've played my cards perfectly with Bryers. She even made me her TA this year. I can never show Cameron how I really feel about her. Mostly I excel at this; sometimes it's a challenge.

We've reached the pub. Its windows are steamy, and live music pulses through the open door. A small line snakes along the sidewalk as the bouncer checks IDs. MRU is small, with only about three thousand students. Even so, the makeshift town of Salt Gulch struggles to serve us all. The nearest "big" town is Arcata, another smallish college town. It's only about twenty minutes south of us, but most of us prefer to walk home after a few beers, so we all cram into the pub every weekend.

We show the bouncer our IDs and push inside the warm, steamy room. I'm glad for the loud music. It will keep conversation to a minimum. If Cameron says anything else annoying, I can just pretend I didn't hear him.